Under the Stars with You

A sweet and entertaining read. The story is entertaining, funny and easy to follow, the characters are likeable and have a great connection.

-Di B., *NetGalley*

...Overall, the story is a compelling and beautifully written romance novel that had me drawn in from the first page. If you enjoy down-to-earth characters, an environment that makes you want to be there and romance with a HEA, this story is worth the read.

-Carol C., *NetGalley*

Over the Moon with You

This story is all about how a relationship evolves, from the initial attraction to moving toward each next step and the delicate balance needed to navigate all the uncertainties that makes up life. I really liked the deep character development of both these characters. This book was also hilarious—from the spicy seniors, Paige's mom to Seren's bff Leslie, they kept me cracking up at their antics and banter. And lastly let's not forget about steam coz it seriously packs a whole lot of fire and is the perfect payoff to the slow burn churning through the story. This was a wonderful weekend read that had plenty of romance, humor, steam and a low angst HEA that made my day.

-D Booker, *NetGalley*

The author takes her time in building the relationship between Paige and Seren even as she is developing her characters. What she has created is one the better LesFic romances so far this year. ...If you like well-written books with characters you'll be sorry to say goodbye to at the end of the story, then this book is for you.

-Abbott F., *NetGalley*

Love, Accidentally

Who doesn't like a U-Haul joke! I really enjoyed reading this book. This is the second book in the "A Mile High City Romance" series, by Rey and Clevenger and once again they show how compatible their writing is. It is also great to see that this is not only a collaboration between writers, but also between publishers. This story runs in parallel with the first book *A Convenient Arrangement*. All in all, this is a happy feel-good book, which I easily recommend. I hope Clevenger and Rey will write a book together again in the future.

-Meike V., *NetGalley*

Just One Reason

I had a lot of fun reading *Just One Reason*. I enjoy diving into a traditional romance where I know exactly what I'm going to get, and then being delighted with a host of clever details that make the story feel fresh and brand new. This book checked all the boxes on my list of what I want in a good book.

-*The Lesbian Review*

I don't want to spoil things, but I was cheering this couple on and I wasn't disappointed. Communication happens and it is beautiful and sweet, but not without a splash of angst. This book gave me all of the feels and really hit a home run with thoughtful, meaningful dialogue.

-Digby M., *NetGalley*

This is the third installment of the Paradise Romance series. I have gotten so much entertainment out of these books. I love the characters and friend group. That while each story focuses on a new budding relationship, the same characters pop in and we see that they continue to progress in their respective partnerships. There is always so much more depth and satisfaction when the writer can put people through the wringer so that they come out on the other side shiny and happy. Overall, this is another great addition to the Paradise Romance series.

-Bookvark, *NetGalley*

All the Reasons I Need

One of the reasons I love *Three Reasons to Say Yes* so much is that Clevenger wrote such strong secondary characters in Kate and Mo. I fell for them almost as much as the main characters, so to have them get their own book I was excited. This is a story about two best friends since college that have a ton of chemistry but have never done anything about it. ...If you are looking for a well-written, angsty romance, look no further. This is an easy romance for me to recommend. I think with this series, Clevenger is at the top of her writing game and I can't wait to see what she puts out next.

-Lex Kent's Reviews, *goodreads*

This book is the second installment in Clevenger's Paradise Romance series. It's not necessary to read the first book, *Three Reasons to Say Yes*, to enjoy Kate and Mo's story ...*All the Reasons I Need* is a thoughtful summer romance full of emotion. It let me imagine myself on a tropical beach, napping in a hammock, and sipping an exotic drink with a little umbrella in it. There's just something about beautiful sunsets and waves crashing on the beach that make falling in love seem easy.

-*The Lesbian Review*

Three Reasons to Say Yes

This is without a doubt my new favourite Jaime Clevenger novel. Honestly I couldn't put it down from the first chapter. ...All in all this book has the potential to be my book of the year. Truly, books like this don't come around often that suit my reading tastes to a tee.

-*Les Rêveur*

...This one was totally my cup of tea with its charming relationship and family dynamics, great chemistry between two likable protagonists, a very convincing romance, some angst, drama and tension to the right extent and in all the right moments, and some very nice secondary characters. On top of that, the writing is technically very good, with all elements done properly. Sincerely recommended.

This was a really easy story to get into. I sank right in and wanted to stay there, because reading about other people on vacation is kind of like taking a mini vacation from the world! It's sweet and lovely, and while it has some angst, it's not going to hurt you. Instead, it's going to take you away from it all so you can come back with a smile on your face.

Party Favors

This book has one of the best characters ever. Me. Or rather you. It's quite a strange and startling experience at first to be in a book, especially one with as many hot, sexy, beautiful women in it who, incidentally, all seem to want you. But believe me, you'll soon get used to it. ...In a word, this book was FUN. It made me smile, and laugh, and tease my wife. I definitely recommend it to everyone, with the caveat that if you don't like erotica you should probably give it a pass. But not only read it, enjoy it, experience it, also find a friend, or a spouse, or even a book buddy online to talk to about it. Because you'll want to, it's that great.

I've read this book a few times and each time changed my decisions to find new and inviting destinations each time. This is a book you can read time and time again with a different journey. If you're looking for a fun Saturday night read that's sexy and hot as hell then this book is 100% for you! Go buy it now. 5 Stars.

The story is told in the second person, present tense, which is ambitious in itself—it takes great skill to make that work and for the reader, who is now the narrator, to really connect to the thoughts and actions that are being attributed to them. Not all of the scenes will turn everyone on, as we all have different tastes, but I am pretty sure there is something for everyone in here. And if you do as you're told and follow the structure the author uses, you can dip into this book as much or as little as you wish. An interesting read with some pretty hot interactions.

-Rainbow Book Reviews

Houseswap 101

JAIME CLEVENGER

Books by Jaime Clevenger published by Bella Books

The Unknown Mile
Call Shotgun
Love, Accidentally
Sign on the Line
Whiskey and Oak Leaves
Sweet, Sweet Wine
Waiting for a Love Song
A Fugitive's Kiss
Moonstone
Party Favors
Three Reasons to Say Yes
All the Reasons I Need
Just One Reason
One Weekend in Aspen
Over the Moon with You
Under the Stars with You

Published by Spinsters Ink

All Bets Off

About the Author

Jaime Clevenger lives in a little mountain town in Colorado. Most days are spent working as a veterinarian, but time off is filled writing, reading, swimming, practicing karate, and goofing off with their wife and kids (both two- and four-legged). Jaime loves hearing a good story and hopes that if you ever meet, you'll share your favorite. Feel free to embellish the details.

Houseswap 101

JAIME CLEVENGER

BELLA
BOOKS
2024

Bella Books, Inc.
P.O. Box 10543
Tallahassee, FL 32302

Printed in the United States of America on acid-free paper.

First Edition - 2024

Editor: Heather Flournoy
Cover Designer: Kayla Mancuso

ISBN: 978-1-64247-542-5

Acknowledgment

Some stories start with a conversation. Others with a picture or a random fun train of thought. This story began with a single word—housebutch. One of my beta readers (Alix) asked me to someday describe a character as a housebutch. I can't pass up a good challenge, but I couldn't think of who would be my housebutch, or what her story would be. Then one day Robbie popped into my head. There was no doubt Robbie was the housebutch I'd been waiting for, and I wanted to drop everything and write her story. Unfortunately, I was writing a different story with no room for a housebutch so I tried to convince Robbie to wait. She wouldn't.

Houseswap 101 came to be because Robbie and Devyn couldn't wait to have their love story. The timing was all wrong but sometimes that's how these things go. I owe a big thanks to my publisher (Bella) for letting me take off on this tangent and for switching manuscripts last minute. Thank you, Linda and Jessica, you are both so understanding and amazing. Thank you also to Becky and Tracie (everyone at Bella!) for all your work behind the scenes supporting authors and making sure our stories and characters meet readers. Without a publisher, people would really think I was weird for talking to these imaginary friends in my head.

Thank you, Alix, for giving me the word housebutch and for the scoop on Seattle and houseboats. Also, of course, thank you for beta reading! Thank you, Aurora, for beta reading this one as well and pushing me to be a better writer. You've almost convinced me that not every story needs lots of angst. Almost. Thank you to Leigh and Rhys for convincing me to go for the story I really wanted to write. Writing buddies are the best. Thank you to my fabulous editor, Heather, for editing me yet again. I may not remember all the grammar rules you try to teach me, but I so appreciate your effort and for being generally awesome. And finally…Thank you, Corina, for reading everything I write. Again and again. Do you know how sweet that is?

CHAPTER ONE

Rain pelted the window, the gale coming in from the north with such force that everything past the flag at the end of the dock was a blur of gray. "Day five of the storm that was supposed to last twenty-four hours," Robbie grumbled, clicking on the link to join the Zoom call. "Hey, Matt. How's the weather?"

"Sunny." Matt Ploughy, Robbie's counterpart in San Diego, did not smile as he delivered the report. He did have the grace to turn the camera angle on his laptop to show off a fountain he was sitting next to. Sunlight sparkled off the cascading water and flowers bloomed in pots around the base of the fountain. Robbie didn't have enough time to fully soak up the blissful scene before Matt's mug was back on the screen. "You got the message about needing to install a hundred new servers?"

"Yep. Already contacted Antonio to let him know he'd be working overtime at the DR site." The disaster recovery site in Phoenix was Antonio's domain, and he hadn't been happy to hear about the increase in his workload. Truthfully his plate was full, and Robbie didn't blame him for griping. "Have you heard anything about when they're hiring a new IT director?"

"Not a word." Matt shifted back on his chaise lounge chair. "One of us deserves that job. Everyone acts like it's the IT director that gets everything done, and we know it's us doing all the work. But as long as no one hacks a bank and everyone's terminal can get online, they forget we exist."

"That's the beauty of working remote."

"I guess so." Matt let out a heavy sigh.

"You doing okay? You've seemed kind of off these past couple weeks."

Matt didn't answer, only turning his gaze to the fountain. His brow creased and Robbie knew something was wrong. She couldn't fathom a guess at what could be amiss, though. Matt was married to a doctor, lived in a big house two blocks from a beach, and had a cute Jack Russell terrier named Angel—who regularly made appearances during their Zoom meetings. As she catalogued the details she knew of Matt's life, she realized it wasn't enough to get the full picture. She'd simply assumed he was happy. "Should I be worried about you?"

"Nah, I'm fine."

"I've dated way too many women to know that when someone says 'fine' they rarely are."

"I'm a dude, Robbie. It's different."

She resisted rolling her eyes but only because she was actually worried. "Talk to me, Matt. What's going on?"

The weekly Zoom check-ins with Matt were at the behest of an IT director who'd been fired two years ago. At first, she'd hated the meetings, arguing that everything they discussed could be resolved faster in a text. But slowly Matt had become her friend through their virtual connection and after her last breakup, she'd appreciated being able to joke about the hassle of dating women with another computer geek who had turned out to be sensitive and understanding.

"Are you quitting? Because I am royally screwed if we lose you at the San Diego site."

"No. This job is the only thing I can seem to do right. I honestly like being a network security engineer." He winked as he added, "Plus, I get you as my friend."

"I'm honored to be a job perk." She flipped her middle finger and got him to crack a smile. If the problem wasn't work, she guessed it was something at home. "Are you in trouble with your wife?"

"How'd you guess?" He let out a long breath. "We're getting divorced."

"Oh, shit."

"Yeah." He scrubbed his face with one hand then straightened in the chaise lounge. "It's not really a new thing. We've been separated for a while but neither of us moved out. Anyway. I was going to tell you, but I didn't know what to say."

"Matt Ploughy."

He chuckled. "Yes, Robbie Price?"

"We're supposed to talk to each other when things go wrong. It's what friends do."

"Well, now you know." He looked from the screen to his yard. "The worst part is I'm stuck here. I hate it, but I can't leave."

"Why not?"

"I'm broke. Until we sell this house, I'm not going anywhere. And there's all these things that have to be done before we can get it on the market." He sighed heavily. "This place was at the top of our budget when we bought and it needed work then." He moved the camera to show a little cottage off to one side of the patio. "I've been staying in the cottage because I can't stand being around my ex, but I have to see her when I go to the main house. And she's got this whole list of projects for me to do."

"Which you aren't doing because you're avoiding her." She'd been through enough breakups to know the avoiding part all too well. "You need to hire someone to do the projects so you can move out."

"I can't afford to hire anyone. I'm telling you, I'm not good with money. Devyn and I split our accounts months ago." He dropped his chin. "Still jealous of me and all this sunshine?"

"I want your weather. I don't want the rest of your mess."

"You sure?" He gave a half-smile. "We could trade places easy."

"You're probably right. No one would know the difference. Except maybe Antonio."

"And he wouldn't say a word." Matt paused. "Wait. *No one would know.* Why didn't we think of this earlier?"

They looked at each other for a moment, neither saying anything, and Robbie knew Matt was seriously considering the idea. "We'd get caught if anyone put in a request for a hands-on at one of the locations." Which happened fairly often.

"Not if we traded badges. We don't look that different."

She squinted at him. "We look completely different."

"You've told me people mistake you for a guy all the time. How tall are you?"

"Five-nine."

His eyes lit up. "So am I."

"And aside from both being white and having brown hair, no one would mistake us."

This cooled his enthusiasm for a moment, but then he said, "We could switch teams."

"Switch teams? I'm not pretending to be straight. How would that even help?"

Matt laughed. "I meant baseball teams. We don't need to look exactly alike. Only close enough for no one to pay attention. You wear my Padres hat. I wear your Mariners gear."

Could it work? They did have similar haircuts and their builds weren't that different. She shook her head, surprised she was even considering the idea.

"You know you want a month in San Diego. I'd do anything to get away from Devyn. Hell, I'll even buy your plane ticket."

"I thought you were broke."

"I've got frequent flier miles."

She eyed the backdrop on Matt's screen—the idyllic yard with trees already leafed out and flowers blooming. Then she glanced at the water droplets racing down the glass two feet from her screen. The constant rain had her in a funk she couldn't seem to break out of, but it wasn't only the weather. For months she'd had the sense that nothing new or exciting was on the horizon. Maybe she needed a change of scenery.

"I have always wanted to check out San Diego."

Matt beamed back at her. "Yes!"

"I didn't say I'd do it. I'm thinking." She tapped the edge of her laptop. "What if we get caught?"

"I'll take the blame. Worst case, they fire me. But we both know that's not happening. We don't have a boss right now."

"Someone's signing our checks." He was right, though. They didn't have a supervisor who'd be paying attention until a new IT director was hired.

"They'll keep signing those checks. I'm telling you, no one will know if we switch. And now's the best time to do something like this. We've got two weeks downtime ahead of those servers." He'd brightened as the plan unfolded and was talking fast like he did whenever he landed on a fix to a network problem. "It's perfect."

"Unless someone at one of the sites figures out we're not who we say we are. The police could get involved. We're dealing with bank security systems."

"No one's calling the police. Have you ever had a conversation with anyone at one of your sites—a conversation that wasn't about a network problem? All they want is for us to get in, fix the issue, and get out."

Maybe the idea of someone calling the police was a stretch. She turned the plan over in her head and then remembered all the things she did at the marina helping her uncle. "What am I thinking? I can't leave. There's too much I do around here."

"But that's why this is perfect. You give me your chore list and I give you mine. I get a houseboat in the rain all by myself, and you get loads of sunshine and my ex-wife."

"Great. Just what I need."

He laughed at her sarcasm. "You might like her."

"I like being free to do my own thing."

"I remember those days. Vaguely." Matt exhaled. "I wish I could walk away and let Devyn deal with everything. I'm so done—with this house and with her. But I don't have money even for a security deposit on a rental. And someone has to take care of Angel."

"You wouldn't take your dog?"

"Angel loves Devyn. He's really her dog."

"I'm sure he loves you too."

"He likes me all right. He loves her." He looked past the screen and presumably at said dog. "I'm the one who's around, you know. Kind of like how things were with me and Devyn when we first got together."

The admission was so sad and honest she didn't know what to say in response.

"I can't figure out if we were ever really in love," he continued. "Mostly I remember being blown away by how beautiful and smart she was."

Robbie had seen Matt's wife pass through in the background of a few of their Zoom meetings and had admittedly lost her own train of thought. Beautiful was an understatement.

"Now it's gotten so bad we avoid being in the same room." Matt shifted out of the screen for a moment and then cleared his throat. "Have you ever wished you'd never met someone?"

"That bad, huh?"

He nodded, and when he took a deep breath, it was clear he was fighting to hold in his emotions. She wished she could give him a hug. "All right. You're pathetic enough that I'm considering this."

Matt sat up straighter. "For real?"

"It's the middle of March and I haven't seen a sunny day since Thanksgiving." Only day after day of gray.

"You need a vacation here." Matt turned the camera to give her a view of his yard. Aside from the fountain and the patio area, there was a fire pit, a hot tub, and a barbeque. Two big trees already dotted with flowers and more flowers in pots spaced around the yard made it look like a spring paradise. As the camera panned, the back side of a tan-colored stucco house with a bank of windows came into focus.

It could be a perfect vacation... "Let me talk to my uncle."

The Zoom session ended with Matt promising again to take the fall if they got caught. She stared at the blue screen for a long moment after the view of Matt's backyard disappeared. The chance of anyone noticing they'd switched places was slim. But not zero. Still, she wanted to help Matt, and when she eyed the pouring rain, a month of sunshine seemed worth a little risk.

She checked the time and decided half past eleven qualified for a lunch break, then went to get her rain gear, still damp from an earlier trip outside. She'd had to go out before dawn to make sure the other houseboats at the dock were still chained securely. Every so often a chain slipped in a storm and a house blew far enough from the dock to snap a utility line. Since the rocking at her house had wakened her from a deep sleep, she'd forced herself out of bed to check everyone's connections.

The downpour hadn't let up and the wind whipped at her jacket the moment she stepped outside. She hurried from her house to the next slip over, giving her uncle's door a perfunctory knock before barging in. "It's me," she called out, quickly shucking her rain gear. "I'm breaking early for lunch. What are we eating?"

"Chili." Uncle Bruce appeared in the hallway. "And it's vegan, so we'll probably starve."

She chuckled. Her uncle was a retired chef and had taken the orders to cut cholesterol out of his diet hard. He waved her to the kitchen, saying, "You'll have to try it and tell me if it needs anything. Other than actual flavor."

His houseboat was slightly bigger than hers—two bedrooms instead of one—but it was still a short distance from the door to the kitchen. He lifted the lid on the soup pot, dipped in the wooden spoon, and held it out for her to taste.

She blew on it and her stomach rumbled impatiently. Before it cooled, she took a bite and then fanned her tongue. "It's good. Did you use a new type of cumin?"

He shook his head, narrowing his eyes as he studied her. "Guess again."

"Chocolate?" He'd been known to add stranger things to his chili, including anchovies.

A smile spread across his face. "Cocoa powder and a bit of yesterday's stale coffee."

"Gross." She scrunched her nose. "Let's eat."

He laughed. "I knew we were related."

As Uncle Bruce dished their meal into their usual blue ceramic bowls, she got their silverware and set out napkins. They didn't share all their meals, but they regularly ate lunch together. She worried about leaving him for a month—although she'd left him alone nearly that long when she'd gone to Europe last summer. Instead of wanting a break from the rain, that time she'd wanted a break from thinking about her ex-girlfriend.

Once they'd settled into their seats, he asked, "Did you find any sexy hackers this morning?"

"Struck out again." She'd explained her job rarely involved personally thwarting would-be hackers, but he was convinced she'd one day meet her match online. "I do have news, though. Or a question, I guess."

As soon as she opened her mouth to mention the month away, her conviction slipped. A month might be too long, especially if Matt didn't keep his side of the bargain.

"Well?" He'd loaded up chili on his spoon but waited for her before taking the bite. "This chili won't taste better lukewarm. And you're not getting any younger."

She rolled her eyes. Uncle Bruce, she decided, could handle bossing Matt around. "If I had someone lined up to do my chores, how would you feel if I went to San Diego for a month?" She might hate living at Matt's house. His ex-wife might be awful. But she felt a zing of excitement as she voiced the idea aloud.

"San Diego? Why would you ever go there? And in spring of all times? I doubt they'll even have rain. You'll have nothing but sunshine."

"That is the risk." She grinned.

"God, a month in San Diego sounds amazing. How'd you swing that?"

"Matt, my friend from work, asked if I'd want to swap places for a while. He's going through a divorce and wants out of his house."

"How old, and is he handsome?"

She laughed. "I think he's in his forties. Sadly straight."

"Everyone has their faults. What about the handsome part?"

She shrugged. "Not my type but he's handsome enough."

"Sold." Uncle Bruce slapped the table. "When's this happening?"

"You really think I should do it?"

"Definitely. You get a vacation in San Diego, I get a handsome replacement for my lunch date."

"Matt has no idea what he's in for." Then again, neither did she. At least her uncle could cook. She didn't know what to expect with Matt's ex, though she doubted there'd be shared meals. Probably the woman wouldn't want anything to do with her.

But all she had to do was keep to the cottage and finish Matt's to-do list. In her free time, she could take walks on the beach with a cute dog. And she'd have all the sunshine she wanted. It really sounded like a perfect vacation.

CHAPTER TWO

Devyn hung her stethoscope on the hook and rubbed the back of her neck. She could use a massage. And a warm bath. Too bad she wasn't getting either of those things tonight.

"Look who's still standing." Kelly reached for her own stethoscope on the hook next to Devyn's. "I heard yesterday was a doozy. Not surprised you volunteered to stay all night—and most of today—but that made, what, thirty-four hours straight?"

"Thirty-six." She'd been on her feet, seeing patients and putting out fires since Friday morning. Now it was Saturday, and dinnertime, by the rumblings in her stomach, and she hadn't slowed down for anything more than a snack break. "Is it April twenty-fifth yet?"

"Still March, last I checked." Kelly stepped out of her sandals and into a pair of Danskos. "Leah better not decide she wants a longer maternity leave. As much as I'm in favor of moms staying home with their babies for as long as they want, we need that particular mom back in this hospital."

"Or we need to clone ourselves." Devyn pulled off the lab coat she'd worn for too many hours and tossed it in the laundry bin. "I'm going home to sleep for a year. See you next Tuesday."

"Did you forget you signed up to be on call tomorrow?"

Kelly's look of concern was warranted. She'd completely forgotten. "Dammit."

"I'll do everything I can to not call you in, but with John out sick and Leah still on maternity leave…"

"It's fine. Call if you need me. And I'm sure you will." She reached for her purse and swung it over her shoulder. "It's not like I have a life anyway."

"Is now a good time to say you're an amazing doctor and you lead our motley team like no one else could?"

"Now is the right time, yes." She smiled. "And thank you. Good luck tonight. Call if you need backup."

"I won't call til tomorrow morning at the earliest." Kelly set her hand on Devyn's arm. "You always look beautiful, but at the moment you look like you've pulled an all-nighter at a swamped and understaffed ER in downtown San Diego."

All-nighter and then some. She numbly thanked Kelly and made her way out the back entrance. With luck, she wouldn't have to interact with another living soul until Angel greeted her at the front door. Dogs she could handle. She was done peopling.

Her dark-blue BMW glistened in the setting sun and she found herself smiling at the sight. "You have no idea how glad I am to see you."

The car didn't respond except to unlock automatically. She settled into the driver's seat, exhaling deeply and letting her eyes close for a moment. She loved her car—it had all the features she wanted and it was all hers, bought and fully paid for after she'd separated her bank account from Matt's—but she was especially happy at the moment because it was her ticket home. With more effort than it should have taken, she opened her heavy eyelids and turned on the engine. She expected thirty minutes of stop-and-go Saturday traffic to make it the five miles home, but then she could collapse in bed.

The radio kept her awake and she sang along to a Backstreet Boys hit from the nineties, grateful no one was around to judge. When her house came into view, she tapped the brakes. A white Honda she didn't recognize was parked in her usual spot.

"I swear to God, if Matt has a woman here…" Her voice trailed. If he had someone over, then what?

Even if it was well within Matt's right to entertain other women, she didn't want to walk in on a dinner date in progress. In her house. Maybe he'd have the decency to keep to the cottage. He seemed to be doing a good job of that lately.

She parked alongside the Honda, too exhausted to search for an open spot on the street, and then hit the garage opener. She stared for a full minute at the empty space where Matt's Range Rover was usually parked. They'd agreed long ago that Matt would always park in the garage and she'd park in the driveway to save them from having to jockey cars if she got called into work late at night. There wasn't room for two cars in the garage because half of the space was taken up with junk Matt had promised to get rid of—including the collection of bikes he never rode. Why he owned three high-end mountain bikes and two racing bikes but never went for a bike ride was something she no longer cared to fight about. The real question was why his car wasn't in the garage.

"Maybe he took his date out to dinner?" She posed the question and immediately hoped that was the case. If so, her plan for showering, microwaving a frozen dinner, and going straight to bed would go off without a hitch.

She went through the garage and into the laundry room, expecting to hear Angel's excited yip. But she heard nothing. "Angel?"

She called for her dog again as she walked down the hall to the kitchen. No scritch-scratch of nails on the tile. No bark. The thought of Matt taking Angel and some woman out for a romantic adventure stung.

As much as she truly felt over their failure of a relationship, Angel was her dog. He didn't get to borrow the dog to woo a date when he acted like it was a monumental ask if she mentioned taking Angel with him on his runs.

The buzz of a Weedwacker interrupted her thoughts and she looked out the kitchen window to the back patio. Angel was stretched out on one of the chaise lounge chairs, his favorite green squeaky ball between his paws and his attention focused on the side yard.

"Did Matt hire a gardener?" Taking care of the yard was the one task Matt seemed to enjoy. Yet he hadn't even seemed to pay attention to that lately. She'd noted the strip of overgrown lawn and the unpruned hedge last week but decided not to bring it up. Every conversation turned into an argument.

She walked around the kitchen island and pushed the blinds open on the window to the side yard. A gasp escaped her mouth as her stomach dropped. "No." She took a shuddering breath. "No, no, no."

It took impossibly long for her to cross through the living room, unlock the sliding glass door, push the broken patio umbrella out of her path, and skirt around the wicker sofa. Angel jumped up excitedly when she passed his spot on the lounge chair, but she didn't slow down to greet him. Instead, she raced to the side yard screaming, "Stop!"

The gardener didn't slow the assault on the plants, not even bothering to turn to face her. She watched, half-paralyzed, as a narrow-leafed milkweed, still yet to flower, crashed to the ground. A stand of buckwheat went under next, followed by some of the showy milkweed. The heartleaf milkweed had already been decimated. That had been the first of the carnage along with the sage, she noted, clutching her chest and fighting back tears.

When she realized the Weedwacker was closing in on the baby lupine pushing up for the sun, she came out of what felt like a trance and barreled forward. She shoved the gardener's arm, propelling them both toward the fence.

"What the—" The Weedwacker motor cut abruptly and the gardener spun round.

"Do you have any idea what a pollinator garden is?" Devyn spat the words, gesturing to the two-foot section of plants still standing.

"What? Hold on." The gardener pulled out earbuds and then held out a hand. "Hey. I'm Robbie."

The woman's bright smile momentarily disarmed Devyn. For one, she hadn't expected the gardener to be a woman. In truth, she hadn't been able to see much beyond cargo pants, a faded gray T-shirt, and a backward ballcap. And she was wearing sunglasses. But when she pushed up her sunglasses it was clear she was very much a woman—and attractive at that.

"I didn't catch what you said. I was blasting my music." She smiled again.

Perfect smile, warm brown eyes, dark lashes, and a look like she was used to winning over everyone who met her. *Well, that's not happening this time.* Devyn shook her head, trying to refocus. "Do you have any idea what a pollinator garden is?"

"Uh, no." The woman's brow furrowed as she looked down at the decimated milkweed. "I mean, I've heard of it. Like a garden for bees?"

"And butterflies." Devyn felt tears spring to her eyes. "Look, I have no idea what you're doing here or why you let out my dog, but—" She realized the woman must have a key to the main house to let Angel out and a bolt of anger shot through her. Matt had let a random gardener have full access to her house. And then left. "You clearly don't know what you're doing."

"I really thought this was a bunch of weeds." The woman pushed a downed stalk of showy milkweed with the toe of her Converse.

"Just give me that Weedwacker and leave." Probably Matt had hired the cheapest gardener he could find. "Are you from Craigslist?"

"What?" The woman seemed legitimately confused now. "I swear I had no idea these were plants you wanted. I was told to mow the grass and take down the weeds."

"These aren't weeds. These are plants the monarchs need so they don't go extinct." She felt her voice rise along with her pulse but couldn't keep either in check. "And don't get me started on the bees. Everything here was about to flower." As soon as she realized that, her anger gave way to grief and she looked down at the fallen plants. "In a month or two, they'd have been covered in butterflies. You whacked them all to shreds."

The woman's face fell. What'd she say her name was? Something ridiculous like Benny or Sammy or… Robbie. That was it. *Robbie.* At least she had the decency to look contrite as she stared at the remainder of the garden and took in what she'd done. Not that feelings mattered at this point.

"Give me that thing," Devyn said, gesturing to the Weedwacker. "Matt can pay you later. I don't even care why you were pretending to be a gardener." She added the last bit as the woman opened her mouth, clearly about to offer an explanation.

"I didn't know—"

"I don't care. Where's the key? You must have one since you let Angel out." She held out her hand.

Robbie dug in her pocket and held up Matt's set of keys. She seemed to hesitate handing them off. "This is probably not the best time to ask, but did Matt tell you about him and me swapping places for a month? I assumed he would have, but now I'm thinking that didn't happen."

"What are you talking about?"

"I work with Matt. We're in the same division—network security. He asked if I wanted to do a house swap and it's been raining nonstop in Seattle."

"A house swap?" She stared at the woman as everything she'd said registered. "As in, you'd be living here?"

"Only for a month."

Only? If she weren't already pissed at Matt, this would do it.

"Matt's staying at my place in Seattle and I'm staying here." Robbie hesitated before adding, "At least that was the plan."

It was unacceptable Matt hadn't asked her permission. Hadn't given her any warning. And this woman thought she had the right to move in because Matt said so?

"He gave me a list of things to do around the house," Robbie continued. "All the projects he hadn't gotten to. Including weeding." She grimaced as she looked at the fallen plants. "The idea was we'd both do each other's chores and get a little break from our worlds."

"I'm sure he wanted a break." She reached out and snagged the keychain. "You can leave now."

"But—"

"I assume you know where the Weedwacker belongs." She turned to the house and called Angel. After a few steps, she looked back at the woman. "You can get your things, if you have things, out of the cottage without keys. You've probably noticed that door doesn't lock. Matt said he would take care of it, but he never did. And you can tell Matt he doesn't need to come back. I'll hire someone and send him a bill for his share."

Devyn didn't look back a second time, relieved when Angel followed her to the house without being called again. "What a mess," she said, pushing the sliding glass door closed behind her. She wanted to be angry at Matt, and angry at this Robbie woman for invading her space, but as she stood in the kitchen, one hand on the cool tile counter and the other reaching down to give Angel a pet on the head, all she felt was exhaustion.

"My gorgeous milkweed." A tear streaked down her cheek and she let out a shaky exhale, then looked at Angel. "Since when are you not barking at a stranger?"

She had no clue when Robbie had arrived or when Matt had left. Sometime in the last thirty-six hours. "My fierce guard dog, who's sent every pet sitter, mail carrier, and repairmen running for the hills, decided this person could stay." She swiped her cheek and cleared her throat. "Well, she can't stay. End of story."

Angel followed her to the pantry and waited as she poured kibble into his bowl. Just as she set down the bowl, the doorbell rang. She cursed out loud, already knowing it'd be Robbie. Angel, on the other hand, didn't make a sound. He simply abandoned his food and raced to the entryway.

"The one time my dog doesn't bark when the doorbell rings." She trudged down the hall after Angel, not bothering to fake a smile when she opened the front door. "Yes?"

"Two things." Robbie stopped abruptly, going down on one knee as Angel circled her feet. She handed Angel's ball to him and grinned when Angel tossed it back for her to throw.

"What two things?" Devyn couldn't keep the irritation from her voice. She was even more annoyed when Robbie tossed the ball into the house and Angel went flying after it. "He's not allowed to have his ball in the house."

"Oh. Sorry."

The apology came at the same moment Angel sailed past Devyn to present the ball to Robbie with an excited yip.

"No balls in the house, buddy," Robbie said. She straightened up, trapping the ball under the toe of her Converse, and met Devyn's gaze.

What adult wore Converse? Devyn reflexively crossed her arms, then wished she hadn't and made herself uncross them. "What did you need to say?"

"The first thing is, I can't actually leave because my key for the rental car is on the ring you took from me. And second—" Angel pawed furiously at Robbie's Converse, trying to free the ball. Robbie looked down, then back at Devyn with a chagrined expression. "One more toss?"

"Fine."

Robbie gently tossed the ball into the foyer and Angel returned almost immediately. Instead of grabbing the ball, Robbie leaned down to scoop up Angel.

"Watch out, he bites—" Devyn stopped short, appalled as Angel leapt into Robbie's arms. To make matters worse, Angel had the nerve to snuggle against her chest. "He doesn't like strangers," she added, feeling ridiculous when Angel licked Robbie's chin.

"Biting's bad. Don't do it," Robbie said, scratching Angel's neck. "You didn't tell me you were a naughty puppy." She gave him another pet before setting him on the ground. "My last dog was a Jack Russell. Maybe Angel figured that out and decided I was an okay stranger."

Devyn knew she was frowning. She also knew she should say something in response but all she could think to say was, "What was the second thing you were going to tell me?"

"Oh. Right. I fixed the lock on the cottage. Had to buy a whole new lock mechanism. And the key is on that ring you took from me, so I can't actually get my stuff out."

"When did you fix it?" She couldn't call Robbie a liar, but Matt had said the lock was unfixable.

"Yesterday afternoon. I didn't know the neighborhood and I didn't know how safe it was sleeping with an unlocked door. No offense, but I didn't want some stranger coming in while I was sleeping."

Pointing out the irony of that statement was useless. "I was told the lock couldn't be fixed because the door didn't close all the way."

"That part took me a hot minute to figure out." Robbie ran a hand through her short brown hair. She had nice hair—which was entirely not important. "I ended up having to take the whole thing off and rehang it. Closes like a charm now."

"Well…thank you. I suppose I should pay you." She shook her head. "I mean, of course I should. I'm sorry. It's been a long day. If you'll hold on a moment, I'll go get my wallet."

"You don't need to pay me. Fixing the lock wasn't a big deal. Turns out I do have some skills. Just not gardening." Robbie's face scrunched up. "I feel awful about your plants. I know you want me to leave tonight, but if I stayed through tomorrow I could buy replacements and patch things up."

"You don't have to do that."

"It's going to be on my conscience forever if I don't."

That wasn't her problem. But when she looked at Robbie, she could tell she felt terrible. Which made it hard to be mad at her.

"I really am sorry," Robbie said. "For being here and for messing everything up. I could stay at a hotel if you'd rather not have me in the cottage, but I want to fix the garden."

Angel took that moment to whine as if he felt bad too. He did seem to be an accomplice. She looked from the dog to the woman who wasn't as much to blame as Matt and felt her resolve crack. "Fine. You can stay one more night. I'll give you a list of plants to buy. But I insist on paying—for the plants and for the door. I won't feel good not paying you for the work."

Robbie bit the edge of her lip. "The thing is, I'm doing this as an exchange with Matt. Also, I should probably tell you I did a few other things on Matt's list. I installed the overhead fan in your guest bedroom—in the main house—and painted the baseboards in the cottage." She hesitated. "And I made a lasagna. He mentioned you never have food in the house. When I realized you hadn't come home last night, I figured when you finally did get here, you were going to be hungry. It's in your fridge with a note."

"You made me lasagna?"

"Matt said you don't like meat so I made it vegetarian." Robbie paused. "You don't have to eat it but I'm a pretty good cook."

There was no reason to make the situation worse by refusing her food. And she was starving. Still, she wanted to scream at Matt for putting her in this impossible situation. "Thank you, but I can only accept if I pay for that too."

Robbie looked like she wanted to argue but said, "We can figure money stuff out tomorrow. I'm guessing you're beat. If I could have that key ring back—"

"Give me a moment." She scooted Angel inside, closed the door, and went to the kitchen island where she'd tossed the keys. As she passed the "guest room" that was now her room, she poked her head in to look at the ceiling. The fan she'd bought two years ago, with a promise from Matt that he'd install it and she didn't need to spend money on hiring a handyman, was hanging in place over the bed. She flipped the wall switch and the fan whirred on.

"Okay. I'm impressed." Not that Robbie had the skills to install a fan but that she'd done so along with all the other projects after only a day and a half. She was almost exhausted enough to consider changing her mind on not letting her stay for the month. But the principle of it bothered her. No one had asked her opinion. And this was a clear invasion of her privacy. The only thing to do was send Robbie packing, hire professionals to finish the jobs Matt hadn't done, and move on with her life.

Convinced she was making the right decision, she stalked back to the front door and tried not to show her annoyance when Angel zipped past her to pounce on Robbie.

"Keys." She handed Robbie the ring. "We can talk in the morning about payment."

"I wanted to ask one more thing." Robbie leaned down to pet Angel, who had gotten insistent for attention. "With Matt gone, who will be taking care of Angel when you're at work?"

Robbie's question stopped her. On one hand it was a relief to have Matt gone, but on the other she would have more things to do herself. "He'll have to go to the boarding kennel when I'm at work. Anything else?"

Robbie's brow furrowed but she only said, "I guess not."

"Let's go, Angel. Inside." Angel looked over his shoulder but didn't move from his spot by Robbie. In fact, he seemed to wag his tail faster when Robbie glanced down at him. "Did you give him treats? He has a sensitive stomach."

"No treats. Matt warned me." Robbie turned Angel around and pointed to the house. "Go inside, buddy. I'll see you in the morning."

This time Angel obeyed, albeit reluctantly. Devyn closed the door, not bothering to wish Robbie good night, and then leaned against it. Angel went to peer through the narrow window at the side of the door, clearly wanting his new friend. "Traitor."

Angel cocked his head and looked her direction, one ear perked.

"But I still love you." She smiled as Angel pivoted his head to perk the other ear. "God, lasagna sounds amazing." Hopefully Robbie was as good at cooking as she was at home repair projects.

CHAPTER THREE

Robbie hit the call button and waited for Matt to answer, debating how much of her anger he deserved. True, the garden disaster was all on her, but things might have played out differently if Devyn had any warning to expect her.

"Hey. How's it going?" Matt sounded more relaxed than even his usual California chill, and Robbie imagined him on her sofa with his feet kicked up. "Your houseboat is the bomb." Matt made a contented sound. "And you didn't tell me I'd be getting gourmet meals. I love your uncle, by the way. I might never leave."

"That's great. For you."

"Why do you sound annoyed?"

"Because, dude, you didn't tell your ex-wife about me. She had no clue who I was—or why I was at your house. She completely freaked out."

"Oh. Guess I should have told her. Honestly, I didn't think she'd care I was gone. And everything happened so fast, you know?"

That much was true. They'd agreed on the plan and bought plane tickets. Forty-eight hours later she was on a flight to San Diego and he was headed to Seattle. "You could have left her a note. Or at least warned me she didn't know what was going on. I assumed you two had talked."

"We haven't talked for a long time, Robbie. She hates me."

"She hates me more."

"No way. She just needs time to process," Matt said. "She doesn't like when things happen that weren't part of her plan. I know she'll come round to liking you."

Robbie thought of the death stare Devyn had given her and doubted Matt's assessment. Her stomach tightened, and she wished she could magically be back in her houseboat, watching the rain and reading a book. She'd traded her perfectly mellow life for Matt's mess. "She might have liked me if she'd known to expect me. Instead she came home to a stranger in her backyard with a Weedwacker."

Matt chuckled. "I'm sure you can charm her. Do a few things on that project list."

"Doing projects isn't going to help. I'm telling you, she's pissed. She said I had to get out."

"Seriously?"

"If she could have thrown me out last night, she would have. She only agreed to let me stay one more night because I begged." She exhaled, eyeing the bed she'd hardly slept in for all the stress. "We need to figure out a plan B."

"Tell her you'll do all the things I didn't do. She'll change her mind."

Her frustration at herself, at Matt, and at the whole situation peaked. "I didn't know what milkweed was, Matt."

"Milkweed?"

"Yes. Milkweed. I knew butterflies needed it, but if you'd asked me to pick one out, I'd have had no clue what it looked like." After spending way too long looking up images of milkweed and researching how to repair the damage she caused, she knew now and felt even worse. "Did you know there's three different species native to California and if you plant the tropical milkweed, it's actually harmful to monarchs?"

"Oh, shit. You didn't touch Devyn's pollinator garden, did you?" Matt's chill was gone.

"It didn't even occur to me that mess of weeds in the side yard was intentional."

"If you pulled anything out—"

"If I'd pulled anything out, I could replant it." She felt tears threaten and scrubbed her face. "I whacked them all down, Matt. I destroyed the garden. Right in front of her."

"Devyn didn't stop you?"

"I think she tried." Robbie had heard someone yell but didn't think it had anything to do with her. "I was listening to music and I didn't notice her freaking out until it was too late."

"Devyn's never going to forgive you. Ever. Monarchs are basically the only thing she likes. Besides Angel."

"Which is why I need to book a flight back to Seattle."

Matt groaned. "You have no idea how much I want to stay here."

"Actually, I have a good idea." She had never wished for a quiet rainy day at home more than she did now.

"I know she'd change her mind and let you stay if you do one of the projects on the list. There's a ceiling fan she really wants put in—"

"Already done. And I fixed the cottage door so it locks."

"You did?" Matt was quiet for a moment. "There's a hole in the living room I was supposed to patch. Maybe you could fix that?"

"She let me stay last night because I begged. Trust me, she's not going to let me stay any longer."

"God, that woman," Matt grumbled. "I swear if something doesn't go exactly her way—"

"She deserved warning." Devyn should have been asked about the plan. She had a right to say she didn't want a stranger on her property. But none of that mattered now. "You need to figure out another place to live. My houseboat only has one room and we aren't sharing the bed."

She ended the call and leaned back in her seat. Light streamed in through the cottage window, and she wished she could appreciate the perfect sunny day. But beyond the sparkling fountain, the main house loomed.

If Devyn didn't so clearly hate her, Robbie could have imagined enjoying getting to know her. The woman exuded confidence and was obviously used to being in charge. And she was even more striking in person than in the brief glimpses Robbie had seen on Matt's Zoom calls. Steely blue eyes, shoulder-length dark-blond hair, sharp features, and a fit body that still managed to have soft curves.

"Plus, she has a cute dog." It was really Angel that made Robbie wish she could stay. She stood and stretched, knowing she shouldn't let herself get attached to a dog that wasn't hers. The problem was, Angel reminded her of Pixie. A year later and she still missed Pixie so much her chest ached when she thought of her.

She checked the time and decided to take Angel for a walk while she contemplated patching the hole Matt had mentioned. Maybe knocking another to-do item off the list would at least smooth over the goodbye.

She'd worried about waking Devyn when she let Angel out earlier that morning. Fortunately, Angel hadn't made a peep, only zipping out the sliding glass door to pee before racing back to the house for breakfast. And there'd been no sign of Devyn, so Robbie assumed she'd stayed asleep.

Now as she approached the house, Angel yipped excitedly and danced on his hind legs. She opened the door and said, "You can't bark. Your owner already wants my head on a platter."

He whined in response and she felt bad. "It's not your fault. I was the one who didn't know what milkweed was. Want to go for a walk?"

Angel immediately took off toward the front door, barking the length of the house. She cringed, expecting to hear Devyn. When she didn't hear anything except more of Angel's barking, she hurried after him. Maybe Devyn was a miraculously deep sleeper.

Angel barked for her to put on his harness and barked louder when she unlocked the front door. "Please, you gotta be quiet. She hates me already."

Whether he understood or not, he stopped barking as soon as the door opened and led the way out, his short tail up like an antenna and his ears perked. She smiled, remembering how Pixie once had walked the same way. When she'd gotten older, she'd gone blind, and although she'd still enjoyed going outside, they rarely walked farther than the patch of gravel at the end of the dock. Then she'd kept her head and her tail down the whole way.

Getting a dog to replace Pixie hadn't been an option. There was no such thing as replacing someone she'd loved that much. But after two days with Angel, she was beginning to think she could make room in her heart for a new dog. "Someone mature like you," she said.

They crossed to the sidewalk and Angel looked over his shoulder as if acknowledging he was mature. The first part of the walk to the beach felt like a stroll through a gated community although there wasn't any gate. All the houses, including Matt's, were fancy and big.

Matt made good money—she knew because she had the same salary—and she guessed Devyn made even more. But Matt had mentioned he'd wanted a nicer house than they really had the budget for. Considering how close they were to the beach, a four-bedroom house with a cottage and a big yard had to be expensive. She wasn't surprised he'd gotten in over his head, but she didn't totally blame him. After only a few days, she was ready to move to the neighborhood, too.

The second part of the walk was a mix of smaller homes and businesses that catered to the beach crowd—a café, a T-shirt shop, and an ice cream place. Beyond that was the beach. A long curve of golden white sand stretching in either direction. The spot was clearly a favorite and plenty of drivers were jockeying for parking places already. "And it's only March." She wondered what the place was like in the summer. "Probably a zoo," she added. "Not that I'll be around to worry about it. You'll have to send me a postcard, Angel."

"Sorry, were you talking to me?" A tall Black woman stood in the open doorway to the café, a crate of produce in her arms. Her eyes squinted at Robbie. "We open at eleven if that's what you asked."

"Oh, no. I was talking to..." She hesitated, wondering if it was better to admit talking to the dog or to herself. "Angel." She pointed to the terrier. "Totally normal, right?"

The woman smiled. "I talk to my dog all the time. She's a good listener. Way better than anyone else in my life."

"Thanks for not thinking it's weird."

"Of course not." The woman lifted a hand. "Enjoy your walk."

It wasn't hard to enjoy a short walk that led to a sun-drenched beach. The brilliant blue ocean glinted beyond the sand and the air felt like a caress—not too hot, not too cold. *Perfect.*

Angel tugged hard on his leash as soon as they got to the sand. "I know the rules. I'm not letting you off." But she did pause to take off her shoes, thinking she should have packed sandals before reminding herself she was leaving soon anyway. With a sigh, she turned to the right and the side of the beach she hadn't explored yet.

More than once she reminded Angel they'd come to get some exercise and not to bark at the sea birds, but she couldn't help smiling. Everyone they passed smiled back. "Too bad this place is perfect." She didn't want to leave but she doubted there was any project on Matt's to-do list that would be enough to convince Devyn to let her stay.

Thinking she might not get another chance to appreciate the beach, she gave in to Angel's request for a long walk. When they got back to the house, she led Angel through the side gate instead of the front door, hoping to avoid Devyn. Unfortunately, Devyn looked up from where she stood in the kitchen at the exact moment Robbie tried to slip past. Then Angel, who she'd unleashed, let out a bark at a pair of finches pecking the carnage of the pollinator garden. Shaking her head, she made her way around the fountain to knock on the sliding glass door.

Devyn took a moment to appear, and when she did, her glare spoke volumes.

"Hi. How's it going?"

Cold didn't begin to capture the temperature of Devyn's responding grunt. Robbie pulled back her shoulders, trying to fortify herself. "I think I figured out which plants I need to replace but I'm worried the nurseries here might not have everything. One of the milkweeds isn't a type that's usually sold for gardens. And they don't sell buckwheat plants."

"I know. I started it from seed."

Was there a temperature below ice-cold? Robbie pressed on. "The good news is I found buckwheat seeds and all the varieties of milkweed in an online nursery. The bad news is the soonest delivery isn't until Thursday." Even with paying for express shipping, there was no chance she'd have the plants or the seeds sooner.

"So you're staying until then?"

Was Devyn suggesting she should stay or annoyed that was even a possibility? From her tone it was impossible to tell. "I know you want me out sooner. I can hire a landscaper—and obviously pay for that—or I can stay."

Angel took that moment to screech across the yard. A squirrel teetered along the back fence and the dog had obvious rules against squirrels. He howled as he pounced on the fence and then continued barking as the squirrel chattered back.

"Angel, no barking." Devyn's reprimand was ignored as was a second reprimand followed by a sharp, "Angel, leave it."

Robbie glanced between Angel and Devyn, remembering Matt's story about getting cited for a noise ordinance when the neighbors complained about the barking. She put her finger in her mouth and let out a loud whistle. Angel immediately stopped barking and spun to look at her.

"Want a treat?" Angel gave up on the squirrel, racing over as Robbie dug in her pocket for a plastic bag full of Angel's kibble, quickly adding, "These aren't actually treats. It's only his kibble."

After catching a few bites, Angel reluctantly obeyed Devyn and trotted into the house. Devyn closed the door behind him and turned back to Robbie. "If you plan on staying, I won't have to take Angel to the boarding kennel."

"Does that mean you want me to stay?"

Devyn crossed her arms. "I didn't say that. I just need to know your plan so I can figure out what I need to take care of. I'm on call today and I'm working all next week. Obviously I never wanted to be in this situation, but here we are."

Making the best of a crappy situation wasn't high praise or encouragement for her to stay. Robbie debated what to say in response. She did want to replant the garden, and getting a plane ticket for the end of the week would be cheaper than a last-minute one.

"By the way, your lasagna was delicious."

"Oh. Thanks." The compliment came as a surprise, but Devyn's voice hadn't softened. "My uncle is a retired chef and he's taught me a lot of tricks. We're always trying to one-up each other."

"If you make other dishes as good as that, I'll pay you to make my meals for as long as you're staying here."

Robbie scratched her head. "Okay, I'm going to be direct. I think you hate me. I don't want to stay if you hate me. Can you tell me if you want me to leave so I don't have to guess?"

"I don't hate you. I don't even know you."

If Devyn had wanted to make her feel completely inconsequential, she'd accomplished her goal. "I took out your pollinator garden."

"And you agreed to replant it." Devyn exhaled. "What's done is done."

Robbie cocked her head. "You're not mad?"

"I didn't say that. I'm upset about what happened, and I'm mourning the fact the butterflies won't have my garden this summer."

Mourning was definitely worse.

"But I overreacted last night. It wasn't simply the garden. It was everything." Devyn met Robbie's eyes. "Finding a stranger in my backyard, realizing you'd been in my house, and then hearing you were planning on staying for a month was a lot."

All reasonable. It wasn't an apology, but Robbie didn't blame her.

"I went to bed thinking I had no idea if you told me your last name or how you knew Matt beyond working with him."

"Robbie Price. I have the same job as Matt but I work at our Seattle site. Since we do the same thing, and we're both mostly remote, we figured we could switch locations and no one would care."

Devyn nodded slowly. "I got a text from Matt an hour ago saying he wasn't coming back."

Where did he plan on staying then? Not in her houseboat if she was going back. She wished Matt hadn't texted Devyn without telling her first. "So you're basically saying you don't want me to stay but you kind of need me to stay?"

"If Angel didn't like you, I'd tell you to leave. I can figure things out on my own and I don't need help from a friend of Matt's."

Ouch.

"I'm pissed Matt pulled this stunt without asking me. And I'm not happy you thought it was fine to come into my house without talking to me first."

Robbie clenched her jaw, fighting back the urge to argue it wasn't her fault.

"But the fan works and no one else was here to take care of Angel. You'll need to keep a list of everything you do so I can pay you at the end."

Robbie shook her head. "If I stay, the work is in exchange for what Matt's doing for me. He's helping my uncle at the marina and taking care of our dock."

"I didn't agree to that plan."

Robbie barely bit back a curse. Somehow Devyn got more under her skin with every passing minute. "You know what? I don't think I want to stay. This is a huge mess and there's a reason I live alone."

"Fine. Leave."

Without another word, Devyn turned on her heel and went into the house, leaving Robbie to stare at her reflection in the sliding glass door.

"Dammit." She rapped on the door and waited. A long minute passed before Devyn reappeared, pushing the door open only a few inches.

"Yes?"

"I want to stay long enough to replant the garden." Hopefully the plants would come by Thursday and she'd be on a flight back to Seattle Friday morning.

"Fine. I want your phone number and emergency contact information. I'm presuming that would be the uncle you mentioned unless you have a significant other."

"No significant other." Robbie almost smiled at Devyn's haughty tone.

"Fine. Your uncle, then. And I'm paying you for any work you do. That's not up for discussion."

"I get the feeling a lot of things aren't up for discussion with you," Robbie said, realizing how her words sounded only after they'd left her mouth.

Devyn stared at her for a moment before clearing her throat and asking, "Is there anything else?"

"No."

"Good. I'll start a list of completed projects. You can add to it and we'll settle up at the end of the week."

Robbie let her shoulders sag when Devyn closed the door and turned away. It was going to be a long week.

CHAPTER FOUR

"He didn't tell you?" Elena shook her head. "Did it not occur to him that this woman would be going in and out of your house?"

"Oh, it occurred to him. He gave her a list of things to do *in* the house. Along with yard work and projects in the cottage." Devyn sank into the open seat at the computer terminal next to Elena's. "The thing is, she's gotten a bunch of things done already and now I'm wondering if I should beg her to stay."

"I'd be too mad at Matt to go along with his plan. Did you tell him not to bother coming back?"

"I didn't have to. He texted me saying he wants to stay in Seattle indefinitely." Devyn exhaled. "Whatever. I'll figure things out on my own. Like usual." She clicked on the patient file for the twenty-three-year-old presenting with arm pain. "I've been doing this job ten years and I still don't understand how someone can be shot in the arm and not know it."

"One of life's great mysteries," Elena deadpanned. "That and how some humans can build rocket ships to take us to the moon and others only manage to get toy rockets stuck up their ass."

Devyn snorted. "Is that a commentary on last night? I heard you got tagged to take someone with a rectal foreign body to surgery."

"It's been my lucky week." Elena grimaced. "I had another on Saturday night too."

"You know these things come in threes."

"Do not tempt fate." Elena pointed to Devyn's computer. "You're supposed to be finishing records so you can get out of here."

Devyn turned back to the screen. "Weren't you trying to get out of here too? Andre took over for you an hour ago, didn't he?"

Elena mumbled, "Too many records," but instead of working on said records leaned back in her seat and closed her eyes. Devyn wondered if she planned on taking a catnap. As far as trauma surgeons went, Elena was one of the best, but she regularly worked double shifts and had seemed more than a little tired lately.

"Are you and Mari doing okay?"

"Define okay." Elena didn't open her eyes but added, "We're fine. Nothing like the trouble you had with Matt."

"That doesn't mean things are good." Devyn studied her friend, noticing the lines on her brow seemed deeper than usual, as did the crow's feet around her eyes. Elena Martinez was not only the best surgeon Devyn worked with, she was her closest friend and it was clear how overworked she was. Her heart clenched in response. "You've had a lot of late nights. Are you working too much for Mari's taste?"

Elena sighed, finally opening her eyes and meeting Devyn's concerned look. "Mari thinks I'm not taking care of myself."

Devyn pointed to the empty Pop-Tart package on Elena's desk. "I'm guessing that was dinner?"

Elena's lips pursed.

"Mm-hmm. And how many days in a row have you been here?"

"Thirteen."

Devyn was on day twelve herself and she knew what that did to her mental health. "When will you admit you're human and give yourself a break?"

"When I die?"

"Don't joke. You know how much I like you—and not only because you're a brilliant surgeon I depend on."

"But mostly that." Elena winked.

"The other surgeons take vacations. And don't agree to work on their days off. You say yes too easily."

"As if you're any better." Elena laughed. "Do you want me to pull up the calendar to mark off the number of shifts you've agreed to work this past month?"

"Leah's on maternity leave and I had someone I was avoiding." She wouldn't have told Matt she was avoiding him before she found out about his yearlong affair, but it was true even then. That was partly why she didn't blame him for finding someone else. She'd almost hoped he would. And since their separation, she'd taken on more responsibilities at work because that meant fewer days—and nights—at home. "You do want to be home with Mari, right?"

Elena was quiet for a minute before saying, "We've been having some hard conversations." She reached for the Pop-Tart wrapper, crumpled it, and tossed it in the trash. "I know I should have expected it eventually. She's always said how much she loves our niece and nephew."

"Wait, she wants kids?" She knew from Elena's tight-lipped look that she'd guessed correctly. "Have you two not talked about this before?"

"Not directly."

When she was trying to get pregnant, Elena had been the one she'd confided in. And Elena had consoled her after the news came that she was infertile. She'd taken comfort in knowing Elena was like her—someone who couldn't have biological children—and eventually she'd realized she was okay with it. But that had taken time and a lot of letting go of expectations.

"I've told Mari I don't understand people who want kids," Elena said. "I guess I wasn't clear that meant I didn't want kids."

"What are you going to do?"

"I don't know." Elena dropped her chin. "I know what Mari wants, and I don't want her to give up what she wants for me. Not something this important. But I also don't want our relationship to be over. Maybe I wouldn't hate being a mom?" Elena shook her head. "I love her. I'd do anything for her."

Devyn set her hand on Elena's shoulder. "She loves you too. And I know she wouldn't want you to go along with something like this if you didn't really want it."

Elena and Mari's relationship was solid. Still, even two people who seemed meant for each other didn't always have the same life goals. Conversely, she knew people could share the same life goals and not be right for each other. When she'd finally told Matt that she not only couldn't get pregnant but didn't want kids, he'd surprised her by saying he didn't want them either. He'd only gone along with it because he thought she wanted kids. That night had been one of the few times she'd felt they'd seen each other clearly. Of course she had no clue then he was already sleeping with another woman.

"Relationships are hard," Elena said, sighing heavily. "Can we go back to talking about Matt's harebrained scheme and this random woman at your house? I don't want to think about my own drama."

"No one wants to think about their own drama." Devyn finished the notes she had to make and then closed the patient file. "I'm so done with Matt. The one thing he promised in the divorce was to finish the projects around the house. I can't believe he passed his to-do list to his coworker. Except it's exactly something he'd do."

"Do you think this woman can do the projects?"

"Yesterday I came home to find her patching a hole in the living room. The hole that's been there since the day we moved in." Matt's promise to fix it that day was a sign of things to come. "She's already mowed the lawn, fixed a lock on a door Matt insisted couldn't be fixed, and hung my ceiling fan. Before I left this morning, I found a note on the fridge asking if I wanted the garage organized."

"Damn. I've got some things I need fixed around my house. Think she wants to come to my place next?"

"Do you want a stranger living in your space?"

Elena hesitated. "If she keeps to herself and gets the work done? I mean, I would obviously have wanted to agree to everything in advance. That's the part that pisses me off for your sake. You had no idea."

"But I don't have time to take care of the yard, I'm not home to take care of Angel, and there's no way I can do all the projects that need to be done around the house. I'm not sure what I'm going to do when she leaves at the end of the week."

"What if you sell the house as is?"

Devyn shook her head. "We bought at the height of the market. If I sell as is, I'll lose too much money."

Elena considered this. "I think you need to convince this woman to stay."

After spending the first night infuriated at Matt for not talking to her about the plan and frustrated at Robbie's very presence, she'd come to the same realization. She didn't want Robbie around, but she was useful.

"You can hide out at work like me while she fixes everything." Elena only seemed to be partly joking.

"I'd miss Angel. And I like taking showers."

Elena lifted a shoulder. "There are showers here. The food's terrible, though."

"True." And she couldn't seem to stop her brain from thinking about Robbie's cooking. "You know that lasagna I made you try a bite of yesterday?"

"God, that was good. Where'd you get that from anyway? Cucina Basilico?"

"Robbie made it." At Elena's look of confusion, she added, "The woman at my house. She said her uncle was a chef and she loves to cook."

"She cooks and does home repairs?"

"And Angel loves her."

Elena's brow furrowed. "That dog doesn't love anyone except you."

"I know. He bites everyone who tries to touch him, but I watched her scoop him up and all she got was a lick on the chin." She still couldn't quite believe Angel's response. "I started calling him a traitor."

"Maybe this Robbie isn't all bad. If Angel likes her…" Elena's words trailed. "Do you know her last name? We could run a background check and make sure she's not a psychopath."

"I don't think she's a psychopath. She seems really normal."

"That's what people say about serial killers."

She rolled her eyes. "Robbie's not a serial killer." Although a background check wasn't a terrible idea. Still, she trusted her gut. Aside from being Matt's friend, there were no red flags or funny feelings with Robbie.

"Matt works with her. He said he's known her for a while. They're both network security engineers but they're based at different sites." She paused, wondering if she should admit her earlier fears which now seemed ridiculous.

After a moment considering it, she continued, "Matt used to talk about this woman he worked with…another network engineer. He seemed really caught up with her. At first I was happy he'd made a friend because he stopped complaining about his job. But then I thought she was the one he'd had the affair with. Now that I've met her, I know there's no way she'd sleep with him." When Elena gave her a questioning look, she added, "I'm sure she goes for women."

"Why didn't you say she was a lesbian to begin with?"

Devyn laughed. "If she's a lesbian, she can't be a psychopath?"

"Oh, she still could be, but this whole mess is more interesting now."

"My problems are only interesting when they involve lesbians?"

Devyn laughed again.

Elena waved a hand in the air. "I said *more* interesting. Don't worry. Your life has been interesting for a while. You know I love drama."

"I'm glad someone's happy."

"Mostly I'm jealous you've got a housebutch," Elena said. "I've always wanted one of those."

"I didn't know a housebutch was a thing." Though the title did seem to fit Robbie.

"I wonder if Mari would be up for a threesome if I told her what this woman can do. Is she good-looking?"

Devyn felt heat unexpectedly rush to her cheeks. She'd been attracted to women before but never felt called out to admit it. And it was one thing recognizing a woman was beautiful and quite another to tell Elena she thought the woman who'd moved into her cottage was hot. But she couldn't deny Robbie was attractive. She'd come home yesterday and found Robbie in her living room stripped down to a tank top and immediately lost all ability to think as she stared at Robbie's sculpted arms and perfect profile. Fortunately, Robbie had been focused on patching the hole and hadn't noticed her gawking.

"Honestly, it doesn't really matter," Elena said, not seeming to notice that Devyn had been thrown by her question. "If she can fix my AC and make me a sandwich, I want her number."

A knock sounded, and both Devyn and Elena looked to the open doorway. One of the new overnight nurses gave them an apologetic smile. "Hate to bug you, Dr. Lancaster, but Dr. Zang is asking for backup."

Devyn nodded. "Tell her I'll be there in five." She turned to Elena. "I'll ask Robbie if she works on air conditioners. She'd probably rather be living at your house than mine." In a lower voice she added, "And I know you love Mari and she loves you. You two need to talk about the kid question. I want you to save your marriage while you still have one."

"Mari and I will be fine. You're right. We do love each other. This is just a bump in our road."

Devyn raised an eyebrow as she reached for her stethoscope. "So why aren't you going home?"

"I'm not leaving until you do. Go help Kelly."

Kelly's relief was obvious the moment she saw Devyn. "I know you were scheduled to be off hours ago, but Malcolm is in with a cardiac arrest and I've got a twenty-year-old male with a tension pneumothorax and a nine-year-old girl with a temp of one-oh-six who started seizing. Plus some guy up front is making a racket about his chest pain."

"If he's making a racket, he's not next in line. I'll take a look at the kid with the fever."

Kelly blew out a breath. "Thanks. I owe you."

An hour later, Devyn found Elena exactly where she'd left her. With another empty package of Pop-Tarts. She pointed to the wrapper and Elena said, "Don't judge. I wasn't going to finish my records without empty carbohydrates."

"Did you finish?"

"Close enough."

Elena was either too exhausted or too caught up in her thoughts to say more. She didn't talk as they gathered their things or as they walked through the parking garage together either. It wasn't until they'd reached their cars that Elena turned to Devyn and said, "I'm sorry about Matt leaving. I know you said you needed his income to pay the bills. If you need any help these next few months—"

Devyn cut her off, raising her hand. "I'll be fine. I can cover a few months on my own." Although after paying off Matt's credit card debt that had become a joint debt with the marriage, she had almost nothing in savings. "Worst case, I tap into my 401K. The only problem is him leaving means I need to sell sooner rather than later."

"Don't pull money out of your retirement. Come to me for help first."

"Elena, I don't want to—"

"Please." Elena met her gaze. "I know you'd only ever need a short-term loan."

She could take out a bank loan if it came to that, and she'd sooner do so than ask for money from a friend. Then again, Elena wasn't simply any friend, and if Devyn could, she'd do the same for her. Finally, she dipped her head. "If it comes to that, we'll talk."

"That was hard for you to say, wasn't it?"

She smiled. "You know me too well."

Elena opened her arms and Devyn stepped into the embrace. She didn't realize how much she needed the hug until her heart tripped over itself to return it.

"See you in nine short hours," Elena said, releasing her.

"Don't remind me."

Devyn followed Elena's car, parting ways only when they reached the freeway. She cranked the volume dial on the radio to stay alert, but her eyelids kept drooping and she breathed a sigh of relief when her house came into view.

The porch lights were on, but the house was quiet when she unlocked the door. She went to the kitchen and called for Angel, worrying when he didn't appear to immediately greet her. Fortunately, she heard the rustle of his tags as he groggily got up from his bed in the living room and shuffled over to see her, tail halfheartedly waving.

"Are you feeling okay?"

At any time, day or night, she usually got an enthusiastic response from him—unless he was outside and distracted. Now all she got was a lick of her hand and a butt wiggle when she gave him a pat on the head. Running through the list of possible ailments he could be suffering from, she spotted a note on the kitchen counter with the title of "Don't worry—Angel is Fine."

She smiled as she read the note that detailed how Angel had made a friend at one of the off-leash parks. "You met another little terrier with too much energy, huh?" She glanced at Angel. He'd taken himself back to bed but wagged his tail at her words. "Sounds like you had fun."

She pushed away a twinge of jealousy at her dog having a fun afternoon with Robbie—because it didn't make sense to feel jealous—and scanned the rest of the note: *Quinoa tabouli in the fridge in case you're hungry.*

She thought of Elena's comment about a housebutch and then the question she'd side-stepped about whether Robbie was good-looking. Even if she did find Robbie attractive, it didn't matter. She wasn't going to act on any attraction. She'd never dated a woman before and there was no sane reason to make the first time be with someone who was Matt's friend.

"She probably won't stay long anyway." Not long enough to worry about a hormonal response. Once the garden had been replanted and Robbie had assuaged her guilty conscience, she'd leave.

Devyn went to the fridge and took out a large bowl wrapped and carefully labeled with a list of ingredients. It seemed like too much work to dish a portion into a separate bowl, so she sat down at the table and dug her fork right in.

"Oh, damn." She took another bite and didn't hold back a moan. Yes, she was still annoyed at Matt, and yes, she felt conflicted about finding Robbie attractive. But the real problem was her cooking. Robbie hadn't left and already she knew she'd miss the gourmet meals.

CHAPTER FIVE

Robbie squinted at the bedside clock, half disbelieving the hour. She forced herself upright, then squished her feet into slippers and blearily made her way out of the cottage. By the time she'd reached the main house, the barking had stopped. She stood still for a moment, considering bringing Angel back to the cottage with her. Matt had been adamant about not letting Angel bark at night, but she'd discovered Angel wasn't happy staying by himself when Devyn worked late. The problem was, Devyn hadn't given her a schedule.

It'd been four days of their awkward co-living arrangement and she'd exchanged less than ten sentences with Devyn—most of which had happened in the fight over the pollinator garden. Since then, Devyn had seemed to go out of her way to avoid interactions. The few times they'd been in the same room together, Devyn had made some excuse for why she couldn't stay and talk. But she'd left Robbie thank-you notes and had a list taped to the fridge of all the completed projects with stars next to each one like some kind of grade school report card. It was oddly rewarding to add a project to the list and find a silver star next to it the following morning.

A loud bark made Robbie jolt. She couldn't see Angel at the sliding glass door and it was locked anyway, so she went to the side yard and let herself in through the laundry room with the keycode lock she'd placed earlier that day. Another to-do item checked off the list.

Angel's barking didn't stop when she called for him, so she shuffled through the kitchen to the living room and turned around in a circle, still confused as to where the sound had come from. Finally, she decided Angel must be upstairs. She started down the hall and paused midstep. The light was on in the guest bathroom, which meant Devyn was home. Before she'd decided what to do, the light switched off and the door opened.

"What the—" Devyn shrieked.

"Shit, sorry," Robbie said, immediately covering her eyes.

A towel was wrapped around Devyn's waist and another was wrapped around her hair, which left her breasts and midsection on full display. Robbie had gotten more than a little peek and…damn. Devyn was gorgeous half-naked.

"What the hell are you doing in here? It's two in the morning."

"Angel was barking. I came to figure out—"

"Go. Now."

"I'm going." Robbie turned around, hand still over her eyes. She took a step toward the kitchen and a howl came from the second floor. "See, he was doing that. I know the neighbors complain if he barks and I didn't know you were home."

"Just go." Devyn's voice was icy. "Angel," she hollered. "Quit barking."

Angel barked again and Robbie stopped walking. She didn't dare turn around. "Can I check and see why he's barking?"

"I can check myself," Devyn said. "And as soon as you leave, I will."

"What if someone's upstairs?"

Devyn let out an exasperated sound. "He's probably spotted the neighbor's cat. I opened the windows up there."

Robbie gritted her teeth but headed for the door, not bothering to keep her hand over her eyes now. She couldn't ignore the protective urge telling her to go upstairs and check for herself, but Devyn left no room for arguing. When she got to the laundry room, she stood for a moment listening. Angel hadn't let up on his barking. "Dammit."

She turned around and called out, "I don't want to leave you alone to be killed by some burglar. If you opened the windows, that means someone could have come in. Please let me check? You can send me back to Seattle after." When no response came, she added, "If the cops show up and I have to explain how I was the last one to see you alive—"

Devyn groaned. "Fine. Go check."

A door slammed and Robbie exhaled. "Remember when you thought San Diego would be a nice little vacation?" She shook her head and reached for the heavy-duty Maglite she'd discovered earlier in the laundry room. As she crossed through the kitchen, she checked to make sure the flashlight worked. "Matt's ex will hate you and you might get killed by burglars but, hey, the weather's great." She lowered her voice, passing by the room she'd assumed was for guests but that Devyn had gone into. A light shone under the doorway, and she imagined Devyn on the other side waiting for her to pass.

Why was Devyn sleeping in the guest room when there were three perfectly good suites upstairs—each with their own bathroom? She didn't plan on asking but she was curious. Now that she'd seen Devyn half-naked, she doubted there would be any further conversations. Not that much had been said, but from Devyn's horrified look she was certain she'd be sent packing by the morning. Too bad, she mused. She'd finally settled in and begun to enjoy herself.

She reached the end of the hall and headed up the stairs. Trying to guess where Devyn slept had been on her mind since she'd hung the ceiling fan. Matt's notes on the house hadn't exactly been clear, and she'd had to go from room to room in order to find the "fan in closet in the guest room."

She hadn't snooped around the rooms on the second floor except to figure out which ones needed paint touched up—another one of the items on Matt's list—and she'd been surprised to not be able to tell which room Devyn regularly used. All the beds were meticulously made and nothing seemed out of place.

What she had noticed was that one of the bathrooms on the second floor had only a plywood base floor and no toilet while another had a tub with no shower door or curtain. None of those repairs were on her project list, however.

She reached the last step and stopped, realizing Angel had switched from his barking to a low growl. "Oh great," she muttered, switching on the Maglite. If someone in fact was in the house, despite all the noise they'd made, the only thing she had to defend herself was a flashlight.

She walked into the first room and swung the beam from the bed to the closet before flipping the wall switch. Then she peeked under the bed and checked the closet, trying not to worry about what she'd do if she met anyone. Once she'd convinced herself no one was hiding in the room or the attached bathroom, she went to the second bedroom. Angel let out an excited yip as she entered but didn't come to greet her. Instead, he pawed the sliding glass door to a balcony overlooking the backyard. The windows were open but the door was closed.

"What's out there?"

To be safe, she checked the closet and the bathroom before going to the sliding glass door. It took a moment to see Angel's perceived threat—a black cat hunched up in a corner of the balcony, eyes wide as it stared back at them.

"You've got that kitty terrified." She shook her head at Angel, who was quite sure she'd come to open the door for him. "I'm not letting you out," she said. "And you're a naughty dog for scaring that poor cat and waking me up." And likely getting her kicked out of the house after she'd barged in on Devyn.

She knew Angel wouldn't follow her willingly out of the room, so she ran downstairs to grab a leash and a few cheese cubes. Angel let her hook on the leash in exchange for a cheese cube, clearly believing the next step would be her opening the door, but then she marched him out of the room and closed the door behind them.

When they reached the bottom of the stairs, she unhooked Angel's leash and tossed him the second cheese cube. "Now go to bed and no more barking."

"Was it a cat?"

Robbie felt her cheeks get hot. From where Devyn stood in the hallway, there was no chance she'd missed seeing Angel scarfing up the cheese. "Yeah. There's a little black cat stuck up on the balcony."

"It's usually a brown tabby. Maybe the tabby invited a friend."

Devyn's voice was surprisingly neutral and since she didn't mention the cheese, Robbie considered not saying anything either.

But her conscience was already on overdrive, so she cleared her throat and said, "I don't usually give him treats—I promise—but I wasn't sure I'd be able to get his leash on. He was all riled up over that cat."

"Can you sleep now that you know there's no burglar in the house?"

"Yeah. Sorry." Robbie ran a hand through her hair, guessing it was a tousled mess since she'd been asleep for hours before Angel's barking and then wondering why she cared. Devyn hated her. For many good reasons. Unfortunately, that didn't stop her body from bringing up the fact that Devyn was a gorgeous woman when she wasn't yelling at her. Actually, she was gorgeous even then.

"You can lock up when you let yourself out?"

"Of course."

"Then good night." Devyn called Angel and the dog trotted to the guest room.

When the door closed behind the two of them, Robbie blew out a breath. She started for the laundry room and then remembered the cat. The balcony was empty, but she poked her head out anyway and scanned the roof to make sure the cat had escaped.

She couldn't blame the cat. Or Angel, really. Once again, her screwing up with Devyn was all on her. She trudged downstairs after she double-checked the other rooms and then made her way back to the cottage.

Hours later, Angel's bark woke her again. This time, though, sunlight shone between the cracks in the blinds and when she eyed the clock, she decided it was late enough that the neighbors would forgive Angel for a few barks.

Still, she pulled the blinds up enough to look outside. She spotted Devyn in jogging pants leaning over to unhook Angel's leash. Devyn's backside certainly was easy to look at. When she stood, Robbie realized she only had a sports bra on her top half.

"Fuck me." Robbie groaned and fell back on the bed, reminding herself she had no business appreciating Devyn's body. What had Matt done to lose Devyn? He'd made it sound like the divorce, though he didn't want it, was his fault. But what had happened?

With Devyn taking care of Angel, she considered falling back asleep but her mind was awake—and now obsessing about Devyn's body—so she got out of bed and headed to the shower.

Days had started to blur, which was a sure sign at least part of her brain considered her on vacation. When she finished in the shower, she had to check her calendar to remind herself of the date. She had a Zoom meeting scheduled with Matt that morning. She'd told him she'd won a reprieve from Devyn and could stay until the end of the week, but after last night she guessed the reprieve would be revoked. Hopefully he had a plan for where he could go. She planned to focus on asking about that while avoiding any questions about why she needed to return early. The last thing she wanted to explain was how she'd seen his ex half-naked.

She finished brushing her teeth as she scanned overnight usage reports and then pulled on a T-shirt and settled in at her makeshift desk. The nightstand had enough space for her laptop, and when she sat crisscross style on the bed she was mostly comfortable. It wasn't ergonomic, but she wouldn't be staying long and she could do most of her work in short bursts.

A rapping on her door broke through her train of thought while she was running a diagnostic check on a set of servers at one of the Seattle locations. She got up, realized she hadn't put on shorts yet, and called out, "Give me a sec."

Devyn had changed out of the workout clothes she'd been in earlier and now wore a light blue blouse with navy pants. The blouse brought out the darker blue of her eyes and Robbie couldn't help staring.

"This may, or may not, be a peace offering." Devyn held up a white box.

Robbie eyed the pastry box. "I think I'm the one who should be bringing peace offerings."

Devyn gave a little head shake and said, "Do you like quiche?"

"I love quiche."

"Good. Then this is my apology for last night." Devyn handed the box to Robbie. "And, rest assured, I did not make the quiche."

"Do you not like to cook?"

She tipped her head. "No one should have to suffer through anything I cook."

Robbie smiled. "You know, you didn't have to get me anything. I'm the one who disturbed your evening and—" She stopped herself short from saying *saw you naked* and instead said, "And made a big deal out of nothing."

"You didn't know I was home. I'd only just gotten in, and if you hadn't stopped Angel I'm sure I would have a noise ordinance violation to deal with. Another one," she added with a sigh. "I also still feel bad for yelling at you about the garden. Most of those plants will grow back on their own." She took a deep breath. "Anyway. I know I've been difficult, but I wanted to ask if you'd consider staying longer."

"Past Friday, you mean?" Robbie couldn't believe Devyn was asking her to stay after last night.

"Your original plan was to stay for a month, right?"

She nodded.

"Having someone here taking care of things is a huge help. And I hate the thought of putting Angel in day care for the long hours I'd need with Matt gone." Devyn paused. "When we talked about this on Sunday, you basically told me to go to hell." She gave Robbie a tight-lipped smile. "Which was reasonable. I blamed you for Matt's mess and that wasn't fair. But if I promise to be nicer, would you consider staying?"

Robbie processed everything Devyn said, surprised they were having this conversation after last night.

"I understand if you want to take some time to think about it. I have to get to work anyway." She shifted the purse on her shoulder and added, "You can tell me tonight."

"Okay. I'll think about it."

Devyn nodded, seemingly understanding, but her expression held a note of disappointment. Her apology hadn't meant an immediate turnabout in Robbie's plan.

"I do still plan on paying you for all the work you've done around here."

Robbie shook her head. "Not if I decide to stay. Those aren't terms I'll agree to if I'm staying here without paying rent."

Devyn looked back at the house and then met Robbie's gaze again. "Look, I'm screwed if you leave. One of the other doctors is out on maternity leave until the end of April, which means I'm working twice as much as usual. But I need to get this house listed and I don't have time to find someone to do the things you can do. So basically tell me your terms."

"I want to think about it."

"Fine." Devyn blew out a breath. "There's two different types of quiche in there. One's spinach Florentine and the other is mixed grilled veggies. I don't think even you—the gourmet cook—will be disappointed."

With that, Devyn turned and left, not bothering with a goodbye or a see you later. Robbie eyed the pastry box, her stomach rumbling. As far as peace offerings went it sounded amazing, but she wasn't ready to say as much to Devyn.

CHAPTER SIX

The kitchen was spotless and someone had vacuumed the living room. That someone wasn't a mystery, though Devyn had no idea when Robbie had found the time.

Last night Devyn had stood for a good two minutes in the middle of the garage wondering how one person could have brought order to a space that had been a complete disaster only the day before. The boxes labeled "donate" were gone, the trash pile including Matt's old bachelor furniture had been cleared out, and her own "deep storage" boxes were carefully stacked along the back wall. Not only that, but the motley collection of bikes now hung from the ceiling and the workout equipment—weights, weight bench, and rowing machine—no longer had cobwebs or a layer of dust. These items still took up a quarter of the garage but there was nothing stacked between anymore and there was more than enough space to park.

She'd made the decision then to call the realtor. Selling suddenly seeming possible. The bathrooms upstairs were still an issue—she needed to either hire an attorney to go after the contractor who'd disappeared with her money and the job half-finished, or she needed to find a new contractor. But all that seemed doable.

Devyn got out the cleaning supplies and headed for her bathroom. She had an hour before the realtor was due and no intention of wasting a minute. There was also something grounding in doing the little things she could take care of, and her nerves needed all the help they could get. The reality of leaving a home that had felt so full of promise at first but quickly became a source of contention and stress was emotionally exhausting. In some ways she didn't blame Matt for wanting to simply walk away. Still, someone had to stay and deal with things.

Her thoughts drifted to Robbie for the hundredth time that week. It was Thursday, which meant the plants Robbie had insisted on buying to replant the pollinator garden were due to arrive. And then Robbie would be flying back to Seattle on Friday. Unless she'd changed her mind about staying. Devyn wanted to ask but worried the answer would be no.

"I'll be fine if she leaves," she murmured. Of course she would. And yet she wanted her to stay.

She'd tried to convince herself the only reason for that was having help around the house. She knew, though, that the way she felt when Robbie looked at her played a part. And how she felt when she looked at Robbie. She couldn't deny the attraction and it'd been ages since her body had noticed anyone. Which made everything more complicated.

"I need to stop thinking about her," she said, spritzing the bathroom mirror with Windex. "And think about the things I should be focusing on." She swiped a paper towel across the mirror and eyed her reflection. "Like what I'm doing with my life."

"First on the list is deciding where I'm moving to." She squirted cleaner into the sink basin and then tugged up her rubber gloves. Of course she could go anywhere and a new ER job wouldn't be difficult to find, but she liked her job and she had friends. "Second on the list…" She'd been about to say she needed to sort through her finances, but her mind had jumped away from the question of her long-term financial stability to what to do about her recent revelation. "About liking women."

As soon as the words were out of her mouth, her hand stilled. She glanced down at the sink basin, sudsy with cleaner, then stared at the sponge in her hand. Robbie wasn't the first woman she'd been attracted to. The stirrings she felt were no sudden epiphany.

But she'd never felt so strong of an impulse to act on any attraction. "If she leaves tomorrow it doesn't matter."

But when she was ready to date, did she want to try dating women? She thought of the TA in her college chemistry class she'd crushed on for a full semester. Anyone would have found Ariana attractive, she'd argued at the time. Then came Vanessa. For the first year of medical school, she'd been infatuated with Vanessa. They were study partners, though, and nothing more. She'd considered reaching out to Vanessa after graduation but couldn't think of what to say.

Months ago Elena had asked if she was ready to start dating again. Between the trial separation and the divorce process, it'd been over a year since she'd slept in the same bed as Matt. She'd told Elena she liked being single. She'd even convinced herself she didn't need company. She had enough peopling at work and liked quiet evenings with Angel.

"And yet I want Robbie to stay." The weight of her words and the meaning sunk in. She wanted Robbie to stay not simply because it was nice having help. "Dammit. I have a fucking crush."

She stared at her reflection, made a look of disbelief, and then laughed. "How old am I?" Too old for a crush.

Maybe it wasn't exactly a crush. If the other person shared the same feelings, what was it called? She thought again of the moment she'd stepped out of the bathroom and seen Robbie. She could have covered herself but she hadn't tried. Robbie had shielded her eyes but not before giving her a once-over that made Devyn feel alive in a way she hadn't felt in years.

Robbie's desire was palpable. But only for a second. Then it was replaced with a look of distress and an awkwardness that took away any anger Devyn felt for the intrusion on her privacy. Robbie hadn't meant to look and had been embarrassed by her own response. That was mostly why she'd given in and let Robbie check to make sure Angel was only barking at a cat. Mostly that. But also she wanted Robbie in her space a breath or two longer.

"Now you're being ridiculous," she murmured.

Once the bathroom was clean, she tidied her room and started a load of laundry. At two minutes to ten, Angel barked and a moment later the doorbell rang announcing the realtor's arrival.

Shania Whitmore looked no more than twenty-five, but she'd come well recommended and it was Southern California—which meant Botox and cosmetic surgery foiled age-guessers everywhere. Devyn took Shania's card as she reminded herself to keep an open mind.

"I can't believe you want to leave this location," Shania said.

I don't. Devyn forced a smile and the words: "I'm hoping you'll have eager buyers because of the location." She loved the location, but she simply couldn't afford to make the mortgage payments alone. There was no use arguing with her bank statement. Besides, the house was too big and she was done with the bad memories associated with it.

She led Shania on a tour, noticing when the realtor's brow bunched and when her lips pursed. She'd planned on updating things when they'd bought but Matt's spending habits had limited what they could do. Together they made plenty, and it had taken her a while to figure out why the balance in their account kept shrinking. Matt liked buying toys for himself like new bikes and the Range Rover, but a good chunk of their income had been funneled to women he met online and eventually the upkeep of his mistress. She was embarrassed how long it'd taken her to realize where the money was going.

"Oh, this is nice," Shania said, stepping out into the patio and eyeing the fountain, then turning her gaze on the hot tub and finally the fire pit.

"The hot tub isn't working. Neither is the fire pit." Devyn quickly added, "Of course I'll make sure both are working before the house is listed."

Robbie came out of the cottage then, bopping her head to a beat and singing. Her voice had an easy, warm timbre to it but Devyn didn't recognize the song. Robbie also wasn't singing loudly and didn't seem to notice she had an audience until she looked up. Then she stopped short and her mouth dropped open. She tugged her earbuds off as she rushed an apology.

"No need to stop," Shania said. "I love Lana Del Rey. You keep vibing."

Devyn glanced from Shania, who was clearly giving Robbie an appreciative once-over, to Robbie, who was very obviously blushing. Devyn clenched her jaw. One, it was annoying to feel out of the loop. Who was Lana Del Rey? Two, it was annoying Shania wasn't being professional. And, three, why did Robbie have to look so good in a tank top and board shorts?

"I'm on a break waiting for some data uploads," Robbie said, ignoring Shania and focusing on Devyn. "Okay with you if I take Angel to the beach for a bit?"

"Go ahead." She waved to the house. "I kept him inside so he wouldn't be racing after the squirrels while I was showing the realtor around. Do you mind if we go in the cottage?"

"It's yours," Robbie said with a shrug.

Shania looked between the two of them, clearly trying to parse out the arrangement, while Robbie headed for the house. "The cottage could use some updating," Devyn began, leading the way between the patio furniture and the fire pit. "But I know it has a lot of potential."

In fact, the cottage looked better than it had in months. Robbie had repainted and the metal blinds that had been on Matt's to-do list to get rid of were gone. Sunlight streamed onto the kitchenette, and aside from an open laptop the countertop was clean. All the clutter Matt had moved into the cottage with was gone. She wondered if Matt had asked Robbie to gather up his things or if he'd cleared out before leaving for Seattle.

"This is a sweet space," Shania said, walking from the kitchen to the one bedroom and then peeking into the bathroom. "And if your tenant is always this clean, I don't think you'll need to worry about listing with her still living here."

"She's not a tenant."

"Oh." Shania hesitated and then said, "You mentioned an ex. Is she—"

"No. And I'm not sure how much longer she'll be here anyway."

Shania's brow creased. "Well, normally I would say it's much easier not having tenants."

"Let's assume she won't be here by the time I'm ready to list."

They stepped out of the cottage right as Robbie and Angel came out of the main house, and Devyn tried to ignore how Shania's gaze zipped right to Robbie. "Have fun at the beach."

"Thanks." Robbie grinned. She dropped down to one knee to latch Angel's harness and the dog kissed her chin.

Shania's eyes followed Robbie and Angel through the side yard to the locked gate. When Robbie stopped to work the combination on the lock, Shania pointed at the remnants of the pollinator garden. "Flowers would look lovely there. I can tell you're in the process of taking out those weeds, but that's one thing you'd want to have done before listing. Flowers are an easy way to spruce up the yard and you've done a good job incorporating flowers in the other areas."

"That's a pollinator garden," Devyn said.

Robbie had paused at the gate and now looked back at Devyn and Shania. "It's my fault it looks terrible. I didn't realize it was a garden. But I'm replanting the milkweed tonight."

Shania turned to Devyn. "You should consider flowers. Everyone loves some colorful pansies."

"Not everyone." The words slipped out before Devyn could stop herself and she heard Robbie snicker. She gave Robbie a sharp look and Robbie cleared her throat in response.

"Actually, I was thinking of suggesting that a coneflower mix might be nice along the edges of the milkweed," Robbie said. "Still pollinator friendly but—"

"Coneflowers will look less like weeds." Shania nodded in agreement.

"I don't think flowers are going to sell this house." Devyn had to stop herself from grinding her teeth. "But I would appreciate a list of things you think should be fixed before I sell."

"Well, definitely those two bathrooms on the second level need to be finished."

"I had a contractor issue." Devyn exhaled. "I can find someone to do the tile and obviously I'll get a new toilet installed."

"I can do those things," Robbie said.

Devyn didn't ask why Robbie was lingering—and now eavesdropping. Angel was peeing on a bush and Robbie seemed to think that was a good enough excuse. "You know how to do tile work?"

Robbie nodded. "I had a job working with a general contractor in college. I learned how to do a little bit of everything. You've got a tile saw in the garage along with a bunch of other tools."

"They're from the contractor who split," Devyn said. "What about installing a toilet?"

"That's easy."

Devyn wished Shania wasn't standing next to her as she psyched herself up for the next question she had to ask. "You aren't leaving tomorrow?"

"I thought I'd stay a while longer if it's still okay with you. I'd like to finish Matt's to-do list. Seems only right after everything."

After everything. Did Robbie mean after swapping houses and no one asking her? Or after Matt deciding he wouldn't come back? Or after the pollinator garden massacre? She hoped it wasn't the part about seeing her half-naked. What more could go wrong if Robbie stayed? Considering how thrown off balance she felt around Robbie, she hated to even ask that question.

"You should take her up on the offer," Shania said. "Finding someone to do the tile and someone else to repair all the other things you mentioned will likely mean we have to push out the listing date. If you have someone willing"—she motioned to Robbie—"you don't want to pass that up. Ideally, we want to be on the market when everyone still has spring fever. I'd recommend listing by May first at the latest."

Devyn agreed with everything Shania said even if something about her was off-putting. She looked at Robbie. "You're sure about wanting to stay?"

"I like getting little silver stars after I complete a project," Robbie joked. "It's kind of addicting. And, honestly, I still feel like I'm on vacation here."

How long would that last? Devyn didn't ask that question or the half-dozen others that came to mind. Robbie was still a stranger. Helpful, friendly enough, and attractive, but someone she really didn't know.

CHAPTER SEVEN

Robbie tossed Angel his ball and then shifted back on the lounge chair. The temperature had dropped noticeably over the past few hours—though Clara from the café had argued the week's weather had been unseasonably warm. Apparently, a morning fog layer with a high of sixty-five was more typical. Grudgingly, she'd pulled on a hoodie and switched her shorts for jeans, accepting she'd gotten lucky with temperatures in the eighties the first several days.

Angel deposited the ball at her feet and she tossed it again. She'd logged off her work computer a half hour ago and was debating checking out the Friday night downtown scene versus working on the hot tub. Matt hadn't left much for her to go on with that repair—only a note saying: *I think something's wrong with the filter.* Since she'd never owned a hot tub and never worked on one, she knew she'd have to start with an online search for possible problems and then watch YouTube repair videos. None of which sounded like an exciting Friday night.

Her phone rang and she smiled as Uncle Bruce's picture appeared on the screen. She'd taken the shot when he was barbecuing on the dock under an umbrella in his daisy apron.

"What's the matter? Couldn't find anything better to do on a Friday night than call your niece?"

"I'm making sure you're getting yourself into trouble and not spending your Friday night alone."

She eyed Angel. "Don't worry. I've got a dog who seems to like me, and he doesn't have any other plans."

"Robbie." He let out an exaggerated sigh. "You're thirty-four. You need to be out meeting people."

"What if I like dogs better?" Angel had been a perfect companion for the week. Not only was he eager to accompany her to the beach on breaks, he stayed at her side while she worked and supervised all the house projects—though mostly this involved trying to convince her it was time for a snack break. "Being with Angel has made me remember how nice it is having company. I think when I get back, I'm going to start checking out dogs at the Humane Society."

"You're young and single. You're supposed to be checking out women."

"I'm not that young. Besides, dogs are easier to please." The woman she'd found herself trying to please all week was particularly difficult. "How's it going with Matt?"

"Someone needed to send him to therapy years ago, but he likes my food and knows how to play poker."

"You know he's straight."

Another of her uncle's classic exaggerated sighs. "Hopelessly."

She laughed. "Some people are born that way."

"Sadly true. It must be a hard life. But hate the sinner, love the sin, right?"

She laughed again. "You're terrible."

"What's his ex-wife like?"

"Also straight." *Hopelessly.* As soon as the thought crossed her mind, she pushed it away. She'd been fighting her attraction to Devyn all week, and the only thing that made it easier were the constant reminders that Devyn was not interested in her.

"I'd take him out to the clubs if I didn't feel too old for that crap."

It took her a moment to remember her uncle was talking about Matt. "You're only sixty-eight. You can still go out."

"Yeah, to a golf club."

She laughed. "You don't golf."

"The point is being seen, my dear."

Her phone buzzed with a text, and she cussed under her breath as she read the message from Matt: *I got a Sev 1 priority ticket – there's a network outage at the data center. In San Diego.*

"You could learn to like being seen yourself."

"By dogs, maybe." She lowered her phone and read the text again. "Hey, Uncle Bruce, Matt texted me about a problem at one of the sites down here. I have to give him a call." So much for being off for the weekend. "Talk to you later?"

"No. Because you'll be out meeting women."

"Sure." She said goodbye, then immediately rang Matt. After confirming there was no option other than her going to the data center—and using his badge to get into the building—she went to trade her hoodie for one of Matt's Padres sweatshirts. He'd loaned her a Padres hat too, possibly as a joke, but she decided to wear it.

As she came out of the cottage with Angel at her heels, she saw Devyn open the sliding glass door and step out of the main house. Devyn narrowed her eyes, probably surprised to see all the Padres gear, while Angel let out an excited howl and raced over to Devyn.

"Someone's happy to see you," Robbie said, then realizing that it sounded like only Angel was happy, she quickly added, "You look nice. Going out?"

Devyn did look nice. Not that she didn't usually, but in place of the dress slacks and blouses she usually wore for work, she was in a dress and heels.

"I'm meeting some friends for dinner. Work colleagues."

"Cool. Have fun." Robbie started toward the side gate, wondering why Devyn had thought it important to distinguish friends as work colleagues and then decided she was overthinking the comment. "Oh," she said, pausing. "I already fed Angel. Didn't know when you would be getting off work. And he's had his walk so he should be set for the evening."

"Great. Thanks."

She'd noticed Devyn had the same response to nearly everything she mentioned even when there was bad news mixed in. *I ordered those tiles you wanted but they won't arrive for a week*—"great, thanks." *I hung the shower curtain you bought but it kind of fights the bathroom wall color*—"great, thanks." Either Devyn had too much on her mind or simply didn't really care what Robbie said. Trying to ignore a twitch of annoyance at this realization, she turned leave when Devyn's voice stopped her.

"Are you wearing Matt's clothes? And...his badge?"

"Uh, yeah." She knew by Devyn's look that she needed to explain. But she suddenly didn't want to explain herself. Devyn would still be annoyed with her—she couldn't seem to do anything right—and likely Devyn would judge her decision to bend the rules as much as she seemed to be judging her outfit.

For that matter, she wasn't simply bending the rules. She could lose her job for what she was about to do. Only, though, if she got caught. With luck, the security guard at the data center wouldn't do anything more than give her a cursory look when she entered the building. The guards at the sites in Seattle often didn't even glance up from their phones when she came to fix something. The only problem would be if Devyn told someone. Which meant she needed to explain.

"There's a network outage at one of the sites down here and since Matt and I swapped places, I need his badge to get in and fix it." No lie there. "It's a high priority that can't wait."

"So you're pretending to be him?"

Robbie dropped her chin. "Sort of."

"You're not going to get in trouble for that?"

"Not if I don't get caught." She tried to lighten the mood with a smirk, but Devyn's brow crease only deepened. "It'll be fine. The guards don't pay attention."

Devyn glanced down at Angel as if the dog should be disappointed in the plan too. She shook her head and murmured, "Whatever" before meeting Robbie's gaze. "When will you be home?"

Whatever. The word and all Devyn meant with it made Robbie want to leave without answering. But she wasn't about to let Devyn think she'd gotten under her skin. Schooling her features, she said evenly, "It depends on what's wrong. Usually the problem is a loose cable. Like something not seated right that I need to reattach. If it's not a quick fix, though, I could be there for a while." She didn't resist adding, "Why do you want to know?"

Devyn opened her mouth but then closed it as if reconsidering what she'd been about to say. "Nothing. Well. Not nothing. I was hoping we could talk."

Devyn sounded almost conciliatory. Likely she wanted to talk about one of the house projects. Probably a new request for the to-do list. "I'll be around all weekend. Will you be here?"

"I'm off tomorrow."

Which wasn't a yes or a no. Robbie almost said as much. Why did every conversation with this woman feel like a tense dance? She was hyperaware of a magnetic pull and at the same time entirely frustrated Devyn couldn't at least pretend to like her. "Should we set up a specific time and place for this chat?"

"I don't think that's necessary. I'll find you tomorrow."

"Great." She forced a smile. "I'll see you tomorrow—unless I get arrested for impersonating your ex-husband."

"I doubt you'll get arrested. You seem to be able to charm your way out of trouble." Devyn raised an eyebrow. "But good luck."

Robbie stared as Devyn turned and headed into the house, calling for Angel with the promise of treat. From the click of her heels on the cobblestones, to her sculpted calves, to where the back of her thighs disappeared under the hem of her dress, to the swing of her hips and the swish of her dark blond hair over her shoulders, Devyn was all that and more. "One minute I think she hates me and the next…" Did Devyn hate her? Or actually like her?

Devyn's look had seemed flirtatious when she'd dropped the grenade about Robbie being able to charm her way out of trouble. Which made no sense. "Unless she actually likes me?" She shook her head, wishing Devyn wasn't a puzzle she wanted to figure out.

"Why do I always have the hots for complicated women?" She groaned as Matt's name popped on her phone. "The fact that she's Matt's ex is only icing on the cake." She answered the call with, "Dude. I haven't even left the house yet. You gotta give me time to get there."

"I wanted to make sure you didn't tell Devyn you were using my badge. I don't know why you would but—"

"Why would it matter?"

"She's a rule-follower. Even if it's something nothing to do with her, she hates it when anyone breaks any rules."

Great.

"I'm not sure how much you two talk, but just don't mention you had to go to the data center."

"Too late."

"What do you mean?"

"I mean she already found out."

Matt cussed.

"Is she going to report me to the data center?"

Matt seemed to consider it for a moment. "I think it'd be too much hassle and I don't think she really cares."

"Then why do you care?"

"Well...You know, I guess I don't care." He let out a short laugh. "I was thinking I didn't want her lecture, but at this point all I'd have to do is hang up the phone." He laughed again. "I'm fucking free. God, it feels good remembering that."

"Yeah, okay, you enjoy that feeling. I have to pretend to be a Padres fan and sneak into a data site." She ended the call and tugged the brim of the Padres hat lower on her head. "Let's hope the security guard isn't chatty tonight."

Fortunately, she didn't have any trouble gaining entry with Matt's badge, and once inside the loud hum of machines in the data center made it impossible to focus on anything aside from finding and fixing the problem. Matt had texted her with directions to go to cage seventy-five on the east wall and then check rack thirty, but it took her a minute to orient in the huge warehouse.

Once she located the rack, she checked the cables and texted Matt a picture of what she guessed was the problem. Loose cable. Maybe a rat had tripped over it? She always wondered how things could be jostled loose in an empty room—empty save thousands of machines constantly running and too many cables to count. The place sounded like the inside of a jet engine but felt more like the inside of an icebox. After a hard power off, seating the loose cable and then systematically checking everything else, she texted Matt and waited for his reply.

As she waited, she thought of Matt's comment about feeling good to be free. He'd made enough comments to convince her he had no interest in getting back together with Devyn. Whatever had happened to bring about the divorce, Matt wasn't longing to fix things. Which was a relief considering how she felt when Devyn had raised her eyebrow at her and called her a charmer. Arguably, it might not have been a compliment.

Her phone buzzed with a text from Matt: *That was it. Thanks.*

You owe me. She snapped a selfie, making sure to look disgusted in the Padres gear.

He sent back a heart emoji and then: *Want to sell your houseboat? I know this was only supposed to be for a month but you look good in a Padres hat and I could stay here forever.*

She sent a middle finger emoji followed by: *No one looks good in a Padres hat. Also—I'm not selling. I can't leave my uncle.*

Everyone looks good in a Padres hat. Matt's text bubble blinked again. *I can't leave your uncle either. I've never eaten so well. So I take the couch and you take the bed?*

She laughed. *The answer's no.*

She gathered her things and made her way out of the warehouse. The guard looked up as she left and gave her a nod when she waved. Apparently, she looked enough like Matt after all. Her phone chimed twice more before she got to the rental car. She settled in the seat and read another text from Matt. This one made her stop mid-reach for the seat belt.

BTW. Got a text from Devyn. She says you're doing all the shit I didn't do. Good job.

Matt's words weren't what stopped her. It was the fact that she immediately wanted to ask what Devyn thought of her.

"She's straight and it doesn't matter." She blew out a breath. "I need tacos." If anything could get her mind off Devyn, tacos from the hole-in-the-wall restaurant she'd discovered near the beach might be it.

After waiting in a long line and then getting caught in beach traffic, her stomach was rumbling by the time she got back to the house. More annoying, her parking place in the driveway was taken and all the street parking nearby was full. She considered who Devyn might have over and then remembered the comment about the work colleague. Had she said that so Robbie would know she wasn't on a date?

She couldn't exactly ask. Asking Devyn anything felt off-limits. Pushing back a wave of annoyance at her crush and Devyn's mixed signals, she parked in the one open spot she found on a street three blocks away. By the time she jogged back to the house and pushed open the side gate, all she was thinking about were the tacos in the take-out bag.

The sound of multiple voices all talking at once—and then a woman's laugh—stopped her. "Great. She's having a party."

She stared down at the take-out bag, debating going back to eat in her car. It was silly to not go to the cottage. She lived there, even if it was a temporary thing. When Angel appeared, giving her a howl of greeting, she had no choice but to pass through the yard and hope what followed wasn't awkward.

"Hey." She held up a hand, surveying the scene. Fortunately, it was only Devyn and two other women seated around the lit gas fire pit. Still, the other women were as good-looking as Devyn and equally as intimidating to walk in on.

One was probably her age—midthirties—but the other she guessed was in her late forties. Both Latina, both looking cozy under Devyn's living room throw blankets, and both holding glasses of wine. Devyn had wine, too, but no blanket. She had a coat instead and an expression that was hard for Robbie to guess at. Annoyance?

"Sorry to interrupt." She pointed to the cottage. "Just need to pass through."

She had to weave around the chaise lounge the older one of Devyn's friends had pulled up to the fire pit. As she crossed in front of the chair, the woman said, "Devyn told us you fixed the fire pit so we had to test it out."

"Glad it's working for you."

The older woman continued, "You're welcome to join our little party."

"Thanks, but I had to work late and haven't had dinner." She held up the taco bag as evidence.

The younger woman on Devyn's right held up her glass. "Tacos and wine go well together—despite what they'll have you believe about beer. We'll save you a glass."

"It's nice having the fire working again," Devyn said, nodding at the fire pit without looking at Robbie as she took another sip of wine. "It's been a while."

"In case you haven't figured her out, that's a sincere thank-you from Devyn." The older woman leaned toward Devyn and poked her shoulder.

Devyn looked at Robbie then, her eyes catching Robbie's. "Thank you. And there is plenty of wine, if you want to join us."

"We'll save you a glass," the woman to the right of Devyn said. "Gina's Tacos are my fave, by the way. Enjoy."

CHAPTER EIGHT

Devyn knew she'd had one too many glasses of wine. She was coming off a hard day at work, which didn't help. Exhaustion and a mild buzz, she argued, were enough to explain why she'd forgotten to make proper introductions—and enough to explain why she'd let her eyes linger on Robbie's retreating backside. She didn't think she'd been obvious, but as soon as Robbie closed the door of the cottage, Elena turned to her and pointedly stared.

"What?"

Elena tapped her nail against her wineglass. "You tell me."

"What are you two talking about?" Mari asked.

"Nothing," Devyn said, knowing she'd answered too quickly when Mari gave her a second look.

"What's her name again?" Mari jabbed her thumb in the direction of the cottage.

"Robbie."

"Right." Mari lowered her voice and added, "It's funny she's a Padres fan. Didn't you say she was from Seattle?"

Devyn nodded. At least Mari hadn't noticed her checking out Robbie's butt. If Mari had seen that, there'd be no end to the questions. Thankfully, Elena was more discreet.

"So why the Padres?"

She didn't want Robbie to get in trouble for something that was likely Matt's problem, but she couldn't see how telling Elena and Mari would lead to anyone else finding out. "She had to pretend to be Matt. Something to do with their work."

"She doesn't look anything like Matt," Elena said.

"I could kind of see it. They're both about the same height. Both white. And I bet she gets mistaken for a guy all the time." Mari leaned toward the fire pit and asked, "Is it weird she's Matt's friend?"

"Why would it be weird?" It was weird. For more reasons than Mari knew.

Mari lifted a shoulder. "She's here in your space, fixing things in your house and…I guess it'd be weird for me? Like if Elena and I broke up and she invited her hot queer friend to move in." Mari shot Elena a look. "Don't do that, babe."

"You can't get mad at me for hypotheticals." Elena laughed. "Anyway, you know I have no interest in us breaking up."

Mari held Elena's gaze for a moment and then dipped her head. "I know."

"I love you," Elena said. "We'll figure it out."

Devyn knew the comment was in reference to the question of kids. Elena had mentioned Mari had tried to bring up the conversation earlier that day and things had ended in another argument. It hurt to see her two friends struggling, though Devyn was momentarily happy for the subject change. Then Elena turned to her and said, "So. Are you going to talk about it?"

Mari's eyebrows bunched together. "Is she going to talk about what?"

"Her housebutch."

Devyn fought back a blush as Elena raised her glass. "Whenever you're ready. You know we won't judge."

"Am I missing something?" Mari asked, glancing between Devyn and Elena.

Devyn shook her head. "There's nothing to say. She's taking care of all the things on Matt's to-do list and I'm obviously happy about that. I'm not sure it wouldn't have been more efficient to hire out the work and I would have liked to have been asked, but—"

"You wouldn't have picked her?" Mari guessed.

"It's not that." She felt her cheeks get hot as Elena studied her. "I don't have any issues with Robbie. At all. She's easy to get along with and gets the work done."

"What about the lesbian part?" Elena asked.

"What about it?" Devyn heard her voice go up an octave. "You know I'm not homophobic."

"That's not what I'm suggesting," Elena said calmly.

"Okay." Mari put both hands on her knees. "Now I know I'm missing something."

Elena met Mari's gaze briefly but didn't offer an explanation. Devyn knew Elena guessed her attraction to Robbie. She wasn't sure if she felt relieved or anxious about her knowing.

"Is it a problem she's a lesbian?" Mari continued.

"Not at all." Devyn motioned to Mari and then Elena. "Have you noticed who my friends are? You two are the only people I hang out with and I love you both."

"You're not attracted to us," Elena said. "This is different."

Elena's comment took the air out of Devyn's lungs. Not because it wasn't true but because she suddenly felt exposed. "Maybe I'm the one missing something here."

"She's your ex-husband's friend," Elena said. "And you two are living together. Not by choice, clearly, but feelings can still develop. With her being Matt's friend…That's a lot to unpack. How close are they?"

"Hold up." Mari sat up straight. "Devyn, are you bi?" She looked over at Elena when Devyn didn't answer right off. "Babe, did you tell me and I somehow spaced that detail?" She huffed. "How the hell could I not have known? God, I swear I have absolutely no gaydar. I'm always the last to figure out this stuff. But honestly, it fits." She nodded at Devyn. "Of course you're bi. Did you date women before Matt? If I'd known you went for women, too, I could have set you up with my old college roommate when she was in town. Lou. The lawyer. I think you may have met her." Mari shook her head. "No, you were working when we had that party she came to. But you two would be so cute together."

Mari not waiting for anyone to answer her questions or interrupt her stream of consciousness at least gave Devyn time to steady herself. She felt Elena's gaze still on her, though, and knew she needed to say something soon.

"Do we need to drop this?" Elena asked, her eyes narrowed with concern. "I don't want to push you to talk about something you aren't ready for."

"I'm fine. It's fine." Devyn felt a pull toward the cottage and gave up resisting looking that direction. "I'm attracted to her, yeah, but she's…This is…Nothing's going to happen."

Elena nodded slowly. "Is this the first time?"

"Sort of. I mean…" Devyn pushed herself to finish. "I've never done anything with a woman, but I've thought about it before."

"Thinking about it is the first step," Mari said. "Next thing you know, your mouth is on some woman's pussy and she's screaming your name and you're wondering why you waited so long."

"Oh, God." Devyn pressed her palm to her forehead as Elena and Mari both laughed. Going down on Robbie had been her fantasy all week. She'd even watched two lesbian movies to study the sex scenes. And she'd never been more turned on.

"I don't even know her. Not really, you know?" She felt like she was spinning but she hadn't moved from her seat.

"That's okay," Elena said. "A passing attraction can be fun and nothing more. Nothing *has* to happen."

She swallowed and glanced again at the cottage. Robbie was still inside. Eating dinner alone. Devyn wished she'd join them even as she worried what her friends might say now.

"How do you feel if you imagine letting something happen?" Mari asked.

"Letting things happen isn't really my style. First I have to analyze, overanalyze, then second-guess…"

Elena laughed. "So true. But when it's the right person, it's surprisingly easy to let things happen. I'm proud of you either way."

"For what?"

"For letting yourself feel again. It's been a long year." Elena patted Devyn's hand. "Feeling things is healthy even if those feelings don't lead to anything."

"I agree with that. And she's cute." Mari spread her hands. "I'd like to officially say I approve of you being bi."

Devyn rolled her eyes. "Thank you."

As Mari laughed, she felt a sense of weight lifting from her chest. It wasn't only admitting her attraction to women. Both Elena and Mari knew how she'd shut her heart down after finding out what Matt had done. This felt like formally stepping beyond all of that. She looked over at Elena and said, "I did consider telling you before."

"That you liked women?" Elena asked.

She nodded.

Mari grumbled. "I would have been the last to find out then, too."

"No, I almost told you both at your wedding. You two were so beautiful and so in love. You still are. I wish I was as brave at going for what I want as you two." She wasn't fearless like Elena, nor as easily loveable as Mari. They both had an energy that everyone around them felt. She worried about admitting her own desires partly because she couldn't imagine ever having what they had. And wasn't sure it was hers to even want.

But then she thought of how Robbie looked at her. From nearly the first time they'd met, Robbie's desire had been plain. There was no threat in it, no pressure, it was simply there. Robbie seemed to sense nothing would happen between them, but she hadn't held back in the way she looked at Devyn. Now the words *what if?* tumbled through Devyn's mind.

What if Robbie was the right person to let go with? What if she got out of her own way for once and didn't think about what might happen next? What if she went for someone she was actually interested in—someone who might not expect anything from her? It sounded nice. All of it. And the idea of wrapping her arms around Robbie? Absolutely exhilarating.

"You're thinking of her, aren't you?" Mari said. "You just smiled."

"I don't know who I am right now." She shook her head. "Clearly I've had too much wine."

"Maybe you want to be someone else for a bit," Elena said. "Or maybe you're letting yourself finally be you. You said you've never had a fling. Maybe now's the time."

"I wouldn't even know how to go about it. I don't know what she wants or if she'd be interested in someone like me." She noticed Elena and Mari exchanging a look. "What?"

"All you have to do is let her know you're interested. I guarantee she'll do the rest." Mari's expression showed how confident she was of that fact.

"You think I should tell her I have a crush on her?"

Mari and Elena laughed.

"Hey, I don't know what to do here. You know I'm used to dating men and things did not start out well between Robbie and me. She's not going to suddenly get the hint I'm into her and ask me out."

The whole week had been one disastrous conversation after another, and she'd done nothing to endear herself to Robbie despite how much Robbie had done for her. Plus, Robbie was Matt's friend. Robbie might not act on any feelings out of respect to Matt.

"Start paying more attention to her," Elena said. "Spend more time with her. Ask about what she's interested in. All the things you'd do with a friend."

"And then brush against her on accident." Mari winked at Elena. "But also completely not on accident."

Devyn smiled. She'd heard the story of how Mari had come on to Elena and how the accidental touches did not go unnoticed. She glanced at the cottage and exhaled, feeling a rush of bravado at the thought of quasi-accidentally touching Robbie. It might be the wine convincing her she could do it, but it still felt good to imagine.

"I never thought I had a type but I'm wondering if I do." She felt almost foolish admitting the thought that had been in her head for days. "Before Matt I dated Amir. He was an IT guy, too. And Robbie has the same job as Matt."

Mari squinted at her. "You think your type is computer geeks?"

"I'm not sure I'd call Robbie a computer geek. But she is quiet and gets really into things." She contemplated what she meant as she stared at the quarter inch of remaining merlot in her glass. When she looked up, she realized both Mari and Elena were staring at her as if they were trying not to laugh. "What?"

Elena looked at Mari before saying, "Most of the time when people say they have a type they mean skinny blondes or strapping Black men or…"

Mari picked up where Elena trailed off and said, "Or short, curvy Latinas." She shot her wife a look and then waggled her eyebrows. "It's possible I have a type."

"But your type is IT people?" Elena asked, clearly trying to phrase the question carefully.

Devyn scrunched up her nose. "Is that weird?"

"Yes. Which is why we're friends."

Mari and Elena both laughed, and she joined in. The door to the cottage opened at that moment, and Angel, who'd nearly fallen asleep at Devyn's feet, hopped up and raced over to greet Robbie.

Robbie had changed out of the Padres gear and into a red flannel button-down with a dark gray puffer vest. Fortunately, she hadn't changed the snug-fitting jeans. When she leaned down to pet Angel, Mari gave Devyn a light push on her shoulder and murmured, "Totally approve."

As Robbie straightened, she looked right at Devyn, then gave a cursory look at the others. "Still okay if I join the party?"

"Pull up a chair." Elena pointed to the patio table with the one remaining seat.

As Robbie went to get the chair, Mari stood and said, "I'll get another bottle of wine."

"And a glass," Devyn said. "You know where I keep them, right?"

"I thought you'd offer to share yours," Mari whispered.

Devyn felt her cheeks heat with a blush but Robbie didn't give any indication she heard, only coming back to the fire pit with her chair and positioning it in the open space next to Elena's. She sat down and held out her hand to Elena, smoothly introducing herself.

As Elena asked Robbie what she did for work, pretending to not know that Devyn had already told her, Devyn breathed out, reminding herself to relax. Mari returned with a glass and more wine, and the conversation flowed to what everyone else did for work. Then to what life was like on a houseboat and where everyone had traveled.

Devyn found herself studying Robbie. She had a relaxed way about her, sitting back in the patio chair with one leg crossed over the other knee and an easy smile that seemed to be always half lifting her lips. She didn't seem to guard anything and her laugh was warm like Elena's. Every so often, the firelight flickered and her fine features were in shadows. Her brown eyes were dark then, and she seemed more serious. Devyn was drawn to her in those flashes and she had to force herself not to stare.

"Venice is still on my list," Elena said. "And Barcelona."

"Mine too," Mari agreed.

"I definitely recommend visiting both," Robbie said. "They're completely different, of course, but both beautiful. And the nightlife's amazing. Italian women are a lot of fun. But so are Spanish women. And the clubs in Barcelona? Yeah. I was not prepared."

"For what?" Mari laughed as Robbie shook her head sheepishly.

"There's a story there," Elena said, laughing too.

Robbie grinned and finally said, "I went to Europe this last time after a breakup. I needed to get someone off my mind. Barcelona took care of that."

The others laughed. Devyn wanted to ask Robbie to elaborate but wasn't brave enough.

"Do you travel often?" Mari asked.

"Not anymore. My uncle and I used to plan a trip to a new destination every year, but we haven't gone for…three years now? That last trip to Europe was solo." Robbie's brow furrowed. "My uncle's getting older. He keeps telling me I need to find a younger traveling partner, but I doubt I'd find anyone who could get me into as much trouble as he could."

"You're definitely holding back on some good stories," Elena said, giving Robbie a conspiratorial shoulder push.

Devyn felt oddly jealous that Elena could so easily touch Robbie. Not because she had any thought that Elena was interested in Robbie. Simply because touching Robbie had been on her mind for too long. She was jealous as well that her friends put Robbie at ease. She'd noticed how stiff Robbie got around her and now she was chatting with Elena and Mari like they'd all been friends for years.

It was notable, too, that in one week she'd hardly spoken to Robbie, hardly knew anything about her, and an hour later her friends knew as much as she did. Of course, Elena and Mari were trying to help, but she wondered if she was fooling herself thinking they had a connection. Maybe Robbie connected easily with everyone she met. Maybe there was nothing between them except a poorly executed house swap.

"I've always wanted to sail in the Mediterranean," Mari said. She mentioned her sailboat and wistfully added there were in fact dozens of places she'd love to sail.

"The Mediterranean is gorgeous," Robbie said. "I don't know a thing about sailing there, though. I've always wanted to try sailing but as much as I love being on the water, a boat in the open sea without a motor kind of freaks me out."

"Most sailboats have motors," Elena said. "Ours does. We use it whenever there's no wind or when something goes wrong."

"And sometimes when we're feeling lazy," Mari admitted.

"Speaking of feeling lazy." Elena didn't bother to stifle a yawn. "Do I need to take you home and put you to bed?"

"Yes, please." Elena smiled at Mari and held up her hands.

Mari stood and tugged Elena up from her chair, then wrapped her in an embrace. They kissed, as they often did, neither shy about showing their affection, but this time Devyn watched their kiss and then looked at Robbie. She felt hot all over as Robbie's gaze locked on hers. Fortunately, Mari interrupted.

"If you're interested, Robbie, we love an excuse to get on the water and show off our sailboat. Maybe we can all go together?" Mari looked to Devyn. "We've been talking about taking another sailing trip for a while."

Devyn nodded. She wasn't particularly fond of sailing, always nervous about not knowing enough in an emergency and fearing capsizing more than was reasonable, but she said, "I'm up for it."

"I'd love that," Robbie said, getting up from her seat. "I basically make my own schedule, so whenever you all have time, I can be free."

"These two are tricky," Mari said, pointing to Devyn and Elena.

Elena looked at Devyn. "I'm off next Saturday."

"I'm on call."

Elena glanced at Robbie. "You've probably noticed Devyn works too much. I can't say much because so do I."

"You two have important jobs. People need you. Sailing would be fun, but it's okay if it doesn't happen."

Robbie's words were exactly what Devyn often wished someone would say in response to the "you work too much" critique. Instead of worrying about letting everyone down if she agreed to a plan, Robbie made her feel like whatever happened would be okay.

And maybe it would.

CHAPTER NINE

Robbie lay in bed, her thoughts as much of a tangled mess as the sheets around her legs. She'd slept, but only in fitful bursts, and a thumping sensation at her temple threatened a full-fledged headache later. She climbed out of bed, grumbling about her low tolerance for alcohol. It wasn't only the wine that had kept her awake until well after midnight, though.

"I shouldn't be thinking about her," she murmured, pulling off the T-shirt she'd slept in and searching for her jog bra.

Devyn did not belong in her fantasies. Why couldn't her body want Devyn's realtor instead? She'd run into the woman at the beach—Shania—and her flirting had been obvious. "Unfortunately, all my body wants is the one person who vaguely hates me."

Vaguely. Devyn had seemed different last night. She still acted annoyed at Robbie's presence but less so. "Now I'm being tolerated." She groaned. Tolerated wasn't a better fate.

Deciding on a run to clear her thoughts, she went to rouse Angel. When she opened the side door to the main house, whistling softly, Angel came barreling toward her. She didn't check to see if there was any sign Devyn was around, hurrying Angel out through the side yard. Devyn had mentioned having the day off, but Robbie didn't want to disturb her if she happened to be sleeping in. At some point Devyn would find her for a conversation. She probably should be dreading said conversation but instead she was looking forward to it.

Devyn had given her so many long looks last night she'd almost asked if there was taco sauce on her face. But she couldn't joke with Devyn. And as much as she wanted to hope the long looks meant Devyn was interested in her, she couldn't completely believe it. More likely, Devyn had been annoyed she'd joined the party. The invitation may have only been issued because she wanted to seem polite around her friends. If that was the case, though, why hadn't Devyn shot down the sailing trip?

Either she genuinely liked sailing or she'd decided to like Robbie. "Or maybe she just likes her friends."

Angel looked up at her, perking one ear as if to decipher her words. He'd led the way to the beach and they were waiting for the light to change so they could cross to the path that ran along the water. The blue ocean spread out before them with sunshine streaming down over everything. Robbie took a deep breath of the ocean scent and exhaled slowly.

"You feel like going for a run?" Despite Angel's short legs, he could outrun her easily and the look in his eyes seemed to say as much.

After a half-hour run, followed by an hour playing in the waves, she pointed them back to the house, her head less crowded with thoughts of Devyn. As they crossed the street by the café, Clara stepped out of the café with the sign for the day's lunch special.

"Hey, Robbie and Angel," Clara said with a smile.

"Hi, Clara. Working again?"

"Six days a week." Clara sighed. "Some days I wish I could work remote like you."

Clara waved her on and as Robbie lifted a hand, she felt as if she'd moved from tourist to local. Home was still Seattle. Home was her houseboat and her uncle. But she could imagine a life here, and it made for a tempting daydream.

When she opened the garage door, she smiled at the sight of Devyn's BMW. Since she'd cleaned out the garage, Devyn had taken to parking in the space. She liked seeing the car because she knew on some level it was Devyn's way of saying she appreciated her hard work. This time the car made her smile because it also meant Devyn was home.

"Come find me whenever you want to talk," Robbie said. She'd been imagining what Devyn might want to talk about but knew none of her fantasies would pan out. Likely Devyn wanted to change the color of the paint she'd picked or she'd decided on a different tile for the bathroom. "Or she wants to tell me she thinks I'm hot."

Angel huffed as if in response and she couldn't help laughing. "All right, not that."

She picked a music station and pushed her earbuds into place. Angel settled on the mat by the door and she wondered if Devyn would come looking for him. The thought crossed her mind that she should throw on a shirt in case Devyn did appear. She'd taken hers off at the beach and was only wearing a sports bra. A sweaty sports bra. Not that Devyn would come close enough to smell her.

"She doesn't want anything to do with you," Robbie murmured.

She'd crushed on other straight women and it had never ended well. It didn't help matters that with Devyn she couldn't seem to have a simple conversation. Even when they were only talking about Angel or the house, there was an underlying level of tension. Last night had been easier only because of Devyn's friends.

She settled in at the weight bench wondering how Devyn could have such chill friends when she was so uptight. But maybe she only acted that way around her because of Matt. If so, how long was Devyn going to not like her purely on the principle of her being Matt's friend?

After three sets, she took a break and closed her eyes. If she could be herself around Devyn and feel no attraction, making it through the rest of the month would be a lot easier. "Maybe I can pretend I'm not attracted to her?" She sighed. "Good luck with that."

She did another three sets, and when she'd finished, dropped back on the weight bench and closed her eyes again. She didn't hear the door open and only jolted alert when the garage door rolled above her head.

She sat up, tearing out her earbuds and searching for Angel. He'd been right by the door. Devyn crossed in front of her headed for her car. "Wait, Angel was in here with me. He's—"

"I sent him into the house." Devyn opened the back seat of her BMW and tossed in a set of reusable bags. She looked back at Robbie. "You were napping."

"I wasn't napping."

"Your eyes were closed."

Robbie felt the tension mount. Every conversation. She shook her head, willing it away. "I don't fall asleep that easy."

Devyn's gaze briefly flitted down Robbie's chest but then she seemed to catch herself and looked at her watch. "I'm going to the store. Do you need anything?"

A thrill went through Robbie when she noticed Devyn's cheeks had gone pink. Something in her shifted, and instead of crossing her arms to cover up, she straightened and met Devyn's gaze. "The grocery store or the hardware store?"

Devyn hesitated for a beat. "I was thinking of the grocery store, but I could go to both. What do you need?"

"Grout. The tile for that upstairs bathroom arrived but there's no grout. I didn't know what color you'd want."

"I don't care. I'm selling the house."

"Then pick something neutral."

"Are there different types of grout?" Devyn sounded as if she'd regretted volunteering but was trying to hide that fact. "I mean, aside from the color."

"There's sanded and unsanded. Sanded would be ideal. I also need caulk. The silicone type. You should be able to find it in the same section." Robbie paused, noticing that Devyn's lips were pressed together in a tight line. "If you don't want to get all that I can run to the hardware store later. But I do need to know what color you want."

"I can do it. I have no idea where I'd find those things, though. Could you put in an order for pickup?"

"The problem is I don't know the color you want." She saw the hesitation in Devyn's expression and guessed the problem. "Hardware stores are great because anyone wearing one of the store vests will help you find what you need. You just have to ask."

Devyn looked at her car for a moment, then back at Robbie. "You want me to walk into the hardware store, find someone in a vest, and ask for help finding the silicone cock?"

Was Devyn playing her? She stared at her for a moment and then said, "Caulk. With an L."

"That's what I said. Cock."

Robbie scratched her head.

"Exactly." Devyn gestured to Robbie. "That's my point."

"I'm not following."

"But I know what you're thinking. I don't pronounce cock right—which is why I'm not asking for it."

"You really can't say caulk?" Robbie sounded the word out slowly, accentuating the L: "Caulk."

"Cah-ock." Devyn held up her hands. "Happy?"

"Huh." Robbie frowned to keep from laughing.

"Great. Now you're trying not to laugh."

"It's just...weird you can't say it."

"I can say plenty of other things. Like, there's no fucking way I'm going to a hardware store and asking someone in a little vest for cock." Devyn put her hands on her hips and stared at Robbie.

Robbie couldn't hold it in then. She burst out laughing, and a moment later Devyn joined in. It was a long minute before Robbie sobered enough to say, "You were playing me."

"Only a little." Devyn had stopped laughing but a smile lingered on her lips. "I can't pronounce certain words. Even after going to speech therapy as a kid. At least I can say cinnamon."

"Impressive." She grinned and Devyn winked back at her. A real wink. They were bantering and the wink probably hadn't meant what Robbie wished it meant, but Devyn opening up and talking about herself was a bombshell all on its own.

"The good news is," Devyn said, "I'm at a point where I can laugh over the words I mispronounce. I don't care anymore if I say things differently than others. I have plenty of confidence in myself when it comes to what I can do."

"You should. You're a badass emergency doctor."

"I don't know about the badass part." She dropped her shoulders. "But I am good at my job."

"I bet you're good at a lot of things." Robbie realized how her words sounded and felt her neck getting hot. She scrambled for what to say to take away the unintended innuendo. "Like driving."

"Driving?"

"I'm sure you're good at other things but I don't really know what else you do and I can see your car isn't bashed up so..."

Devyn laughed again. Robbie didn't care if she'd sounded ridiculous. She loved hearing Devyn laugh, and when she shook her head and laughed too, all the tension from the past week seemed to release.

Finally, Devyn cleared her throat and said, "I know you're working out now, but I did want to talk to you at some point. Will you be free later?"

"Right. That."

Devyn tipped her head. "You're not in trouble."

"You sure? I seem to be pretty good at getting in trouble with you."

Devyn rolled her eyes. They were bantering, at least, but if Devyn had any idea about the thoughts in her head, she'd definitely be in trouble. She added, "I was hoping to start the tile project but we can talk any time."

"You know you don't have to work all the time while you're here. I appreciate everything you've done but—"

"I know. I've seen the silver stars."

"I probably should be better about saying thank you directly."

Robbie shrugged. "I like our system. I check off one of the to-do items, the next day there's a little star from you." She smiled, wondering at the look in Devyn's eyes. "What?"

"Nothing. Well, not nothing." Devyn took a deep breath and exhaled. "It's been an odd week."

"No kidding. A random stranger showed up at your house and took out your garden."

"I wasn't happy at first." Devyn seemed to need to acknowledge the truth they both knew. "But now I feel incredibly lucky you're here taking care of everything. It's a huge weight off my shoulders. That's what I wanted to talk to you about. I'm afraid you aren't going to let me pay you, and I don't quite know how to thank you for everything."

"You just did." Robbie held Devyn's gaze for a moment and then extended her hand. "Hi. I'm Robbie Price. I'll be enjoying your cottage for the next few weeks and—in exchange—doing a few projects around your house. This is my San Diego vacation."

Devyn looked down at Robbie's hand. "Is this our fresh-start handshake?" At Robbie's nod, she clasped her hand. "Hi. I'm Devyn Lancaster. Thanks for not leaving after I yelled at you."

"I considered it," Robbie admitted. She smiled to soften the words and Devyn's gaze met hers. The handshake was brief, but the feel of Devyn's hand was enough to clog up all other thought processes. The look of apology on Devyn's face tipped the scales.

"Whenever I don't have to work on Saturdays, I treat myself to a bagel from my favorite place over by the library," Devyn said. "Can I pick one up for you?"

"Sure. I like the everything bagels."

"Me too." Devyn smiled. "So you're not going anywhere for a while?"

"I'll be here googling everything I need to know about tiling. I want to make sure there isn't anything else I need before I go to the hardware store."

"You sure you want to take on this project?"

"What, tiling doesn't sound fun to you?" Robbie grinned. "Don't worry. I promise I've done it before and I'm only looking things up as a refresher."

"Okay." Devyn turned to the car but then turned back. "I feel like I should go to the hardware store with you. It's all the way across town and traffic is going to be awful on a Saturday."

"As much as I'd love to hear you ask for cock, I got this."

Devyn grimaced. "Why do I feel like I'm going to regret telling you I can't say that word?"

"I don't regret it one bit."

Devyn only shook her head and headed for her car. As she backed out, she lifted a hand and smiled. So much had changed in one conversation. Their tension had turned to warm banter, and the idea of a friendship seemed suddenly possible.

But there was no use pretending the attraction didn't exist. At this point, it was all about damage control.

CHAPTER TEN

Robbie looked good in a T-shirt and jeans, but the loose clothing had nothing on the sports bra she'd worn earlier. Now her muscles and abs were all covered up and Devyn had to stop herself from imagining taking off the shirt.

Which was ridiculous. Never had she been the one to make the first move. To take off anyone's shirt. Or any item of clothing, for that matter. There was no reason to think she'd be any different with Robbie. Except her attraction to Robbie was so different from any attraction she'd felt before, she didn't know what to expect. From herself or from Robbie.

Probably, she shouldn't expect anything. Despite how certain she'd been they were flirting earlier, how certain she was of her own attraction, she didn't know if Robbie would be interested in a fling and there was no way they could have anything more. Aside from that, she knew she wasn't brave enough to broach the subject. The next step to their flirting, if there was one, was all up to Robbie.

She crossed the backyard to the patio table where Robbie had set up her computer under the shade umbrella. Angel was in Robbie's lap and looked up at her approach. He hopped off, wagging his tail almost guiltily. His traitor status had turned to accomplice.

"Ready for a snack break?"

"I'm always ready for snacks." Robbie pushed back from the table and stood, stretching as she did. "My stomach has been thinking about bagels nonstop since you left."

Meanwhile, she'd been thinking about Robbie nonstop. "I didn't know what type of cream cheese you preferred so I got you the same as mine." She passed Robbie one of the everything bagels with strawberry cream cheese, hoping she'd be okay with the choice. Strawberry was riskier than going with a plain spread since she didn't know if Robbie would like the combination of sweet and savory, but she'd picked it anyway. It'd felt like a test. Could she take a risk with Robbie? Now, as she waited on the verdict, she felt silly for overthinking something as inconsequential as cream cheese even while she worried about her pick.

Robbie unwrapped the bagel and took a first bite, moaning as she did. "Mm. So good."

She enjoyed Robbie's moan more than she should. Nervous her response would be noticed, she gestured to Robbie's laptop. "Learn everything you need to know about tiling from YouTube?"

Robbie chuckled. "Let's hope so. I spent the rest of the time researching a new garbage disposal for your kitchen sink."

"That's not on the to-do list." It should have been. The garbage disposal hadn't worked since a month after they'd bought the house. She'd simply forgotten the sink was supposed to have a disposal.

"I tried fixing yours but the motor's done. It'll need to be replaced before you sell." Robbie spun the screen toward Devyn and sat back down. "What do you think about this one? If it's okay with you, I'll pick it up when I get the grout. And the caulk."

Devyn sat down and pretended to look at the device on the screen. "Looks fine to me. Thank you for taking care of that."

Robbie nodded. "I never get strawberry cream cheese. This combination is amazing." She took another bite and moaned again.

One point in favor of taking risks. Not that she was keeping score. But maybe she was. She unwrapped her own bagel and took a bite. "I want to give you a credit card."

"First I impersonate your ex, now you want me to impersonate you?" Robbie laughed. "Fine by me. But I think I can pull off looking like Matt more than I can look like you."

She was tempted to say Robbie looked nothing like Matt but that seemed like a slippery slope. She'd add how much better looking Robbie was and then she'd really be in trouble. "You don't have to try impersonating me. Just swipe the card at the self-checkout. They have those at hardware stores, right?"

"Yes." Robbie studied her. "Tell me you've at least been to a hardware store."

"Do I lose points if I haven't?" She realized what she'd said a moment too late but didn't take it back.

"No." Robbie hesitated. "Maybe."

She rolled her eyes. "It's been a while, but yes, I've been to a hardware store."

"A while as in?"

"Med school. I needed a hammer." At Robbie's furrowed brow, she laughed and said, "Not for school. Elena and I shared an apartment but we were both so busy the place was basically a bachelor pad with nothing on the walls. One day Elena took out the trash and came back with all these oil paintings a neighbor had dumped. She called it our rescue art." She smiled at the memory. "I volunteered to hang the paintings and realized we didn't have a hammer."

"It's cool you've known Elena since med school."

"We met the summer before classes started. She posted about needing a housemate and I responded to her ad." She smiled again. "We were instant friends."

"Do you still have the hammer?"

"I do. It's in the garage along with our other tools. Elena kept the paintings. She was more attached."

"You don't like art?"

"I got a minor in art in college."

Robbie's mouth parted. "Wow. Didn't expect that. So you're a doctor and an artist?"

"No. Not even close. I wasn't very good to begin with and I haven't done anything even artsy for…I don't remember the last time." She was embarrassed they were even talking about it and then wondered at that embarrassment. Was it a problem she wanted to impress Robbie?

"I consider myself an excellent paint-by-numbers artist. If you want, I can show you how to get started."

Devyn laughed and Robbie grinned back at her, adding, "I'm only partly joking."

"Paint-by-numbers?"

"They have ones for adults. You might not want to judge before you try it. I could see you being into it."

"Why?" She was genuinely curious. Not because she had any intention of picking up a paint-by-numbers project, but because she wanted to know what Robbie thought of her.

"Well..." Robbie scratched her head like she regretted saying anything. "For starters, your furniture is nice, but it's also pretty basic."

"Basic?" She made a mock gasp.

"Simple, clean lines, you know? Not boring basic."

"Okay. I might believe you. But what does my furniture have to do with paint-by-number art?"

"I wasn't done." Robbie feigned frustration but a smile edged her lips.

"Fine. Go on."

"I don't know you that well, obviously, but I can tell you like order. Your house has no clutter, and you don't like it when things are off even a little bit. Like if I move Angel's food bowl a few inches one way or the other, you'll move it back. You always make sure it lines up with the edge of the dishwasher. And I don't think it was Matt who labeled the pantry shelves."

She cringed. "That was me."

"You like everything to have a place. It's okay."

Robbie wasn't wrong, but her assessment made her sound like her OCD was over the top. And like she was boring. She wondered if she should argue that work was a state of constant, barely managed chaos, and coming home to simplicity and order helped her relax.

"Also, I knew you were happy about the garage being organized because I got three stars for that. All the other projects only got one star."

"It was a huge relief to have the garage cleaned and organized," she admitted. "But that has nothing to do with paint-by-number."

"Sure it does," Robbie said. "You like order. But you also like pretty things—things other people might not notice. Or look at twice. Like milkweed. And that scrawny Japanese maple tree." She pointed to the tree in the one shady part of the yard. "Nearly every time you walk past it, you reach out and touch the leaves."

Devyn didn't know what to say. She loved the tree. Particularly this time of year when the new leaves seemed so fragile. Beautiful, but delicate. But that Robbie had noticed?

"Plus, you have neat handwriting even though you're a doctor. Paint-by-numbers could be right up your alley."

She smiled at the last part, relieved Robbie was lightening the conversation after making her feel almost too seen. "I guess I shouldn't judge something I've never tried. Although, I'm pretty sure I've done an entire paint-by-numbers book. I think I was six at the time."

Robbie chuckled. "This is different."

"Have you ever painted anything without the numbers?"

Robbie shook her head. "I'm not that creative. I bought a canvas and some oil paints to try one time, but…"

"It's still blank?"

Robbie scrunched up her face. "How'd you know?"

"Art minor. I have more than one blank canvas in my closet. I never was much of a painter, though. Sketching was my thing. Unfortunately, I wasn't very good at that either. Not as good as I wanted to be, anyway."

"Did it make you happy?"

"Sketching?" She considered the question. "I don't know if happy is the right word. Sketching made me feel…grounded. Or centered. Whatever you want to call it. I used to love losing myself in a project and forgetting everything else."

"You know what else can do that? Paint-by-numbers."

Robbie's knowing smirk was way too attractive. She wanted to drink in the sight of it, but she made herself look away, feigning annoyance. "Whatever."

"You don't even have to pay attention to the numbers," Robbie said, clearly undeterred. "Just swirl the paint wherever you want— whatever color makes you happy."

"Now you're going too far."

Robbie laughed and took another bite of her bagel. She leaned back in her chair, catching the sunlight on her face. "This bagel's hitting the spot."

"I bought another dozen to freeze. You're welcome to anything in my freezer or fridge, you know. I've noticed you always buy the groceries yourself whenever you cook. You could use what I have already since you're making me dinner, too."

"That might get complicated."

"The money part? I'm not worried about what you use, and if you keep receipts for what you buy, I'll pay you back for everything—including your time."

Robbie shook her head. "We've been through this. Matt's helping my uncle, and I'm helping you."

"I didn't sign up for that exchange."

"I know, but that's the deal. You aren't paying me."

She started to argue, but Robbie only gave a half shrug and then closed her eyes, tilting her nose to the sun.

"I hate to pull the doctor card, but you should be wearing sun protection here. You've already gotten more color on your cheeks than you had when you first got here. With your complexion, I'm surprised you haven't burned."

"Doctor card?" Robbie chuckled.

"I am a doctor."

"I know. And I'm sure you're right, but I hate being told what to do."

Devyn narrowed her eyes. "You've had no problem doing everything I've told you to do on the list."

"Matt gave me the list."

"Are you always this difficult?"

"Yes."

"I'm not letting you buy things for the house with your own money." She was done with their back-and-forth on the subject and done being powerless in the plan Matt had concocted. "I don't want to feel indebted to anyone and certainly not my ex."

"I'm not your ex."

"By extension you are." She could tell she'd landed a hit. Robbie's jaw clenched and her body tensed. When she didn't argue, though, Devyn pushed on. "You're here because of Matt. It's one thing to do the work he agreed to do—because of some deal you two made—and another to do extra projects for me, spend your own money on things, and cook for me."

Again, Robbie didn't have a response. This time she wouldn't even meet Devyn's gaze. "We can argue later about me paying you for your time, but I'm going to insist on you using my credit card whenever you buy anything going further."

Robbie's lips pressed together, but still, infuriatingly, she said nothing. "Is there something you want to say to me?" Devyn asked.

"Lots of things." Robbie shifted forward in her chair so the sun was off her face. She leveled her gaze on Devyn. "But I'll start with this. I'm not your ex. Or any extension of him. If you want to pretend that's the case, fine, but I'm not accepting that role."

Robbie's obvious challenge along with her calm, cool look was both irritating and had Devyn's whole body on fire. When had she ever been so thirsty for someone? She swallowed, trying not to let on her internal fight.

"Now that we've cleared that up, let's move on." Robbie cocked her head. "Am I someone you only want to hire to do a job? Because if so, you don't need to worry about me getting a sunburn."

When Devyn didn't answer—because Robbie did have a point and because she didn't think she could manage words with her damn hormones raging—Robbie continued, "I will agree to use your credit card to buy supplies, but you're not paying me for the work. That's the deal or I'm not staying."

Robbie's tone was insolent, and she felt her anger pique again. When Robbie pointedly pushed her chair back, tilting her face to the sun, she caught herself grinding her teeth.

"Are you trying to be frustrating? Is this some sort of power play for you?"

"Not trying at all." Robbie didn't meet her gaze. "It comes naturally. And I don't do power plays."

She cussed under her breath. Of all the people in the world, why was she drawn to this woman? Why did she have to like someone who was Matt's friend—and only in her orbit because of Matt?

One minute she wanted to throw Robbie out, and the next she wanted to ask her all about her life. Had she grown up in Seattle? Where had she gone to college? Was she dating anyone?

This is ridiculous. She finished chewing her bite, then stood and adjusted the umbrella so the shade fell on Robbie's face.

Robbie looked over at her. "Can't help taking care of people, huh?"

"It is literally my job." She didn't consider it a flaw, but Robbie had said the words as if it was, which annoyed her even more. "Look, I need you to do all the things on the list. And, yes, I understand you have a deal with my ex, but I doubt that included making me meals. Or doing anything extra for me. I think we can both agree the lines are not clear."

"You're right." Robbie nodded slowly. "So should I pick up one paint-by-numbers or two when I go out?"

Devyn didn't answer for a moment, then she shook her head. "You're impossible."

"I'll get two and you can decide later," Robbie said.

She wanted to spend more time with Robbie, but she couldn't imagine doing a craft project. Her body flushed when she thought of what she could imagine. After a beat, she cleared her throat and said, "I don't think I'm in the right headspace for an art project. Even that kind of art."

"That's fair." Robbie finished off the last bite of her bagel and stood. "I'm going to the hardware store. But first I'm going to grab a hat so I don't get skin cancer on the way."

"You're welcome."

Robbie didn't look back as she headed to the cottage. If she had, she'd probably only do so to give Devyn a middle finger. Or one of her crushing smiles. The cottage door opened and closed behind Robbie, and Devyn sank back in her chair. She looked down at Angel, lying belly up in the sun.

"You could get skin cancer, too, you know." She glanced at the cottage door but looked away a moment later. "I can't think about kissing her." And yet, that's exactly where her thoughts went.

CHAPTER ELEVEN

Installing a garbage disposal was easier, as it turned out, than slicing a bagel. Devyn had been gone most of the afternoon—Robbie hadn't asked where she was going when she'd left—but she'd picked the worst moment to come home.

Devyn walked into the kitchen, took one look at Robbie, and cussed. She set down her shopping bags and strode forward. "What the hell happened?"

The sharp words and Devyn's taut expression made Robbie's knees feel even more weak. "The knife slipped."

Devyn reached for her hand, but Robbie turned before she could touch it. "Don't." She'd wrapped her hand in a white dish towel and it was a mess of red now.

"Let me see. I need to know how bad it is."

"I don't want to know." Robbie leaned against the counter, her words sounding far away. The realization she was going to faint if she didn't do something came at the same moment Devyn's hand steadied her, bracing her at the elbow.

"Sit down. Now."

She saw Devyn's lips form the words, knew what she'd said, but also knew she hadn't heard her. That was a bad sign. She followed the orders, thinking that Devyn telling her what to do, and taking care of her, was not how she wanted things to go. Not at all.

Devyn guided her to the ground and she settled into a crouching position, her back against the kitchen cabinets. Her vision tunneled to the only thing in front of her. *Devyn.* Devyn's hands were on her shoulders holding her in place.

"Do you have any medical issues I need to know about?" Devyn raised her voice. "Robbie, answer me."

She managed to shake her head, but a wave of dizziness followed.

"Are you on any medication?"

"No."

"You sure about that? I will make you take a drug test if I think you're lying."

Robbie grumbled. "My mom had an overdose when I was a kid. No drugs."

"I'm sorry about your mom." Devyn's voice softened. "Can you open your eyes and look at me?"

She pushed her eyes open, forced a smile, and said, "Hey. How's it going?"

Devyn choked out a laugh. "You tell me. I come home to find blood everywhere, a bloody knife on the floor, and your ass fainting on me."

"Sorry about the mess."

Devyn murmured, "What am I going to do with you?" and then in a louder voice added, "I need you to sit all the way down. On your butt."

Robbie obliged, half falling onto her backside. She didn't let go of her left hand. If she did, she knew the blood would start spurting again. "I've been told I have a nice butt."

"You do," Devyn said evenly. "At the moment, however, I only care about your hand."

She'd been trying to lighten the mood and hadn't expected Devyn to comment. The response only scrambled her brain more.

"Your hand, Robbie."

Reluctantly she held out her hand. "Sorry about ruining your towel."

"Stop apologizing." Devyn grasped Robbie's left hand between the two of hers and then began unwrapping the towel. "Don't pay attention to what I'm doing. Focus on breathing. You look like shit."

Robbie wanted to argue she couldn't look that terrible considering Devyn had checked her out plenty in the last twenty-four hours, but the words didn't come. She took a deep breath and exhaled, feeling her chin tremble as she did.

"This is more blood than I'd expect. Do you have any bleeding issues?"

Robbie made a sound she wasn't proud of. Something between a whimper and whine.

"I didn't say you were dying. Any bleeding issues?"

"No...I tried to wash the cut, but blood was squirting everywhere."

"Either you nicked a vessel or you're not very good at applying pressure. I hate to say it, but you need this sutured."

Robbie's stomach turned. "Let's wrap it back up again and pretend it didn't happen." She tried pulling her hand back but Devyn's grip on her wrist only tightened.

"No."

"I think it will be fine when the bleeding stops."

"Robbie, look at me."

Robbie pushed her eyelids open. "I don't want to go to the hospital."

"No one said you had to go to the hospital." Devyn held her gaze. There was no harshness in her eyes now. The gentleness, though, was almost worse. "Remember how I'm a doctor? I happen to have everything I need here. Call me paranoid, but you never know when the zombie apocalypse is going to hit."

Robbie squinted at her. "Are you...Was that a joke?"

Devyn smiled. "Maybe."

"I'm bleeding out and you're joking about the zombie apocalypse?"

"You're not bleeding out. You've got a three-centimeter laceration on your middle finger. I think you cut off a little bit of the tip but the bleeding has mostly stopped. Look."

Robbie didn't want to look, but Devyn insisted so she risked a glance. The towel was soaked in blood and her hand was a mess, but the flow from the cut had slowed to a trickle. She went to touch it and Devyn pushed her away.

"Don't touch. You'll make it start gushing again."

"I wasn't going to."

Devyn tipped her head. "You sure? Because I'm not." She paused. "Unless you want me to drag you to the hospital, you're going to have to do what I say. Which means no touching."

"Okay."

"Are you sure you want me to take care of this here?"

Probably Devyn was bending some rules for her. Robbie dropped her shoulders. "Yes. Thank you."

"Don't thank me yet. I don't have any lidocaine."

After another cursory inspection, Devyn went to get supplies. When she returned, Robbie only extended her hand.

"At any point, you can change your mind," Devyn said, clasping Robbie's wrist and positioning the injured hand palm up on the back of her knee. "Remember to breathe. This is going to hurt."

Robbie focused on Devyn. Her gloved hands, deft despite the pain they inflicted, her scent, faintly sweet vanilla mixed with jasmine, and her look of studied concentration. When Devyn moved from cleaning the wound to suturing, Robbie had to close her eyes. The needle pierced her skin and she breathed through the pain that followed, keeping Devyn's face in her mind. Dangerous, but effective.

The seconds ticked by slowly, but then it was done and Devyn let go of her hand and cleared her throat. "You can open your eyes."

Robbie peeked at the stitches. "It looks good."

"You sound surprised." Devyn swabbed away a bit of blood. "Maybe you should be. Most of the time I'm not the one suturing up wounds. Other people get all the fun."

"Sewing someone up is fun for you?"

"I probably shouldn't admit it." A smile turned up the corners of her lips. "Don't move. I still need to bandage you."

The bandaging didn't hurt but Robbie closed her eyes again. She didn't trust herself not to say something she'd regret with Devyn kneeling in front of her. When all was said and done, her hand was wrapped with the middle finger jutting out from the rest on a splint.

"How's that feel?" Devyn asked, tugging off her gloves.

"Not bad."

"It'll start pulsing soon." Devyn went to one of the drawers in the kitchen island. She took out a bottle of Tylenol and tossed it to Robbie.

Robbie caught it with her right hand and Devyn nodded. "Good. You're ready to stand and take that."

"I should have gotten up earlier so you wouldn't have to work on the ground."

"It was safer on the ground. Less chance of you cracking open your head if you fainted again."

Any chance of impressing Devyn was gone. She got up carefully, aware Devyn was watching. "By the way, I replaced the garbage disposal before I tried to hack off my middle finger."

"Thank you. And I saw you got some cock."

Robbie chuckled. "There is no good way to respond to that."

"No problem using my credit card?"

"No. I've now successfully pretended to be you and your husband."

"Ex." Devyn stiffened at Robbie's slip.

"Sorry." *Dammit.* "Ex."

"I'll let it slide this time." She put her hand on Robbie's arm. "You almost bled out on my kitchen floor." Her hand slipped off Robbie's arm as she said, "I was thinking of making dinner. How do you feel about shrimp scampi? It's the only gourmet thing I know how to make."

"You don't have to make me dinner."

"And you didn't have to replace my garbage disposal. Are we going back to arguing now that you're standing, or do you think we could come to a truce?"

Robbie dropped her shoulders. "I'd like a truce."

"Me too." Devyn's chin dipped. "There's chardonnay in the fridge. Pour us two glasses and then have a seat." She gestured to the barstools on the other side of the kitchen counter. "I'm not letting you help tonight, so don't even ask."

They polished off the open bottle of chardonnay and the dinner Devyn cooked over a discussion of politics. Not the conversation Robbie would have expected, but Devyn had started it, asking somewhat offhandedly if she voted. Then Devyn had pressed further, asking who she'd voted for in the last election.

It came out that Devyn's whole family was Republican and staunchly conservative. Devyn seemed relieved Robbie wasn't—as if that would be harder to take than having a stranger move in unexpectedly. It also came out that Devyn was active in the local League of Women Voters and had considered running for office.

Then, without any obvious segue, Devyn asked, "How old were you when you came out?"

"Eighth grade. I probably shouldn't have come out that early." She shook her head. "Things did not go well."

"What happened?"

Robbie exhaled. "I was living with my dad and his new family. My dad wasn't really part of my life when I was little, but he showed up when I was in middle school. Anyway, one day he picked me up from school and he saw me holding hands with a girl. On the drive home, he asked if I was gay. I didn't think to deny it." She paused. "That same night he gave me a box to pack up my things. He said he didn't want me around his kids. He had two other kids with his second wife and he thought…Well, I don't know what he thought. I didn't ask."

"He kicked you out?"

Devyn's dismay brought up a rush of old emotion. "It wasn't that big of a deal. I'd lived with my uncle before, and I just moved back in with him."

"Robbie, getting kicked out by a parent is a huge deal. Especially after you'd lost your mom." Devyn reached out to touch Robbie's good hand. "I'm so sorry."

"It's not your fault." She swallowed, trying to block her response to Devyn's touch.

"No kid should be kicked out for that. For any reason." Devyn pulled back her hand and looked over at Angel. "The more I know about people, the more I like dogs."

"Same. But not all people are assholes."

"Most seem to be." Devyn shook her head. "Do you want kids someday?"

"No. I've got nothing against kids, but I like my life the way it is. And my parents didn't set a very good example. I'm sure I'd screw up any kid who came my way."

"I doubt that," Devyn said.

"Do you want kids?"

"I thought I did. I changed my mind." She seemed to hesitate and then added, "It turned out me not being able to have kids wasn't the problem."

Robbie wondered what Devyn meant, but her face had clouded and she didn't want to push the subject. Maybe Matt had wanted kids? She'd never thought to ask.

"Since we're asking random questions—"

Devyn smiled. "I guess we are. What do you want to know?"

"Did you always want to be a doctor?"

"I wanted to be a firefighter when I was four." She laughed. "Then my grandmother taught me how to sew. One afternoon we were sewing together and I told her I wanted to be a seamstress. She said, 'Why not a doctor?'" She paused for a moment. "I never looked back."

"But you didn't want to be a surgeon?"

"Emergency medicine was a better fit. I could sew all day, but I love being there for someone right when they need me. And I love the rush."

Robbie held up her injured hand. "In that case, you're welcome."

"Yes, thank you. Although I could have done without so much blood on the tile."

Robbie cringed. "I'll clean it up."

"No, you won't." Devyn's eyebrow arched as if daring Robbie to argue. "I don't want that bandage getting wet. And, although you might not believe it, I know how to use some tools. Like a mop."

Robbie laughed, wondering even as she did at the coquettish look Devyn gave her. How was Devyn straight? It wasn't fair.

"Don't believe me?"

"No. It's…Nothing." She shook her head, knowing she needed to get the conversation back to something neutral. "So you like your job even with the long hours?"

"It's been hard lately, but I don't usually work this much. One of our doctors is out on maternity leave. Speaking of." Devyn leveled her gaze on Robbie. "Do you avoid doctors entirely or just hospitals?"

The question was warranted given her earlier freak-out. "Just hospitals." Even after months of counseling she'd made no headway in her hospital fears. She didn't want to tell Devyn all the reasons for that, however. Bringing up her mom was always hard. Especially any conversation that involved the day she'd lost her.

"Okay. I'll let you off the hook as long as I know you don't have an aversion to all doctors."

"Not all doctors."

Devyn tried to stifle a yawn but Robbie noticed. She would have happily spent the rest of the night talking but she said, "It's getting late."

"Not for normal people," Devyn returned. "Unfortunately, I have about ten years of missed sleep to catch up on."

Robbie stood and started clearing the plates but Devyn got up, too, and shooed her away from the sink. "Remember I don't want that bandage getting wet. No shower for you tonight, either."

Robbie leaned against the counter, watching Devyn scrub the dishes. "I took a shower after my run. I can handle skipping tonight." She looked down at the bandage. "I'm not sure about starting the tile job tomorrow, though."

"You might have to take the day off."

"Are you going to be around?" She felt sheepish asking. She wanted to spend the day with Devyn but had no right to expect Devyn would want to spend any more time with her.

"I'm on call. There's a slim chance I won't have to go in."

"You're on call all day?"

"No rest for the weary. Or the wicked. Or anyone who works in a hospital." Devyn finished cleaning the saucepan and set it on the rack to dry.

"I'll keep my fingers crossed you don't get called in." She quickly added, "For your sake. I'm sure you could use a break."

"Not because you want to keep me around in case you slice something else?"

"I should probably avoid sharp objects for a while…I really wanted to start the tiling project tomorrow but I don't know how I'd manage a tiling saw like this." She held up her hand, her middle finger jutting up, and Devyn quirked her lip like she was trying not to laugh. "I'm pathetic. That's what you're thinking, right?"

"No. Well, maybe a little." Devyn smiled. "You could be a tourist for a day or two. There's always the Aquarium. Or you might like checking out one of the art museums. I recommend the Timken but it doesn't have any paint-by-numbers. You might be disappointed."

Robbie laughed. "That's a low blow. And I'm injured."

"I know. You're entirely defenseless. I kind of like you this way."

"Whatever." She didn't care how pathetic she was if it meant Devyn was openly flirting. Unfortunately, she was still straight.

Plenty of straight women flirted and it meant nothing. She pushed on. "One day you're going to try paint-by-numbers and love it."

Devyn rolled her eyes. "You could also check out Balboa Park. Or go up to the Hillcrest neighborhood. That's the gay part of town."

"You know the gay parts?"

"My two best friends are gay," Devyn said. "And married to each other. Yes, I know the gay parts." She turned to pick up the breadboard, setting it in the sink and not looking Robbie's direction. "Also, just because a woman married a man does not mean she's straight."

Damn. Okay. Robbie was momentarily disarmed. Both by Devyn being clearly upset and by the answer to her unasked question. Devyn wasn't straight. At least, not completely. But Robbie had no idea what to say to fix things now. She scratched her head. "You're right. I assumed you were straight. Dumb assumption."

Was Devyn bi? Or had she realized she was a lesbian and that was one of the reasons she'd ended things with Matt? "I'm sorry for assuming instead of asking."

"People make assumptions all the time." Devyn finished with the cutting board and leaned it against the drying rack. She turned to face Robbie. "I made plenty about you."

"Do I want to know what assumptions you made?"

Devyn pursed her lips. "You're friends with my ex, so…no."

"We're work friends. I don't know Matt that well."

"You know him well enough to decide to swap houses."

"I needed a break from the rain. Are we really fighting about this again?"

Devyn held her gaze for a moment and then turned the water on at the sink again as she leaned past Robbie to flip the power on the sink's disposal. The motor cranked and in seconds, the sink drained. She looked over at Robbie. "That's satisfying."

The tension was still palpable between them, but Robbie forced a smile. "Do I get a star?"

"You might get two." Devyn flipped the switch and rinsed her hands. She looked back at Robbie. "We didn't last long with that truce."

Not long at all. "I think we're still figuring out how to talk to each other."

"I'm not sure why it's so hard."

"I frustrate you," Robbie said.

Devyn narrowed her eyes. "You do."

"You frustrate me too."

"Think we have a chance at being friends anyway?" Devyn's question seemed sincere but as if she already doubted the outcome.

"Friends would be a step up from where we started." Robbie had meant to lighten things but Devyn didn't seem to take her comment as a joke. She wanted to admit she'd prefer being more than friends. There was a slim chance Devyn would ever get past seeing her as Matt's friend, though, and an even slimmer chance she'd want more. "I'd like to be friends."

Devyn nodded slowly, then looked over to where Angel was sleeping on the couch. Her shoulders dropped and she said, "I think I'm ready to call it a night."

Robbie wished they could get back to the friendly flirty banter they'd enjoyed earlier, but she dipped her head and said, "Thanks again for sewing me up."

"My pleasure."

"I believe you. Which is a little weird."

Devyn smiled. "Just take care of my hard work."

When Robbie got back to the cottage, she was still digesting everything Devyn had said. "She's not straight." She rocked her head to the side. "But that doesn't mean she's interested in you."

For a brief moment, she'd hoped otherwise. Then Devyn had brought up Matt and everything had gone sideways. Again. Did Matt know Devyn wasn't straight?

As soon as she thought of Matt, she regretted it. She didn't want the reminder that she had no business lusting after his ex-wife. "But would he actually care?"

The question gave her pause. She'd been fighting the attraction because Matt was her friend—and Devyn was straight. But Matt had made it clear he was done with the relationship, and Devyn wasn't straight. So what was holding her back from trying to win Devyn over now?

She looked down at her bandaged hand and shook her head. Fate had to be laughing.

CHAPTER TWELVE

Devyn didn't want to answer the call but she felt childish for avoiding Matt. "I don't feel like talking to you," she said, staring at the phone as it rang again. "But thanks for sending Robbie."

Angel looked up at the word *Robbie*, his right ear perking as he tried to decipher her words.

"Think I should say that?"

Angel studied her, seemingly debating his answer.

"Probably not a good idea." Thanking Matt for Robbie was opening up a bottle she wasn't ready to uncork. "Although having Robbie here means I don't have to badger Matt. And no one enjoyed that." She sighed and wrapped her wet hair in a towel before hitting the green button.

"What's up?" Hopefully her tone conveyed exactly how much she didn't want to spend any part of her day off in a conversation with an ex.

"Hey. How are you?"

Matt's upbeat tone was a change—so much so she didn't know quite how to respond. "I'm fine." She heard the wariness in her voice. God, they'd become a total mess. "Did you have a reason for calling?"

"I wanted to check in."

Matt wanted to check in? That hadn't happened ever. "Why?"

"Because of the house and everything."

"Oh." Weird. And vaguely annoying that he cared now. "Everything is fine. Thanks for checking in."

"I was feeling guilty for how nice things are here. It's so peaceful kicking back on the water. I love Robbie's houseboat. And Seattle's amazing."

She wanted to ask about Robbie's houseboat but caught herself before she did. "That's great. I'm happy for you."

"Are you mad about something? You sound mad."

"I'm not mad." Probably she should be. But she wasn't. Because…Robbie. "I'm just doing something at the moment."

"You're always doing something."

His comment should have ticked her off. She'd heard it before, followed up by "you don't know how to relax" when she'd ask him to help her with any project around the house. Now she only shrugged it off. "You're right. I'm a busy person."

"Sounds like Robbie's been busy too. How's that going?"

"Good. Actually, great."

Matt let out a sound of relief. "I told Robbie you'd get to liking her. She was sure you were going to kick her out."

"Technically I did."

Matt chuckled. Fortunately, he had no clue about her feelings now. She opened her underwear drawer, not letting her eyes linger on any of her sexier panties. Her night had been consumed with the question of acting on her desire for Robbie. She didn't need sexy underwear spurring her to skip the part where she analyzed the repercussions of sleeping with someone she still hardly knew— and who wouldn't be staying.

"My mom might call you."

"Why would Tina call?" And why now? The news made her immediately choose her most conservative cotton underwear. She'd never disliked Matt's mother. In fact, she'd thought they had a good relationship. They weren't particularly close, but they'd gone to lunch without Matt multiple times and the conversations always flowed easily. She'd felt Tina understood her, even liked her, and she'd cared for her in return. Which made it especially hard Tina had cut off all contact after Matt announced he wanted the divorce.

"She's having surgery on her gall bladder. I told her she should call you about some of the things she's worrying about."

"Of course."

"You wouldn't mind?"

"No. Not at all. I've always liked your mom."

"That's what I told her." Matt paused. "But, well, I guess I should tell you…It doesn't really matter, but she thinks you broke up with me. I didn't tell her that exactly. She made the leap on her own and…well…"

"You didn't correct her." Devyn exhaled, sitting down on the edge of the bed. She set the underwear on the comforter next to her and pressed her hand to her head. "Why can't you talk about things, Matt?"

Maybe she was being harsher than necessary, but his obstinance to talk about problems, or to tell the truth when called out, was something she no longer had patience for. "I'm sure it was easier to let me be the fall guy."

"You know she makes everything into a big deal. I didn't want a class action lawsuit. Anyway, at the time it didn't matter what she thought."

"So you lied." She sighed. "On one hand, I don't care what you lie about at this point. On the other hand, I hope you grow up before you try marrying someone again. Being in a relationship with someone who can't tell the truth because they're scared it might make them look bad is annoying as shit."

He laughed. "I've always appreciated how honest you are. Robbie was joking about how much she liked it, too."

Joking?

"By the way, I think she has a crush on you."

"I'm sure that's not the case." A tingly sensation went through her though, followed by a wave of heat. Thankfully Matt couldn't see the blush she knew would be on her cheeks. "Anyway, I'm happy to talk to your mom. Do you know which hospital she'll be at? I can check in with her surgeon if she wants."

"I don't know which hospital, but I know she'd appreciate you talking to her surgeon."

"I'll call today and figure it out. Anything else?"

"No. Well…I wanted to apologize for not telling you Robbie and I were swapping houses."

The apology was overdue by a week, but she could hear the sincerity. That was something at least. "Thank you."

"Being up here, away from everything, has been good for me. I've had time to think." He exhaled. "I didn't deserve a second chance with you. I'm not really sure why you gave me one, to be honest. And then I fucked up again. You were right when you said we never should have gotten married. You would have been better off without me."

Matt's words sank into her. She'd only known for sure about the one affair—the one that lasted a year and involved him buying the woman a car and renting an apartment for her. She'd wondered if there'd been other women, had partly guessed it, but hadn't wanted to ask. The truth was it didn't matter. Not now and not a year ago.

"We both made mistakes, Matt."

Neither spoke for a long moment. She wanted to end the call but didn't feel like taking the initiative. He'd been the one to call, he could hang up. They hadn't had many conversations that didn't involve yelling. And none that involved an apology that wasn't followed with an excuse. This time, she believed he truly was sorry about all of it. She didn't have to forgive him. He wasn't asking for that anyway. But she felt strangely better all the same. Maybe they should have tried talking on the phone two years ago.

It wasn't the cheating or their inability to communicate that had spelled the end of their relationship though. Matt wanted someone she could never be. Someone she never wanted to be. Unfortunately, it took him taking on a mistress for her to recognize that. She'd been angry at first—mad at herself for not seeing obvious signs, mad he'd asked her to quit her job so they'd have more time together, mad they'd gotten together in the first place, and mad she'd wasted so much energy trying to make something work that had never felt quite right. She'd realized Matt had gone looking for company because their relationship wasn't giving him what he needed. And she felt the same. The divorce had been a foregone conclusion after that, but she'd still waited for Matt to ask for it.

Realizing the relationship was an empty void had helped her move on—and why she'd let him off the hook after his yearlong affair. She pushed down a sick feeling as she reminded herself there'd been more than one.

"Not that it matters, but I won't tell your mom you were the one to ask for the divorce. It really doesn't matter at this point."

"You can tell her whatever you want. I can handle it. I really appreciate you talking to her. She trusts your medical advice. Speaking of, Robbie says you bandaged her up." He whistled under his breath. "She sent me the picture of her hand."

She couldn't stop the image that came into her mind. Robbie, ashen-faced, clutching her hand and blood everywhere. She'd gone into work mode, scanning the scene, taking in all the details, and immediately deciding on a plan. Her brain had ticked off the checklist of the supplies she'd need, the questions she'd have to ask, and everything had gone accordingly. Right up until the moment Robbie slumped in her arms.

As she guided Robbie to the ground, her heart had launched a campaign. She was no longer in work mode by the time she'd taken Robbie's hand in hers. She steadied her thoughts to casually say, "She was slicing a frozen bagel. Apparently, you were right and one shouldn't bother freezing bagels."

"She didn't tell me she did that cutting a bagel." He chuckled. "Man, all of your bagels taking up freezer space used to annoy the shit out of me. I don't know why I made such a big deal about it."

It'd been a source of contention—one of dozens of little things they couldn't see eye to eye on. "We could have done a better job talking to each other about our real problems instead of fighting over the little stuff."

Matt snorted. "Damn. Philosophical Devyn. Never thought I'd see the day."

"Well, I never thought we'd talk on the phone like normal people and you'd apologize for something."

"Yeah…That's real." He chuckled again. "While we're on the subject, I'm sorry I didn't explain your pollinator garden to Robbie."

Before she had a chance to say she was over that, Matt continued, "I know you don't think Robbie has a crush, but I'm telling you, she does."

"She doesn't have a crush," she said, worrying even as she said it she'd been maybe too fast to deny it.

"I don't blame her. For what it's worth, you're still the hottest woman I've ever been with."

She barely suppressed a groan. "Thanks, Matt, but I'm not ready for a breakdown of the women you've fucked."

He laughed. "Fair. Go easy on Robbie, okay?"

"What do you mean?" She was certain her pulse had shot up along with her heart rate. On some level, she knew it might be a good idea to talk about her feelings with regard to Robbie instead of wrestling with it all in her head. But that conversation did not need to involve Matt. In fact, he was the last person she wanted to talk to about it.

"She's a good person."

"So?"

"Well, I know if you don't like someone in your space you can be kind of…"

"Bitchy?" She knew that was what he was going to say. "None of this situation is her fault. And, yes, I like my privacy, but I appreciate everything she's doing here. We have no issues." Not any she wanted to discuss with Matt, anyway.

"I'm just trying to watch out for my friend."

She tried not to be rankled with his reminder. "You know me. I get over being mad faster than most."

"You really do. Ever wonder why?"

"Now you sound like my therapist. I think Seattle is getting to you." She shook her head. "Is there anything else, Matt? I've got a million things to do today."

"Sometimes I forget you save the world on a regular basis. Thanks again for calling my mom. And for everything with Robbie."

She shook her head after they'd said goodbyes, realizing it was the first time in a long time that she didn't feel worse after having talked to him. Which didn't mean she wanted to talk to him again any time soon. But maybe they wouldn't need to fight anymore.

She picked up the underwear she'd chosen, thinking longingly of the sexier possibilities she'd prefer wearing around Robbie. "The world is full of possibilities," she said, smiling to herself.

Angel hopped off the bed and ran to the door. He pawed at the doorframe and whined. Robbie must have come into the house.

She started to put the cotton underwear on but then changed her mind and padded over to the dresser, shushing Angel when he whined again. No chance was she opening the door until she was fully dressed. Having Robbie catch her once in a towel was once enough. The embarrassing experience had made for amazing fantasy material—she'd let herself imagine the towel slipping off while Robbie watched and all sorts of dirty things had followed. But fantasy and real life were two different things.

Picking sexy underwear didn't mean she'd decided to do anything with Robbie, she told herself. She could still get called in to work at any minute even if she was pretending she had a full day off and could do whatever she wanted.

She reached for the silky black thong. The only thing sexy underwear meant was that she could feel sexy, she decided. The fact that she wanted to feel sexy around Robbie was something she could dissect later.

By the time she'd thrown leggings on and settled on a loose knit shirt that showed off enough cleavage to make her worry she was being obvious, Angel was fit to be tied. She opened the bedroom door and he raced out, howling a greeting. She followed, smiling when she saw Robbie in the kitchen, bent down to pet Angel.

"Hi." Robbie stood and gave her a wave with her still bandaged hand. "You didn't get called in to work?"

"Not yet anyway."

"I hope I didn't wake you."

"I've been up for a while. Angel and I took the paddleboard out early."

Robbie looked between her and Angel. "The two of you go on the paddleboard?"

"Angel loves being on the water. It took me a few times to get the balance right with him on the board, but now I take him whenever I can."

"I'd love to see that." Robbie grinned down at Angel. "You're a cool dog."

"He knows it. You know, you can come out with us the next time we go. If it's not too windy, I go every morning I don't have to work. But we go early—usually right after dawn."

"Isn't that when the sharks are out?"

She shrugged. "I've got Angel with me. He's my official shark guard."

"All right, Angel, I'm impressed. I thought you were only good for barking at stray cats and squirrels."

"He has many talents. Including helping me maintain my sanity when random women appear in my yard with Weedwackers."

Robbie frowned. "I can't imagine how that would happen."

"You'd be surprised."

Robbie held up a grapefruit. "On that note, want to split this with me?"

"Changing the subject?"

"One hundred percent."

Devyn laughed. "I'd love some grapefruit."

Robbie went for a knife but Devyn stopped her, holding out her hand. Robbie dipped her chin and glumly passed her the knife. As she split it in half, Robbie asked. "Any big plans for your day?"

"I was wondering if I could help you with the tiling. Since you're down a hand—and didn't seem all that interested in being a tourist today."

"You want to spend your day off tiling?"

"I need to get this house sold." She sighed. "I might get called in, but I can help as much as I can while I'm here. And, I hate to break it to you, but you're going to be down a hand for a while."

"It's only my middle finger," Robbie said. "In fact, it hardly hurts. I was going to ask you if I could take off the bandage today. I could do a lot more without the splint."

"Why do you think I splinted it?" She gave Robbie her best stern look. "I'll change the bandage today and take a look at the wound, but the splint stays on for three days."

"Three days?"

"You'll survive. I don't want you overdoing it and opening the wound." She offered a sympathetic smile to Robbie's whine. "What, were you planning on a hot Saturday night out on the town?" As soon as she asked, she knew she wanted the answer more than she wanted to admit. "I bet you could still make the women swoon. Or at least have them feeling sorry for you."

Robbie held up her hand. "This is basically the worst thing to happen to lesbian mojo."

"Are you left-handed?"

"No, but a lot of things work better with two hands."

Devyn swallowed, outplayed, and knowing a blush was working its way up to her cheeks. Robbie sounded more disappointed than cocky, though, and Devyn realized then how much more experience Robbie likely had when it came to sex.

"I'll take your word for it." She dropped the two grapefruit halves into bowls. "What else are we having? Something tells me you might not want a bagel."

"Actually, I'd love one. I get it if you don't, but I didn't get blood on any of the others. I only took one bagel out and I tossed it after I failed the part where I tried cutting it in half." Robbie made a face. "Blood got everywhere."

"I know. I mopped last night."

"I'm sorry. That was probably gross."

"Don't worry. I deal with blood all the time." She opened the freezer and took out the bag of bagels. "Just in case, any communicable diseases I need to know about?"

"No. I got tested after my ex and I broke up."

"Me too." Devyn felt a flush for being so quick to mention her own status. "I'm going to make eggs too. Want some?"

"Sure." Robbie reached for the egg pan but got out of the way when Devyn shooed her off. She leaned against the counter opposite the range looking uncomfortable.

"Not used to letting others do things for you?"

"No." Robbie chuckled. "But I can accept help. I don't know if this is something I should say or not, but…Matt and I talked about you last night."

She waited for Robbie to go on, focusing on cracking an egg.

"He said you had the biggest heart of anyone. But you act like a b-word sometimes as cover."

"It's not only my cover." She smiled at Robbie. "Do I want to know what else he told you about me?"

"That was basically it," Robbie said. "I told him how you stitched me up."

She wondered if Matt had called Robbie out on having a crush then. If so, what had she said in response?

"Matt said you won some doctor award and I probably owed you tons of money for this." She held up her splinted middle finger. She smiled. "We can settle at the end of the month."

"I'm not going to touch that topic. I want our truce to last at least a day." Robbie grinned back at her. "So you don't mind talking about Matt? I was wondering if it's weird because him and I are friends, and you're well, you know."

"Exes?" She shrugged. "Matt's not my favorite topic. I'm sure I'm not his, either."

"I get not wanting to talk about exes."

"Too bad. I was about to ask for a full rundown of yours." She waved off Robbie's look of surprise. "I'm teasing." In fact, she was curious but not brave enough to ask outright. She wanted to know a lot of things about Robbie but all the questions she really wanted answered felt off-limits. "Preference on cream cheese?"

"Do you have more of that strawberry kind?"

She held up the container and then closed the fridge. "Want to tell me about tiling while I make us breakfast?" Better to stick with the safe topics.

CHAPTER THIRTEEN

No daylight seeped between the blinds, but Robbie was wide awake. She lay on her back, aware she was wet, and stubbornly refused to slip her hand between her legs.

Every morning for the past week she'd found herself with the same problem—uncomfortably aroused after a dream involving Devyn. The dream was never exactly the same. This time she'd walked in on Devyn with another woman between her legs. Devyn hadn't told her to leave so she'd stood in the doorway and watched. She'd jolted awake when the Devyn in her dreams had climaxed, arching off the mattress as she grabbed a fistful of the woman's hair.

Had Devyn been with a woman before? The question circled in her mind. What was her type? Someone like her or someone more femme like the woman who'd been between Devyn's legs in the dream?

Robbie reached over and picked up her phone, checking the time. Half past five. She sighed, tossed the phone aside, and dropped back on her pillows. "Go to sleep."

A minute passed, then another. It seemed wrong to think of Devyn when she touched herself, but the temptation was hard to resist. What would Devyn say if she knew her thoughts? Her fantasies?

Groaning, Robbie rolled on her side. If today was a repeat of yesterday, she'd spend it in a state of near constant arousal no matter what she did. Between the close quarters of the bathroom they were tiling and the sight of Devyn on her hands and knees, she'd been wet for hours on end. Fortunately, they'd made good progress on the tile and Devyn hadn't gotten called into work. If that luck held today, they'd finish the job.

The memory of Devyn, sweaty, leaning against the bathroom counter and looking down at Robbie, came to mind. Her clit pulsed with need. She balled her fingers into fists as she imagined getting up from the tile floor and Devyn reaching for her. She imagined her hands settling on Devyn's hips, her lips brushing Devyn's neck. When she imagined sliding her hand between Devyn's thighs, she had to clench her legs together.

It didn't seem fair to Devyn to have a fantasy about her. Thinking of a past or present lover, someone imaginary or a celebrity, was one thing. But fantasizing about someone real and someone who she'd have to face in a few hours?

She flopped onto her back. *No fantasies about Devyn.*

Devyn had made it clear yesterday she wasn't looking for a relationship. She'd even said marriage was an unhealthy trap and didn't think most committed relationships were worth the stress and heartache. Then she'd said how much more fulfilling her friendships were than her other relationships and Robbie knew she was sunk. Any thought of hooking up had gone out the window when Devyn had added, "Even this right now. I like being with someone when there's no expectations. When you can relax and just be yourself. It feels good, right?"

Classic friendzone.

As soon as she'd confirmed Devyn's interests weren't the same as hers, she'd had to scale back the flirty banter. Then, because her attraction wasn't going away, she'd made herself avoid any accidental touches. She'd also tried to avert her gaze whenever she thought Devyn might have noticed her paying too much attention to what she was saying. Or doing. The problem was, she couldn't spend the day with Devyn and not notice everything about her.

She exhaled and got out of bed, pushing herself into the shower despite the early hour. She wanted to be ready when Devyn and

Angel went out paddleboarding. Even if she couldn't admit why aloud, even if it was torture being close but not touching, she was hungry to spend every waking moment with Devyn again today.

The shower managed to yank her out of her dreamlike state, but when she went to turn off the spray, she accidentally got her bandage wet. She got out of the shower, tied a towel around her waist, and unwrapped the wet gauze. Devyn had redone the bandage only last night and now she'd have to ask her to do it all over again. Not that it was a problem having to ask Devyn to bandage her, but her libido had been out of control. Especially when Devyn had bent her head, leaning close to study the wound and giving Robbie a full whiff of the scent of her shampoo. When she'd prodded a reddened area with the lightest of touches, Robbie had pulled her hand back a fraction of an inch, her body zinging, and Devyn had worriedly asked, "Does that hurt?"

Robbie had only managed to shake her head in response, willing her hormones to behave as she forced herself to submit to the rest of the examination. And then the bandaging. Medical stuff had never been easy for her. With Devyn it was a complicated mess.

She pulled on a pair of boxers and then her cargo pants, gingerly avoiding brushing anything against her wound. Before she'd finished dressing, she heard a scratch at the door. Often Devyn let Angel out to pee and without fail he'd come right to the cottage after finishing his business. This time when she opened the door, Angel bolted right inside. Unfortunately, he wasn't alone.

Not once had Devyn come outside when she'd let Angel out to pee. But this time she'd not only come out with him but followed him to the cottage. Robbie reflexively crossed her arms and then instantly regretted the move. The pressure on her unwrapped wound sent a spasm of pain through her.

"Fuck." She pulled her left arm away from her chest and grimaced as she looked at her hand.

"What happened?"

"Nothing." Robbie shook her head. "I got the bandage wet in the shower so I took it off because you said it couldn't get wet and then…I squished my hand."

Devyn held out her hand. "Let me see."

"I'm sure it's fine. I don't—"

"Robbie."

"Ugh. Fine." She kept her right arm across her chest as she let Devyn examine the wound. Devyn in a wetsuit that outlined every bit of her gorgeous body was not what she needed to see while half-dressed herself. Devyn holding her hand, with her cute worried expression, was even harder to take.

"It looks good." She let go of Robbie's hand, a noticeable blush on her cheeks. "I'll have to bandage it again, though." She closed her eyes for a moment, shaking her head slightly. "I was coming to ask if you wanted to go down to the water with Angel and me. If it's too early—"

"I want to come. Let me throw on a shirt."

"We'll get the paddleboard." Devyn called to Angel and he dashed past Robbie's leg. "Oh." She'd started to the garage but stopped to look back at Robbie. "You might want to throw a glove on your hand, too. If you get sand in the wound, you'll really be flinching later when I make you hold still to clean it."

What Devyn said shouldn't be a turn-on. And yet Robbie instantly had the desire to build a sandcastle barehanded. "Right. Okay."

Devyn started walking again, calling over her shoulder, "And don't forget the shirt or I'll have to give you a hard time about applying sunscreen to your sensitive bits."

Robbie rolled her eyes but Devyn didn't look back to see it. Neither did Angel, hot on his favorite person's heels. Despite it being his fault there'd been now two half-dressed awkward interactions between her and Devyn, he did not seem the least bit apologetic. Typical terrier.

When Devyn was nearly to the garage, Robbie closed the door and dropped her right arm. Her breasts weren't big but her nipples had always been sensitive and they weren't happy about being smashed. She sighed and got the sports bra she'd meant to put on earlier along with the last of her clean shirts. Laundry would have to happen soon. "But first I get to try admiring Devyn in a wetsuit without it being awkward." She grabbed a hat as well as one of her work gloves, thinking she couldn't handle sitting still while Devyn picked sand from her wound. She only had so much self-control.

The walk down to the water was quiet. Devyn seemed introspective and Robbie was glad she didn't have to make small talk while pretending she wasn't still embarrassed at being caught half-naked.

Angel howled with delight the moment the paddleboard splashed into the water and there was no holding him back as Devyn pushed the board past the breakers. Robbie laughed as Angel, clad in a bright orange life vest, launched himself onto the front of the board.

Devyn looked back at her and smiled. "He thinks he's the captain."

"More like a little pirate," Robbie added.

Devyn's smile widened. "That's what I call him when he's naughty. You can head back to the house anytime. Don't feel like you have to stay out the whole time with us."

Robbie had no intention of going back. She waved as they pulled away from the shore, watching as Devyn nimbly went from a kneeling position to standing and Angel settled into his captain role. For a while she could follow their progress walking along the beach, but then Devyn turned the paddleboard west toward the open ocean.

"Damn, that's gorgeous," Robbie murmured, not sure if she meant the layers of blue sky merging with the deeper blue water to the west, or the sun pushing above the horizon in the east, or Devyn's profile catching both the golden light and the glittering water.

"You sure you only want a friend, Devyn?" Robbie sighed. Devyn's response to seeing her without a shirt made her question everything all over again. Devyn had given her a once-over that said she wanted to be more than friends. "And you flirt with me."

Robbie shook her head. Maybe Devyn wasn't over things with Matt. Maybe he was the reason Devyn didn't want another relationship. She could understand needing time. After her last breakup, she'd gone a full year with no interest in any women she'd met. "Apparently I'm over that now."

She eyed Devyn again and then pulled out her phone. As Devyn coasted over a wave, she snapped a picture, telling herself she was only doing so to share with Devyn later. Angel stood like a sentinel at the front of the board and Devyn stood behind him, her paddle held across her chest as she seemed to pause midstroke to watch the rising sun. Robbie smiled at the image and then took several more before jamming her phone back in her pocket. When it came time to go home to Seattle, she wanted to remember the view at least.

When the wind picked up, Devyn turned the paddleboard back to shore. Robbie met her at the same spot she'd pushed in at and they walked back to the house with Angel bouncing between them and Devyn gushing about the bay. She said it was her happy place, and Robbie could see it in the way her eyes shone after getting out of the water. When Robbie asked about the wildlife in the area, she got even more animated. Today had only been birds but she'd had seals try to play with her, sea lions bark at her, whales wave, and plenty of otters pop up with seashells to show off.

Then Devyn asked about the wildlife Robbie came across living on a houseboat. The conversation felt easy. Comfortable. And Robbie could almost imagine simply being friends. Almost. Then Devyn traded out her wetsuit for a spaghetti-strap tank top and shorts that showed off her legs.

The next eight hours passed with Robbie trying not to overtly stare at Devyn's body. Fortunately, the tiling project took some concentration—especially since she only had one hand to work with—and the day slipped away with breaks for snacks and a few "recesses" outside with Angel.

They worked well together. Devyn easily took direction and seemed happy to be the pair of hands Robbie didn't currently have. And Devyn was even chattier on day two of the project than she'd been the first day. After a while, Robbie couldn't deny that Devyn sincerely wanted a friendship—opening up about all kinds of things friends would share. Unfortunately, the feeling of a budding friendship only brought on more guilt for her body's response when she looked at Devyn. Or when Devyn looked at her.

By the time they'd finished sealing the edge of the tile against the tub with an outline of caulk—Devyn joking Robbie was in charge of the "cock"—she'd decided she needed a cold shower and to spend the evening alone. Otherwise there was a good chance she'd fess up to her feelings and that would ruin everything.

She wiped a bit of caulk that had oozed over the tile with a rag and then straightened up and surveyed the work. "What do you think?"

Devyn had cleared the rest of their tools and supplies and was wiping dust off the counter. She scrutinized the line of caulk Robbie had finished with a squint before nodding. "I'd hire us."

Robbie chuckled. "I'm not sure you should give up your day job for this."

"Why not?"

"For one thing, you wouldn't be able to afford a place this nice two blocks from the beach if you spent your days doing tiling work."

"I can't afford it now. Not without Matt paying half. We bought when the market was at a peak. The house is too big for me anyway."

"Where do you think you'll move when you sell?"

"I'm not sure. I love being close to the water and being able to walk with my paddleboard to the beach. There's an apartment complex near here…It's small, but they allow dogs."

"You wouldn't have a pollinator garden if you lived in an apartment."

"I know, but you would not believe the prices on houses in this neighborhood."

She'd seen the prices, actually. Still, she wished she'd kept the comment to herself as Devyn frowned when she looked from the bathroom to the open sliding glass door leading out to the balcony where Angel was positioned. He'd been on guard duty the entire time they'd been tiling—likely hoping the cat he loved to bark at would saunter into his yard.

"Want to see something?" Robbie didn't wait for an answer, pulling out her phone, tapping the unlock code, and handing it to Devyn. "Check out the last picture on my roll." She washed her hands, trying not to focus on Devyn as she did.

"I love this. Angel is so adorable, isn't he? So photogenic. I swear he can't take a bad picture. Wait, where were you when you got this shot?" Devyn asked, glancing from the picture to Robbie's reflection in the bathroom mirror.

"I walked out on the jetty."

Devyn looked at the phone again and smiled. "I've never had a shot of Angel and me on the board together. Do you mind if I text this to myself?"

"Go ahead. You can check out the other pictures I took too. You might like one of those better." She paused. "Angel's not the only one who's photogenic."

Devyn's lips lifted at the corners but she kept her focus on Robbie's phone as she said, "I take bad pictures all the time. This one was a fluke."

"You're gorgeous in every shot."

Devyn shook her head but didn't say anything more, seemingly busy studying the other pictures on the phone. Robbie was well aware she was in dicey territory mentioning anything about Devyn's appearance. She didn't think Devyn was upset, but she didn't seem to know what to do with the compliment.

"I made myself only take a handful of shots. I didn't want to seem weird," Robbie admitted.

Devyn raised an eyebrow. "But you thought telling me that doesn't make you sound weird?"

Robbie grinned. "Well, since I'm already in a hole, you look good in a wetsuit."

"That's clearly why I wear them."

Robbie chuckled. "I figured. For the record, I wasn't the only one who thought you looked hot in that wetsuit."

Devyn shook her head. "No one thought I looked hot."

"If you honestly think that, you weren't paying attention. Two guys practically ran into each other because they were so busy staring at you they didn't look where they were going. And about a dozen people checked you out when we walked from the beach back to the house. Including Clara."

"Who's Clara?"

"The Black woman who owns Good Tides—that café at the end of your street. She's asked about you. And she hinted she was interested."

"Really?" Devyn paused, seemingly surprised by the news. "I think I know who you're talking about. She's really pretty."

"I could introduce you, if you want."

Devyn seemed to consider the offer but then shook her head. She handed Robbie back the phone. "Thanks for the picture."

"You're welcome."

"It's funny. I've walked past that café three times a week at least the last two years and I've never thought to stop and talk to the owner."

"Like I said, I don't mind making the introduction." Robbie lifted a shoulder. "I'm not a matchmaker, but—"

"I'm not in the right headspace to date anyone."

Robbie wasn't surprised at the news, but her heart sank anyway. Another confirmation that nothing was going to happen between them. She gestured to the newly tiled floor to change the subject. "Hey, look what we did."

"I'm impressed." Devyn eyed the bathroom floor again. "Can I buy you dinner as a thank-you? This was above and beyond—and before you say it—tiling was not on Matt's to-do list, which means this had nothing to do with your deal with him."

She smiled. "Dinner sounds nice." *Too nice.* If she made it through without thinking about anything inappropriate, her libido would deserve a star after.

"Maybe we should shower first."

"Are you saying we stink?"

"Probably." Devyn shrugged. "I have no problem with that, but I'm in the mood for the Water Grill and our waiter might. It's a little fancy. Do you mind?"

"I'm not sure I can do fancy with what I packed. I think the best I can do is business casual." She'd brought one nice outfit on the off chance she got called in for an in-person meeting. It wasn't what she'd pick for a date, however. Not that this was a date. Still, she wished she had more than slacks and one nice dress shirt.

"That's perfect." Devyn's phone buzzed with a text. She'd left it on the back of the toilet and the sound rebounded off the porcelain. When she reached for it, her brow furrowed. As she read the words, Robbie knew it wasn't good news. "I have to go in to work." She cussed under her breath. "I'm sorry."

"It's not a problem. I'll take a rain check."

"You don't mind?" She seemed truly surprised.

"Of course not. You're on call. Do you need to leave right now?"

Devyn nodded.

"Then while you change, I'll throw together a little dinner for you to eat on the way."

"That's really sweet of you." Devyn's shoulders sagged. "But I wanted to buy you dinner and instead you're making me dinner. And I'm leaving."

"I won't forget you owe me," Robbie teased.

Devyn smiled. "Deal." She glanced at the bathroom one last time. "I may regret spending the last six hours on my hands and knees if I'm stuck at work late, but this tile looks amazing."

"It does. We make a good team." Which made everything that much harder.

CHAPTER FOURTEEN

After leaving Robbie to clean up their tiling project alone, Devyn promised herself she'd make it up to her. Unfortunately, the next five days did not allow for any makeups. Kelly went down with COVID. Then Malcolm caught it. Having two of the other doctors out sick meant Devyn hardly had time to go home to sleep. Fortunately, she did make it home and each night dinner was waiting for her. Robbie and Angel were always waiting for her, too. She usually had an hour or two before she crashed from exhaustion, and she loved spending that time with Robbie.

The wound on Robbie's hand looked better each day and when she'd last checked it, she'd teased Robbie about being an eligible date. Robbie had only rolled her eyes in response, which made Devyn tempted to say more. She hadn't, though, and she'd spent that night regretting it. Robbie made her want to push her usual boundaries, made her want to say the things she thought of instead of biting her tongue, but wanting something and going for it were two different things.

As soon as she'd convinced herself she was ready for a fling, she'd started overthinking. Not because she didn't want it. The problem was she liked Robbie—more than felt right for a fling. And the more time she'd spent with her, the harder it was to deny that feeling. Yet she knew she was still in no place to start a relationship. If something happened, could she manage to not get attached? One minute she thought she could and the next she'd gone back to telling Robbie she was only interested in friendships.

"If I weren't stuck here day after day, I might get desperate and just kiss her." She said the words aloud, but the hallway was empty.

She'd come to a quiet part of the hospital—quiet at least at this time of day—to check her phone, and she smiled as she opened a waiting text message from Robbie. It was a sunset picture with Angel at the beach, shimmering water behind him and one of his favorite fluorescent green balls between his front paws. In the shot, his eyes were half-closed and he looked as if he'd fall asleep any moment. Below the picture were the words: *We're sure you're working hard too.*

"What are you smiling about? This is a serious place." Trudy held up her clipboard. She'd come around the corner of the empty hallway so quickly Devyn hadn't had any warning of her approach. Now she stopped in front of Devyn and said sternly, "No smiling allowed."

Trudy was one of the nurses who loved to joke. She was also a big gossip. Devyn tucked her phone in her pocket and casually said, "Someone sent me a silly picture. That's all." Hoping Trudy wouldn't pry further, Devyn started past her. "Don't worry, I won't get into the smiling habit."

"Someone who makes you smile is a good thing," Trudy said, hinting she knew Devyn was hiding something. "Does the always-serious-doctor have a new boyfriend?"

Devyn wished she could ignore the question, but the ramifications of doing so could be worse than addressing it. "It was a picture of my dog. From the woman who's taking care of him."

"Oh." Trudy's face fell for a moment but then brightened the next. "You know, I have a cousin who's single. He's very handsome."

"Thank you, but I'm not interested in dating right now." That was still true.

Devyn started walking again and didn't look over her shoulder as Trudy called out, "If you change your mind, let me know. Plenty of men will be lining up once that divorce is finalized."

Thankfully, the hallway was empty and no one else heard Trudy. Devyn hadn't said anything to her about the divorce and didn't make a habit of sharing her private life at work. Which meant the news had gone through the gossip chain. Fighting a surge of annoyance, she quickened her steps and turned the corner past the nursing station. She stopped short when she saw a nurse with her hand on her chest and a chilling look on her face.

"What's wrong?"

"There's been a shooting at the mall. Multiple victims." The nurse's voice broke. She took a shaky breath and added, "They're sending half here and half to Memorial."

Devyn touched the woman's shoulder. Clarisse. She was one of the new intake nurses and had only been on staff for a week. "We'll be ready to do what we can. Let ICU and trauma know what's happening."

The blur of adrenaline, tears, and blood that followed were nothing Devyn wanted to remember. Elena was called in as was anyone else who might be needed. Six victims. Three in serious condition. And that was only a fraction of the lives changed by one kid with a gun.

When Clarisse, the new nurse, touched Devyn's shoulder fourteen hours after the call had come in, she startled and then pushed back against a wave of dizziness.

"Someone brought in donuts." Clarisse gave her a concerned look. "I think you could use a break and some sugar."

She nodded and promised she'd grab a donut. But they all needed a break.

An hour later, Ian found her at one of workstations. He cleared his throat and said, "I'm pretending I'm in charge and sending you home."

"I can't leave."

"We've got enough hands to manage things. You've been on for too many hours."

She knew what he was telling her. *This is when mistakes happen.* But a list of reasons to stay pushed up in her mind.

"Please go home," he said. "You can come back in eight hours. I'll need a break then."

Ian was right. She'd been on for too many hours and someone still had to work tomorrow. "Fine."

She wasn't sure how she made it to her car. Once she was there, though, she couldn't manage to turn on the ignition. She stared at the steering wheel, trying to will her body to drive as her mind filled with images of the shooting victims. A wave of nausea hit and she had to open the door and lean out of the car to breathe.

Of the six victims the ambulances had brought, five were still alive. Countless nurses and doctors had been involved trying to save the one life they'd lost. She'd been the one to stare at the monitors long after the call had been made—arguing with the machines and arguing with herself. She'd known the patient likely wouldn't survive the moment he'd come in and yet she hadn't wanted to accept the truth in the end. All of the other patients had been passed to other doctors while she spoke to the young man's family.

The waiting room was full. *Triage.* Some days she hated the word. There was no way to keep up, no way to make everyone happy. And no way to save every life. Her chin trembled and finally she let the tears fall.

She couldn't drive home. But she couldn't stay. She needed a break. A few hours to close her eyes. Then she could come back and take over. For better or worse, her guilt over leaving wasn't as strong an emotion as her fear of making a mistake.

Her phone rang and she stared at it for a moment, swiping away tears and trying to think why Robbie would be calling at two in the morning. She steadied her voice as she answered.

"Elena texted me an hour ago," Robbie said. "She told me you were leaving the hospital and wanted to make sure you got home okay…I heard what happened. It's awful. I'm so sorry."

Devyn couldn't answer. The tears she'd thought she had under control now streamed down her cheeks accompanied by choking sobs.

"Where are you? I'm coming to get you."

She wanted to tell Robbie she was fine. That she could drive herself home. But she couldn't. "I'm in the parking garage. At the hospital."

"I'll be there in twenty minutes."

She ended the call and dropped her head on the steering wheel. Relief mixed with embarrassment. She should still be working, still helping. Instead, she was sitting in her car crying. And she needed someone to drive her home.

Tomorrow she could be annoyed at Robbie for not asking if she'd wanted her to come. For assuming she needed help. Tomorrow, too, she could be annoyed at Elena for texting Robbie. Now she had no energy to be annoyed.

She closed her eyes, slowed her breathing, and begged her mind to go blank. Had it been the right call to increase the dose of the lidocaine drip? The kid had the same color eyes as her father. Same shade of brown with flecks of gold. And the light had gone out after only nineteen years. Was there anything else she could have done? Her mind spun through everything that had happened and then brought up the cases that had come and gone earlier that day. The girl who'd grimaced when she'd suggested pink as the color to bandage her ankle. The man who'd slipped in the shower and was still in ICU with a bleed that wouldn't stop. Had she remembered to double-check his medications?

Her phone beeped. *I'm at the garage. Which level are you on?*

Three. She stared at her text and then scrolled up to the picture of Angel at the beach. One day had never seemed to last so long. Though, technically, the picture had been taken on Sunday. Now it was early Monday.

She startled when Robbie tapped her window. The worry on Robbie's face broadcast more than she could handle. She looked away, fumbling to unclip her seat belt and then slipping her keys and her phone in her purse.

Robbie opened the door and stepped back, not saying anything. Probably she could tell words were impossible at the moment.

She looked for Robbie's car and then numbly walked to the white Honda. Robbie didn't try to open the door for her, which she was grateful for, and still didn't speak as they drove out of the parking garage.

When they got home, Robbie led the way inside, glancing back a few times as if to make sure she didn't lose her charge. She set her keys and her wallet on the kitchen counter and said, "I'm going to make us tea."

Devyn didn't feel like tea but didn't say so. She went to the living room and sank down on the sofa. If Robbie had said it was late and she should sleep, she would have cussed her out for telling her what to do, but tea was hard to get into an argument over. She closed her eyes, dimly aware of Angel hopping up to settle on the sofa on one side of her. It was late for him, and he did little more than nudge her hand for a pet. She indulged him and her mind finally went blank. After a few pets, he cuddled up closer, sighing softly as he closed his eyes. Her chest tightened. He always seemed to know exactly what she needed.

Robbie appeared with two mugs of steaming tea. She handed one to Devyn and said, "It's chamomile. My uncle says tea doesn't fix anything but if you make it hot enough, you'll burn your tongue."

"Why is that a good thing?"

"Because it's hard to think of anything else." Robbie offered a sympathetic smile. "You don't have to talk, but if you want to, I'm here."

"I don't want to talk." She also didn't want tea, but she made herself take a sip. Immediately the liquid scalded her tongue. She pulled the mug away from her lips, cussing.

"He's got a point, doesn't he?" Robbie raised an eyebrow.

"Smart old bastard."

Devyn looked at Robbie, and despite everything, found herself laughing. Robbie pointed to the space next to her. "Okay if I sit next to you?"

She nodded and Robbie settled in, leaving a few inches between them. She took a sip of tea and made a face. "I don't even like tea."

"Me neither," Devyn admitted. "I only keep it on hand for when my mother insists on coming over. But I think this is what I need." She blew, then took a shallow sip, aware of Robbie watching her and likely worrying. "I'm fine," she said. "I know you want to ask."

"You're not fine. And that's okay."

She didn't argue. Instead, she pointed to Robbie's hand. Over the last five days she'd graduated from the bandage with the finger splint to a simple Band-Aid. "How's that feel?"

"Good. It's nearly healed. I had a good doctor." Robbie added, "I still can't believe I cut my middle finger. Of all fingers."

"Sucks to be a lesbian who won't be getting lucky anytime soon, huh?"

Robbie held up her middle finger but grinned as she did it. She lowered the injured hand and then looked at the other. "I'm right-handed anyway. Probably could still get lucky."

"I'm ambidextrous." A moment after she said it, she realized it sounded like a brag and she added, "Not that it matters because—"

"Braggart." Robbie chuckled. "I already know that if we went to the clubs, you'd get all the women. And the men."

"I don't go to clubs."

"Me neither." Robbie took another sip of her tea and then set it down. She shifted back on the sofa cushions and exhaled.

Devyn knew Robbie was tired. She considered saying she wanted to go to bed purely so Robbie would feel she could as well. But she didn't want to be alone. And Robbie wouldn't think of going to bed with her. As soon as the thought crossed her mind, she knew that was what she wanted. To cuddle up against Robbie, wrap her arms around her, snuggle close, and breathe in her scent. The strength of the desire to do everything she'd imagined for the last week and a half rolled through her. She set down the tea, her hand trembling as she did.

"Do you want—" Robbie cut off when Devyn stood.

"I want a shower. Can you stay for a bit?"

Robbie nodded, brow knit together but not asking why.

Devyn didn't offer an explanation, only heading to the bathroom and flipping on the light. She closed the door and leaned against it, taking a deep breath. *First, a shower. Then you can decide if asking her to sleep with you is a terrible idea.*

She shed her clothes and stepped into the water before it'd gotten hot. The cold brought her immediately to her senses and she asked the question out loud. "Is it a mistake sleeping with her?"

No. There was no hesitation in the answer from any part of her. She scrubbed down, not bothering with shampoo but washing every part that felt tinged with what she'd been through.

After she dried off, she brushed her teeth, avoiding eye contact with her reflection in case she lost her nerve. Then she wrapped a fresh towel around her and opened the bathroom door. She looked down the hall to the living room. Angel was still asleep on the sofa but Robbie had gone and their mugs of tea had been cleared.

"I'm right here," Robbie said.

Devyn turned and saw her leaning against the wall next to her bedroom. Waiting for her.

"You asked me to stay. I wouldn't leave."

Devyn's throat felt tight. She forced herself to say, "Will you lie down with me?"

Robbie seemed to consider the request for a moment and then nodded. Questions had to be running through her mind, but she didn't ask.

"I'll only be a minute," she said, padding across the hallway to her room. As much as she wanted to lie naked with Robbie, to finally feel her body, she closed the door to her room and took pajamas from the drawer. She tugged on a T-shirt and sleep shorts and then opened the door and briefly met Robbie's gaze.

Robbie didn't say a word, only pushing off the wall and stepping forward. Devyn turned back into the room as she fought the impulse to reach for Robbie. If she touched Robbie, she knew she'd kiss her. How much she wanted that felt dangerous. Heart hammering, she went to her usual side of the bed and pushed down the covers.

She'd never shared the bed with Matt. It'd been the guest room and then when she couldn't bear to sleep with him anymore, she'd left their shared bedroom and this space had become hers. As she lay down now, she wondered if she was truly ready to share a bed with someone again. But even if she wasn't, she wanted Robbie.

"Okay if I turn off the lights?"

She nodded and the room went dark. She heard a rustling sound and guessed Robbie was undressing. Should she have offered Robbie something to wear?

"I'm keeping my T-shirt on, in case you're worried," Robbie said.

"You don't need to." She'd whispered the words but knew Robbie had heard when the sound of her movements stilled. Could she ask Robbie to take off everything and lie with her naked?

She held her breath as Robbie's weight made the bed give ever so slightly. The sheets shifted but she didn't move from her position despite how much she wanted to turn toward Robbie.

"Can you…" Her voice trailed as she lost her nerve asking for what she wanted.

Robbie touched her shoulder and she trembled. The sheet was over her and she was wearing a T-shirt, but still she felt stripped bare by Robbie's gentleness. She knew if she turned to Robbie, she wouldn't stop herself from taking the next step.

One second passed and then another. She took a long, shaky inhale and then turned, moving into Robbie's embrace. Robbie held her for a moment, not saying anything, and she wondered if she'd have to ask for what she wanted. Then Robbie brushed a fingertip lightly across her cheek and she held her breath. Waiting.

"I want to kiss you," Robbie said softly. "I want to make everything better, but I know a kiss won't make anything better. It'll only make things more complicated. And I don't know exactly what you want from me."

"I don't know either." She clenched her jaw, straining to hold in her emotions. She couldn't see Robbie to know her response. The room was too dark to see anything. The windows all had blackout curtains so she could sleep at any hour.

"Will you kiss me anyway?" She couldn't hold the question back.

Robbie caressed her cheek again. "This will change things, you know."

"Are you warning me or yourself?"

"I'm not sure."

When Robbie shifted forward and met her lips, the kiss was gentle. Soothing. Exactly what she should have wanted if the only thing she needed was to be cared for after what she'd been through. But she wanted more. As Robbie started to pull back, she slipped her hand behind Robbie's neck.

She couldn't see Robbie, but she knew she had her attention. "One more."

Robbie pressed into her lips then with a full deep kiss that took away her breath. Made her forget she needed air.

This. This is what I want.

Every part of her wanted Robbie's kiss. She reveled in it, didn't want it to end, and when she parted her lips, Robbie's tongue darted against hers. Everything she'd wanted to feel from every kiss before rushed through her. Red-hot desire. A perfect match. A feeling of being safe in wanting more. In taking more. When Robbie pulled away for a breath, she was the one to lead with another kiss.

The desire to be touched and to feel Robbie everywhere came on suddenly, overwhelming her ability to rationalize it. Between kisses, she found Robbie's hand and guided it under her shirt. She gasped as Robbie's warm hand grazed the cool skin of her belly. Then, her heart lodged in her throat, she moved Robbie's hand to her breast.

Robbie grazed over her nipple and she barely held in a moan. When she pushed herself into Robbie's hand, needing more than a light touch, she heard Robbie's breath catch. She knew she'd been understood. She moved against Robbie, no longer able to hold back, and Robbie responded with a roughness in her touch that made it clear she'd been holding back for too long. Robbie's touch awakened every part of her.

As Robbie's hands stroked over her body, she felt every part ignite. She'd imagined what it would feel like with Robbie, with a woman, but this was more than she'd expected. More emotion, more desire. She'd never been so turned on.

When she shifted on the mattress, Robbie moved on top of her. She breathed Robbie in, loving the feel of her weight and how she seemed to know exactly what to do. When Robbie straddled her, she was acutely aware of how wet she was and of what she wanted.

Five minutes ago she'd thought she'd only needed to be in Robbie's arms. She'd wanted a kiss, but she hadn't been certain if she'd want more. Now she wanted everything—wanted Robbie with no clothing between them and wanted Robbie's hand between her legs. Desire pulsed through her as she moved to take off her shirt.

Robbie caught her hand. "I need to ask." Her voice sounded hoarse as if she were fighting against her own need. "We're taking things fast. Are you sure?"

She didn't blame Robbie for asking. It was their first time. And her first time with a woman. After the day she'd had, was it a good idea? Should they rush in without a conversation first?

But she had no doubt about what she wanted. After everything that had happened—not only in the last twenty-four hours but in the last year—she needed Robbie. She needed someone to take hold of her in a way only a lover could. She pushed up to kiss Robbie's lips. As she pulled away, she said, "I'm sure."

"You have no idea how much I hoped you'd say that."

CHAPTER FIFTEEN

As soon as Devyn returned her kiss, Robbie couldn't hold back any longer. All the reasons for not taking things too far, all the risks, didn't matter. Devyn moved against her body and every part of her wanted to jump off the cliff she'd been carefully avoiding the last two weeks. She didn't care what happened next.

Devyn stripped out of her T-shirt and pajama shorts and desire blinded everything else. Her body was ready to explode for all the waiting. She shifted back to take off her shirt and Devyn's hands were on her in the next breath. Devyn, mapping out her body in the dark, and drawing in lungfuls of air like she couldn't get enough.

When Robbie lowered herself again, pressing her naked body along the length of Devyn, she couldn't hold in her gasp. Devyn was silk and sinew. Smooth but taut. Sharp angles and rounded curves.

She learned every part of Devyn with her hands and her lips. Caressing down her body, then kissing her from the arch of her foot, up her calf, and darting to the inside of her thigh. She skirted over the part she wanted most, the scent of Devyn's arousal making her heady as she kissed the curve above her hip.

Devyn moaned with every place she touched. She could lose herself in Devyn's sounds as much as her kiss. When Devyn's lips pressed against hers with more need, she wanted to give her everything.

"I need…" Devyn's voice trailed but before Robbie could ask, she shifted and parted her legs.

Robbie didn't need to see Devyn to know exactly what she wanted. She leaned down and kissed her again. "I'll get there."

Despite Devyn's insistence that she did not need to go slow, Robbie wanted to savor her. She couldn't dismiss the thought this might be the only time. She knew she could walk away from Devyn but not without the memory following her. And she wanted Devyn to remember her too.

That thought battled with the reality that what had happened at the hospital had shaken Devyn to her core. Tonight wasn't about making a point. Devyn needed to let go and be taken care of. She traced the curves of Devyn's breasts, then shifted down and took a nipple between her lips. Devyn pushed up with a moan.

"You like that?" Robbie didn't wait for an answer. She already knew and she gave in to what they both wanted.

Devyn's nipples were perfect. Responsive and sensitive. But when Devyn's wet center brushed her thigh, her attention shifted. The feel of silky legs, along with Devyn's sounds—pants and whimpers and groans—was too tempting. She pushed away from Devyn's breasts and settled between her legs, one hand resting on each hip.

Devyn reached for her hand, fingers encircling her wrist. "I want this."

Robbie couldn't help smiling. She should have guessed Devyn would want to be in charge in the bedroom. "I want something too," she returned.

Her senses were filled with Devyn, but it wasn't enough. She wanted to taste her. She kissed the inside of Devyn's thigh and then moved her lips closer to what she wanted. Devyn tensed and she knew in that moment she'd overshot. Devyn didn't simply want to be in charge. She needed to be.

"I know what you want," Devyn said. "But I'm not sure if—"

"It's okay." She pulled away from Devyn's center and moved to kiss her neck, checking her disappointment. "There's lots of things I want."

When they kissed again, Devyn rocked her hips, pushing against Robbie. "I want your hand."

"You mentioned that." She smiled as she pulled back, then touched Devyn's lips with her index finger. Devyn opened her mouth and licked her fingertip. "Good thing I'm right-handed."

Devyn started to laugh but then gasped when Robbie parted her.

"Fuck, you're wet." She let Devyn's wetness coat her fingers and then stroked inside.

Devyn moaned, and the sound only amped up Robbie's arousal. She thrust in and out, and Devyn moved with her, the room filling with their panting breaths. When Devyn moved her knees farther apart, Robbie took the cue and stroked deeper.

She brushed over Devyn's swollen clit and felt need build in her. Devyn writhed under her at the touch, then bucked her hips up. Her arousal consumed Robbie's thoughts, making her own throat dry. She couldn't completely ignore the longing to go down on Devyn, but this was a close second.

When she stroked inside again, Devyn wrapped her fingers around Robbie's forearm. "You show me how you like it," Robbie said, knowing Devyn wanted control.

Devyn's grip on her forearm tightened. She took over then, guiding Robbie's thrusts, her breath coming faster. She easily took three fingers and Robbie brushed her thumb over her swollen clit with each stroke. The sounds Devyn made pushed Robbie on, making her own vision starry. When Devyn bucked her hips again begging wordlessly for Robbie to be rougher, there was no holding back.

She gave Devyn what she needed, knowing it wouldn't take long for her climax. Not nearly as long as she wanted. Devyn's body responded to every little thing. So wet. So ready to be taken all the way. Robbie pumped harder and Devyn's nails sank into her arm. In the next breath, Devyn's orgasm hit.

Devyn clenched on Robbie's fingers and moaned. Bringing Devyn to a climax made her own clit quiver. She was hungry for a release, but she focused on Devyn, moving with her as pleasure rolled through her.

When Devyn collapsed back on the pillows, her breath still ragged, Robbie wished she could see her face. Wished she could see the beauty she could feel. A minute passed and then another before Devyn's grip loosened on Robbie's wrist. Slowly, Robbie eased her fingers out. She pressed once more on Devyn's clit, making her squeeze her legs together and groan with an aftershock.

It took Devyn a long minute to relax. When she did, Robbie shifted off her and found the sheet that had been pushed to the foot of the bed. She covered them both, then settled back on the pillow, her mind spinning with what had happened as need pulsed through her—manageable but not something she could ignore.

"That was…I don't have words." Devyn's voice was slurred with sleep. "I want to return the favor, but I don't think I can move."

"If I do my job right, you aren't supposed to want to move after." She waited for Devyn to say more but she didn't. Slowly Devyn's breathing lengthened, and Robbie tried to quiet her need.

"Do you mind staying with me for a while?" Devyn asked.

"As long as you want." Robbie felt a tightness in her chest as she realized how true the words were.

Devyn rolled onto her side, reaching for Robbie's hand as she did. Robbie settled in against Devyn's back, wrapping her in an embrace. Devyn sighed softly and then snuggled closer, her butt pressing up against Robbie's center.

Robbie begged her body not to respond. With Devyn's backside pushing into her, unfulfilled need strained every part of her. She steadied her breathing, timing it to the rise and fall of Devyn's chest, forcing her mind to focus on something other than the feel of Devyn's smooth skin under her palm, the jut of her hip bone and the curve below it.

Devyn shifted a half inch and her butt pressed fully against Robbie. It was too much. She had to pull back, had to separate the contact. It didn't last long. Devyn moved to follow her, fitting their bodies together again. They fit together too well. Robbie held her breath, wondering how long she could hold still.

"I should sleep, but I don't want to." Devyn caressed Robbie's hand, still on her hip, slowly stroking to the tip of Robbie's index finger. "I've thought about touching you nonstop for the past week."

Robbie's clit twitched as if to say, "I told you so." Her heart, too, seemed to bump up in her chest with a similar response. She kissed Devyn's shoulder. "You've had a crazy day. Two days, really. And you're exhausted."

"Are you going to tell me to go to sleep?"

When Robbie didn't answer, Devyn rubbed her butt against her center.

"I wouldn't try to tell you to do anything. But if you keep doing that…"

"Doing what?" Devyn's tone was innocent but she clearly knew what she was doing.

Devyn repeated the move, and Robbie didn't hold back her groan. Her clit was pulsing, begging to be satisfied, and she was embarrassingly wet. Still, she pulled away, murmuring, "There's only so much I can handle."

Devyn lay still for a moment, then said, "You probably think I'm a tease."

"I didn't say that."

She rolled to face Robbie, then touched Robbie's lips with a fingertip. "I want to do everything right but…I probably should have told you I haven't been with a woman before."

Robbie found Devyn's hand and brought it to her lips. She kissed Devyn's knuckles. "I'm so turned on you really don't have to worry about doing anything wrong."

Devyn shifted up onto her elbow, and even in the dark Robbie could feel Devyn sizing her up.

"Where can I touch you?"

"Anywhere you want."

"Anywhere?" Devyn didn't move for a moment, maybe thinking or maybe trying to break away from her inhibitions, then she put a hand on Robbie's shoulder and pushed her onto her back. "You mean it?"

"No rules for a first timer." Robbie felt a tremor race through her as Devyn moved her hand from the point of her shoulder to between her breasts. "But it is late, and you were exhausted about two minutes ago."

"That was two minutes ago." Devyn moved to straddle her, smooth thighs sliding into place on either side of Robbie's hips.

When Devyn's center brushed against Robbie's, she quivered. "Mm. That feels good."

"I agree." Devyn lowered herself to kiss Robbie's lips.

Robbie wanted to be the one who could lie still and let a beginner figure things out. She even believed she could up until the moment Devyn's mouth parted. Then her tongue darted in and she found herself flipping the dynamic. She found Devyn's hand and shoved it between her legs. Her hips hitched when Devyn's delicate fingers stroked over her swollen clit.

"Like that," she managed.

Devyn circled her opening, her touch tentative. "Can I..."

"You can do anything." *But please don't stop.* She pushed up, bumping Devyn's hand and silently urging her on. Devyn's fingers slipped through her folds but didn't push inside.

She tried to be patient, setting a rhythm with her hips as Devyn explored her, but after a while she couldn't handle the gentle teasing. "Try going inside," she said, bumping up her hips again. "You might like how wet you've made me."

Devyn didn't hesitate. She slid inside and her breath hitched. "Oh. Fuck." She stroked back her fingers, nearly pulling out only to go deeper at Robbie's next hip thrust.

"Feels good, doesn't it?"

"Amazing," Devyn said, letting out a little laugh followed by a moan. "How much can you take?"

"You'll know when I come." Robbie couldn't help pushing up to take Devyn's fingers again. "I'm close, so don't get lazy."

"I don't do lazy." Devyn seemed to take Robbie's words as a challenge. She leaned down to kiss her again, then shifted position and stroked deep into Robbie, groaning with pleasure as Robbie clenched on her again. "Show me how to get you off."

Robbie was so close she knew it wouldn't take much. She moved Devyn's hand a fraction of an inch, placing her thumb on her clit. "Keep your hand right there and ride me a little more."

Devyn did as she was told. Obedient, even if she wouldn't admit it, and for once clearly wanting to please. Robbie bucked under her, loving the sounds Devyn made in response. She took Devyn's hand and showed her how she liked the thrusting, forgetting that she was teaching when she felt her orgasm building fast.

"Keep going," she said, her voice low. "Don't stop."

They were both covered in sweat, but Devyn rocked into her faster and harder when she asked for it. Her clit pulsed, nerves firing in rapid succession as her vault tightened on Devyn's fingers.

As the climax hit, Robbie didn't hold back. She wanted Devyn to hear everything—to know what she'd done to her. The sounds of their pleasure filled the bedroom and Devyn cried out as if she'd been the one to come when Robbie clenched down hard.

The wave rolled through Robbie, bringing delicious aftershocks. She savored the orgasm, but before she'd relaxed completely, she pulled Devyn into a deep kiss and then flipped her and settled on top.

Devyn laughed. "That didn't last long."

"But just the right amount of time," Robbie said, spreading her weight over Devyn and pinning her hands as she kissed her lips. She pulled back and said, "Nice job, rookie."

Devyn laughed again. She wiggled out of Robbie's hold and pushed up to return the kiss, murmuring, "You're so fucking hot."

"That's my line."

"I said it first."

Robbie shook her head. "You always need to be in charge?"

"Who's on top right now?"

Robbie kissed her in answer, but when she pulled back, said, "That's your last one for the night. I'm going to leave if you don't try and sleep."

"It's funny you think you can tell me what to do," Devyn said, her tone playful.

Robbie smiled. "I really should know better." She rolled off Devyn and pulled the sheet up over them. "Good night."

Devyn didn't echo the comment. Instead, she found Robbie's hand and guided Robbie's arm around her as she again shifted to her side. "It was your fault I couldn't fall asleep after the first time."

"You can blame me." Even seconds after her climax, she was itching to pleasure Devyn again. But now it was so late it was in fact early, and she forced her mind to ignore the feel of Devyn's soft belly under her palm.

"Thank you for giving me a ride home," Devyn said quietly. "I don't think I was safe to drive."

"Thank you for letting me be with you tonight." Robbie meant that in a dozen different ways. She wondered if Devyn had any idea.

CHAPTER SIXTEEN

Devyn wasn't sure what she'd expected. To wake in Robbie's arms and have a deep conversation about feelings? To have Robbie profess what they'd done together had felt transformative because that's what it had been to her? To have torrid sex again?

She didn't know what she'd expected, but an empty space next to her in the bed wasn't it. The pillow Robbie had used was rumpled as were the sheets on that side, so she knew she hadn't imagined the night. Though maybe she had imagined more existential meaning out of it than was warranted. Maybe it had only been sex. Sex that made her feel…Desired. Sexy. Fun. Powerful. Alive.

Her mind stumbled on the last word. *Alive.* She tried to block the image of the young man who'd died and yet it came anyway. She'd seen plenty of death and still yesterday had been crushing. His pulse had been too weak when he'd arrived. Of course they'd tried anyway. So many people had come together to help. Too little, too late. Too many bullet wounds.

She wished she could accept absolutes like death, but she couldn't understand the why part. Why did death have to claim a body that was perfect before the bullets entered it?

One thing was certain—there was no chance she would have slept at all if not for Robbie. Robbie had given her something even the trazodone she sometimes took to quiet her mind couldn't. A complete break from reality. But she knew that wasn't all last night had been. Being in Robbie's arms, being kissed by her, had felt like an answer to a question her mind had struggled with for years— why didn't she like intimacy the way others did? She'd thought she was simply wired differently. Now she knew it wasn't that.

She rolled over and looked at the bedside clock, then bolted upright when she saw it was half past eight. "Shit."

As she reached for her phone, she wondered if she'd forgotten to set the alarm or unconsciously turned it off and debated the apology text she'd need to send. A handful of texts greeted her, including one from Elena that read: *Don't come in. Leah's working your shift.*

She stared at the words, rubbing sleep from her eyes, as she tapped a text back to Elena: *Leah's on maternity leave.*

She came back early.

Devyn dropped back on her pillow trying to decipher why Leah would have come in. *Did someone ask her to cover for me?*

When Elena didn't immediately respond, Devyn guessed the answer. But who would have called Leah? Nothing made sense. For one, she'd never slept through her alarm.

Elena: *She heard what happened and showed up. Said she wanted to help.*

Typical Leah. God, Devyn had missed her. Before Leah had gone on leave, she'd said she'd be surprised if she survived staying home for eight weeks. *Are you still at the hospital?*

About to leave. Two of your patients are out of ICU and the third is looking good after surgery.

She exhaled, more relieved at the news than she could say. What had happened in the last forty-eight hours and the patient they'd lost wasn't something she'd ever completely let go of. But for now she could stop worrying about the others. She glanced again at the pillow Robbie had used and the empty space. She hadn't slept in the same bed with Matt in over a year and waking up alone was something she'd gotten used to. So why was there a gnawing feeling of missing something—something that wasn't hers to miss?

Can I call you? Even as she sent the text, she wondered if it was a mistake to talk to Elena about Robbie. She wasn't sure she was ready to talk. Her phone rang before she could change her mind.

"Last night was rough on everyone," Elena said. "I'm guessing you're upset I asked Robbie to check on you. And, listen, I don't totally blame you. I'd probably be pissed."

"I'm not upset."

A beat passed before Elena said, "You're not?"

"No. I was a mess. I needed a ride home."

"Robbie gave you a ride?"

"Yeah. And then—" Devyn had absently looked up at the ceiling and the fan Robbie had installed caught her focus. She'd come so close to sending Robbie back to Seattle. It seemed ridiculous how she'd blown up about the garden and how annoyed she'd been at Robbie's very presence. An interruption in her shitty status quo.

"And then?"

Elena's question brought her back to the call. "Then she stayed with me until I fell asleep."

"In your room?" The skepticism in Elena's voice was almost comical.

"I know I've said I don't like cuddling, but I guess last night I needed it." The memory of how good it had felt being in Robbie's arms bumped the questions of what it had meant to Robbie.

"Oh, Devyn, that's so healthy. I've been worried about you." Elena sounded genuinely relieved. "Not only with everything you've taken on here, but all the other stuff you've been dealing with—the divorce, Matt moving out and not paying his share, and all the issues with the house. I can't say I'm not surprised you let Robbie stay with you, but I am happy."

"We had sex."

Elena made a sound like a half laugh, half snort. "Holy shit, Mari called it."

"Mari called what?"

"She said you two would be sleeping together before we saw you again."

Devyn pressed a hand to her forehead. "Elena, I don't know what I'm doing."

"You haven't been with a woman before. It's okay to not know."

"I don't mean that part." She did have questions, but Robbie had made her feel more than competent. "I don't know where this is leading. Maybe we shouldn't have had sex?"

"It doesn't have to lead anywhere," Elena said. "Sex can simply be fun. I think that's what you need after everything Matt put you through."

"The divorce isn't even finalized. Do I need to tell Robbie? I mean, I don't know if last night was a onetime thing or if it will happen again but—"

"Do you want to?"

"Well, yeah. I know it was exactly what I needed, but it was also...really good sex."

Elena laughed. "I'm happy for you. But what I meant was, do you want to talk to Robbie about the divorce?"

"Oh."

"For the record, I don't think you need to. It's only on paper that it isn't final."

True, and once the house was sold, they'd sign to finish everything. But she wasn't in any position to start something new. "I don't know if..." She shook her head, trying to gather her thoughts. "I wouldn't start anything with someone in the middle of a divorce, and I don't know if Robbie should either."

"Robbie's a grown adult. She can make her own decisions. And she's only here for another few weeks, right? I'm sure she's not expecting a long-term thing. Besides, if she's friends with Matt she probably already knows plenty about the divorce. I don't think you need to bring it up."

The idea of Matt talking to Robbie about the divorce details hadn't occurred to her. Would Matt have admitted his affair? Or talked to Robbie about the other woman? She felt sick thinking of it, imagining what Robbie knew and thought of her. Between that and everything that had happened at the hospital, she wondered if Robbie had slept with her out of some sort of feeling of pity. It was awful to even consider.

"I don't know what's going through your head right now, but I can tell you're overthinking even from here."

"You're annoying sometimes."

"My wife says the same thing. What would happen if you stopped overthinking and just enjoyed this?"

"You make me sound like I never have fun."

"You are fun. You're my best friend and I wouldn't trade you for the world, but you keep yourself on a shorter leash than you keep Angel."

Elena's words rang true. Too true.

"I want you to enjoy whatever this is with Robbie," Elena continued. "And enjoy your day off. You earned it."

After Elena had hung up, Devyn got out of bed. She went to the bathroom, noticing that Angel didn't greet her as she opened the door, which meant he was with Robbie. Angel never let her sleep in and usually hopped on her bed around six in the morning. Unless he had a chance to be with Robbie.

Devyn got in the shower and let the water stream on her head for a full minute before reaching for her washcloth and the soap. Elena's advice repeated in her head—*enjoy whatever this is with Robbie*. Maybe she could. Still, she wanted to be clear about what she was doing. Even if Elena didn't think it was necessary, she felt obligated to tell Robbie that whatever they did, it couldn't lead to anything serious.

She finished showering and pulled a towel around her. As she dried off, she caught her reflection in the mirror and noticed a red mark on her breast. She touched it and the memory of Robbie's mouth on her came back with a flash of heat. She circled the mark with her fingertip. No one else would be able to see it, but she relished it all the same.

She'd loved everything Robbie had done to her. And it was amazing touching Robbie. She couldn't decide which she liked more. If she could avoid overthinking and not worry about how she would feel in two weeks when Robbie left, *and* if she could let herself go again like she'd done last night, there was plenty more she wanted to try.

She eyed her reflection and said, "So I go up to her and ask—how do you feel about having lots of sex over the next two weeks?"

She felt a quivering sensation at her clit and resisted the urge to check if she was wet. She knew she was. "You might want more sex, but are you brave enough to ask for it?"

She finished in the bathroom, started a load of laundry—including the sheets she'd stripped from her bed—and then went to the kitchen when her stomach reminded her she hadn't eaten a real meal in days. A note in Robbie's handwriting was on the counter. She felt a moment of worry that she was about to read a Dear Jane letter but was quickly relieved. *There's a frittata in the fridge with your name on it. I turned off your alarm because you don't have to go to work—Elena texted me to tell you. Also, I'm keeping Angel with me so he doesn't wake you. R.*

It was short and could almost be traded for any other note they'd exchanged except the tone felt entirely different. Or maybe the difference was only in her head. She brushed her finger over the letter R, realizing she wanted to see Robbie more than she wanted food. She debated for a moment and then decided the sex conversation had to happen before she could do anything else.

Robbie looked up from her computer when she opened the cottage door. She hadn't knocked and, second-guessing that, paused to rap on the doorjamb.

Robbie smiled. "Come in."

Angel hopped up from Robbie's bed and ran over to her, dancing on his hind legs for a pet. She indulged him, then let him slip past her to race outside.

"He thinks I've been holding him hostage," Robbie said. "He's had a walk and breakfast, and he's fine, but he wanted to bark at the squirrels and I wouldn't let him. I didn't want him to wake you."

"Thank you." She glanced over her shoulder when Angel barked and then looked back at Robbie. "Right on cue."

"He's kind of predictable." Robbie looked through her window to spot him and then narrowed her eyes when he barked again. "Should I call him back?"

"I usually give him three barks."

Robbie nodded, then met her gaze. "How are you this morning?"

She wanted to say "good," but the word didn't exactly cover the mix of emotions she felt and her confidence had only carried her as far as the doorway. She glanced back at Angel, then at Robbie, feeling ridiculous for the urge to walk over and sit in her lap, and feeling more ridiculous thinking she could waltz in and flatly discuss the idea of their spending the next two weeks in a purely sexual relationship.

"You okay?" Robbie asked, clearly sensing a problem. When Devyn only nodded, she pushed back from the table she'd made into a workstation and stood. "I'm guessing you want to talk about last night." Robbie seemed to hesitate. "It's okay if you want to pretend last night didn't happen."

"That's not what I want at all." She shook her head. "I'm standing here feeling awkward because I'm not good at these conversations." She knew she sounded nervous. Awkward and nervous. *Great.* "Maybe now is a bad time to talk. I don't want to interrupt when you're working. Will you have a break later?"

"Now is good. I'm running some diagnostic system checks."

Robbie stared at her expectantly and she wished she were the type who could simply step forward and kiss her. Or suggest a replay of last night and not worry about repercussions. But that wasn't her. She straightened and said, "I think we should discuss expectations. Obviously last night changed a few things, and I'm not sure I've fully processed all of those things." Too bad she couldn't simply say she'd liked what they'd done and wanted more.

"Do you want me to promise not to tell anyone we slept together?"

"No." She realized the leap Robbie had made and cringed internally. Robbie probably guessed she was hung up on processing the part about how she'd slept with a woman. Which was something she wanted to process but only because of how good it had felt. "This isn't about other people knowing. I mean, I don't know who you'd talk to about it."

"I won't tell Matt if that's what you're worried about. It's not his business anyway since you two are divorced and I can sleep with whoever I want."

"The divorce isn't finalized."

"Oh. I didn't realize—"

Devyn held up her hand, seeing the worry cross Robbie's face. "It's only not finalized on paper because of the house. Matt and I separated over a year ago. And I don't care what you tell him. I guess I don't really want him thinking about the two of us having sex but…" She shook her head. "This is not going how I planned."

"I think it's my fault for interrupting you."

"It's no one's fault." She took a deep breath. "You're going back to Seattle in two weeks and obviously we aren't starting something serious."

She waited for Robbie, but she didn't respond to agree or disagree. "I'm going to be one hundred percent honest here and admit I've never had a fling. Or a one-night stand. I've never had sex with someone I wasn't in a committed relationship with—and I've only had sex with two people." She tipped her head. "Now three."

Robbie scratched her head. "What are you worrying about?"

The question didn't seem to carry any judgment and yet Devyn heard Elena's voice in her head chastising her for overthinking. "I want us both to be on the same page."

"That's fair."

"I don't know if last night was typical for you, but it wasn't for me, and I don't know how we go forward." She'd rushed the words and felt a need to add, "If we go forward."

"Do you want to go forward?"

"Do you?"

"Yes. But I don't need a plan for that, and I think you do." Robbie seemed to study her for a moment. "What do you want, Devyn?"

A rush of longing pushed through her. "I want to spend the next two weeks having as much sex as possible."

Robbie laughed. "I wasn't expecting that. I can't say I mind the plan, though. It's a hell of a lot better than what I thought you were going to say when we started this conversation."

Robbie's laugh loosened the tension in the room and Devyn found herself smiling. "What'd you think I was going to say?"

"That last night was a mistake and it couldn't happen again." Robbie lifted a shoulder. "Which would have been fine, but then I'd have to spend the next two weeks pretending I didn't like you. I'd rather spend that time showing you all the things about you I like—and all the things you make me think of doing."

Robbie's words were simple, but the meaning burned through Devyn like a flare. She felt a pulse at her center and shifted her legs closer together. "Last night wasn't a mistake."

"I'm happy to hear that. So…we're good?"

She nodded. "I'll let you get back to work. Thanks for not saying I was being ridiculous."

"You aren't. Weren't. Not at all."

She believed Robbie, and maybe that was what pushed her to say, "When do you plan on taking a real break?"

"I've got another few hours on this diagnostic run. Should I come find you then?" Robbie's look was cocky—like she knew exactly what Devyn was thinking of.

Devyn didn't mind. She needed cocky. "You should. I have a project I want to add to your to-do list."

Robbie nodded, all seriousness now. "How long should I expect to be busy with this project?"

"A few hours, at least." Devyn prided herself on keeping up the cool business tone and even raised an eyebrow when Robbie winked. "I don't know what you're thinking."

"You'll find out."

Robbie's promise made Devyn convinced she would have a hard time keeping herself focused on anything except sex for the rest of the morning. "A little part of me was sad you weren't in my bed when I woke up."

"I had to log in early to get these tests run. Can I make it up to you later?"

When Devyn nodded, Robbie stepped forward. She held out a hand and Devyn clasped it, her heart racing. A rush went through her simply holding Robbie's hand, and when Robbie moved closer, she felt her breath catch. It was one thing kissing Robbie in the dark. Another in the full light of day.

"Is this okay?"

She nodded, wishing Robbie couldn't read her so easily. She steadied her breathing and met Robbie's gaze. "I'm not used to wanting someone so much."

Robbie's lips turned up in a subtle smile. "That's a hard problem to have."

When Robbie closed the distance between them, Devyn moved into the kiss. Desire burned through her as Robbie's lips pressed against hers. Yes, this was okay. More than okay.

CHAPTER SEVENTEEN

If anyone asked—and no one would—Robbie would tell the truth. Her brain had stopped working when Devyn returned her kiss. All thoughts short-circuited.

"Schedule change," she said, pulling Devyn toward her. "I'm on break now."

"You won't get in trouble?" Devyn asked.

"No one will know." She didn't hold back her moan when Devyn pressed against her. "And I can't wait for you." She took another step toward the bed but felt Devyn hesitate. "What is it?"

"All the windows are open."

"Angel's on patrol," Robbie said. "We'll be fine. But I can close the blinds if you want."

Devyn glanced at the windows, sunlight streaming in, and bit her lip, clearly thinking. "I want to try new things. Maybe this is one of them."

Robbie chuckled. "Sex with the windows open is new for you?"

"I usually like it to be dark. But I have a feeling you could make me like a lot of new things." Devyn dropped onto the bed. She pulled off her shirt and looked up at Robbie. "You might not want to pass up this opportunity." She licked her lips, her expression knowing. She was clearly aware of the effect she had on Robbie. "I don't often go around stripping off clothes." She unhooked her bra. "Or throwing myself in other people's beds hoping I can distract them from their work."

When she dropped the bra on the floor and shifted back on the pillows, her breasts were on full display. The dark pink nipples drew Robbie forward. "You are my new favorite distraction."

"You've been mine since you showed up here," Devyn returned.

"I don't think I was your favorite in the beginning," Robbie said, taking off her shirt and sports bra. She enjoyed the way Devyn watched her undress and decided to lose her shorts as well. When she straightened up, Devyn was full-on sizing her up. "Like what you see?"

Devyn seemed to hesitate. "I do."

"Not used to admitting these things?" Robbie held Devyn's gaze as she came to the side of the bed. "What do you want?"

"You." Devyn pulled her into a kiss.

Devyn's lips, and the slip of her tongue, rocketed up her arousal. She moved onto the bed and pushed Devyn's legs apart, shifting into the space she'd made.

"You're on top again." Devyn stroked Robbie's arms. "I think you like that position."

"Maybe. But you can still call the shots."

"Is it still okay for me to touch you anywhere?" Devyn asked.

"I'm yours to play with."

Devyn's lips parted, her desire obvious.

"You like the sound of that, don't you?" She smiled, knowing she was right. "What else do you like?"

"Your butt."

Robbie started to laugh but stopped short when Devyn cupped her butt cheeks. A thrill raced through her as Devyn said, "Anywhere I like?"

"Anywhere." Robbie pressed a kiss to Devyn's lips as her hands roamed down the back of her thighs.

While Devyn explored her body, Robbie drew a curve under each of Devyn's breasts. Under her touch, each nipple hardened. When she pinched, Devyn pulled away as if caught off guard but pushed back into Robbie's hands a moment later.

"I found something else you like."

"Maybe."

Devyn gasped when she repeated the move and she realized how sensitive Devyn's nipples were. "Too much?"

"Mm. Not at all."

"Good." She took a nipple between her lips and forgot about being gentle.

Devyn didn't stop her again. She didn't stop touching her, either, and her hands were as sensual as her lips. When Devyn tugged at the band of her underwear, Robbie pulled away long enough to take it off. Then she moved between Devyn's legs, shifting her knees apart and giving Devyn full access.

Devyn slid a finger inside and moaned. "You're so wet." She pulled back and then pressed in with two fingers.

"Do you like knowing I'm all turned on because of you?"

"So much." Devyn stroked another finger inside and made Robbie clench. Devyn sucked in a breath. "I love when you do that."

"Then keep going," Robbie murmured, grinding on Devyn. "I like being your new toy."

Devyn stroked faster and Robbie rode her hand, panting into her mouth between kisses. Her orgasm came quick and hard, and she drenched Devyn's fingers when she climaxed.

"You can't come that quick," Devyn said.

"Sorry." Robbie caught Devyn's wrist, pulling fingers away from her clit and giving her body time to readjust.

"You sure you came?" Devyn moved her hand back to Robbie and started stroking again. As good as it felt to be pushed further, Robbie could only handle it for a minute before she stilled Devyn's hand.

Devyn grumbled and Robbie chuckled in response. "You're mad because you got me off too fast? I think you should blame your hands for that."

"I barely got to touch you."

Devyn pouting about not getting enough sex wasn't what she'd ever have expected. She grinned, wondering if she could take more. "Try me again. I'll tell you if I can take another round."

"Really?" Devyn didn't hesitate. Her hand moved to Robbie's center. She circled Robbie's clit and then pushed inside again. "I love when you clench on my fingers."

"Me too. But go easy on me."

"You really want me to go easy?" Devyn asked. "You seem to like it hard."

She wasn't wrong. Robbie groaned with pleasure when Devyn pushed deep. She felt another spasm and didn't fight it.

Devyn shifted up to kiss her. "So agreeable."

Robbie rode Devyn's hand harder the second time. She'd orgasmed easily the first time, keyed up on Devyn's attention and with a lingering wetness from last night, but the second go took more work. Devyn only seemed to be more turned on with every passing minute, though.

"Don't come," Devyn said. "I don't want to take my fingers out of you. I want you to keep using me."

Robbie felt the climax push up in that moment. "Sorry." She kissed Devyn and seconds later the orgasm caught her.

As she tensed, Devyn's arms wrapped around her. Devyn kissed her neck, her chest, her arms, anchoring her even as the climax swept through her. She collapsed a moment later, unable to hold herself up any longer, and Devyn's embrace only tightened.

"I love when you come hard like that."

Robbie steadied her breathing and said, "I love it too, but you have to give me a break after that one."

"I want to give you a present after that one." Devyn laughed, kissing Robbie's cheek.

"Mm. You know what would be a present?"

"Letting you go down on me?" Devyn asked.

Robbie hadn't planned on saying that. She'd planned only to say a present would be her having a turn. She met Devyn's gaze, searching her expression to decide if she was serious.

"I feel bad I stopped you last night," Devyn admitted.

"It's okay if you don't like it or—"

"That's not it." Devyn looked up at the ceiling, breaking their eye contact. "I haven't done it a lot but...I think it'd be different with you." She met Robbie's gaze again. "Do you like doing it?"

"Are you kidding? I love it. It's on my list of favorite things. And it's really close to the top. Basically right after kissing. I don't have the list with me to prove it, but I promise you it's there."

Devyn smiled. "I believe you. Which makes me consider it. Even if I'm a little nervous."

"I don't want you to feel pushed to do anything you don't want to do."

Devyn's lips pressed together. "Do you really think I'd be a pushover?"

"No."

"Good. Also…I'm tired of wearing pants." Devyn started to push down the waistband herself but didn't argue when Robbie helped her out of them, snagging the thong underwear she was wearing at the same time.

When Devyn was naked, she shifted back against the pillows looking almost smug. "That's better."

Robbie stroked a hand up each leg, beginning at the ankle. She reached Devyn's upper thighs and stopped. "Can you think of being at the beach?"

"What?" Devyn's eyes narrowed. "Why?"

"It'll help you get out of your head."

Devyn bit the edge of her lip.

"Imagine you're kicking back on the sand with your eyes closed. Just listening to the waves. No care in the world."

Devyn hesitated for a moment but then closed her eyes. "I love listening to the waves."

"I thought you might." Robbie kissed Devyn's lips, then kissed her neck, circling her nipples with light fingertips. She kissed her way from Devyn's breasts to her belly, her fingers plying her nipples until they'd hardened with arousal.

"I love when your hands are on me," Devyn murmured, moving into her touch.

Robbie wanted to memorize every part of Devyn. She was gorgeous with the sunlight bathing her skin, her complexion almost the color of amber, and her dark-blond hair shining like gold.

"I can't wait to taste you." Robbie knew it was a risk saying the words aloud. She was fully prepared to have Devyn change her mind, to feel her tense and pull away, and if Devyn's response was another no, she would accept it. But desire burned through her.

She moved lower, kissing haphazardly as went—the side of Devyn's ribs, the space below her belly button, the curve above her thigh, and then her smooth slit. Her first kiss was light, questioning, and she glanced up at Devyn after. Devyn's eyes were still closed.

She knew she had to take a chance. She kissed the same spot but firmer this time, her tongue barely parting Devyn.

Devyn gripped Robbie's shoulder.

"Are you stopping me?"

"No." Devyn licked her lips and took a shaky breath, her eyes still closed. "It's warm on this beach."

"So warm." She pictured Devyn lying on a beach towel. The sun warming her skin and her legs parted…

She kissed Devyn's slit again, not pushing inside this time, only waiting and stroking Devyn's thighs with her hands. "I want you to want it."

"I do," Devyn breathed.

When Devyn's fingers threaded through her hair, hips bumping into her, she slipped between Devyn's folds, tasting what she'd longed for. Devyn sucked a breath in and then pushed herself into Robbie's mouth with a low moan.

Robbie let go then, sliding her tongue over Devyn's heat. Devyn's salty musk was everything she wanted. She licked and sucked, wanting to drink her in and knowing she'd never get enough. Devyn said her name between panting breaths, arching into her. She didn't let up as Devyn's grip moved from her shoulders to her neck, hips thrusting rhythmically. When she felt Devyn getting close, she slid two fingers inside.

Devyn pushed herself hard into Robbie then, begging, "Don't stop."

Robbie licked faster, pumping her fingers deeper. She loved the feel of Devyn tightening, and the sensation of being pulled in. They were both covered in sweat, both panting hard, but Devyn's building arousal and the wetness dripping from her only pushed Robbie on.

As Devyn's climax hit, she arched up from the bed and cried out her pleasure. Robbie held tight, moving with her, not pulling out or letting up on her clit. A breath later, Devyn slumped back, quivering and clenching her legs.

Robbie didn't ease up until Devyn's grip loosened. Then she moved to kiss Devyn's cheek. Devyn let out a trembling sigh and wrapped her arms around Robbie. They lay together, Robbie careful to spread her weight so Devyn wouldn't feel crushed, and it was several minutes before the room was quiet from their heavy breathing.

"I should trust you when you say you like things," Devyn said, sighing. "That was nothing like what I've had before. I didn't even know it could feel that good."

"I'm happy to hear that." Robbie enjoyed the pride that flowed through her. "Thanks for letting me do that."

"You're welcome. But I think it's the other way around. Ten out of ten recommend."

Robbie chuckled. "Does that mean you'd let me do it again sometime?"

Devyn opened her eyes. She kissed Robbie lightly. "That depends. Are you going to keep letting me get you off?"

"You know I'm yours to use as you like." Robbie was turned on all over again when Devyn gave a little moan of approval.

"Why does it sound so good when you say that?" Devyn's head rocked side to side. "A little part of me is worried there's something wrong with me for liking it so much."

"I'm giving you permission to like it and no one else is here." Robbie kissed Devyn's neck and nuzzled closer.

"I like that, too."

Devyn relaxed as Robbie traced the outline of her curves. In the afterglow of sex, all tension was gone from her body and she was truly breathtaking. "I love seeing you like this."

"Naked and stretched out on your bed unable to move?" Devyn smiled, but it was a lazy sort of smile. "You made me like this. You might as well get to enjoy it."

Robbie noticed a red mark on Devyn's breast and circled it lightly.

"That's your fault, too," Devyn said. "From last night. I rather like it."

Robbie wanted to admit she liked it as well but held back the words. Admitting she liked having left a mark on Devyn wouldn't be in keeping with the agreement they'd made. *Only two weeks of sex.*

"I rather like a lot of things you do," Devyn continued. "Like how you hung my fan."

Robbie chuckled. "You make that sound dirty."

"I don't know what you're talking about. There's clearly nothing sexual about me liking how you do all the things I've fantasized about for years."

"Sure."

"Although someone might assume I was saying something dirty if I bragged about the cocking job you did in the bathroom."

"Caulking." Robbie knew Devyn fully intended to mess up the word this time.

"Mm. I loved watching you with that cock."

Robbie laughed. "You've gotta stop."

"Do I? Hmm. I don't think I do." Devyn reached up and stroked her thumb over Robbie's cheek. "You're very attractive, you know."

"Not compared to you."

"I beg to differ." Devyn arched an eyebrow. "And do you really think you'll win an argument with me on this subject?"

"I don't think I'd win against you on any subject."

"There's a few I'd let you win."

Robbie laughed. "Okay, what subject?"

"Sex."

Robbie opened and then closed her mouth, not sure what to say.

"You look surprised."

"I thought we were going with you being in charge."

"I think I go both ways with you." Devyn touched Robbie's lips, looking thoughtful but also nervous. She pulled her hand away and said, "I'm not a prude, but I haven't been exactly adventurous in bed before. In my defense, it's been a long time since I've had anyone around I truly wanted to have sex with. And…You make me want to be brave and try new things."

"I like that." Her appetite for Devyn amped up all over again. She went for another kiss but Devyn's stomach growled.

"Ignore that," Devyn murmured, returning the kiss.

"When was the last time you ate?" Robbie continued. "I made you a frittata—it's waiting for you in the fridge."

"God, that sounds amazing." Devyn sighed. "I'm not sure how I'm going to feel when you go back to Seattle."

"Let's not think about that yet." Robbie wasn't sure how long she'd last pushing it from her mind, but she intended to try as long as possible. She leaned down and kissed Devyn. "We've got plenty of time."

"I want to make you come again," Devyn said, her fingers straying down Robbie's back side. "You're kind of addicting."

Robbie smiled. "You'll be able to fuck me better if you eat something."

"So crass." Devyn shook her head. "How do you know exactly what to say to get me out of bed and make me want you again in the same moment?" She wiggled out from under Robbie and stood. As she leaned down to pick up her shirt, she added, "For the record, this is not usually me."

"Dropping your clothes on the floor or hopping into someone's bed in the middle of the day?"

"All of it."

Which could be a problem. For both of them.

CHAPTER EIGHTEEN

Work was a hard reality to face after two days with Robbie—two days spent almost entirely in bed. Robbie did convince her to leave the house to go to the beach, and they'd had several long walks and deep conversations that were almost as enjoyable as the sex. *Almost.*

The part she kept coming back to was how she'd never much been into sex before. She'd told Robbie the truth—jumping into bed with someone wasn't usually her—but there was more to it. She had felt like a prude for not thinking about sex or wanting it as often as others did. And she'd worried what that meant with past partners. But with Robbie she couldn't seem to stop thinking about sex.

Now the only thing she wanted was to fast-forward to the end of her shift. She knew Robbie had been checking out sex toys because she'd gotten a text with a picture of a harness and the question: *When you say try new things...how do you feel about strap-ons?*

She'd had to squeeze her legs together as arousal flared. She kept her answer short: *I'm open.* Very open.

"Want to hear about your next patient?" Tiana, one of the intake nurses, stood in the doorway to the office.

She wanted to keep thinking about Robbie and the fantasy of coming home to find Robbie lounging in her house in nothing but a strap-on. But she had two more hours of work to get through. She closed the picture of the leather harness and set her phone down. "To be one hundred percent honest, I want to go home."

Tiana laughed. "You can't leave until I do, and I'm sorry to say we've got a smart-ass who tried a new TikTok challenge." She glanced at the chart in her hand and added, "He was pretty proud of himself for eating three wasps before his tongue started to swell."

Devyn swung her stethoscope around her neck as she followed Tiana out. "I don't even want to ask what dumb thing they'll think of next."

Tiana grimaced. "Me neither."

Eating wasps wasn't the first mindless trend she'd come across, and the reaction was fairly mild all things considered. Fate seemed to be smiling on her, too, because the next several patients were all in and out quickly. Nothing critical came through the door for the rest of the evening, and she almost questioned her good luck aloud as she rounded with the doctor taking over for her. But she knew better. Instead, she simply sent a quick text to Robbie saying she was on her way home.

She almost added that she hoped Robbie was wearing leather, but before she got up the nerve, she got a text back. Robbie: *I'm worried something's wrong with Angel. He skipped dinner.*

Skipping meals wasn't typical for him. Still, she tried not to be overly concerned as she drove home. Angel wasn't in the main house and she found him curled up in Robbie's lap in the cottage. Robbie was at her computer but didn't seem to be actively working. Instead, she was eyeing Angel with a furrowed brow.

"Angel, I hear you're worrying Robbie." Angel lifted his head but didn't bother with a tail wag. She went to him and touched his head. He made to lick her hand but then the effort seemed too much. "Something's wrong."

"I know," Robbie agreed. "He hasn't moved from my lap since I tried to get him to eat dinner. Whatever this is came on all of a sudden—he was fine two hours ago. Can you take a look?"

Devyn scooped Angel up and took him to the bed. He didn't feel warm but his stomach was tight. As Robbie watched, concern lining her features, she said, "You know I'm not a vet."

"You're a doctor. What do you think?"

He did seem lethargic. No tail wag. And when she picked him up again, she got a whiff of foul breath as he yawned. "Maybe he ate something gross?"

"Not that I know of, but he keeps acting like he's about to get sick."

He belched and Devyn hurried him outside. Two steps out the door and he hacked hard but only brought up bile. "He's done this before when Matt gave him too many treats."

"I haven't given him any treats."

When Angel vomited again, hacking harder this time, she noticed a blood tinge even in the weak light of the cottage's porch lamp and felt sick herself.

"Is that blood?" Robbie asked, worry edging her voice.

Angel took a few steps away from the vomit, stumbled, and collapsed. Devyn's heart lurched in her chest as she scooped him up. "Oh, baby." When he'd gotten sick before, she'd worried she lose him. He'd gone downhill quickly then, too. "Let's take him to the vet."

Robbie volunteered to drive so she could hold Angel, and she didn't argue. Angel shivered in her arms, groaning every few minutes. She cursed the traffic slowing them down and tried not to think about worst-case scenarios.

Angel was sick a third time as they got out of Robbie's car, but thankfully there was no sign of more blood. Still, by the time they walked into the ER's waiting area, she was too worried to answer the receptionist's questions and Robbie had to fill out the paperwork. Angel's groans had turned to weak whimpers, and as they were led into a room for triage, she couldn't stop horrible worries from filling her head.

"Maybe he ate something on his walk?" Devyn asked.

"He is always trying to grab trash when we go to the beach." Robbie shook her head. "But I really didn't see him eat anything."

Devyn felt a press of tears and had to take a slow breath to steady herself.

"I feel terrible that he got sick on my watch."

The vet tech came into the room and Devyn didn't get a chance to tell Robbie it wasn't her fault. It was all she could do to hold in her tears as the vet tech's expression turned from businesslike to concern when she checked Angel over.

The vet tech stepped out of the room saying, "I'll be right back. I'm going to go get the doctor."

As confident as Devyn was making decisions for others, everything fell apart when the veterinarian examined Angel. First Angel screamed, then he tried to bite the vet's hand. She rushed an apology, regretting she hadn't warned anyone.

"He's painful," the vet said. When she suggested lab work and radiographs to rule out a mass or an obstruction, it was Robbie who gave the approval and signed the paperwork.

As soon as she heard the word *mass*, everything else blurred. Angel was whisked away and Robbie reached for her hand. She clasped it tight but couldn't stop the tears.

"What if it's cancer?" Shouldn't she have been able to feel something? Shouldn't there have been other signs? But he rarely stayed still for longer than a brief cuddle. He was a terrier through and through.

"Let's wait for the x-rays," Robbie said.

She nodded and tried to slow the what-ifs buzzing through her mind. Minutes passed and she was grateful Robbie didn't try to start a conversation, only holding her hand. Finally, she said, "Thanks for taking care of the paperwork. I'm ordinarily the best person to have when shit hits the fan, but—"

"It's okay. I know how important Angel is to you." Robbie was quiet for a moment and then added, "I was the same way when Pixie got sick." She pulled out her phone and handed it to Devyn, pointing to a picture of an older graying Jack Russell. "This was Pixie." She smiled but then clenched her jaw, clearly trying to keep her emotions in check. "She was the best little buddy." She smiled again. "Want to see an adorable picture of Angel I took?"

At Devyn's nod, she scrolled for a moment and then handed the phone back to Devyn. Angel filled the screen. He was curled up on the bed, and it took her a moment to realize he was snuggled up next to her feet.

"When did you take this?"

"Yesterday morning. I meant to show you." Robbie took her phone back. "You know, whenever you leave, he sits by the door for about twenty minutes before he'll accept you're gone for the day. He loves you so much."

Devyn didn't bother fighting her tears. She let them slip down her cheeks as she stared at the image of Angel. Robbie got up to get a box of tissues in the corner of the room and after handing it to her, said, "I don't think it's cancer. Obviously I'm not a doctor, but I bet he ate something. We both know how sneaky he is."

Robbie's confidence gave her hope. "He's always been sneaky." She shook her head. "I got him when he was a year old. I had no business getting a dog…You know Elena and I lived together in med school and we had this neighbor with all these kids. They got a puppy and it was a huge mistake. They didn't have time for him and he was so naughty. Tearing up everything. I volunteered to walk him and it became a regular thing.

"Then they moved out and left Angel behind. I heard him barking…I found him all alone in the apartment waiting for me to take him on his morning walk the day after they'd gone." She paused. "I didn't need a dog. I didn't have time for one."

"We make time. And they make it up to us tenfold."

She let the tears fall then and Robbie wrapped an arm around her. Angel had made it up to her in so many ways. When the veterinarian came back into the room, the look on her face was hard to gauge. It was Robbie who asked, "Bad news?"

"More like surprising news." She had an iPad in her hands and she turned it to show them the screen.

Robbie squinted at the x-ray image. "Are those—"

"Bones. Lots of little bones. All through his intestines." She drew a line on the screen, tracing a loop of intestine filled with bone fragments. "His stomach is empty but the rest of him sure isn't. The question is, what did he eat?" The veterinarian squinted at the image. "My tech guessed a rat, but I think it's something bigger."

"Could it be a squirrel?" Devyn hated to ask the question, picturing the fluffy-tailed cuties that raced from the trees to the fence tops.

The vet nodded thoughtfully. "Definitely possible."

"He couldn't have eaten a whole squirrel though, could he?" Robbie looked appalled at the thought.

"Never underestimate a Jack Russell," the vet said. "The good news is there doesn't seem to be an obstruction. At least not yet."

"What about the blood in his vomit?"

"He might have been retching hard enough to cause some bleeding because his stomach was empty. Not a great sign, but his lab work is perfect." The vet flipped the screen to the lab values and gave Devyn a moment to scan the numbers.

"What do we do next?" Robbie asked.

"I want to give him something so he's not nauseous and get him on fluids. I'm not ruling out surgery yet, but if he can pass this, that's better news for everyone." Her gaze moved from Devyn to Robbie, clearly trying to figure out who would be making the decisions. "I'd like to keep him for the night and retake x-rays if it's okay with you two."

"I don't want to leave him," Devyn said, feeling ridiculous even as she felt the tears start again.

Robbie clasped her hand but didn't argue. The vet glanced at the iPad before saying, "He's dehydrated and needs fluids. Especially if we want to avoid surgery." She softened as she added, "I know he's going to miss his moms, and I know you two are going to worry about him, but it's really best if you let us take care of him."

"I understand it's better if he stays, but I don't want to leave him."

"What if I stay here with him?" Robbie looked to the vet as she asked, "Is it okay if I stay in the waiting room?" The vet nodded and Robbie turned to Devyn. "I brought my laptop in case we had a long wait. I've got to log in at midnight to do some work and I won't be able to sleep anyway. You can go home and get some rest. I'll call if there's any problem."

"But what if—"

"I'll be here," Robbie said. "If he has to go to surgery, or if he gets worse, I'll call you."

"I will need a primary contact," the vet said. "And authorization to get started on treatment."

Robbie looked to Devyn. "Let me do this. If you stay, you're not getting any sleep."

"You won't get any sleep, either." She did need to sleep. But what if something went wrong and she couldn't get back fast enough?

"I've got to catch a maintenance window to perform a fail-over," Robbie said. "I have to stay up anyway. If anything happens, I promise I'll call. You can trust me."

Despite how rare it was for her to trust someone, she did trust Robbie.

"If you're okay with the treatment plan, I'd like to get started." The vet looked expectantly from Robbie to Devyn.

"Please go ahead. Do everything you need to do." She paused and added, "Robbie will be the primary contact."

The vet nodded and turned to Robbie. "I'll let my tech know you're planning on staying in the waiting room. She'll give you updates there."

After the vet left the exam room, Robbie reached for Devyn's hand. "Angel's going to be okay."

She kept hold of Robbie's hand as they walked out of the room, her mind running scenarios of what might go wrong. Robbie led them right to the receptionist and handed over her credit card before Devyn realized what was happening.

"Wait, you're not paying for this."

"We can argue about it later, but this happened on my watch." Robbie turned back to the receptionist and signed for the deposit.

"He's my dog," Devyn argued.

Robbie tipped her head. "When do you think he ate that squirrel?"

"That little Jack Russell you brought in ate a squirrel?" The receptionist looked impressed. "You two raised a beast." She laughed. "Don't worry. He's in good hands."

Robbie thanked her, mentioning she was planning on staying, and then headed for one of the open corner seats.

"You know, it would have been okay if you'd corrected the vet and told her we weren't together," Robbie said, slipping her laptop out of her messenger bag.

She wasn't surprised Robbie brought it up, but she didn't know what to say in response. The truth was, she'd felt fine with the doctor's assumption and the receptionist's as well. "I'm fine with people thinking we're together. I'm not okay with you paying for this."

"I feel responsible, but honestly, I'm not in the right headspace to fight over who pays."

The comment stopped her. "I don't want to fight either."

"We can split the bill later if it makes you feel better." Robbie met Devyn's gaze. "I want Angel to be okay. That's all I care about right now."

She dropped her shoulders, the will to argue gone. "Angel's been the center of my world. This past year especially." She glanced at the two open seats on either side of Robbie. "I know you're right and I should go home and there's nothing for me to do here, but I don't know if I can leave."

"Do you trust me to call?"

She nodded.

"Then there's tomato soup and cheesy bread waiting for you at home. If anything happens, it won't take you long to get back here." Robbie waited for her to agree before adding, "You don't have to go to sleep, but we both know I've been keeping you up late these past few nights."

"Actually, I've been keeping you up." She smiled, despite everything. "You have no idea how few people I trust in this world." She leaned down and kissed Robbie, not caring that they weren't alone. "Thank you."

"I haven't done anything yet."

"Yes, you have."

She started crying the moment she stepped out of the waiting room. Angel was in good hands, Robbie would call if anything changed, but still the tears came. As she drove Robbie's rental car home, she knew the tears weren't only her worries about Angel. She walked into the empty house, found the dinner Robbie had made for her, and then admitted the truth.

"I don't want her to leave." She stared at the sticky note and the words "yummy dinner" with a cartoon heart on the container of tomato soup. Robbie would be gone in ten days. She'd tried to push it from her mind every time she thought of the ending that would surely come. Tonight had made her realize exactly what she would lose. A chance for something real with someone who had thrown her world into chaos—and then stayed to reorganize everything.

"But she lives in Seattle and I live here." She set the container of soup in the microwave, careful to remove the sticky note. She had a collection of notes from Robbie in the junk drawer on the far side of the fridge. She'd argued she was saving them as a reminder for what was owed, but she knew it had nothing to do with settling any balance. Robbie would refuse her money anyway. She simply wanted the notes because Robbie wasn't staying and the notes were what she'd have in the end.

She closed her eyes and took a deep breath. If Robbie was there, she'd make some joke about how she could tie her to the bed and not let her leave. The problem was, things went beyond sex and had for a while. After tonight, she couldn't pretend anymore. "I've totally fallen for her."

The microwave beeped as if weighing in on her declaration. She took the soup out and stirred, not resisting the temptation to inhale deeply. Of course it smelled amazing.

CHAPTER NINETEEN

The time passed quickly enough, but there wasn't much news. Robbie sent Devyn nearly the same update every hour—*no word yet*—until eleven, when she added she wouldn't message again unless something changed. She hoped Devyn would sleep but knew worry might keep her awake. Angel had looked so sick and weak. And the possibility of having to go to surgery still hung in the air. Unfortunately there'd been no sign of the doctor, and given how busy the waiting room stayed, Robbie doubted she'd be able to pop out for a chat.

After Devyn had left, a dog that had been hit by a car was rushed in, followed by a cat wailing in distress. In both cases, Robbie's heart went out to the families. She chatted with a guy waiting to have a fishhook pulled out of his retriever. They both felt lucky in comparison.

As she watched the other two families file out crying, she couldn't help thinking about the last time she'd been at the ER for a dog—for her Pixie. She'd known walking into the waiting room she might not leave with a dog in her arms. The memory brought back an onslaught of tears she didn't do a good job of hiding. When the receptionist came up to her with a box of tissues, she pulled herself together enough to thank the woman, but her heart felt heavy even after the tears had stopped.

"Angel will be fine," she whispered to herself. He'd walk out of the ER with his tail held high. Devyn wouldn't have to go through what she'd experienced. Not yet anyway.

Work was the last thing she felt like dealing with, but it was a good diversion. She started the security updates right at midnight and crossed her fingers there wouldn't be any hiccups in the system. When Matt's number flashed on her phone ten minutes later, her stomach clenched. She'd avoided any direct conversation since she'd started sleeping with Devyn, and as much as she believed who Devyn slept with wasn't any of Matt's business, she still didn't want to talk to him about it.

"Hey," Matt said, his voice groggy with sleep. "We've got a maintenance window for that, uh…you know, the thing."

"I'm already on it." Ordinarily she would have teased him more, but their exchanges felt complicated now. *Because, by the way, I'm having sex with your ex-wife.* "Security updates are installing now."

"Ah, man, thanks." He groaned. "Your uncle introduced me to his whiskey collection, and I was out cold by round two. He's got some seriously strong shit. I thought my head was gonna explode when my alarm went off."

"I think it's funny how much you two have bonded." She'd gotten a call from her uncle earlier that day and he'd mentioned how he was looking for a houseboat Matt could rent long term and how he hoped he could find one close. She'd teased her uncle for having a crush on a straight guy, but he'd cheekily returned he wasn't the one with the crush. She hadn't asked if her uncle meant Matt had a crush on him or if he was referring to her crush on Devyn. She also hadn't told him things had progressed and her feelings were way more complicated than a crush.

"He's got me cooking dinner and playing cards every night with him." Matt yawned. "Tomorrow we've got a big poker game with his friends."

"I know that crew. You'll be broke by the end of the night." She checked her laptop at the sound of a ping from a completed scan. "All right, Matt, go back to sleep. I got this."

"Thanks, dude. One more thing I owe you for," Matt said. "I'm screwed when you need a favor. I'll have to do whatever you ask."

"Watch that whiskey. You sound like hell."

She ended the call and blew out a breath. Would it count as a favor if she asked him to not be mad she'd had sex with Devyn? She wasn't the type to keep secrets, and as much as she argued it wasn't Matt's business who Devyn slept with, her conscience wouldn't let her off the hook entirely.

She tossed her phone on the empty seat next to her and then scrubbed her face. In a few weeks, she might be neighbors with Matt if her uncle had his way. She wasn't sure she could handle being around Matt and not Devyn.

Her phone rang a minute later, and she answered with, "What'd you forget to tell me?"

"Was I supposed to tell you something?"

Devyn's voice jolted Robbie. *Devyn.* Not Matt. She cursed silently before saying, "I'm sorry. I didn't look to see who was calling me. Thought you were Matt."

There was a long pause before Devyn said, "I can't sleep. I know I should be sleeping, but Angel's not in his bed and the house feels empty."

Robbie's chest tightened. She wanted to wrap Devyn in an embrace and curl up next to her so she'd fall asleep. "I didn't sleep right for a month after I had to let my dog go."

"What was your dog's name again?"

"Pixie." Robbie let the memory of the last few weeks with Pixie settle over her and then said, "She was a lot like Angel when she was younger. But she lived on a houseboat, so she chased birds instead of squirrels."

"Did she ever catch one?"

"No. She was all bark and no bite. She did get into a fight one time with a duck—she lost."

"Oh, poor baby."

"Don't worry. She was fine." A smile worked up to her lips as she remembered the duck who'd been Pixie's nemesis. "The duck loved to hang out on our dock and Pixie obviously hated that."

"Obviously. Jack Russell."

"Exactly. So she got it in her head that if she barked enough, she'd chase him off."

"Completely logical. And ducks can be annoying little shits."

Robbie chuckled. Of course Devyn would side with Pixie. "One day, the duck finally had enough of Pixie's barking and went after her. She was so surprised that she lost her footing running away and slipped right off the dock."

At Devyn's gasp, Robbie quickly added, "It wasn't a big deal—she'd fallen into the water before and knew how to swim—but her ego took a hit. I had to fish her out of the water while the duck laughed."

"Angel would have been mortified."

"Pixie totally was. For about an hour. Then she was right back to barking at the duck."

Devyn laughed and Robbie felt her smile stretch her cheeks. When Devyn's laughter stopped, she sighed softly and said, "Thank you for that."

The line went quiet and Robbie shifted back in her chair. She pictured Devyn's room and the bed they'd shared for the last several nights. Then she imagined Devyn lying on her back, staring up into the dark. The room was impossibly dark. How no light got in was a testament to blackout curtains. At first she'd found it unnerving to not be able to see her own hand if she held it in front of her face, but she'd quickly come to like the peacefulness of the pitch black. She realized she was timing her own breath to Devyn's on the other end of the line when Devyn shakily exhaled.

"It's hard waiting, but I know he's going to be okay." She didn't know for sure, but she had a sense that this time everything would work out. *At least for Angel.*

"Thanks for being there," Devyn said. "If there's any update—"

"I promise I'll text right away." She waited until Devyn ended the call to set down her phone. Then she stared at the dark screen for a long moment, wondering how her heart had decided on Devyn so quickly. As much as she wanted to believe things would somehow work out for them, her conscience kept reminding her about the sex-only agreement. Sometimes things didn't work out.

A little after two in the morning, she got up to fill her paper cup with her fourth round of watered-down coffee. Aside from a woman praying over rosary beads because of her sick poodle, the waiting room had emptied out and she was struggling to keep her eyes open. The tech who'd checked Angel in hours ago met her at the coffee station with an upbeat look.

"Good news. We took another set of x-rays and Doctor Andreas wanted me to tell you that things are moving. Nearly all the little bones are in the colon."

"Really? That's...disgusting. And amazing!"

The tech laughed. "I know he's feeling better, too, because he didn't try to bite when I took his temp this last time. Then I turned my back and he tried to steal one of my Cheetos."

Robbie cringed. "I'm sorry—about the Cheetos and about him biting." She'd been surprised at Devyn's comments about him not letting strangers touch him, but now she'd seen how fast he could turn into a shark. "We should have warned you."

"Oh, I'm used to it."

"Still not cool." Robbie made a mental note to drop off a big bag of Cheetos in apology. "So does this mean surgery isn't likely?"

"Yep. As soon as he poops, we think you'll be able to take him home."

She'd never been so happy to hear the word *poop*. As she headed back to her seat with her refilled coffee cup, she debated the text to send to Devyn. If Devyn had fallen asleep, she didn't want to wake her. But she knew how worried she was. Finally, she decided on a brief note, hoping Devyn would quickly read it and fall back asleep. She'd been amazed at how fast Devyn fell asleep and even joked with her about it. Devyn had claimed sleep was usually a struggle, but she'd added with a smile that apparently sex fixed everything.

We got an update. Angel's feeling better and XRAYS show bones are in colon. Waiting for him to poop.

Devyn's response was immediate, which confirmed she'd been awake and waiting for word. *Thank God. Text me when (poop emoji) happens.*

Robbie smiled as she read the text and then pocketed her phone when her laptop dinged to announce the next round of updates were complete. She had at least another hour of work to do, scanning the system and testing for problems, but as she tried to focus on the screen, her thoughts zipped back to Devyn.

Lately it was impossible not thinking of Devyn. She told herself she couldn't get attached about a dozen times a day and chastised her mind every time the words *love* and *Devyn* popped up together in her thoughts—even if it was something silly like thinking she loved the way Devyn bumped into her and pretended it was an accident. Or how she loved Devyn's laugh. And how much she loved that Devyn always wanted one more kiss after they had sex.

Tonight, she didn't bother with the mental gymnastics her mind did to keep her heart in line. For one thing, she was worried about Angel. For another, she was worried about Devyn. She understood how close a bond someone could have with a dog. But had Devyn let Angel be the center of her world because she didn't want anyone else close? She couldn't ask that question—or any of the others that fell into the too-personal-but-not-about-sex category.

Aside from Elena and Mari, Devyn had openly admitted she didn't have other friends. And she'd said that she'd had no interest in dating. The question of why the divorce had come about rattled round in Robbie's mind. Matt seemed like a good guy—not as perfect as who she'd picture Devyn with—but not terrible. What had made Devyn hate him enough to end the relationship?

She shook her head, reminding herself she didn't need to know the whys of the divorce. As much as she wished she'd have some place in Devyn's life when she went back to Seattle, she'd agreed to not get attached.

Two hours later, she shook herself awake when the door to the hospital treatment area swung open and the same vet tech who'd chatted with her earlier appeared with a plastic Ziploc freezer bag in her hands.

"Guess who pooped?"

Robbie reflexively covered her eyes. "Please don't show me."

"You don't want to see all the little bones?"

"Not even a little bit. My girlfriend's the doctor and she could probably stomach it, but not me." *Girlfriend.* The word had slipped out. Thankfully Devyn was not around to hear it.

"I can save it for her. It's pretty impressive."

"Does that mean Angel's cleared to go?"

"The doctor's ordered one more set of x-rays. I'll let you know as soon as those are reviewed."

Robbie downed the last of her now-room-temperature coffee and stood to pull out her phone. Waiting room chairs weren't ergonomic and every muscle groaned. She didn't care. It'd been worth it to stay, and now all she wanted to do was share the good news.

* * *

Robbie jostled awake at the sensation of someone touching her shoulder. It took her a moment to realize where she was—Devyn's bedroom—and what she was holding—a can of dog food.

"I'll admit I've got questions," Devyn said, a half-smile quirking her lips.

Robbie sat up and looked around. "Where's Angel?"

At the sound of his name, he hopped up into the bed, raced a circle around Robbie, and then let out a howl. When Robbie laughed, Angel's whole body wiggled as he wagged his tail.

"Someone's definitely feeling better," Devyn said. "I came home and found the two of you snuggled up here together. Angel woke up faster than you did."

"He's had less to stress about," Robbie said, setting the dog food on the nightstand and stretching before falling back on the bed. "What time is it? I've got to give him that medication at eight."

"Seven thirty. I got home a little early."

After Angel had passed the bulk of the bones, the vet had agreed to let him go home as long as he was closely monitored. That was what she was supposed to be doing. She ran a hand through her hair, knowing it was a tousled mess, and said, "I'm guessing you wouldn't hire me to be a nurse."

"Because I found you sleeping with the patient you were supposed to be watching? Or because I couldn't handle working with someone I wanted to sleep with?" Devyn arched an eyebrow. "I saw you made him a little chart for his meds, and you've been tracking what he's eaten. I'm certain you'd be an amazing nurse if you wanted the job."

Robbie shook her head. "I'm not cut out for nursing. I've been so worried."

"Look at your patient." Devyn nodded at Angel, who had found one of the stuffie toys Robbie had brought into the bed.

Earlier he'd ignored the toy, settling in alongside Robbie and only sleeping. Now he tossed it in the air and attacked it as it landed on the covers, happily growling as he shook the fox stuffie side to side.

"He's definitely feeling better," Devyn said. "Were you going to feed him some of that?" She pointed to the can of dog food.

"Not in your bed. I'm not sure why I brought it here."

Devyn smiled. "You two were both exhausted when I picked you up this morning. I'm glad you got some sleep. And now I'd like to feed both of you." She narrowed her eyes. "But not in my bed."

Angel hopped up when Devyn asked if he wanted dinner, eagerly wagging his tail as she held up the can of dog food the vet had given them, but Robbie still struggled to sit up. She rubbed sleep from her eyes and felt Devyn touch her chin. When she looked up, Devyn closed the distance between them with a deep kiss.

"After I feed you, I promise I'll let you go right to bed." Devyn kissed her again, lighter this time. "But I'm not promising I'll let you go right to sleep."

"Mm. Suddenly I'm not so tired." She stood, stealing a kiss before Devyn made it out of the room.

As Devyn pulled back, she shook her head. "Food first. Kisses later. And you should prepare yourself. I plan on properly thanking you for everything you've done in the last twenty-four hours."

"Properly?" Robbie affected an English accent. "Are we having tea and crumpets?"

"No crumpets. And you might not want to joke. I'm currently scheming exactly how I want to thank you, and I have a very devious mind when I let it have its way."

Robbie laughed. "I'm not usually nervous about being thanked."

Devyn headed down the hallway toward the kitchen, swishing her hips and saying, "Guess I'm not your usual."

"Not even close."

Devyn stopped to shoot a look over her shoulder. "Is that a good thing?"

Robbie's heart tugged at her chest. Devyn's tone was flirty and light but the look in her eyes was different. She wanted Robbie's answer. Needed it even. "It's a very good thing. I still don't know how I got so lucky."

"I know how," Devyn said, adding a wink. "And you're not the only lucky one." She turned the corner and disappeared from view, leaving Robbie to wrestle with emotions on her own.

She glanced at the rumpled sheets and the pillow she'd taken to using. When Devyn had dropped Angel and her off at the house she'd considered going to the cottage, but Angel had wanted to go to his bed in Devyn's room and she hadn't wanted to leave him alone. She hadn't planned on falling asleep, however. She wouldn't have thought she'd be comfortable in Devyn's space without her. Not enough to fall into a heavy, dreamless sleep. Her subconscious should have kept her alert for the sound of Devyn's return at least. But she'd gotten comfortable in Devyn's house, in her room, in her life.

Maybe it had happened fast because the relationship had a designated endpoint. Maybe that was why her heart had jumped so quickly to Devyn as well. Maybe there was no risk when nothing could last.

CHAPTER TWENTY

"This smells amazing." Robbie lifted the spoon to her lips. "Oh, that's good."

"Tom kha is my favorite comfort food." Devyn was happy Robbie approved of her choice. Thai takeout was her favorite, but she'd settled on it mostly because it was quick and she wanted to spend as much of her evening with Angel and Robbie as she could. Fortunately, Angel was feeling better—enough so that he was begging for a bite of the soup.

"Sorry, Angel," Robbie said. "This food does not qualify as a bland diet."

"I feel bad he's stuck eating stuff that smells like gross baby food, but also…he ate a whole squirrel."

"You know he's going to be bragging to every dog he meets for the next week." Robbie looked over at Angel and added, "And I was impressed you rode a paddleboard."

Devyn angled her glass to Robbie. "When am I getting you on a paddleboard?"

"I don't think I've got the balance to pull it off."

"It's not as hard as you think. Can you swim?"

Robbie nodded. "I grew up on a lake."

"And I already know you're in good shape. We can work on the balance part. Unless you're scared to try new things."

Robbie opened her mouth but closed it a moment later.

Devyn smiled. "I've got a second paddleboard and I'm off tomorrow."

"You're hard to say no to." Robbie laughed. "The thing is, I've felt that water. It isn't that warm and there's a very good chance I'm going to fall in."

"I've got a second wetsuit." Devyn finished her last sip of wine. "What are your other excuses?"

Robbie grinned. "I guess I'm out of excuses."

"Do you really want to say no?"

Robbie shook her head.

"Good. Paddleboarding in the morning then." She held Robbie's gaze, enjoying the what-just-happened look on her face. "If it makes you feel better, I'm feeling nervous about this new thing I want to try, too."

"What new thing?"

Saying it out loud was one step further than her confidence could take her. "It's an after-dinner thing. Anyway, I want to do this new thing a lot more than you want to try paddleboarding, so I'm not sure how fair it is."

"Okay, I'm intrigued. Am I allowed guesses?"

"No. Maybe." She felt heat climb up her neck.

"A sex thing?"

"Maybe. But no more guesses. I won't be able to get through dinner."

Robbie picked up her spoon and took another bite. Devyn did as well, but she felt Robbie studying her. "What?"

"I want to know all the things you want to try."

She wanted to joke she'd start a list, but her breath caught in her chest and words wouldn't come. The way Robbie looked at her made everything else slip away.

Robbie's gaze dropped to their soup bowls. "I think I want to save the rest of my dinner for later."

She couldn't hold back the smile that tugged at her cheeks. "You're distracted."

"Completely."

She stood and held out her hand. "I promise I'll give you pointers tomorrow if you give me pointers tonight."

"I don't usually make a deal without knowing what I'm getting into." But Robbie clasped her hand.

"I'm not your usual, remember?" She pulled Robbie into a kiss. Robbie deepened it before she could and then pushed her back a step toward the hallway.

"I thought I was in charge here," Devyn murmured.

"You are." Robbie pushed her back another step until she was against the wall. "But I need something."

When Robbie kissed her neck, heat flooded her body. "This was not part of my plan."

"Mm. Sorry." Robbie kissed her exposed collarbone. "I tend to mess up plans."

Robbie's hands moved down her chest, thumbs grazing her nipples and making them take notice even through the layers of her bra and her blouse. "It's something easy for you to give me," Robbie continued, her hands settling on Devyn's hips. "Do you mind if I show you?"

The pulse at her clit argued it was a shared need. "If you don't show me, I think we'll both have a problem."

"Good answer."

Robbie's lips met hers. Between kisses, she managed to get under Robbie's shirt to feel the warmth of her body, but then Robbie undid the clasp at the side of her skirt and the material dropped to the ground.

"That's better," Robbie said, her voice husky. She stroked up Devyn's legs. "You really are gorgeous, you know."

"Half naked and letting you do whatever you want with me?" She was teasing Robbie, but her pulse raced in anticipation. "I do have a bedroom, you know."

"I don't want to wait." Robbie pressed against her again, pinning her to the wall.

"Good because I'm already wet." She sucked in a breath when Robbie pushed her underwear aside, giving her full access.

"You could tell me to stop."

"You know that's the last thing I want to do." Devyn moved to kiss Robbie, but then Robbie's fingers stroked inside her. She parted her mouth in a silent gasp and Robbie's tongue followed.

There was nothing she could do but move her legs farther apart. Nothing she wanted to do but let Robbie take her. Robbie thrust into her with a deep, firm stroke, glancing over her clit and making her immediately wet. In no time, a climax threatened. She didn't try to slow Robbie down. She didn't try to do anything but hold on to Robbie's shoulders.

"Don't stop."

"I won't." Robbie kissed her and shifted her hand, adding more pressure to Devyn's clit as she stroked again.

"Can I have more?"

"Please?" Robbie's question held her playful smile. "Always."

Every part of her seemed to moan the word, "Yes," when Robbie pushed another finger inside. She let her head rock back against the wall as Robbie fucked her. Their bodies moved together, their breath coming in pants, and she let Robbie have her completely. She didn't need to pretend she was in control. She didn't want to be.

Tears came to her eyes as the nerves at her clit began to fire. She'd never wanted to give herself over completely because she'd never trusted anyone enough. Until now. She gave in to the orgasm, saying only, "More."

When the climax hit, she gave herself one breath to enjoy it before telling Robbie she wanted more. Robbie obliged and her center clenched around Robbie's hand. She pushed through a spasm, feeling her wetness drench Robbie's fingers.

"You are so damn sexy," Robbie said. "I can't get enough of you."

"I'm the one who can't get enough."

She felt the shift then in Robbie's body and in her own. Robbie kissed her cheek, her neck, her lips, but didn't stop thrusting. Heat filled her body as the next orgasm gained on her. She knew she couldn't hold it back, didn't want to, but she also knew it wouldn't be enough. Now the truth was out in the open. *I can't get enough of you.*

If Robbie pulled out, let her step away from the wall where she was pinned, she'd only long to be back in the same place. Letting everything happen all over again.

The second climax hit and there was no pushing through. The first had been like a rolling wave but the second crashed into her, making her knees go weak. She squeezed her legs together, cussed and apologized in the same breath, and then collapsed in Robbie's arms. She shivered, tensed, and shivered again. But she wasn't cold. She was coated in sweat and panting for air.

"You're amazing. I hope you realize that." Robbie kissed her cheek and then her lips. The kisses were gentle and sweet, and a relaxed warmth filled Devyn.

"I wasn't joking about never being able to get enough. I love fucking you."

The words could have felt crass, but Robbie's tone was reverent. And she understood. "I love you fucking me." Her body felt used in the best possible way. "But I don't think I'll last much longer standing." She took a deep breath and straightened. "You're going to have to be okay with a bed."

Robbie smiled. "Your bed?"

"Yes. And I want you naked and stretched out on it."

Robbie's smile widened. "Who says I'll do what you want just because you tell me?"

"I say." She pressed her index finger on Robbie's chest. "And as I recall, you gave me permission to use you as I like. Is that still our agreement?"

Robbie laughed but said, "Yes, ma'am."

"Good. Go to my room and strip."

She needed water and to pee. Once she'd taken care of both of those needs, she went to her bedroom but stopped in the doorway. Robbie was, as requested, naked and stretched out on her bed. Her hands were clasped under her head and her ankles were crossed, but she was plainly not using the sheet to cover up.

Devyn stared, taking in the sight that still felt like a guilty pleasure—like something that shouldn't be for her to enjoy even as much as she craved it. Robbie had muscles in all the right places. Not bulky, but tone. And she had a solid thickness about her body, a strength that Devyn loved.

Robbie tipped her head, and the look in her eyes said she knew Devyn liked what she saw. "Now that I'm lying here naked, what's your next request?"

"You have to do something very difficult. Lie in that position and not do anything unless I tell you to."

"That does sound hard. Very. Hard."

Devyn arched an eyebrow. "I want to try something I've never done." She stepped up to the bed and slowly took off her blouse, knowing she had Robbie's full attention.

"You are so hot." Robbie groaned. "I know this isn't news to you but...Damn."

She had doubts about her body. About if she was sexy or attractive enough. After everything that had happened with Matt, it would be impossible to not have doubts. But Robbie had swept all those doubts away the first time they'd kissed.

"I'm keeping the lights on tonight. I want to see you when I thank you."

"You're welcome," Robbie said.

"I haven't thanked you yet." She pushed Robbie's knees apart. "Are you nervous?"

"A little bit." Robbie chuckled. "I have no idea what you're going to do to me."

"You can be nervous. I get to be confident." She settled between Robbie's legs, a feeling of confidence washing into her as if the words alone had manifested the emotion. "Should I ask if what I want is okay?"

"I'm so unbelievably turned on right now I'd agree to anything."

She stroked a fingertip lightly up Robbie's shin, stopping at her knee. "Anything?"

"Now you really have me nervous."

"You don't need to be." She stroked slowly from Robbie's knee to her upper thigh. Instead of being waxed smooth like she was, Robbie's center was neatly trimmed. She liked the difference, liked how Robbie looked similar but not the same. She traced the triangle of trimmed hair and then stroked down the opposite leg. "Close your eyes."

Robbie held her gaze for a moment, as if seeking something. Maybe a sign she could trust her. In the next moment, her eyes closed and Devyn's breath caught in her chest. She thought of Robbie as sexy and strong. Capable in ways she wasn't. But in the moment, there was a vulnerability in her that made her simply beautiful.

"There are a lot of things I like about you," she said. "How brave I feel around you is one of them." She bent her head and breathed in, savoring Robbie's scent. When she looked up, Robbie's eyes were still closed. Trusting her. She felt a tightness in her chest as a knowing settled over her. She couldn't say the thought that crossed her mind, but that didn't mean she didn't feel it. *I love you. But I can't tell you.*

She parted Robbie with her tongue and found her swollen clit. The taste of Robbie, her arousal rich and sultry, filled her senses as Robbie's voice filled the room. She loved the wetness that spilled onto her tongue. Loved how swollen and hard Robbie was, loved how Robbie couldn't help pushing into her mouth. Loved how Robbie responded as if everything she did was exactly the right thing.

Robbie hitched up her knees, but Devyn held her hips in place. She circled Robbie's clit, stroked her folds, and pushed her tongue deep inside. She wanted to explore every part of her. Wanted to know all of the secrets that turned Robbie on, all the ways she liked to be appreciated.

"Devyn, please," Robbie said, quivering on the sheets. "Can I move my hands? I want to touch you."

Robbie's eyes were closed, but her mouth was open and she was breathing hard. She'd kept her hands folded beneath her head as Devyn had ordered, but the rest of her had hardly held still.

"You'll distract me." She licked Robbie again, lazily this time. "I want to see if I can make you come."

"I'm so close. If I could just touch you—"

"After." She flattened her tongue on Robbie's clit and felt a spasm in response. "How close?"

"So close," Robbie said, bucking her hips up.

She had seen it done in movies and had tried to pay attention when Robbie had gone down on her, but there was no way of knowing what someone liked. Not until she tried. She licked faster and then shifted and pressed one finger to Robbie's opening.

"Oh, fuck," Robbie moaned.

"You like that?" She didn't need the answer but Robbie nodded, panting faster. She slid her finger in, not letting up on Robbie's clit.

Robbie reached for her wrist, shoving the finger deeper inside and then clenching down. In the next breath, and before she was ready, Robbie cried out with her climax.

"Fuck. Yes."

The words roared through her ears. She felt every muscle twitch, the gush of Robbie's arousal, and the wave of the climax. She felt it like it was her own and she savored every second. Every ragged breath Robbie drew, every tremor. Before she was ready for it to end, Robbie abruptly pulled away from her and curled on her side, shaking and sweaty.

"Was that…okay?" She touched Robbie's shoulder but didn't get a response. Robbie's breathing was still heavy and maybe she hadn't heard. Was it too much? God, and she wanted more.

"Mm. Yes." Robbie flopped on her back and exhaled. "I just needed a minute to regroup. You kind of undid me."

"Is that a good thing?"

"Definitely." Robbie opened her arms. "Come here. I'm sweaty but I want you."

Devyn moved onto Robbie's chest. "I made you sweaty. I should get to enjoy it." She kissed Robbie and then remembered her plan. "Thank you."

Robbie laughed, and the sound rumbled through her chest. Devyn kissed her again. "Do you like how I say thank you?"

"So much." Robbie's arms tightened around her. "Are you tired? Because I'm suddenly exhausted."

"Go to sleep. I want to stay up for a while to keep an eye on Angel." She kissed Robbie's cheek and noticed it was already slack.

"Wake me if he needs anything?"

Not tonight. Tonight, she wanted Robbie to sleep. She rested her head on Robbie's chest, feeling the rise and fall time to her own breathing. She spotted Angel in his bed next to her nightstand. He wasn't asleep yet, but he seemed as close as Robbie.

She looked between Angel and Robbie and then closed her eyes. With the light on she wouldn't sleep, but she wasn't ready to break the spell she felt in the room. She didn't need anything. Didn't want for anything. Her mind, for once, was at peace. This was how *perfect* felt. "Or maybe this is how love feels."

"What'd you say?" Robbie rustled awake, rubbing her eyes. "Sorry I drifted off. I fall asleep quick when I come hard."

"Go back to sleep. I'm going to take Angel outside one more time, but I want you to be right here when I come back."

Robbie kissed her, murmuring, "Okay."

It was better than okay. And it was also, possibly, a complete disaster.

CHAPTER TWENTY-ONE

"You look good in a wetsuit."

Robbie glanced down at the black-and-white wetsuit she'd squeezed herself into and then at Devyn's svelte all-black wetsuit. "*You* look good in a wetsuit. I look like an awkward penguin."

"Aren't all penguins a little awkward?"

"You could have tried denying it."

"I was joking." Devyn laughed. "You look nothing like a penguin. Except when you walk like that. Why aren't you bending your knees?"

Robbie exaggerated the penguin walk. "Because this wetsuit is too tight. I'm bigger than you."

"That's Matt's old wetsuit."

Robbie cringed. "Great. So I'm bigger than your ex, too."

"Which I love." Devyn touched Robbie's chin. "In case I didn't make it abundantly clear this morning, I love everything about your body. Were you not paying attention when I listed all the parts I liked?"

Robbie couldn't help a sheepish smile. "I was paying attention. It was sweet to wake up to a list of things you like about me."

Devyn bumped against her. "I'll have to add your penguin walk to the list."

"Please don't." Robbie still had a buzzy feeling inside her body from the night they'd shared and she loved the way Devyn kept stealing glances at her as they walked. She'd wanted to convince Devyn to spend the day in bed, but Devyn was too excited about paddleboarding. "It feels almost warm enough to skip the wetsuit."

Devyn looked at the waves. "When the wind picks up, it gets chilly on the board. If you want to try without the suit, I won't stop you. But I think you'll regret your choice if you fall in."

Probably that was true. Still, she wished she weren't wearing Matt's wetsuit. She was used to her body and liked it well enough, but it had taken some work and a lot of letting go of what society and her dad had told her—about her legs that her dad had called stocky, about her broad shoulders that friends in high school had said made her look like a football player, and about having hips so the men's jeans she preferred didn't quite fit unless she went a size up. She was in good shape and reminded herself of that fact, but not quite fitting was an old thread. Matt's wetsuit picked up the thread and tugged on it.

They stopped walking when they reached the dark line of wet sand and Robbie glanced from the waves to the paddleboard she'd carried. "Is this Matt's, too?"

"No. It's my old board. Matt never liked paddleboarding. He tried surfing for a while but wasn't really into that either. He sold his surfboard but never got rid of the wetsuit."

They'd avoided talking about Matt for so long it felt weird hearing his name in their conversation now. Still, Robbie asked, "I thought Matt was a beach guy."

"I think he liked the beach, but we moved here because of me." Devyn met Robbie's gaze. "Running is his thing. He's not much into watersports. I thought about telling him to sell the wetsuit but...we reached a point where the only way we communicated was in text messages and I let go of discussing anything that wasn't really important." She narrowed her eyes. "It feels weird talking with you about Matt now."

"I agree. Can we go back to how hot you look in a wetsuit?"

Devyn smiled even as she rolled her eyes. "I think we should move on to a paddleboard lesson."

"Good idea. Angel won't be here to rescue me if I sink." They'd both decided it would be better leaving Angel home. He was seemingly back to his usual self with no obvious sign of the ordeal he'd been through, and his appetite that morning had been ravenous. Still, the vet had warned not to let him overdo it.

"You won't need rescuing. It's really not hard." Devyn set her board on a flat section of sand and motioned for Robbie to do the same. "I know you've got nice muscles. Let's see if you can use them."

After that comment, Robbie had trouble focusing on the rest of the paddleboarding lesson. She wanted to impress Devyn—even if she didn't want to think about all the reasons why. Fortunately, paddleboarding seemed like a sport anyone could pick up.

"Ready to give it a try?" Devyn's eyes lit up as she lifted her board.

"Let's do it."

Robbie was a confident swimmer and wasn't a novice when it came to the ocean. Still, she managed to get knocked on her ass trying to get past the breakers. Devyn cruised right over the waves, moving smoothly from standing in the knee-deep water to being on her stomach on the board, and as she paddled out called over her shoulder for Robbie to catch up.

After one wave knocked her on her butt, another one added a mouthful of salt water. At least Matt's wetsuit did help buffer the cold. She pushed herself onto her feet, set the board level in the water, and then belly-flopped on—much less gracefully than Devyn had. She paddled hard with her hands and didn't stop until she'd made it to the calmer water beyond the surf.

When she stopped to catch her breath, Devyn was waiting for her, already standing up on her board. A smile stretched across her face. "Now get up on your feet. I want to show you a few things."

Sunshine sparkled on the brilliantly blue water and Robbie would have been content lying on her belly watching Devyn against that backdrop, but she pushed up to her knees and then, not smoothly, scrambled onto her feet. Devyn cheered, lifting her paddle in the air even as Robbie felt her board rocking side to side under her feet.

"Keep your knees bent until you get the feel for the water," Devyn said. "And keep your eyes on the ocean. Sleeper waves can come out of nowhere and you need to be ready."

"How can I be ready if they come out of nowhere?"

"Don't stop paddling," Devyn continued. "It's harder to stay up if you aren't moving. Like riding a bike."

"It's funny how people say that and almost nothing is like riding a bike." She dipped her paddle in the water, trying to keep up with Devyn, and nearly lost her balance, righting herself at the last minute.

Devyn circled round her. "Lost your sea legs?"

"I never really had sea legs."

"You live on a boat."

"In a lake. Besides, houseboats are different." Robbie didn't want to let on how hard it was talking when her concentration was solely focused on not falling. "They bob up and down. Not this side-to-side stuff."

"I like up and down but side to side can be fun, too. As long as I'm getting rocked, I'm not going to complain."

Robbie glanced at her. "Is that a sex reference?"

"I have no idea what you're talking about." Devyn's look was not at all innocent.

"I can't believe you're trying to make me think of sex right now." Robbie laughed and nudged Devyn's board with her paddle. "You're supposed to be teaching me tips so I don't sink."

Devyn laughed, too, giving Robbie's board a nudge back and saying, "Keep your knees bent."

As Robbie struggled to stay standing, she remembered Devyn's earlier comment about using the paddle for balance. Once she'd steadied herself, she shot a look back at Devyn. "What's your next tip?"

"You're fighting against the water when you hold your paddle like that." Devyn adjusted the angle of her paddle and dipped it in. "Stroke like this and you go with the waves and there's less resistance."

"Wait, how am I supposed to stroke?" Robbie smirked.

"I think you were paying attention the first time," Devyn returned. "But you should know you'd have no resistance if you wanted to do some extra work on your stroke later. I'll even spread my legs to help."

Robbie knew she'd straightened her knees. She'd also turned her focus away from the ocean to look at Devyn. Still the wave that lifted her board came out of nowhere. She lost her balance, tried to overcorrect, and the next thing she knew, her board was going right and she was going left.

She didn't mind getting dunked with the wetsuit on, but there was nothing to be done about embarrassing herself in front of Devyn. The fact Devyn looked so worried when she surfaced made the situation worse. "I'm fine, I promise."

Thankfully, she hadn't let go of her paddle and her board was leashed to her ankle. She swam up to it and then heard a splash behind her. When she looked back, Devyn was in the water. Devyn swam up to her in three strides.

"I promise I'm fine," Robbie said, already half up on her board. "I live on a lake. If I couldn't swim—"

"It's my fault you slipped. And saying sorry isn't the same as this." Devyn braced one hand on Robbie's board and then shifted up to kiss her.

The kiss was quick and salty and it shouldn't have taken her breath away, but it did. Blame the sleeper wave for throwing everything off. Although really it was the look on Devyn's face before the kiss. And how she'd closed her eyes as she'd leaned in.

"I shouldn't have distracted you," Devyn said. "I'm the worst teacher ever."

"If I agree, will you kiss me like that again?"

Devyn laughed but kissed her again. As she pulled back, she said, "Now get back up on your feet. I am not going to mess around anymore."

When Devyn decided on something, Robbie realized, she followed through. They spent the next hour crisscrossing the little bay and talking very little. Devyn did give hints on technique and pointed out the parts of the bay that were her favorites, as well as all the animals she'd come across, but she didn't joke and looked nervous whenever Robbie's balance wavered.

After they'd paddled for a while, Devyn suggested a break and sat down on her board, hooking her paddle through a loop of rope at the front of Robbie's board to keep them close together. Robbie sat down too, dangling her toes in the water and thinking of all the questions she wanted to ask. Had Devyn grown up in San Diego? Would she ever leave? What about her family? Did she want a partner in life, or had marriage ruined that for her? And what had happened with her and Matt?

She thought of those questions, but when she looked at Devyn she didn't want to disturb her peaceful look. Her eyes were trained on the horizon where the distant line of deep blue blended with a pale blue sky. The sun bronzed her skin and lit her hair. Her profile was stunning, and Robbie wished she had a camera. She didn't think she could hold the sight in her head for as long as she wanted it—which was longer than she had any business wanting.

"I never get tired of this," Devyn said. "Sometimes I think it's silly how much time I spend staring at the water, but the ocean never stops being gorgeous. Even when it storms. I feel…" She gave a slight head shake and looked at Robbie. "Like this little bay is part of me. I know that's a ridiculous thing to say."

"It's not ridiculous."

The ocean was part of Devyn. Robbie could see and feel how true that was, and by the time they'd pulled the paddleboards out of the water she knew Devyn had shared something personal with her. Maybe even more personal than sex.

Which didn't mean Robbie wanted sex any less. Especially when Devyn gave her a deep kiss at the water's edge. She wanted sex more than ever then, even as she wondered how her heart would fare after.

As they made their way home from the beach, Devyn said, "I don't suppose you've spent any time thinking about what you want to do this afternoon."

"Well, there's some touch-up painting on my to-do list, but I've got a few other ideas of things I'd like to do even better."

"Things?" Devyn arched an eyebrow. "Hmm. Sounds interesting. Maybe you'll include me in your plans?"

"I'm hoping to." Robbie smiled.

"Good. I don't think I'd let you get many to-do items checked off if I wasn't on the list."

Robbie laughed and Devyn gave her a knowing look. "I'm not joking. And, if I take up as much of your day as I'm hoping I will, you might need to push that painting project to tomorrow."

Robbie laughed again. They passed the café and Clara, who was setting out the lunch specials sign. She straightened as she saw them and put her hands on her hips.

"Look at you two all blissed out." Clara smiled. "How was the water?"

\
Houseswap 101   181

"Perfect," Devyn said.

Robbie nodded. "Perfect." Like the past evening she'd spent with Devyn and the day that stretched in front of her.

Clara sighed. "Go on before I start wishing I had a girlfriend, too."

Robbie and Devyn both laughed as Clara waved them off, turning back into her café with a smile. "We could rinse off and go back to the café for lunch," Robbie suggested as they started walking again.

"I love that idea," Devyn said. "Except for one thing." She bit the edge of her lip as she glanced at Robbie. "After we rinse off, I want you between my legs, so it will have to be a late lunch."

Robbie grinned. "I can't argue with that."

They crossed the street and came up the block to the house. Devyn's steps slowed and then stopped in front of the neighbor's magnolia tree. She squinted at something and Robbie followed her line of sight to a red Mercedes sedan parked on the street.

No one was in the car, but by the look on Devyn's face, she knew who owned the car. Devyn didn't offer any information, however, only murmuring, "Shit," and then heading for the side gate at a fast clip.

Robbie followed. Before she could think of what to ask Devyn, a woman opened the front door of Devyn's house and called out, "I was about to send out a search party." She gave an exaggerated sigh and crossed her arms. "I'm assuming you forgot about our lunch at the yacht club? From what I can see, you aren't too busy with work to cancel this time."

Devyn had one hand on the gate, but it looked as if she wished she could bolt the opposite direction. "I need to change."

"Obviously." The woman's voice set Robbie's teeth on edge, but the sneer she gave Devyn was worse. "I'll call Laurel and let her know we're running late."

Devyn set her board on the ground in the side yard. She keyed in the code to the garage door, still not offering any explanation. Robbie left the second board with Devyn's and followed her into the garage.

Devyn stripped out of her wetsuit and then looked over at Robbie. "I hate to ask you to do this but…could you rinse off the boards and the wetsuits?"

"Sure. Who is she?"

"My mom."

Robbie didn't see much resemblance between Devyn and the sixty-something bleached-blonde who'd sneered at her. There also didn't seem to be many warm feelings between them.

Devyn closed her eyes and took a deep breath. "You have no idea how much I would rather spend this afternoon with you."

"Instead of your mom?" Robbie lifted a shoulder. "She doesn't seem like a ton of fun."

"She's not. But I didn't mean instead of my mom. I meant instead of anyone else." Devyn had only worn a rash guard and bikini bottoms under the wetsuit, and when she stepped close for a kiss, it took all of Robbie's willpower to not beg her to cancel the yacht club.

"I wish I could tell her to go to lunch without me."

"I wish you could, too," Robbie said. "But I understand."

Devyn gave her another quick kiss before heading into the house and leaving Robbie to wonder how much she did understand. She still knew so little about Devyn. But family dynamics were always tricky, and Devyn's relationship with her mom seemed complicated even in the short exchange she'd witnessed.

She rinsed the boards and then set them in the sun to dry before doing the same with the wetsuits. As she headed to the cottage, Angel came tearing out of the house, yipping with excitement. She went down on one knee, and he leapt into her arms. It was good to see him so energetic, and his recovery took away some of her disappointment.

"Put him down. He bites."

Robbie looked around to localize the voice. She knew it was Devyn's mom but she couldn't tell where she was. Finally, she spotted the woman through the window screen in the living room.

"He can be nasty and he hates being picked up."

Devyn's voice came next. "Angel knows her, Mom. She's staying in the cottage."

Robbie couldn't see Devyn, but with the windows open, voices carried. Devyn's mother had turned away from the screen, but her words were still distinct when she said, "You didn't tell me you'd rented out the cottage. When did that happen?"

"When Matt left—three weeks ago."

"I don't like you having someone we don't know in that cottage. Where'd you even find her? I hope you didn't post something online."

Robbie waited for Devyn to say she was Matt's friend. Or, even better, her friend.

"You didn't let her sign a year lease, did you?" Devyn's mother continued. "Does she know you're selling? And wasn't that Matt's wetsuit she was wearing? Did she tell you she was going to borrow it?"

Robbie wished Devyn would say something, but only silence came after the questions. Then Devyn's mother added, "Do you know what a squatter is? People move in and then the landlord can't get them out. What are you going to do if you can't get her to leave? She's already using your things and—"

"Can we not have this discussion right now? I thought you were worried about being late."

"If that dog bites her, she could sue. She certainly doesn't look like she has money and I'm guessing that Honda out front is hers. If she has to rent that little cottage…Was this a Craigslist thing? You know murderers find their victims on Craigslist."

"Seriously, Mom, stop. She's not a murderer."

"Well, she looks…tough."

Devyn didn't argue. It made sense Devyn wouldn't admit they were sleeping together. But she wished Devyn would at least say she was getting the projects done around the house that Matt hadn't.

"How much are you charging her?"

"I'm not charging her," Devyn said.

"You've taken in a charity case? Oh, my God. What if she's into drugs? What if she has a record?"

"You need to stop watching Fox News."

Robbie glanced at Angel and whispered, "Something tells me your grandma would be happier about a police record than knowing I'm gay and her daughter went down on me last night."

CHAPTER TWENTY-TWO

Lunch at the yacht club wasn't an hour affair. It was an afternoon project. And the last thing Devyn wanted to do was spend the afternoon with her mother, her mother's two friends, and the son of one of those friends—who'd definitely been brought for the purpose of being set up with her. Andrew, also divorced, pale complexioned, and forty-something, was allergic to shellfish, but at least told a few jokes that weren't awful. Under other circumstances, Devyn might have tried to like him. But not today. Not after everything her mother had said about Robbie—and continued to bring up during the course of the two-and-a-half-hour-long lunch—and after everything she'd realized about herself.

Andrew had clearly come to placate his mother and Devyn almost felt sorry for him. Almost, until she realized he'd had a heads-up on the scheme. Which was why when he suggested a walk along the harbor after lunch, she'd avoided a direct answer and was thankful when the childless friend of her mother's suggested ordering more cocktails and dessert. She desperately wanted an excuse to leave. Getting called into work would have felt like a blessing from the universe, but of course no call came when she wanted it.

Once dessert was ordered, she managed to slip away to the bathroom. She immediately texted Robbie: *Ever rescue a damsel in distress from a yacht club?*

I've been waiting for this moment. Polishing my armor now.

Devyn smiled at the screen.

I don't have a white horse. Do you think a white Honda will work?

Devyn laughed. A woman coming out of one of the stalls looked at her with a raised eyebrow before heading to the sink to wash her hands. Devyn stepped away from the basins and sat down in the pink chair in the corner by the door. Likely the chair was intended as a nursing station, but it served the dual purpose of affording a quiet space away from dull yacht club conversations.

I'm allergic to horses.

Lucky me. No other strapping knights will have a chance.

She smiled again, but her chest tightened. She missed Robbie and they'd only been apart for a few hours. There was no use pretending—she was in deep. *Anything I can do to convince you to spend the evening with me after I flaked on our afternoon?*

You didn't flake. You were abducted.

Which is why I need to be rescued. She didn't want to beg, but she was tempted. Yes, she could make it through dessert and a ride home in her mother's car—where she most definitely would be pressured about getting herself "back on the market." But she didn't want to.

Is there some emergency at the house?

Robbie took a moment to text back. *You want me to come up with an excuse so you'll have to leave the yacht club?*

Maybe.

You have to leave because a package was delivered. A very important package.

Robbie had mentioned ordering a strap-on. Her mouth went dry as she realized that had to be the delivery.

I hope you like the fit as much as I do.

Did you already try it on? Devyn pressed the send button as a flush heated up her neck. She'd imagined Robbie with a strap-on, knew it was something Robbie liked, but she hadn't expected it yet.

I might be wearing it now.

Robbie was at home, alone, wearing a strap-on. Was she walking around naked with it? Was it hidden under her clothing? Was she playing with it—without her company? All of the possibilities made Devyn wet. Undeniably, hopelessly wet.

Were you serious about wanting me to rescue you?

Yes. Hell yes. Devyn took a deep breath. She couldn't say that. She didn't want to sound as desperate for Robbie as she felt. But, also, yes. *Only if you don't mind. I hate to bother you if you're busy.*

Pulling up the yacht club address now. There was a pause and then a second text from Robbie. *Looks like I can be there in ten minutes.*

Devyn returned to the table and gave the explanation of not feeling well before excusing herself with a halfhearted apology to Andrew. Half, because she didn't like disappointing anyone. But only for that reason.

Robbie was parked at the curb waiting for her when she stepped outside. She couldn't help staring at the bulge in Robbie's cargo pants. At least she held herself back from reaching to feel it as she came up to the car.

"You requested a knight with a white Honda?"

"I did."

Robbie opened the passenger door with a flourish. She waited for Devyn to get in and then went around to the driver's side. As she settled into the seat, she said, "This seems too easy. Isn't there a dragon I'm supposed to fight?"

"She's inside eating dessert."

Robbie laughed. "So, all I need to do is take you back to the castle?"

"Trust me—you're saving the day." She buckled her seat belt and then reached across the console to set her hand on Robbie's thigh. "I'm having trouble not feeling you up."

"You know we still have an agreement," Robbie said, pulling away from the curb. "I'm yours to play with for another week."

Only one more week. She hated the reminder. That couldn't be all the time she had with Robbie. Not when every step they took together felt like they were building something—something she'd always wanted. How could they not talk about what would happen next? She wanted the conversation, needed it, even if she'd been the one to set the ground rules of nothing but sex. Rules changed.

But she didn't want to start that conversation today. She had other things in mind. When she moved her hand up Robbie's thigh, Robbie looked away from the traffic long enough to flash a smile. "Go ahead. I think you'll like what you feel."

She felt the bulge at Robbie's groin and moaned softly. In response, Robbie pushed into her hand. "I'm so ready to be home." Especially now.

"I may be secretly hoping you're feeling drained from that dragon ordeal and ready to collapse in bed."

"With a knight on me?"

"Maybe."

She traced the outline of the cock down to the head and her body quivered with desire. She glanced up and Robbie was waiting for her. "You're so hot."

"Because I'm packing?"

"That too. But you have this look…" Devyn searched for the words. "Like you know you have something I want."

"Do I?"

"Yes." Devyn gripped the cock through Robbie's pants. Emboldened by Robbie's quick intake of breath, she stroked the shaft and imagined it inside her.

"What do you think?" Robbie asked.

"I think if you weren't driving, I'd be in your lap right now." Devyn reached for the zipper on Robbie's pants.

"You do want us to get home, right?"

"Focus on driving." She reached through the opening of the boxers and found what she wanted. "I know you can be very focused."

Robbie groaned as Devyn wrapped her hand around the cock. Her center pulsed in anticipation. Robbie, to her credit, kept her eyes on the road, but her breathing hitched when Devyn stroked again.

"Can you get off with this?"

"If you keep doing what you're doing. Though I was hoping to wait until I was inside you."

The words were simple but Devyn felt every part of her flare. She reluctantly stopped stroking and tucked the cock, then pulled the zipper halfway up and shifted back in her seat. "You have no idea how wet I am."

Robbie looked over at her. "Maybe you'll let me find out when we get home."

She didn't notice the rest of the drive, her mind spinning from the yacht club to everything she wanted to tell Robbie, to the need simmering in her. Robbie parked and Devyn was out of the car before the engine cut. She unlocked the front door, but as she reached for the handle, Robbie sidled up behind her.

"You in a hurry for something?" Robbie kissed her neck and ran her hands down Devyn's arms. "I like you all dressed up for the yacht club."

"You say that like you can't wait to take off what I'm wearing."

"I can't." Robbie reached past her for the door handle. "But you know someone's going to be waiting for us."

Angel. As much as she loved him, she needed him to be occupied with something for the next hour. Or two. "I've got a plan."

Angel was indeed waiting for them, but Devyn found one of the special chew treats he loved and handed it to him, saying, "I need you to give us some quiet time."

"Is that what we're calling it?" Robbie asked. "I don't know how quiet we'll be."

Devyn touched Robbie's lips. "You don't need to be quiet." She pulled her finger away and Robbie moaned softly. "I like it when you make noise. Especially when I have my way with you."

"What if I have my way with you?"

She shrugged, pretending she didn't care, but a thrill went through her at Robbie's words. She turned, heading down the hall to the bedroom, but stopped when she felt Robbie's hand circle her wrist. When she looked back, Robbie's arousal lit the space between them.

"Remember how I rescued you from the dragon?"

She wanted to give herself over with Robbie's look alone. Her body was impatient with all the waiting. Impatient and wet. But she narrowed her eyes and said, "Do you plan to take advantage of me?"

"I think you're hoping I will."

"Maybe." She closed the distance between them with a kiss, melting as Robbie moved against her. "Please."

"Please take advantage of you?" Robbie pulled her through the doorway into the bedroom. "Don't mind if I do."

Robbie swung the door closed behind them and then pushed her against the wall with a hard kiss. As Robbie deepened the kiss, she undid the zipper she'd pulled up only ten minutes ago. The cock sprang up and she stroked it, pushing the base against Robbie and loving how Robbie moaned in response.

After a few more strokes, and more kisses, she said, "I can't wait to feel you inside me." She felt brazen saying the words aloud and even more so with the look Robbie gave her. Pure desire.

Robbie kissed her all the way to the bed, undoing the buttons running down the front of her dress. The fabric fell open and Robbie lifted it off her shoulders before taking them down to the bed.

Robbie hooked Devyn's underwear and pulled it off, then caught her gaze and said, "I don't feel like I did enough to deserve this reward." Robbie's hands moved up her legs. "You were the one stuck with the dragon. And the rest of the yacht club."

"I almost told her about you," Devyn admitted. She'd wanted to tell her mom that Robbie was her girlfriend partly because of how rude her mom had been. But she knew there was more to it. "I wanted to tell her. But I lost my nerve."

Robbie leaned over her, one hand on either side of her shoulders. "You know you don't have to tell anyone. I can be your secret."

"I don't want you to be a secret." Devyn felt her heart race as she admitted the truth.

"What do you want me to be?" Robbie grinned, and Devyn wondered if the almost flippant attitude was a cover.

She held Robbie's gaze for a long moment before saying, "I want you to be exactly who you are. I want..." She wanted Robbie to be her girlfriend, but she stopped herself from saying the words. She didn't know how they could go forward. Or if they should.

"What do you want?" Robbie reached down and angled the cock toward Devyn's slit.

Devyn licked her lips. *Fuck.* She was so ready for Robbie. "Lots of things."

Robbie leaned closer to her, brushing her lips against her neck. "What's one thing?"

She pushed up and reached between Robbie's legs to feel the strap. Robbie subtly shifted her hips forward at the touch.

"Are you going to tell me?"

She didn't answer, only running a light fingertip down the shaft to the sculpted tip. She liked the length and the weight and loved how it fit Robbie perfectly. The soft tan color was a close match to Robbie's skin. The width was bigger than the dildos she'd used on her own but that didn't change how much she wanted it. "I want this."

"Lie back down," Robbie said, her voice low and commanding.

She didn't often like following orders, but this time she wanted to comply. Especially when Robbie pushed her knees apart. "Let me know the next time you need to be rescued."

Tremors raced through Devyn when Robbie touched her. She moaned as Robbie's fingers slipped through her folds, shifting her knees farther apart as Robbie moved between her legs.

She shivered when Robbie licked her clit. Not because she was cold but because every nerve was on notice. It hadn't taken long for her to be comfortable with Robbie going down on her. Everything Robbie did felt unbelievably good, but she knew it was more than that. She trusted Robbie and knew Robbie liked what she was doing.

When Robbie circled her clit and sucked, she nearly forgot about what she'd wanted to race home for. Nearly. She felt the start of an orgasm build, but before she could say she didn't want to come without Robbie inside her, Robbie pulled away.

Breathless, she looked up and watched Robbie adjust the cock. "You were right. You're nice and wet for me."

Robbie moved on top of her again and she felt the tip of the cock nudge her opening. "We can do this slow or fast. I like it both ways." Robbie shifted and the head pushed inside.

She gasped and reached for Robbie's hips, needing something to hold on to.

"Slow or fast?" Robbie held in place, waiting on her answer.

She had to will her mind to form words, her thoughts focused on how much she wanted Robbie all the way inside. "Slow."

"Nice and slow." Robbie moved the shaft an inch deeper and kissed her.

She felt her center spasm. "More."

"All of it?"

She nodded, knowing it would hurt. Wanting the pleasure of that pain. Robbie pulled back a bit, then readjusted and sank inside her. She gasped again and tightened her grip on Robbie's hips. As much as she'd thought she'd been ready for full penetration, she wasn't. The cock was thick and her body wouldn't relax.

"Too much?"

She forced herself to breathe and then shook her head. It only hurt a little and she wanted it. More than Robbie could know.

"You sure?"

She jutted her hips against Robbie's in answer. Robbie pulled back and thrust again. She didn't resist a long, low moan when Robbie moved deeper inside her. Robbie set a slow pace as promised. An almost hypnotic slow rhythm. With each stroke, the full length of the shaft filled her.

She was pinned to the bed under Robbie's weight but didn't want to be anywhere else. All she could do was move with Robbie. And it was all she wanted. When she felt the earlier hint of an orgasm build again, she managed to say, "Faster."

Robbie responded with a kiss. "I was hoping you'd say that."

Robbie's own desires seemed to take over then. She thrust in and out, faster and harder. Sweat covered them both. Devyn was panting and shaking, delirious with satisfaction when Robbie said, "I want to come inside you."

She managed to nod and Robbie held her index finger to her lips. She licked Robbie's finger and then shuddered as Robbie swiped it over her clit. Robbie kept the finger on her clit, and then pumped the cock. Their hips smashed together with every thrust and her clit took everything Robbie gave.

"Don't stop."

"Not until you come," Robbie promised. "But I can't wait for you."

She hadn't realized Robbie was close, but she felt it now, felt the climax coming. "Use me."

Robbie thrust again and her orgasm hit. The climax caught and held them both, destroying Devyn's ability to think or to resist. Then in the next breath, Robbie stroked her clit hard and her own orgasm rolled through her. Robbie knew exactly what she needed. Knew exactly the right spot. She couldn't do anything but give herself over.

Aftershocks followed, then a stillness disrupted only by their heavy breathing. They lay together for several minutes, Robbie deep inside her, pleasuring her simply by not pulling out. She relaxed completely then, satisfied in a way she'd never fully been, and soundless tears slipped down her cheeks.

"Want me to pull out?"

"Not yet." She swiped away the tears, grateful for the darkened room that kept Robbie from seeing her emotion. *Only sex.* That was laughable now.

Robbie kissed her cheek. "Was I too rough?"

She rocked her head side to side. "Not too rough." She sighed into the curve of Robbie's neck. "I love this." It wasn't what she wanted to say, but it was close. "When you're on me like this. Inside me."

"I love it too," Robbie said.

"I don't want you to pull out." Her body was still clenched on Robbie, but it wasn't only that. She wanted to hold on to everything about the moment.

"I promise you can have more later." Robbie kissed her again. Light kisses. "But you'll be sore if I don't pull out soon."

She knew she'd be sore anyway. The best kind of sore. She tried to relax as Robbie pulled out but her body spasmed. When she shuddered, Robbie pressed a hand over her, gently soothing the need that quivered through her.

"I want more."

Robbie laughed softly. "Give me a minute."

Her body had been satisfied. It was everything she wasn't admitting that made her reach for Robbie again. "You're still hard."

"Always. It's kind of how it works."

"Wait. Should I not have said that?" She felt her cheeks heat with an immediate blush.

Robbie pushed up and met her gaze. "You're good. Don't worry."

"I don't want to say the wrong thing. I feel like I'm still clueless about…all of this."

"You don't need to stress about what you say with me. And, this"—Robbie reached down to stroke the cock—"is always ready for you. One of the perks of a strap-on."

"It's a good perk."

"You really want more?"

"I really do," she said. "I don't know what I'm going to do when you leave." She'd meant the words as light banter, but she heard the catch in her voice and knew Robbie had heard it too.

"Let's not worry about that part yet." Robbie shifted and the cock nudged Devyn's opening. "Let's just enjoy each other."

She closed her eyes, realizing that was all they could do. Enjoy each other. Nothing had changed. Robbie's life was in Seattle and hers was here. In San Diego. And the divorce still wasn't finalized. She had no business falling in love. But she couldn't help it. She wished away feelings she could do nothing about and willed her body to relax as Robbie eased inside.

CHAPTER TWENTY-THREE

A wet nose woke Robbie from a deep sleep. Angel nudged her elbow a second time before she rolled over and rubbed her eyes. With the door cracked there was some light in the room. Enough, at least, to make it clear Angel had to pee. Robbie glanced at Devyn, still soundly sleeping, and pushed herself out of bed.

"You know you could have woken Devyn instead of me," Robbie whispered as she stepped out of the room. Part of her was happy Angel had picked her—Devyn needed the sleep more than she did—but she still grumped about the hour as they passed the clock in the kitchen. A quarter after five.

Devyn's blackout curtains always made it hard to tell the time, but without the clock Robbie wouldn't have been able to tell the hour even outside. A dense fog had settled over everything and the sun had yet to rise. She hugged herself, shivering in the cool air. After Devyn had fallen asleep, she'd gotten up to use the bathroom and put on her T-shirt before going back to Devyn's bed. She'd considered going to the cottage then, but the temptation to snuggle with Devyn had been too strong. Now, though, she led

Angel back to the cottage and gave him a small handful of kibble before heading for the shower.

She was sore from all the sex but guessed Devyn would be even more so. After several rounds with the strap-on, they'd shared a nap, woke to have dinner, and walked to the beach. They'd enjoyed a gorgeous sunset and gone back to Devyn's bed for more sex. Sometime after midnight they'd finished, sated and exhausted.

Robbie braced one hand against the tiled wall, letting the water pelt her head and trickle down her neck and chest. She couldn't remember ever having so much sex in one day. And still her body craved more. She didn't move to touch herself, though. What she wanted was more of Devyn. Not more of a simple thing like an orgasm any vibrator could give.

"I want more of what I won't have after next week."

One more week. That's all she'd get. Then what? Would they simply part ways and never see each other again? Or maybe there would be texts and emails for a while before those dwindled away to a memory of something they'd shared. Something amazing and unexpected but something that wasn't meant to last.

She sagged against the tiles, wishing she could have held on to the euphoria from last night and not have the longing for more lessen what had been a perfect thing. Devyn was a perfect thing.

In her arms, Devyn was supple and soft and strong all at once. Last night Robbie had questioned if she had any right to hold someone so beautiful. To be gifted something so perfect. And maybe she didn't have the right. But Devyn had given herself freely over and over. Devyn's craving kept pace with her own. Last night they'd needed each other's breath. Each other's sweat. And each other's cum.

She finished in the shower and got dressed. Angel had made himself comfortable on her bed. He had a plush dog bed in Devyn's room, but in the cottage he'd simply claimed her bed as his. She sank down next to him and patted his head. "What am I going to do when I leave you and Devyn next week? Should I get my own dog?"

Angel jerked his head up at the question, seeming to almost glare at her. She smiled. "Okay, it's too soon to talk about that." She chuckled as he pushed her hand for more pets. "But I do have to leave. This isn't my world. I've got my uncle to take care of, and my houseboat."

She reminded herself she had a life in Seattle beyond the obligations she'd abruptly abandoned. She had friends, habits, and things she loved about Seattle.

It'd been three weeks since she'd been in touch with anyone aside from her uncle and Matt. The friends she talked to every day knew where she'd gone—after telling Uncle Bruce about the opportunity she'd ran it past her two closest friends before making the spur-of-the-moment decision to come to San Diego. Barb, who lived two slips over and was a close friend despite a thirty-year age difference, had shouted "Oh my God! Go!" Stacy, who was an ex-girlfriend but two exes ago, which qualified her as a friend, had a similar response.

She grinned now, remembering the conversation. She'd told Stacy about Matt and the house swap idea and Stacy had simply said, "Of course you're going. I hate that I'm not going with you. Screw you."

Stacy never pulled any punches or said anything she didn't mean. Which had been a problem when they'd dated but was a bonus for a friendship. She hadn't thought they could be friends after their breakup, but Stacy had convinced her. Partly it was Stacy's two degrees of separation rule: "If you've dated two other people since you've broken up, your ex can now be your friend. Or your therapist. Because who else knows all your issues and will hold you accountable?"

She'd laughed then because it was a ridiculous rule, but like all things Stacy said, it panned out. She wondered now what Stacy would say about her falling for Devyn.

It was early, but Stacy woke up stupidly early and Robbie decided to call her and check in. She wasn't ready to tell Stacy everything about the situation with Devyn, but she could definitely use some advice.

After a minute hunting for her phone, she realized it was in the back pocket of the pants still in Devyn's room and decided to send a text from her computer instead. As soon as she opened her laptop, a string of text messages she'd missed from last night popped on her screen. In one glance, Stacy was gone from her mind.

* * *

Robbie straightened at the sound of the cottage door opening. She looked up from her laptop to Devyn's face. Devyn's hair was wet like she'd stepped out of the shower minutes ago, but she otherwise seemed ready to leave in her business-casual attire, purse swung over her shoulder and travel mug in hand.

"I kind of hoped I'd wake with you still in my room." Devyn glanced at Angel, who'd come up to her, tail wagging. "You, too, mister."

Angel wagged his tail faster and Devyn set her travel mug on the windowsill before leaning down to pet him.

"Angel got me up to pee. I think we forgot to let him out last night."

Devyn made a cringing expression before cooing to Angel, "I'm sorry, sweetie. I can't remember the last time I've slept that deeply. Good thing you have Robbie."

"I have to tell you something." Robbie stood, then exhaled.

Devyn's demeanor immediately changed. Gone was the happy relaxed look she'd come into the cottage with. Now she seemed to be bracing for impact. "What's wrong?"

"I have to go back to Seattle."

Devyn's brow creased but her voice was level when she asked, "When?"

"Today. You said you've taken Angel to a boarding facility before for day care. I can drop him off on my way if you've got a long shift."

"Did you change your plans because of something to do with us?"

Robbie shook her head as tears came to her eyes. She blinked them back, looked up at the ceiling, and swallowed. She did not want to break down. Not now. "My uncle went to the hospital last night. I've been texting back and forth with Matt. The doctors say he had a stroke."

"Oh, shit, Robbie."

"There was a storm, and he went out to salt the dock. It can get really icy. It's my job but I wasn't there. And I forgot to put it on Matt's to-do list. Uncle Bruce slipped and..." The lump in her throat got too big to push past. A moment later, Devyn's arms were around her. She clenched her jaw, fighting back tears again. "I don't know how long it was before Matt found him."

"He's at the hospital. I'm sure they've got good people taking care of him."

Robbie nodded but didn't say what was on her mind. What if it was too late? What if he'd been out in the storm for too long?

"Have you booked a flight?"

She took a shaky breath. "Direct to Seattle. Leaves at eleven."

Devyn seemed to be about to say something but then only nodded. She lightly swiped her thumb across Robbie's cheek, carrying away tears, and then kissed the same place. "You need to take care of your uncle."

"He's my family. I don't speak to my dad and you know my mom's gone. It's just been him and me for a long time."

"I get it." Devyn took a deep breath. She held Robbie's gaze and then closed the distance between them with a kiss.

Robbie didn't realize how much she needed the kiss and needed Devyn's comfort. She wished she could hold on to it, but Devyn pulled away and she had to open her eyes. When she did, her heart sank. What if this was goodbye?

"Don't worry about Angel. I'll take him to day care and they can board him overnight if my shift runs late. You have enough to worry about."

"Are you sure?"

She tipped her head. "I can do some things on my own."

She doubted Devyn meant the words to be brusque. Devyn seemed to be trying to keep her feelings out of the picture, which made sense but still hurt. Robbie took a steadying breath, wishing she could ignore the premonition that things would be over once she got on the plane. "I feel bad leaving so many things undone. I never got the painting finished and the hot tub still isn't fixed."

"Don't apologize for anything. I can hire people for what isn't finished."

Outsourcing. It's what Devyn and Matt should have done in the first place. Then she'd gotten involved and now she wanted to keep the job. But she couldn't.

"Hey." Devyn touched her shoulder. "Things here are going to be okay. I do change of plans and emergencies better than most."

She smiled wryly. "I want you to call me. Or at least send a text. I want to know as soon as you get to Seattle."

"Okay." Robbie looked from Devyn to the room that had been home and office in one for the past three weeks. "I'll clean up here before I leave."

Devyn shook her head. "You've only got a few hours before you need to be at the airport. And Matt's not great with medical stuff. Call the hospital and find out what you can about your uncle directly from the nurses on duty. Even better if you can talk to a doctor." She seemed to notice Robbie's hesitation and added, "It happens all the time that next of kin has to fly in from somewhere else and we're used to having the same conversation twice. But with something like this, timing is important. You need to know what's going on. Let me take care of everything here. You focus on what's important."

What was important? Her uncle's health was the most important thing at the moment, of course. A month ago she'd have said he was the most important person in her life. He was still her only family and she loved him dearly. None of that had changed. But what she had with Devyn was important too. She wanted to admit that but worried Devyn might remind her of their agreement.

Devyn clasped her hand. "There's probably a million things running through your mind right now, but sometimes a stroke is mild. If he got treatment quickly, there's a good chance he'll be okay."

She nodded numbly. "You're right. But he's got diabetes and a heart issue." She squeezed her eyes closed. "I know you have to go."

"I do." Devyn looked between her and Angel, her shoulders dropping. "I'm going to be sending your uncle all the good energy and believing this is a mild stroke until we know otherwise." She seemed to wait for Robbie to respond and when she didn't, said, "We'll talk later."

Robbie nodded and Devyn kissed her again. The press of Devyn's lips, the scent of her shampoo, the heat of their bodies, and the essence that was uniquely Devyn weren't things she could hold. But she wanted to.

She pulled back and exhaled slowly, an ache filling her chest. This was goodbye. Devyn had softened it with a phrase anyone would say without thought. *We'll talk later.*

"Bye," she said, pushing the word against a new lump in her throat. She dropped to one knee, called Angel over, and kissed the head she'd gotten so used to having under her hand. He seemed mildly annoyed at all the fuss but licked her chin anyway. "I'll miss you," she murmured.

When she straightened, Devyn was already reaching for the door. "Text me when you get to Seattle."

Robbie nodded and Devyn called for Angel. She watched the two of them leave and didn't look away until they were gone. Gone from the cottage and gone from view, disappearing into the garage to take Devyn's car to the boarding facility and then to work. Robbie dropped onto the bed.

She had a little over two hours to clear her things out of the cottage, check the main house for anything she'd left there, take the rental car back, and check in for the flight to Seattle. Then she'd have three hours on the flight to do nothing but think.

CHAPTER TWENTY-FOUR

Devyn schooled her features as Elena came down the hall toward her. Given the number of times she'd poured her heart out to her best friend and been consoled, she knew she didn't have to hide anything. But what had happened with Robbie—or not happened—was still too fresh a wound for Elena's bandaging.

"Hey, lady," Elena said, flashing a smile. "Are you done for the day?" At Devyn's nod, Elena brightened. "Me too! Let me grab my things and we can walk out together. I can't believe we're leaving this early on a Friday." She laughed, then added, "I guess I shouldn't say that until we're out the door."

"You are tempting fate."

Elena lifted a hand. "I'm not superstitious. I called Mari and told her I'd be home for dinner. She said I shouldn't make promises until I'm in my car, but she's making her grandmother's sopa de mariscos and nothing's holding me back."

It took a few minutes for Elena to gather her things and then they headed out together. "You're quiet tonight," Elena said. "Everything okay?"

"Long day."

"We're still leaving before eight."

Every hour of the day had seemed to drag, though, and her free moments were spent checking her phone. She hated how many times she'd checked for a message only to be disappointed.

They stepped through the double doors and Elena gave an exaggerated exhale, followed by a shoulder shimmy. "I love leaving work while the sun's still shining."

The sun was indeed shining, although low in the sky, and Devyn wanted to enjoy the moment at least for Elena's sake. She forced a smile as she took in the view. The streaks of clouds to the west had taken on light shades of pink and orange. In a half hour, at the water's edge, she knew the sight would be breathtaking. But the last sunset walk she'd taken with Angel had left her feeling painfully lonely. Before Robbie, she'd had moments of loneliness but nothing like the weight she couldn't seem to get out from under now.

"Are we still on for tomorrow?"

"Tomorrow?" Devyn stopped walking. "Oh my God. Sailing."

Elena laughed. "How much fun have you been having with Robbie? You never forget plans." When Devyn didn't respond, Elena turned to her. "Does *oh my God* mean we need to reschedule?"

"No. Well…" Devyn took a deep breath. "Robbie had to go back to Seattle. Her uncle had a stroke."

"Oh, no. How is he doing?"

"He's still in the hospital but that's basically all I know."

Elena studied her. "I'm sorry. I completely missed how worried you were."

"Mostly I'm worried about Robbie. She's so close to her uncle. He's her only family. And I wish I knew more of what was going on, but Robbie's shared almost nothing. I hate being completely out of the loop—then I feel ridiculous for thinking I have any right to be in the loop."

Elena pressed her lips together.

"Since Robbie's gone back to Seattle there's only been three texts. Literally."

"I know you're worried but she's probably just focused on her uncle."

"And I want her to be focused on him. But this is a medical thing—and she's told me hospitals and medical stuff freak her out. So why isn't she talking to me?"

"Maybe she's overwhelmed?"

It was a reasonable explanation and exactly why Devyn had tried to give Robbie space. "I keep thinking that the one time we hear from distant relatives, exes, anyone, is when someone is in the hospital."

"True." Elena made a cringey face. "And we get asked to be a remote second opinion."

"I know that's not fun, or easy, but I expected it. I thought she'd want to talk to me about what was going on." Tears welled in her eyes, but she clenched her jaw, keeping them at bay. "I want to know how she's doing, but we aren't in a relationship. We're not... anything."

She hadn't told Elena everything that had happened, but she'd admitted enough—including how happy she was with Robbie. Now Elena's look of sympathy made her wish she'd kept that to herself. Sympathy made it harder to pretend her heart hadn't gotten involved. "Anyway. I'm sorry, but I don't think I'm up for sailing." She started walking again but Elena caught her arm.

"You're not getting out of this conversation that easily. Where's Angel?"

"At doggie day care."

"Go get him. The two of you are coming over for dinner." When Devyn started to argue, Elena held up her hand. "I know the look on your face. I've seen it before. We are going to open a bottle of wine and talk and Mari is going to feed us an amazing dinner. End of discussion."

She sighed. "You're such a surgeon sometimes." Arguing was pointless and she knew it. "But, also, thank you. Dinner with you and Mari is probably what I need."

"Of course it is. I know what I'm doing." Elena opened her arms and Devyn stepped into her embrace. The hug almost pushed her emotions to the brink, and she broke away before the tears came.

Angel didn't leap into her arms like he did when he saw Robbie. She'd taught him not to jump but he also had never tried the move. Still, he was excited to see her, hopping up and down on his front feet and howling for good measure. He didn't mind going to day care, which helped make it easier on her emotions having no other option, but he loved leaving. She didn't try to tamp down his excitement as they headed to the car.

Devyn checked her phone after snapping her seat belt. The checking and hoping for a text had become too much of a habit. She knew that and yet she couldn't bring herself to break the habit. Five days had gone by and she'd reread the three texts Robbie had sent too many times. The first simply said: *Landed.*

She'd given Robbie grace, and space, when the next text said: *The doc says it was a mild stroke but Uncle Bruce looks terrible. I need to focus on getting him better and not on how much I hate hospitals.*

She'd expected more news to follow. Like she'd told Elena, she'd expected Robbie to want to talk to her about what was going on. She'd hoped for updates as well as some peek into Robbie's world in Seattle. And she'd desperately wanted some sign that what they had wasn't over. Blown out as easy as a candle.

Mari opened the door in an apron. She took one look at Devyn and pulled her into a hug. "Elena told me."

Devyn returned the embrace but let go before the tears escaped. She rubbed at her eyes and said, "Thanks for having us over last minute. Angel got excited as soon as I turned down your block. I hope I'm not—"

"Stop," Mari said, waving off her words. "You know I always cook for a family of six. And I would have made Elena drive over to get you if you hadn't come on your own." She crossed her arms, studying Devyn. "Why didn't you call?"

"There wasn't much to say."

"You and I both know that isn't true."

"Are you two coming?" Elena's voice came from somewhere in the house. "Mari, I'm not sure how long you wanted to keep this bread in the oven."

Mari sighed. "The woman does complicated surgeries all day, but put her in front of an oven and she folds under pressure."

Devyn felt a smile lift her lips. She needed her friends tonight. "Elena's never been much of a cook."

"I can hear you two, you know?" Elena called. "How brown should this bread get?"

Mari motioned Devyn to follow, calling to Elena that the dinner rescue crew was on its way. Angel felt nearly as comfortable at Mari and Elena's as he did at Devyn's. Fortunately, he didn't feel comfortable enough to bark at the cats who were the kings of the house. Both cats appeared as they entered the kitchen, and each issued a hiss in response to the sight of a dog. Angel took the advice to heart and wagged his tail between his legs.

"Look who's feeling meek all of a sudden," Mari said, looking at Angel but swinging her hip to bump Elena's as she moved her away from the oven.

"These are the only two cats Angel won't bark at," Devyn said. "He knows he's in the presence of royalty—who will kick his ass."

Elena, who'd handed off the oven mitt she'd put on, pointed at Angel. "We know when to bow down, don't we, buddy?"

"Bow down?" Mari scoffed. "You know when to call for help."

"That too." Elena laughed easily. "Dev, red or white?"

"Whatever's open."

"Chardonnay. Because there's fish in the soup and Mari insists we have to drink white wine with fish." Elena raised the open bottle, waited for Devyn's nod, and then poured her a glass. "Sit. Talk."

"Or the interrogation will begin," Mari added jokingly.

Elena joined Devyn at the table, arguing there wouldn't be any interrogation. Devyn believed Mari more than Elena in this case and said as much. She wanted to open up and talk. She wanted to admit to the feelings she'd been holding in for the past few weeks. But she couldn't think of where to begin.

"Do you think Angel misses Robbie?" Mari asked, spooning the soup into three bowls. "You said he really took to her."

She glanced at Angel. "I don't know. He's gone to scratch at the cottage door a few times, but I don't know what he's thinking. I know I miss her." Emotion hit like a sleeper wave. She clenched her jaw and set down her wineglass. "I can't believe I let myself fall in love. It was stupid in so many ways."

"What ways?" Elena asked gently.

Devyn looked up at the ceiling. "I told myself I didn't want to date anyone after Matt. I didn't want another relationship that I didn't have the time for. You know what our job is like. I don't want to let someone else down when I can't meet their expectations." She took a deep breath. "And the divorce isn't even finalized until we sell the house. I didn't plan on this. A month ago, I would have sworn I didn't want anything like this. It just…happened."

"So you think it's stupid you fell in love without planning on it." Elena nodded. "What else?"

The way Elena rephrased her words made her realize how ridiculous it was to give her heart a hard time. Who planned on falling in love? She'd tried to love Matt and it had never happened. "She lives in Seattle. Not once did she give me any hint that she wanted to move here."

"And you'd never do a long-distance relationship?" Mari asked, setting a bowl of steaming soup in front of Devyn and another in front of Elena. "Wait for the bread."

Elena pulled back her hands and Devyn said, "It's funny you think you're in charge."

"I am in charge."

"In the bedroom." Mari arched an eyebrow as she set the bread basket in the middle of the table. She playfully scooted it out of Elena's reach, offering it to Devyn when Elena tried to get a piece. "Guests first."

"Devyn's not a guest," Elena argued. "She's family."

"True. And I'm in charge in the kitchen."

Elena dropped her chin in acquiescence.

"But you're cute." Mari handed Elena a hunk of a baguette and kissed her. "And if you play your cards right, I might let you pretend to be in charge later and do the dishes."

Devyn smiled at Elena's mock gasp. She knew her friends had their ups and downs, but she admired the relationship they'd built. She admired it, and she wished she had something like it.

"Devyn," Mari said, motioning to her with the remainder of the baguette. "You didn't answer the long-distance question."

"I've thought about it. I'd consider long distance but not without some chance for a future that wasn't long distance." Before Robbie's abrupt departure, she'd given it plenty of thought. The problem was, she knew long-distance wouldn't work for more than a short period. She could only imagine doing it if she knew that at some point they'd live in the same place. And call the same spot home.

"You both know I can't get away for a weekend the way some people can. Robbie could, but I wouldn't want to ask her to be the one always traveling to see me. And, honestly, I want someone I can come home to. The past month has made me realize that more than ever."

Life with Matt had been a roommate situation for so long she hadn't realized how nice it was coming home to someone she wanted to see. The realization that she liked regular intimacy came as even more of a surprise. She'd never thought she'd crave more than hugs and occasional kisses. With Robbie, she'd craved sex and thought of it more than she had at any other point in her life.

"I couldn't do long distance either," Elena said.

Mari sat down with the last bowl of soup. "It works for some couples." She reached for her spoon. "So we've decided it was stupid to fall in love because you didn't plan it, aren't sure you want a relationship, and because she doesn't live here. Is that it?"

"That feels like enough."

"Maybe it is," Elena conceded. "If neither of you can move and you don't want long-distance forever…"

Devyn felt a heaviness settle over her. Having her friends confirm everything she'd wrestled with over the last week made her feel more hopeless than ever.

Mari gestured to the food, saying, "Bon appétit."

Elena took a bite of the soup, complimented Mari, and then turned back to Devyn. "Did you ask her if she'd ever move here?"

"They were only together for three weeks," Mari chided. "You can't ask someone that after only three weeks. Dev, try the soup."

Devyn didn't have an appetite now, but she picked up her spoon. The soup scalded her tongue and she instantly thought of the night Robbie had made her tea. Robbie's words repeated in her mind: *If it's hot enough, you'll burn your tongue and you won't think of anything else.*

"You okay?" Elena touched her arm.

"I will be." She forced herself to take another bite, careful to blow on it first. "This is delicious, Mari."

"My abuela's recipe." Mari tasted hers and murmured her approval. "She would tell me I added too much spice, but I love the kick the cayenne adds."

Devyn wondered what Robbie would say about the soup. They'd had more than a few conversations about the food Robbie made and the unique ingredients she'd add to typical meals, making them feel entirely new. Like green salsa mixed in tuna salad. And molasses in whipped cream.

"I'm not saying it would be wrong to ask Robbie if she'd move here," Mari said. "But I think it's early. You two would need to figure out a lot of other things first, I'm sure."

Devyn nodded. "And I've hardly heard from her since she went back to Seattle. I know she's helping her uncle, so I don't want to bother her, but the reality is she's gone back to her life." Her stomach tightened and she set down her spoon. "I think whatever we had is over. My life is here, and even if she wanted to, I don't think Robbie would ever leave Seattle."

Mari and Elena looked at each other. Something passed between them and Devyn wondered if they agreed with her assessment. She stopped herself from asking. She didn't want confirmation.

"Maybe a relationship with Robbie can't work, but you could give someone else a chance," Elena suggested. "You've been so happy this past month. Happier than I've seen you in a long time."

Mari nodded her agreement. "Would you consider something with another woman?"

That was hard to answer. Her heart was stuck on Robbie and she didn't want to think of anyone else. "I don't feel ready to think about that yet. I didn't even want Robbie."

"And look how well that turned out."

Devyn narrowed her eyes at Elena. "I wouldn't say it turned out well."

"I meant you had fun. You let loose and enjoyed yourself. It was pretty incredible to watch from the outside. Even if it hurts now, I think you'd say it was worth it." Elena continued, "What if the next step is looking for something more serious? Maybe Robbie was your rebound and the next step is a real relationship."

She felt a lump in her throat. She couldn't think of Robbie as a rebound. The word alone tore apart what they'd shared.

What she'd had in three weeks with Robbie was more than what she'd had in six years with Matt. And she'd had plenty of time to get over things not working out with Matt on her own. She hadn't needed a rebound.

She thought of suturing Robbie's hand and then trusting her to take care of everything at the ER with Angel. She thought of the tiling project they'd done together and how much she'd enjoyed the work because she was with Robbie. Then she thought of the moment she'd realized she was in love as they'd paddleboarded around the bay. Even without the best-ever sex, she couldn't call Robbie a rebound. But that didn't change the reality that there seemed to be no future together.

"Do you have other parameters for a relationship beyond the no-long-distance part?" Mari asked.

"Watch out. She'll have you set up with someone in no time," Elena joked.

"Well, now that we know she likes butch women," Mari said, "I happen to know someone who's single and moving back to San Diego."

"Who?" Elena asked.

"Lou." Mari turned back to Devyn and added, "My old college roommate. I've told you about her. The lawyer?"

Devyn vaguely remembered Mari mentioning her lawyer friend.

"She's a bit of a player but I know she's ready to settle down."

"A bit of a player?" Elena raised an eyebrow. "I don't know about setting Devyn up with Lou. Do I have veto rights?"

Mari ignored Elena's question. "Lou used to live in San Diego but she moved to San Francisco when she fell for this woman she shouldn't have looked at twice. There were so many red flags." Mari looked to Elena for backup. "Then the woman cheated on her. It was a whole thing."

"Lou makes everything a whole thing," Elena said. "She's a lot of drama, Mari."

"That was the old Lou. She's matured." Mari pointedly looked at Devyn when she added, "Anyway, she's in town this weekend checking out rentals. You two would be perfect together." She waited for Devyn to show some interest. "I could see if she wanted to have dinner with us. Double date?"

She didn't want to think about anyone besides Robbie—even if it wasn't healthy pining for someone who didn't return her messages and who couldn't ever be in her world.

"What if it's not a date?" Elena asked. "We could all go sailing. If Lou's in town this weekend the weather is supposed to be perfect tomorrow." To Devyn she added, "Lou and Mari used to sail together in college."

"I thought you were the one who didn't want to set me up with this person."

"It'd only be sailing," Mari said, latching on to the idea. She leaned close and kissed Elena's cheek. "You always have the best ideas. What do you think, Devyn?"

"I want to stay home and mope with Angel." Pathetic, but true.

Elena set her hand on Devyn's. "You know moping won't help. At least sailing might get you out of your head for a while."

"It'll be nice out on the water," Mari added.

Maybe she did need to get out of her head for a while. "I'll think about it."

CHAPTER TWENTY-FIVE

Robbie finished adding the last of her uncle's pills to the container and snapped the lid closed. "One week of meds. Look how easy this is going to be."

Uncle Bruce didn't make eye contact. He shifted back in the recliner and studied the scene out the window. *Rain.* Again.

"You happy to be home?" She'd tried engaging him for the past hour, but her questions were met with one-word answers or, as he demonstrated now, an unconvincing nod. The speech therapist who'd checked on him the day after the stroke had happily reported no problems, saying he was lucky to have fared so well. She was the one, though, who had mentioned depression often followed a stroke event. Robbie knew she was seeing the signs. Uncle Bruce had always been moody but nothing like now. Fortunately, one of the meds in his mix was an antidepressant. Hopefully it would kick in soon.

"I know you're not happy they've got you restricted to the house, but another fall—"

"I know. I don't need to hear it again."

"Wow. That's more words than you've said all day, Mr. Price. Progress." She hoped the sarcasm would at least get an eye roll, but his gaze didn't leave the window. She never called him anything except Bruce or Uncle Bruce—though they both knew *Dad* would have been a more apt title.

She cleared her throat. "I'm all set to sleep in my old room. Cleared out some of the things you'd wanted to send to Goodwill. Cleaned up your room, too. Hope you don't mind sleeping in fresh sheets."

When he didn't respond, she stood and stretched, setting the pill organizer on the kitchen table next to the alarm she'd preprogrammed. Twice a day an alarm would signal for him to take his medications and she would be there making sure all went according to plan.

Even if he wouldn't admit it, she knew he was happy to be out of the hospital at least. She was happy too. In the past five days, she'd lived through all the reasons for her anxiety about hospitals, including misdiagnoses and medication errors. She knew mistakes happened, but it'd been one worry after another feeding a constant underlying layer of anxiety. The what-ifs had kept her in a sleepless daze. But now he was home. And, in the end, the doctors had given him a good prognosis—albeit with restrictions.

The stroke had been mild, but when he'd fallen he'd injured his leg. One doctor had been concerned he couldn't bear weight on the leg because of something to do with his diabetes. Another thought he might have a tumor. Two days in the hospital and two MRIs later, consensus was he needed a total knee replacement. He'd managed to tear all the ligaments in his knee, but surgery couldn't happen right after a stroke. The list of reasons why included death. She'd stopped listening when they'd said that.

After it was decided he wouldn't have surgery but would be sent home with a walker, she'd gone to his house to gather a few of his things and measured to make sure he could get around the tight corners of the space with a walker. Matt was still living in her house, and they'd agreed he would stay the remainder of the month as originally planned. She'd checked in on him, avoiding any topic that might bring up Devyn, and then headed back to the hospital.

In the few hours she was gone from the hospital, Uncle Bruce had gotten out of bed and fallen again. It wasn't another stroke, but he managed to hit his head. That meant another MRI.

The next few days were a blur. All the tests and exams took an emotional toll on him. It took a toll on her, too, though she couldn't admit it. Then on day five he was standing—with assistance—and could mostly use the walker he detested. The neurologist had determined he hadn't suffered any significant damage after the second fall but said, "Use the walker or you'll be back to see me when you fall again, and I know you aren't a fan."

The neurologist's dry humor reminded Robbie of Devyn. But lots of things reminded her of Devyn. She'd gone between desperately wanting to call her to wanting to push away all memories of San Diego. After the news that Uncle Bruce was being discharged with the plan for surgery on the knee in six months, she felt like her fate was sealed. He didn't have to go to a rehab facility as long as he used the walker and had supervision.

Supervision had been the word that hadn't sat well with Uncle Bruce. Supervision also meant no chance she was going back to San Diego.

"It's not so bad living with someone else, you know. I got used to it with a woman who hated my guts." Robbie sat down on the sofa opposite the recliner. "She kind of liked me by the end of it. It was probably only my cooking."

He looked away from the window finally. "First time you've mentioned her. I was wondering when you'd decide to talk."

"We've been talking."

"About nothing important."

The medications and the diagnoses as well as the future care plan were all important, but Uncle Bruce wanted nothing to do with any of it. Which meant all decisions fell to her. She'd longed to call Devyn simply to discuss the plan and the recommendations, but she didn't want Devyn to think she was using her simply for medical advice. When she was ready to talk to Devyn, she wanted to do so without any other motive. The problem with that plan, though, was she didn't know what to say. Did Devyn want a real relationship? She desperately wanted one, but for anything to work it'd have to be long distance and she had no idea if Devyn would be interested in that. Was what they'd had together important enough to Devyn for her to want more than sex? She worried the answer was no.

"You miss her. I can tell." He could read her like no one else.

"I was getting too attached." She shrugged, trying to act nonchalant. "Better to cut ties early, you know?"

"No."

"No?" She squinted at him. "Meaning you think I would have been better off staying another week and getting more attached? Or worse, pouring out my heart to her?" She shook her head. "We had a talk after we first slept together. She set the boundary lines. She didn't want a relationship. Only sex."

"Then why would it have been a problem if you'd stayed longer?"

"If I stayed another week, I would have crossed the lines we agreed on."

"What lines?"

She blew out a breath. "I fell in love. I was too close to telling her. It's better I left before that happened."

He nodded slowly. "Guess that makes sense if you didn't want her to know you were in love."

"I didn't want to be in love." And she'd tried fighting it. "It's better I left. To be one hundred percent honest, I'd rather it not have been because you decided to have a stroke. But you like risking your life to save mine." She winked.

"That wasn't saving your life."

"Saving me from heartbreak, then." Her heart ached more with every passing day, however, and she wasn't sure he'd saved her fully from that fate. She longed to hear Devyn's voice. Longed to wrap her arms around Devyn. Longed to simply be within five feet of Devyn. She hadn't anticipated how much she'd miss her nor how gutted she'd feel. She tried blocking a swell of emotion and said, "A relationship wasn't going to happen. Not the type of relationship I want, anyway."

"Why not?"

"Because she's in San Diego and I'm here."

"End of story?" He lifted his eyebrows. When she nodded, he said, "Didn't know I raised you to be so scared of getting hurt."

She locked eyes with him then, feeling the weight of his words. He had raised her. More than her mother who gave her life to drugs, more than her absent father who only showed his face long enough to be an asshole, and more than any teacher or coach or anyone else who'd come in and out of her life. "You didn't raise me to be scared of getting hurt."

"You sure about that?" When she didn't answer, he continued, "I used to say, 'Who needs love?' Love never did me any favors." He took a deep breath and gazed out the window again. "So. Good riddance."

They sat in silence for a long moment after that. The words good riddance ran back and forth through her head. Nothing about leaving San Diego had felt good. She'd cried on the flight but the tears hadn't brought any relief. She felt hollow. Like something she hadn't realized belonged to her had been taken away and she couldn't go after it. She had to simply sit with the emptiness and pretend she was fine.

Devyn wasn't hers. She knew in her heart she wouldn't be back to the house two blocks from the ocean with the dog she'd come to love and the woman she'd fought hard to keep from loving. After she'd landed, she'd sent Devyn a text and then tried to push San Diego out of her mind. For better or worse, as soon as she arrived at the hospital she'd been too caught up with worrying about her uncle to do anything about the gaping hole in her chest.

"Want me to start dinner soon?"

He shook his head. The old clock on the wall tick-tocked the passing seconds and Robbie couldn't help wondering if Devyn was at work or off today. If she was off, what was she doing? Was she out walking Angel?

"I was on the phone with Paul when I fell," Uncle Bruce said. "Matt found me, but Paul had already called the ambulance. He knew something was wrong with my voice."

She waited, expecting more, but Uncle Bruce only closed his eyes and leaned his head back on the recliner's head rest. Paul was his long-term on-again off-again boyfriend. When Paul had moved from Seattle to Palm Springs, Bruce had gone into a dark depression. She'd suspected the only reason he rallied was for her. She also suspected the reason he hadn't followed Paul was because of her. "I didn't know you and Paul were talking again."

"He called me the day after you left for San Diego. We've been talking every day since." He stopped, again studying the rain pelting the window. "Love. A lot of good it did me."

"Are you being sarcastic right now or…" Her words trailed as she realized he was crying. Not sobs. Just tears slipping down his cheeks slowly like a faucet that couldn't quite be tightened. She got up and went for the tissue box, handed him one, and sat down again. Now she understood who had ordered the roses that had awaited them when they'd come home from the hospital and who had called Uncle Bruce twice a day for the past five days. He'd asked for privacy when he'd taken the calls, and she hadn't pressed.

"I'm sorry."

"For what?" His voice was hoarse but he'd swiped the tears away.

"For sending your life in a different direction when I showed up on your doorstep."

When he looked at her this time, there was no harshness in his eyes. Only tenderness. "Robbie, you have no idea how much you changed my life. And it was all for the better."

"You gave up things. I know you did."

He shook his head. "I made choices. You know who named you?" He tapped his chest. "I've loved you from the moment you came into this world. Your father wasn't at the hospital—they'd broken up by then. So it was only me and your mom. The doctor thought I was the father and it was awkward explaining I was the gay uncle." He smiled wryly. "But that's what I said and the doctor laughed. Then I admitted I wanted to be a dad and the doctor looked around the room—your mom was passed out and it was just me and a nurse and the doctor—and he said, 'Looks like you're the only candidate who showed up for the job.' Then he put you in my arms."

She felt a press of tears. "You never told me that."

"Sometimes we don't tell the stories that are the most important."

She reached out and grasped his hand. "Thank you. For a thousand things."

He nodded. "Same." After a deep sigh, he added, "I'm tired, Robbie."

"You rest. I'll start dinner. We can eat when you need to take your meds." She made to get up but he held out a hand. "What?"

"I've loved you like my own daughter. I know how lucky I am you've loved me in return—even when I'm a cranky bastard. I don't have any regrets for the direction you took my life. But I am tired of working the marina." He glanced out the window at the gray water and added, "I'm tired of owning this dock. Tired of the rain. I'm even tired of this houseboat."

She waited for him to go on, but when he didn't, she asked, "You want to move to Palm Springs?" As soon as the question was out of her mouth, she knew his answer. She couldn't imagine Uncle Bruce, who'd always been a boat guy, in the middle of a desert. She could, however, imagine him back with his old boyfriend.

A picture of Paul and Uncle Bruce collected dust on the wall adjacent to the window. There were more pictures of Uncle Bruce and her, but her eyes went to the one with Paul. Twenty years at least had passed since the shot had been taken. Two men in their forties, both balding, both laughing. Paul was bigger than Bruce and had a mustache. His arm was slung around Bruce's shoulders. Uncle Bruce looked as handsome as he ever had, shirtless and with a sweetness in his eyes that had hardened with the years.

"Is Paul still sober?"

He nodded.

While the effects of the stroke had been minimized because of how quickly Uncle Bruce had gotten treatment, his other health issues weren't minimal. On his own, he wasn't doing a good job of taking care of himself. The internist had given him a list which included getting his diabetes under control and giving up alcohol. She knew he would be better off around Paul than his poker friends who all loved whiskey and cigars.

"I know what you're thinking. Being around someone sober would be good for me." He grumbled. "Paul wants to come for a visit."

"That's a great idea. When?"

"I haven't said yes. I don't like the idea of him seeing me with the walker."

"The walker's temporary. He'll understand that. You should let him come."

He eyed the walker with a grim expression. "This whole mess of getting old is bullshit."

"It is." She smiled when he scrunched up his nose, making a stink face. "You should get a refund."

"I should," he agreed. After a moment he added, "I don't want to die here. Not without trying a few other things first."

"Like living in Palm Springs?" At his nod, she asked, "You still love Paul?"

"Always have."

She wondered if Paul had asked Uncle Bruce to move to Palm Springs with him years ago. Had he asked him to try long distance? Or to leave everything and take a chance on being with him? She didn't have a lot of memories of Paul, but she remembered his deep voice and how he always made everyone laugh—and how he made Uncle Bruce light up like no one else could.

"Once we're through with all of this," she said, gesturing to the walker, "you could go there and try it out. I wouldn't mind visiting you in Palm Springs, that's for damn sure."

He held out his hand and she clasped it. "We have to talk about the marina and the dock. Someone needs to take over management."

"I can do it."

"And keep working your other job full time? You won't have any time off."

"You'd be surprised what I can get done on the side." She smiled. "Do you think I can't swing it?"

"I know you can. The question is, do you want to?"

All along, Robbie had understood that the marina and the dock would be hers when her uncle was gone. It'd belonged to Uncle Bruce's father first—the grandfather she'd never known—and even if she hadn't always lived on a houseboat at the dock, the lake had always been home. It was her responsibility to step up to the plate next.

"What about San Diego?"

"What about it?" She shrugged. "I can't rethink my whole life plan because I spent three weeks living a vacation dream."

"Huh."

"What's that 'huh' supposed to mean?"

"Nothing."

She tipped her head. "Tell me."

"I didn't return Paul's letters for years. I couldn't see how we could be together. I couldn't see a way to make it work. Then I got to missing him, so I sent him a card. He called when he got it." He shifted in the recliner. "Anyway. You'll make your own choices."

"There's not a choice to make."

"There's always a choice." He turned his gaze to the window, effectively ending the conversation.

She stood for a moment watching him. He didn't look relaxed like she would have expected now that they were home. His brow was furrowed as if particularly cross at the rain and his fists gripped the recliner's armrests. What was worse, he seemed to have aged ten years in the space of a month. She'd noticed how much older he looked in the hospital, but she'd guessed it was the lack of rest and the stress about his health. Now she knew there was another layer.

She headed to the kitchen with her head full. She wanted to call Devyn but still couldn't think of what to say. "Hi. How are you? I miss you. And, by the way, I can't leave Seattle again so this should be goodbye." She sighed as the words landed in an empty room.

Uncle Bruce wanted to move to Palm Springs, which meant her future was on the lake. The marina, the dock, the houseboat. It was her turn to manage it all. She couldn't sell, because if things didn't work out with Paul, Uncle Bruce would need a place to come back to. She also couldn't rationalize giving everything up for someone who'd set the ground rules of no attachment. All that was true, and yet she knew she'd find a way to have a relationship if Devyn asked.

CHAPTER TWENTY-SIX

Devyn had no excuse to not be having a good time.

Mari and Elena were joking about making babies as they took turns at the grill, and both were in the best mood she'd seen either of them in a long time. The wine tasted delicious. Mari's old college roommate, Lou, was attractive and funny, not to mention obviously interested in her. And the sailing had been perfect. They'd had enough breeze to fill the sails but not so much to make the water choppy, and enough cloud cover for a break from the sun but not so much to have everyone shivering.

"Are you always this quiet?" Lou asked, claiming the space on the bench next to her. "Or should I be worried?"

Loaded question. She took a sip of her wine as she considered her answer. "I'm often quiet."

"As long as it's not the company." Lou's smile seemed tentative.

"Not at all." Her mood had nothing to do with Lou, and she felt bad if she'd given that impression. She couldn't well admit the problem concerned someone who wasn't there, however.

"I told you she can be quiet until you bring her out of her shell," Mari said, jumping into the conversation from the grill.

"It's the quiet ones who can be trouble," Elena added, bumping Mari's hip. The two waggled their eyebrows at each other, making everyone laugh.

"I can handle quiet." Lou's look was cocky now. "Anything else I need to know?"

"Oh, there's lots more you need to know," Elena said. "But don't expect that one to give up anything because you ask."

Elena wasn't wrong. It had taken years before she'd let Matt close enough to share anything personal. The same went for her other ex. Even Elena had to work to get past her walls. Robbie was the only person who she'd opened up to without thinking about the decision. Everything had happened easily with Robbie.

"Was today your first time sailing?" Lou asked.

"No. Mari and Elena have taken me out several times. And each time I'm just as freaked out about capsizing as the last, if that's what made you ask." She smiled and Lou laughed. "This time I was brave enough to stand up a few times. So. Progress."

Lou grinned. "You'll be a sailor before you know it."

"I think I'll leave that to the three of you. I loved watching you and Mari work the sails together. You two have clearly done that before."

Lou nodded. "I convinced Mari to join the sailing team in college. She'd never sailed before but she was a natural."

"That sounds like Mari. I bet you two had fun in college."

"We did. Sometimes too much fun. We definitely got into our share of trouble. Mari seems innocent now, but—"

"Hey, I'm standing right here," Mari said, raising a pair of tongs in a teasingly menacing way. "And, Lou, you know I've got more dirt on you than you have on me, so watch it."

Lou chuckled and held up her hands. "I know when to back away slowly."

"Mm-hmm," Mari said. "You better."

Elena came over and slipped her arm around Mari's waist. "I like knowing I married a bad girl. Makes you even hotter. Which I didn't think was possible."

They shared a deep kiss, and Devyn smiled. Even if she wasn't able to shake her gloom, she was happy to see her friends happy together. She felt Lou's gaze on her and met her eyes. A hint of a flare went through her as she saw the desire in Lou's expression.

Nothing like the fire that rushed through her when Robbie looked at her, but maybe something could build with time?

Her phone chimed with a text but she resisted checking it. Likely it was work, and if they truly needed her, the text would be followed with a phone call. When a second text chimed, she pursed her lips.

"Work?" Lou guessed.

Her phone was face down on the patio table in front of them. "Probably."

"Are you on call tonight? Mari told me your job is intense. She also mentioned your ex didn't like that."

Devyn wondered what else Mari had said. She would have trusted Elena to keep the details to a minimum but Mari, as much as she loved her, was more open about everything.

"I've had to deal with something similar," Lou continued. "The last woman I dated only worked a few hours a week. She came from a wealthy family and didn't really need to work. Which meant she wanted me to be available all the time. When you're a professional, and your career is important to you, you can't take days off whenever it feels good."

Devyn nodded.

"I had a case I was working overtime on. Lots of late nights. After the trial, I decided to surprise her and come home for lunch. I found her with another woman. Someone who had more free time, I guess."

Devyn knew then Mari had told Lou that Matt had cheated on her. She schooled her features as she said, "People can be awful. I'm sorry."

"She had the nerve to call me last week to ask if I'd help her get out of a speeding ticket."

"Wow."

"Yeah." Lou shook her head. "Now I only date busy people with full-time careers."

Devyn smiled. "Good plan." Her phone chimed again.

Lou motioned to the phone as she reached for her wineglass. "You really can check. It won't hurt my feelings."

Devyn hesitated, not wanting to think about work. Finally, guilt pushed her to check the texts. She wasn't prepared to see Robbie's name on the screen. Nor was she expecting paragraphs in multiple messages. She wanted to read through everything but couldn't do so with Lou sitting right next to her. A new text popped on the screen that read: *I want to give you space to think about everything. Don't feel any pressure to respond until you're ready. I hope you're okay. I miss you.*

It was the last line that made her heart clench.

"Is Robbie someone from work?"

"What?" Devyn looked up at Lou's question. Had Lou read the text or only seen Robbie's name? Either way, she was taken aback by the intrusion. "Robbie is—" Before she could decide what to call Robbie, her phone rang.

"Robbie apparently really wants to get ahold of you."

The ringing cut off abruptly and her phone switched back to the home screen image—a shot of Angel. Robbie had taken the picture and texted it to her while she was working weeks ago. She stared at the screen for a moment, wishing the phone would ring again and feeling all the implications of that wish.

"Everything okay?"

"Yeah." She nodded, probably unconvincingly. Why would Robbie have called only to hang up? The list of possible reasons, including some emergency, made her want to read all the texts. Or she could call Robbie back. As soon as the thought crossed her mind, it was the only thing she wanted. "I'm sorry. I'll just be a minute."

She got up from the bench, motioning to Elena and Mari that she was heading inside. As soon as she stepped through the French doors, she pressed the call button. Robbie answered on the first ring.

"I accidentally dialed you. I'm sorry."

"Did you accidentally text me, too?"

"No. That I thought about long and hard." Robbie paused. "Did you read the texts?"

"Not yet."

Robbie was quiet for a moment. "I didn't want to call you because I wasn't sure I could get all my thoughts out if I heard your voice. And I wanted to give you space to think about everything I said without you having to respond right away."

"Thanks for knowing I'd need that." Robbie had figured out what she'd learned about herself only after months of therapy. "Do you want me to hang up and read your texts?"

"No. I probably shouldn't say this, but it's really nice hearing your voice."

"Why shouldn't you say that?"

"Because. I know I haven't been very good at communicating this past week." Robbie blew out a breath. "And I took off before we had a chance to really talk about us. Now things feel complicated."

Understatement.

"It's been intense with my uncle in the hospital and not knowing how things were going to go."

"How is he now?"

"He's okay. Considering everything, he's lucky. It could have been a lot worse. But he screwed up his knee and he can't walk. And he's been told he has to stop drinking and get his blood sugar under control. Which he isn't happy about. He also wasn't taking his cholesterol medication—now he's on that along with a bunch of other meds.

"Thankfully the stroke part was mild. Probably because he got treatment right away. Anyway. We're back home now. Tonight's the first night out of the hospital." Robbie exhaled and her relief was obvious. "How are you?"

She hadn't realized she'd been pacing until she stopped. Pieces that had been jumbled up inside her seemed to settle into place as she listened to Robbie's voice. Robbie's exhale made her feel like she could relax, too. But that didn't mean anything about their situation was fixed. She didn't even know what fixed meant in this case.

"You still there?"

"Yeah." She debated how to answer Robbie's question. "I'm fine. I've had better weeks." Answering honestly was all she could do. "How are you?"

"Better now."

She wanted to sink into Robbie's words, her voice, and everything she felt in that moment. *Better now.*

A sound of a teapot whistling interrupted and then came a shuffle of sounds. "I'm making my uncle tea. Give me a second here."

She wished she could be in Robbie's kitchen, but she couldn't even picture it. Robbie had shown her an aerial photo of the marina and the dock with a hodgepodge of cute houseboats all painted in bright colors and with flags waving. It was a clear day with the sun shining when the picture had been taken, and Robbie had joked it was false advertising. Robbie had pointed out her uncle's houseboat and her own, his green with bright purple trim and hers blue with white trim.

The clatter of dishware went quiet, and Devyn held her breath as she waited for Robbie.

"There's so many things I want to say to you."

"Same. I don't even know where to start." She waited to say more, hoping Robbie would take over, and she longed for Robbie to ask her to come to Seattle. Invite her into her world. But what then? Instead of offering any words to fill the space, she simply listened to Robbie's breathing. The French door opened and she looked up to see Lou.

"I was watching you pace in here and figured the conversation wasn't going well. I came to get you out of it."

She opened her mouth to say that wasn't necessary, but before she could get out the words, Lou reached for the phone. "I got this."

There was no time to warn Robbie. Devyn's throat tightened as Lou started to speak.

"Hey, Robbie, Devyn's on a date and can't talk right now."

No. Please, no. She wanted to yank the phone out of Lou's grasp but couldn't seem to move.

"Also, no one wants a selfish ex who only comes back for attention."

Fuck.

"My advice, not that you're asking, is move on. I think it's safe to say Devyn can do better." Lou ended the call and smiled. "Damn, that felt good. Why is it so much easier to tell other people's exes off than your own?"

Devyn held out her hand, her body vibrating with anger. "Give me the phone."

Lou's brow bunched together. "Are you really still caught up on that guy? Mari told me he treated you like crap and then cheated on you. For like a year, right?"

"Give me the phone," she repeated.

"Fine." Lou dropped it in her hand. She stared at Devyn for a moment, then shook her head. "It's not my place to—"

"You're right. It's not your place."

"Whatever." Lou walked past her and out the French door without bothering to close it.

As soon as Lou reached the patio, Devyn heard Mari and Elena both ask, "What's going on?"

"Don't ask me," Lou said.

Devyn walked over to the French door and closed it, then took a steadying breath and pulled up Robbie's number. She waited for the ring. One ring. Then two, then three. "Shit." She pressed her hand to her forehead. "Robbie, please pick up."

The call went to voice mail and she listened to the recording, unable to stop the tears. When the beep came, all she could manage to say was, "Please call me. That was a misunderstanding."

A misunderstanding. She ended the call and then set the phone on the coffee table, wishing she hadn't checked her phone in the first place. And wishing she hadn't called. But she'd needed to hear Robbie's voice. She sank down on the sofa and dropped her head in her hands.

What a mess. She hated to think of what might be going through Robbie's mind, but she desperately wanted to know, if only to try to right things. She straightened and picked up her phone again, pressing the call button and sending out a plea to the universe that Robbie would answer.

When the voice mail picked up, she ended the call and opened Robbie's text messages. This couldn't be how things ended. Not when she knew Robbie cared as much as she did. She could hear it in Robbie's voice. Her eyes filled with tears as she read the first text message:

I'm going to try to explain why my texts this week have all been brief. I owe you more. You asked me if I was okay and if there was anything you could do. I said I was fine and didn't need anything. That wasn't true. But I couldn't think of how to say what I was feeling.

I didn't mean to fall for you. I knew you wanted to keep things casual. But I completely fell. I knew when it was happening and I didn't try to stop. We both know the problem. My life is in Seattle and yours is in San Diego. Before I left, I wanted to ask you if there was a chance you'd be up for something long distance. I don't know what that would look like exactly. Especially now. But it's either that or we say goodbye. Which hurts so much to write.

Devyn took a shaky breath. What Robbie said was true and not any different from what she'd been wrestling with all week. Still, it wrenched her to read the words. She wiped away tears and kept reading.

My uncle wants to move to Palm Springs to be with his boyfriend. I think it's a good idea, but it means I'll be taking over management of the marina and the dock. Between that and my job, I won't have time for vacations. This will be my world. I could swing a long weekend away occasionally but that's it. And I know how busy your job keeps you and I know how important it is so I would never ask you to come to me.

I wish we could be in the same room having this talk. It's hard over text. Also I want to be in the same room because I want to hug you. I've wanted to call you so many times the last few days. I've wanted to hold your hand even more.

"Oh, Robbie." She sniffed and pushed herself to finish reading.

As I'm writing this, I keep thinking how hard it'd be to do long distance. I don't know how it would work or even if you'd want to try. All I know is what we had was perfect and I can't just walk away from it.

I want to give you space to think about everything. Don't feel any pressure to respond until you're ready. I hope you're okay. I miss you.

"Hey," Elena said, touching her shoulder. "What's going on?"
"Robbie…" She shook her head, not sure how to go on.
"Did something happen with Robbie's uncle?"
She swiped her eyes, but more tears came.
Elena sat down next to her. "Tell me."
"I don't know what to say." Devyn handed Elena her phone.
Elena scanned the texts and then pointed to the last few sentences. "She called after sending you this?"

"On accident. I called her back, and while we were talking, Lou came in and took the phone out of my hand." She swallowed. "Lou told Robbie I was on a date."

"Shit." Elena grimaced. "Did you call her back?"

"Twice. She's not answering."

Elena seemed to contemplate that and then said, "I know you said you wouldn't but…would you do long distance for her?"

"I don't know. I miss her so much."

Elena nodded. "Text her an apology about Lou and tell her you need time to think."

"Instead of jumping on a plane and showing up at her front door?" She wanted Elena to tell her to go for what she wanted, but Elena's expression was grim.

"That's only going to mean more heartbreak if you don't know your next move after that."

Elena always thought of every possible scenario when she made any decision. Only then did she act. It was what made her an incredible surgeon. But sometimes it was impossible to know all the outcomes and risks. When Devyn had announced she was marrying Matt, Elena had been dumbstruck she hadn't processed her own feelings, or lack thereof, before saying yes. And this time she had no idea what her next move would be if she went to Seattle.

"As much as I want to be in the same room with her right now, I almost wish she'd never shown up in my life."

"She was a perfect housebutch." Elena smiled sadly. "I think Mari was jealous when she heard all the things Robbie took care of." She wrapped an arm around her and pulled her into a hug. "Even if nothing more happens, she was good for you. She pulled you out of that place you were hiding."

Devyn let the tears fall again. Robbie had been good for her. She knew it the first time she'd felt heat spread through her after a look Robbie gave her. But was that all Robbie had been—a dose of what she needed?

CHAPTER TWENTY-SEVEN

April 13 Saturday at 8:13 p.m.

Devyn: *Please can we talk? At least text me back?*
I'm not actually on a date. That was Lou—Mari's friend from college. She thought you were Matt.

Devyn: *I mean she knew your name was Robbie but she assumed you were my ex-husband.*
Please say something.

Robbie: *I figured she didn't know who I was.*

Devyn: *Can I call you?*

Robbie: *I don't think I'm in the right headspace tonight.*

April 13 Saturday at 11:13 p.m.

Devyn: *Can I call you tomorrow? I have to work but I think we should talk.*

Devyn: *Everything has felt off this past week. I haven't known what to think. And I know I made everything worse tonight. You have no idea how terrible I feel.*

Devyn: *I promise I would have told you if I was on a date. Mari and Elena wanted to go sailing like we'd planned and Mari invited her friend Lou. I told Mari I wasn't interested in dating anyone but I don't think Lou got that message.*

Robbie: *I'll be around tomorrow.*

April 14 Sunday at 9:15 a.m.

Devyn: *I reread everything you texted me last night. I don't know what to say other than I miss you. Well, that and I'm sorry about what happened with Lou.*

Robbie: *It's all good—I get that it was a misunderstanding. But I wouldn't get on the wrong side of that woman.*

Devyn: *I think I accomplished that. I told her off for grabbing my phone and she stormed out. Trust me, that's the end of that.*

Devyn: *I want to call you but I'm at work and it's crazy here. For the record, you can text me anytime (or call) about your uncle—if you're worried about meds or how he's healing or whatever. Medical stuff is the one time I can be useful.*

Robbie: *You don't give yourself enough credit. I've seen your tile work.*

Devyn: *How is it you can make me smile even when I still feel awful?*

Robbie: *I don't want you to feel bad.*
I'm the one who's done a shitty job of communicating this past week. I miss you, too. I keep thinking—I just wish we could be in the same place again.

Devyn: *Same.*

April 14 Sunday at 9:25 a.m.

Devyn: *I wasn't going to tell you this but I talked to Elena about us. I told her I wanted to jump on a plane and come see you. She said I should figure out my next step before I do that.*

Robbie: *Elena's probably right.*

Devyn: *Does that mean you don't want me to come?*

Robbie: *I think we need to figure out what we both want before anything else happens.*
We had an agreement. I know I didn't keep up my end of it but it was still probably a good idea.

Devyn: *I don't know if it was a good idea or not. I know it wasn't fair to ask you to keep things sex only.*

Robbie: *Why not?*

Devyn: *I already knew I liked you.*

Robbie: ...
What do you want now, Devyn?

Devyn: *You. But I know you need to be with your uncle.*

Robbie: *We could try long distance.*

April 14 Sunday at 9:39 a.m.

Robbie: *Are you thinking or...?*

Devyn: *Someone coded. I'll call when I can.*

April 14 Sunday at 8:32 p.m.

Devyn: *I'm sorry. I wanted to call earlier but I didn't get a break.*

Robbie: *Don't be sorry. Is everything okay?*

Devyn: *No. Nothing feels okay.*
I don't want what we had to be over.

Robbie: *Me neither.*

Robbie: *Do you want to try long distance?*
Or talk about some other type of relationship?

Devyn: *I don't know.*

Robbie: *We knew we had an end date all along.*
Maybe we're at a point where we need to try being friends.

Devyn: *Ouch.*

Robbie: *I'm not saying that to be hurtful. I don't want to hurt you at all. I'm just putting all my cards on the table. I like you. I like us together. But I can't see an option for us if you don't want to do long distance. And I'm not getting the sense that you want long distance.*

Robbie: *Honestly I think you need to figure out what you want— what would be good for you. I know long distance isn't ideal but that's all I've got to offer.*

Robbie: *Can I call you?*

Devyn: *I'm still at work. Today was hard. I don't think I can have the conversation we need to have here tonight.*

Robbie: *I'm sorry. I wish I could give you a hug.*

April 14 Sunday at 11:45 p.m.

Devyn: *It's late and I'm guessing you're already asleep. The thing is…You're right. I need to figure out what I want for myself before I get someone else involved. I know I'm not in a place where I can be in a serious relationship. I knew that from the very beginning.*

April 15 Monday at 6:45 a.m.

Robbie: *I get that you aren't ready for a relationship.
It makes me sad, but I understand.
Do you think we could try being friends?*

Devyn: *I think I need to step back.*

Robbie: *Okay. I'll give you some space. You know where to find me.*

CHAPTER TWENTY-EIGHT

Six months later

Fall was gorgeous on the lake. The leafy trees bordering the water were in peak color, bright patches of yellow, orange, and even some red mixed in with the evergreens, and the air felt crisp and clean. Sunsets were especially nice. Brief but brilliant.

"Enjoy this—it won't last," Robbie murmured.

"Nothing lasts," Uncle Bruce said, sounding more pleased than mournful about what time stole.

Robbie glanced over at him, half surprised he'd heard and half surprised to see him beaming as he gazed out at the lake. She'd asked if he wanted to keep her company while she grilled their dinner, but he'd acted like he had better things to do. Apparently, he'd changed his mind. She pushed her Mariners ballcap back on her head. "You need anything?"

"Not a damn thing." He settled in on one of the deck chairs and closed his eyes, tilting his face to the sun and repeating, "Not a damn thing."

The knee surgery had finally happened. He was a grump for the week following and she'd been exhausted, constantly tending to him. But the second week things improved, and by week three, he was in a better mood than he'd been in for most of the last several months.

Now four weeks out, he was getting around on his own and even taking little walks along the marina. She turned the corn on the grill and glanced back at him. His legs were stretched out and he seemed about to doze off, but a smile pulled up the corners of his lips.

She grinned and asked, "What's up with you tonight?"

"Nothing."

"Not buying it. You're happy about something."

He chuckled. "I'm such a pain in the ass, you don't know what to do if I'm in a good mood."

"So why are you in a good mood?"

"No particular reason."

"Liar."

"It's Thursday. When are you meeting up with Stacy?"

"You're changing the subject. Not subtly, by the way." She knew something was up even if he wouldn't say it. "Stacy's at a conference. No friend-date tonight."

Since moving in with her uncle full time, her best friend, Stacy, had instituted regular friend-dates on Thursdays. Stacy's friendship, and ironically Matt's, too, had gotten her though the long months of wishing things could have worked out differently with Devyn. "If you want me out of the house, I can ask Matt if he wants to do something tonight."

"You two need to get out more."

"So you do want me out of the house?"

He lifted a shoulder. "I only said you needed to get out more. You're both single and not getting any younger."

"Who's coming over?" When he didn't deny it, she knew she'd landed on the reason for his goofy happy look.

"I don't want to jinx it."

She shook her head. "You have the strangest superstitions of anyone I know."

"Considering how small your social circle is, that's not saying much."

She had plenty of friends. Or at least plenty of friendly acquaintances and a few friends. "I like my social circle. I don't need a ton of friends."

"You could use one more."

He meant she could use a girlfriend. "I'll put up a notice." Unfortunately, the sarcasm didn't do a thing for the ache in her chest. "Should I have made more kebabs for our mystery guest?"

"No. He said he'd get dinner at the airport. Anyway, he's vegan." Instantly she knew. "Paul's coming? Tonight?"

"He's not here yet. I won't say it." The smile reached Uncle Bruce's eyes as he added, "But it might be Paul."

Robbie let out a whoop, then tossed the tongs on the hook of the grill. She came over to where he was sitting and held out her arms. "Get up and let me hug you, Grump."

He grumbled she was making too big of a deal out of nothing but stood anyway. Paul had visited a few weeks after the stroke. Things hadn't gone well. Uncle Bruce had at first been receptive to talking about a future and a serious relationship but then he'd changed his tune when Paul tried to lay out specifics. Robbie knew it was the uncertainty of the health issues. The last thing he wanted was to be a burden to Paul. But he hadn't said that, and Paul had taken his reluctance to agree to any plan as a sign he wasn't interested.

Robbie had driven Paul to the airport and asked him not to give up. Still, he'd left Seattle heartbroken. A month later, Uncle Bruce reached out and apologized. They'd had breakfast together on videochat every day since.

Uncle Bruce only briefly accepted any hug and let go, saying, "Get the kebabs off the grill. The chicken won't be any good overcooked."

"Don't let anyone see you get too emotional," she said, poking his arm. "Should we go back inside, or do you want to eat out here?"

"Here is good."

She didn't complain. The water was smooth as glass, and it truly was a perfect evening. The kebabs and corn were gone before Uncle Bruce cleared his throat and said, "Speaking of emotional, you haven't mentioned Devyn in a while."

"What does that have to do with being emotional?"

"She's the only one I've seen you cry over. How is she?"

"She's fine." Robbie stood and held out her hand. "Give me your plate. I want to get the dishes done before Paul gets here." In fact, all she wanted was out of the conversation.

He didn't hand over his plate. "When was the last time you called her?"

"We don't talk on the phone. We text."

"Fine. When was the last time you texted her?"

"I don't know." She knew exactly. Six days ago.

"What happened?"

"Nothing. Give me your plate."

"You think I don't know you after all this time?" He shook his head and handed her the plate finally. "You want to call her. So call her."

"I didn't say I wanted to call anyone." She clenched her jaw, frustrated he was getting under her skin and more frustrated that he could. "I'm going to clean up before Paul gets here."

"You know they don't give martyr awards for not calling."

"Whatever." She wasn't a martyr. She was simply a realist.

She went inside and dropped the dishes in the sink and then closed her eyes for a moment. Not thinking of Devyn was a lost cause, but she wished her mind would give her a break. So much of the last seven months had consisted of trying not to think about Devyn and failing spectacularly.

They'd only spoken once over the phone. That was the call that ended with a virtual throat punch. When Devyn had denied she'd been on a date, despite what the woman who'd ripped into Robbie had said, Robbie had wanted to believe her. But they'd gone sailing. The same sailing trip she'd planned to go on with Devyn.

After the ill-fated call, and a rush of text messages, Robbie had pushed through the hurt to again ask the question Devyn never directly answered—do you want to try long distance? The moment Devyn sidestepped answering, she knew how things were going to go. She pulled away then and texted something she'd often wished she could take back: *I think you need to figure out what you want— what would be good for you. I know long distance isn't ideal but that's all I've got to offer.* At the time, she'd been trying to mitigate her own pain. It was only afterward she'd realized what she'd done. She'd offered the bare minimum and placed everything on Devyn's shoulders.

She couldn't forget Devyn's response: *You're right. I need to figure out what I want for myself before I get someone else involved.*

Being right about what Devyn needed had felt worse than anything else. Devyn didn't need her.

After that, a month passed with no messages. Then Devyn started texting again, but the mood had changed. Their exchanges were more like check-ins. They chatted about their plans for the day or some annoyance or something good that had happened. Nothing wildly important. It was nice keeping in touch, but the texts only drove home the growing separation between them. She started thinking that if Devyn didn't ever want a relationship, she wished she'd stop messaging. But she couldn't bring herself to say as much.

Then out of the blue—last week—Devyn had asked if she was dating anyone. Robbie told her she wasn't, thinking it would have been strange to not mention it until she realized Devyn might be dating someone and looking for a way to tell her. When she'd asked, Devyn's response kicked her in the stomach: *There is someone I'm interested in.*

Thankfully over text Robbie could hide her feelings and she'd simply said: *That's great. I'm happy for you.*

Devyn had sent a few more texts and Robbie had given only cursory responses. She knew she needed to step back and Devyn seemed to have gotten the hint. She'd stopped texting and six days had gone by without a message.

Her phone vibrated in her pocket and for a moment she wondered if it could be Devyn. Was Devyn texting now to tell her about whoever had stolen her heart? She finished cleaning the kitchen before checking her phone.

Matt: *I have to go shopping. For clothes. FML.*

Robbie felt a twinge of disappointment that the message wasn't from Devyn. *I'm sorry for your loss. What's the occasion?*

Have to wear business casual beginning Monday.

That sucks. Since Matt had wanted to stay in Seattle, he'd had to find a different job. It hadn't taken him long, but the new company insisted all "remote" workers be in the office three days a week. He'd only recently, and grudgingly, begun wearing pants. *I won't go shopping with you, but I'll buy the ice cream. Molly Moons?*

Now? I can beat you there.

A half hour later she pulled up to Molly Moons and easily picked out Matt waiting for her with a grim expression. "Still mad about the business casual?"

"I've been given a list of acceptable clothing items."

She laughed. "Let me guess, *Star Wars* T-shirts and Padres gear aren't on the list?"

"And no cargo shorts."

"You need ice cream." She reached for the door, catching a whiff of the ice cream shop's distinctive sweet scent, and moaned. "It's a good thing we don't live closer to this place."

"Are you getting something besides melted chocolate?"

"Nope."

He snorted. "Gourmet cooking until it comes to ice cream?"

"Molly Moon's melted chocolate ice cream is gourmet." She'd introduced Matt to Molly Moons not long after she'd come back from San Diego. He'd been excited to try all the flavors but she always got the same thing. "I know what I like."

"Boring."

"Maybe." She didn't care. "I don't like being disappointed."

"I'm not disappointed trying all the flavors." He winked, and she knew he wasn't only talking about ice cream. He'd gone on two dates that week with different women and was baiting her to ask about said dates. She was half-interested but only because he told good stories about dates gone wrong. If either had gone well, she'd only be more depressed about her own fortune. Thankfully, he got distracted eyeing the list of new flavors. "Ooh, blueberry pie ice cream?"

"All yours."

She stepped up to the counter and ordered her usual. Matt went for the new flavor, making a point of moaning over the first lick.

"Stacy would tease you endlessly about that moan."

Matt stopped mid-lick. She'd suspected Matt had a crush after she'd introduced the two but now she was sure. "Good thing she's not here. I can tease you about your crush."

"Whatever." He grinned, but the blush was obvious. "Where is she, by the way? Aren't Thursdays the day you two hang out?"

"She's at a conference."

"Oh." His downturned look said plenty.

"Why haven't you asked her out yet?"

"I did. She said no." Matt's brow furrowed. "I really like her, too."

"If it's any consolation, she turned me down the first time I asked. But I was drunk and naked."

He laughed. "Why'd you two break up?"

"We were better friends than lovers." It was depressing to admit but also the truth. And it made her think of Devyn. With Devyn, they'd been better as lovers. The friendship wasn't going well at all.

"Maybe I'll ask a second time."

"Never hurts. If she turns you down twice, though, let it go."

He nodded solemnly and she knew he was serious about liking Stacy. They left the ice cream shop and wandered toward the park. The sky was darkening and they wouldn't have long before it got too cold to be outside. They reached a bench and Matt sat down. She took the space next to him.

"You remember Uncle Bruce's friend Paul from Palm Springs?"

Matt nodded. "I lost fifty bucks to him on one round of poker."

"He's in town again." She paused. "I'm pretty sure he's going to convince Uncle Bruce to move to Palm Springs."

"Would he sell his houseboat? What about the marina?"

"I'll take over the marina officially and probably buy his house." She wasn't ready to deal with that part yet, however. She hadn't completely accepted the reality of being fully in charge. Still, she knew Uncle Bruce belonged with Paul. "Sometimes I think relationships aren't worth the trouble, but then I hear Uncle Bruce talking with Paul. They make me think it's possible being happy with someone for the long haul."

Matt nodded but his look was distant. Either he agreed or he was still thinking about his chances with Stacy.

"Anyway. I thought you should know."

"Thanks for the heads-up. How much notice will I get if I have to move?"

"You can stay. I've got money in savings to buy my uncle out and still keep my houseboat."

"Wish I could say that. I never had a savings account until Devyn. I'm better at spending." He sighed. "After the house sold, Devyn sent me an email of ways to invest my half of the money."

Hearing Devyn's name brought a swirl of emotion. She fought to hide her reaction and said, "Did you invest it?"

"One thing about my ex-wife—she's always fucking right. I decided to finally listen. You know, Devyn said you were the big reason we got the house listed in time for the spring buyers. We got fifty thousand over the asking price."

She wasn't sure how to respond. It would have been nice hearing the news from Devyn.

"It's weird. Devyn's been really nice to me lately. I think if I was still down in San Diego, we'd be friends like you and Stacy. Maybe more."

"More than friends? I thought you hated her."

"Everything's changed since I came up here. There's no stress now. Or not like it was. We talk. It's nice." He paused to lick his cone. "I'm not saying I want to be in a relationship with her—fuck that. But I wouldn't say no to hooking up. I still think she's hot."

A wave of heat flushed through her. She clenched her teeth, knowing she couldn't say anything.

"What?"

"Nothing. Well…I guess I figured you were done with that relationship. I mean, you said you were separated for a year before the divorce."

"I am done. But that doesn't mean I'd say no to sex." Matt chuckled. "Devyn doesn't do emotional attachments anyway. I think she could be poly."

"Being polyamorous has nothing to do with whether or not you form emotional attachments. In fact—"

Matt held up a hand. "Chill, dude. What I meant is Devyn could totally hook up with someone and move on the next day. She doesn't get emotionally invested. She keeps everyone at a distance. Even her family."

The words rang true, but Robbie's heart battered against her chest arguing she knew Devyn better. Did she? Better than someone who'd been married to her for six years?

"I thought I was the problem in our relationship," Matt continued. "After a while I realized it was her. There's a wall. She doesn't let anyone in. But you know how she is. You had to deal with her."

"I think things were different when I was down there."

"Well, yeah, she was focused on getting the house ready to sell. You did get a dose of the real Devyn when you cut down her garden, though." He laughed. "Remember how she tried to kick you out?"

"Yeah." She felt her throat tighten and knew she couldn't keep the secret any longer. "Matt…We hooked up."

Matt's eyes narrowed. "You hooked up with who?"

"Devyn."

He seemed to register what she'd said, but it was as if he expected her to follow up with "Just kidding." When she didn't, he only stared at her.

"I wasn't going to tell you because it really didn't matter, and I figured you wouldn't want to know. But now it feels like I should have told you."

He shook his head slowly like he was still processing. "Devyn's straight."

"Technically she's bi. Same as Stacy." She waited for him to say something, wishing she could tell if he was pissed or hurt or what might be going through his head. "Anyway, nothing came of it." That truth felt heavy now.

"I can't believe you had sex with her."

"You told me you were done. You said you hated her."

"I don't hate her. I never did."

"Wait, are you still in love with her?"

His jaw muscles worked but he didn't answer. After a moment, he said, "You know what sucks? Whatever happened between you two meant nothing to Devyn. And it won't matter who you sleep with after her. You're still going to miss her."

She couldn't argue, couldn't say a thing. All she could do was watch him get up from the bench and walk over to the trash can and toss the remainder of his ice cream. As he walked away, she found her voice. "I'm sorry."

She thought of going after him, but the words he'd left her with had her feeling empty and cold. She got up and tossed her cone, then went back to the bench and dropped her head in her hands.

In the space of one conversation, she'd alienated Matt and had her doubts about everything with Devyn confirmed. Her first impulse was to call Stacy, but she couldn't without then hearing Stacy's take on Matt. And Uncle Bruce was with Paul.

Her phone vibrated. She ignored it for a moment before worrying it was Uncle Bruce. The last thing she expected was what she read on the screen.

Are you free next weekend?

For as many times as she'd hoped to get a text exactly like the one on her screen, she couldn't think of a response. She was still reeling from what Matt had said and now her equilibrium was off. Everything was off.

A new text blinked on the screen.

I'll be in Seattle and I'm hoping I can see you.

CHAPTER TWENTY-NINE

Devyn checked her phone three times before setting it face down on the table in front of her. Robbie wasn't due until seven, but for the last hour she'd alternated between anxious excitement and plain anxiety. The stress level in the hotel bar wasn't helping matters.

At least the bartender was a sweet gay guy. He'd listened patiently to an older man who'd come to Seattle to see the son he'd been estranged from, and offered encouragement and a gin and tonic to a woman who'd lost her job. When he got to Devyn, he'd given her a worried look after she'd said she only wanted a ginger ale because her stomach was off. She'd had to reassure him she was fine. Which she was. Mostly. Then her phone beeped and she nearly knocked it off the table reaching for it.

Robbie: *On my way. Should take twenty minutes if I don't hit traffic.*

Twenty minutes. As soon as she'd sent the text last weekend and gotten the short reply of "yes" to her question of whether Robbie was free to meet up, she'd done nothing but count down the minutes. She knew Robbie might have other plans which was why she hadn't simply shown up—despite how many times she'd imagined the scenario of knocking on Robbie's door unannounced. It was nice as a fantasy, but Robbie deserved warning. As well as a chance to say no. Fortunately, Robbie hadn't said no.

She glanced at the doorway as a couple filed in. The bartender followed her gaze as he wiped down the table next to hers. "Waiting for someone?"

She nodded.

"First date?"

"No…It's…well, complicated."

"Sounds like all the dates I've been on lately." He chuckled. "I'd say good luck, but I don't think you'll need it—not if they have any sense at all. You look gorgeous."

"Thanks." She appreciated the pep talk. He gave her an encouraging smile and then went to check in on the couple who'd taken seats at the front counter.

The bar wasn't big and it filled quickly when a group who'd clearly been at conference together showed up. Devyn alternated between checking the time on her phone, checking the door, and scanning the crowd. Nothing prepared her for how her heart seemed to fill her chest the moment she spotted Robbie.

In the three weeks Robbie had been in San Diego, she'd never gotten dressed up. Now she was wearing a perfectly tailored suit coat and slacks along with a button-down. She'd been attractive before, but the outfit made her and Devyn couldn't help staring.

Robbie glanced around for a moment, then her gaze locked on Devyn and she strode forward. Devyn's pulse raced but she made herself stay seated until Robbie reached her table. When she stood, Robbie suddenly in arm's reach after all this time, she forgot everything she'd planned to say. Instead, the only thing that came to mind was the memory of their last kiss.

"Hi."

Robbie smiled. "Hi yourself. You came a long way to say hi."

"It's not so bad if you get a direct flight." She felt emotion press through her. For the last six months she'd been trying and failing to tell Robbie how she felt. She'd convinced herself the conversation needed to happen in person, but now she wasn't sure she'd say the right thing and Robbie wasn't leaping forward to embrace her. "How are you?"

"I'm fine. You look amazing."

The compliment was said easily but not in an offhand way. She knew Robbie meant it and the words buoyed her. "Thanks. You too."

Robbie glanced down at herself. "Turns out I do own some clothes besides the old T-shirts and shorts you saw me in." She smiled again—her same easy smile that Devyn had fallen for months ago—and then motioned to the chair. "Okay if I sit?"

"Please." She sat down as well, remembering the speech she'd planned. When she looked at Robbie, though, the words slipped away.

"How are things back in San Diego?" Robbie asked.

"Busy. You know how it goes." That was the expected response, and Robbie nodded as if she knew the script.

"I was surprised to hear you were coming to Seattle. Did you have a conference or something here?"

"No. There's something I have to do for work, but…mostly I had time off and I wanted to get away." She hoped that answer would suffice. She needed a better sense of how Robbie was feeling before she wanted to admit more. "And you're here, so I figured it must be nice."

"It's not San Diego, but Seattle does have its charm." Robbie glanced at the crowd from the conference when someone cheered and another started to clap. She looked back at Devyn, held her gaze for a long beat. "I don't know if I should say this or not, but I've missed you."

"I've missed you, too."

She didn't look away from Robbie's warm brown eyes, and a familiar warmth spread through her. The feeling almost brought tears—she'd missed Robbie so much. "Six months is a long time."

"It is. And a lot has changed in both of our worlds."

Robbie seemed to be allowing that their feelings for each other may have changed as well. The time apart hadn't changed anything for her. Or if it had, that was only because she knew more than ever how much she wanted Robbie in her life. She'd tried to move on, but her heart wouldn't. Couldn't. She couldn't go back to the life she'd had before. She couldn't forget their time together. Or how hard their time apart had been.

"How's Angel? Has he caught any more squirrels?"

"No more squirrels. Thankfully."

Robbie cocked her head. "He probably wouldn't agree."

Devyn smiled. "Probably not. I thought about bringing him, but he hates flying."

"You'll have to tell him hi for me."

The tension between them was palpable, yet the conversation was like the texts they'd exchanged the last several months—glossing over the big issues in favor of small talk. Small talk was the one thing they'd skipped in the three weeks they were together.

"How do you like your new place?"

She lifted a shoulder. "I'm getting used to it. Angel doesn't like the tiny yard but it's less work. The nicest part is being done with the divorce. Selling the house was the last holdup."

"Congrats on that. Matt seemed happy about the sale, too."

She thought of all the times she'd wanted to complain about Matt to Robbie and had held back because of their friendship. Matt had been a complete pain throughout the listing and the sale. The deal had only closed because her realtor had wrangled Matt for her.

"Should I not have mentioned Matt?" Robbie clearly read her hesitation. "He's made it sound like you two have patched things up and are friends, but—"

"We're not friends," she cut in. "We haven't been friends for a long time."

"Oh." Robbie paused, seeming to work something out in her head. "I thought maybe you were coming to Seattle to see him, too."

"No. Matt is…" Again she found herself needing to bite her tongue. "Not in my Seattle plans."

Robbie's lips turned up subtly.

"What?"

"I forgot how good you are at taking the high road even when you don't want to. Like letting me stay when you wanted to send me packing."

"Angel liked you. And you hung that fan." She tried a smile, hoping that would make Robbie realize how far past all of that she was.

"It wasn't that you thought I might be fun to look at for a while?" Robbie tipped her head. Devyn couldn't help thinking it was the same expression she used to have when they'd played around in the bedroom. The I-know-what-you're-thinking look.

"I'd say it was a combination of things."

Robbie grinned. "I like knowing I wasn't the only one distracted."

"At first I was mostly thinking you could be useful." Devyn tried to fend off a blush as Robbie's eyebrows went up. "Not like that."

"Sure." Robbie laughed but she turned serious a moment later. "So what are your plans while you're here?"

Besides you? If she were more confident, she'd have voiced her thought aloud.

"You said it was something for work?"

"I have a job interview on Monday. I haven't decided what else I want to do yet." She couldn't decide on plans that didn't include Robbie.

"You have a job interview here?" Robbie's surprise was obvious. "You're thinking of leaving San Diego?"

"There are other nice places to live, you know."

Robbie didn't look like she believed her. "You love San Diego."

"I do." Now was the time to say why she'd really come, but the words stuck in her throat. In the same moment, the noise in the bar increased—two men boasting loudly and a woman laughing. She suddenly wished she had suggested somewhere more private.

"It's kind of loud in here. Do you want to go somewhere else?" Robbie asked.

"How is it you can read me so well?"

"If it makes you feel any better, I can't read you at all over text."

Which was why she knew she had to come to Seattle. She glanced at her empty glass and then realized the bartender hadn't come to their table to take Robbie's drink order. "You didn't even get a drink."

"I don't need a drink." Robbie stood. "It's a nice night. We can take a walk."

A walk sounded perfect, though outside the sun had set and dusk had given way to a cool evening. They only made it a block past the hotel when she wished she'd brought a jacket. She tried to discreetly cross her arms against a shiver, but Robbie took one look at her and shrugged out of her coat. She handed it off, saying, "Don't worry, it's clean. I only wear it for interviews or important meetings."

Which one was this? She considered asking but was distracted when she caught Robbie's scent mixed with a faint cologne on the jacket. She couldn't help pulling it on. "You sure you won't be too cold?"

"I'm used to Seattle. And I'm in long sleeves."

Meanwhile, she'd gone for her favorite black tank dress which made more sense in San Diego. "Nights are still warm in San Diego."

Robbie took a deep breath and exhaled. "The weather there is hard to beat."

She brushed the back of Robbie's hand as she stepped around a light post and Robbie's gaze went right to her. A zing went through her, but she didn't say a word and Robbie looked away quickly.

"So, the job interview. Do you want to talk about it?"

"There's not much to say yet."

Robbie waited, not pushing her to go on, only waiting—the way she had so many times before.

Devyn cleared her throat. "A month ago I got an email about a position in Seattle. Elena has a friend who's a surgeon at a hospital here and my name was passed along." She paused. "I did a lot of research before sending in my résumé. It's a move up for me, and I think it could be a good fit."

"Wow."

Robbie looked like she was having a hard time believing the news and Devyn couldn't tell if she was happy or not. They'd stopped at an intersection, but the walk sign came on a moment later and as they crossed, she organized her thoughts. When they turned down a residential street, she said, "Aside from the job, Seattle seems like it'd be a nice place to live. There's people here I like." She smiled at Robbie and then felt a flush of nervousness. "But I haven't agreed to anything yet. I'm here to check things out."

"The person you said you were interested in…do they live here in Seattle? Is that why you're thinking of taking a job here?"

She knew Robbie was thinking of the text she'd sent almost two weeks ago. The one Robbie had glazed over—which had sent her into a spiral of worry about her decision to come at all. She'd thought Robbie had known the person she was interested in was her and hadn't considered there'd been a misunderstanding. Before she could explain, Robbie started talking again.

"I want to be happy for you. You moving here and a new relationship has got to be exciting. And I'm not going to tell you what to do, obviously. But you'd be giving up so many things. I mean, your whole life is in San Diego. Your friends, your job, your family. I know how much you love that little bay by your house."

"By my old house. I moved, remember?" She stopped walking and turned to Robbie. "You're here, Robbie. You're the person I'm interested in." She searched Robbie's face, hoping she'd understand—and that it wasn't too late. The last thing she wanted to see was a sign that Robbie had moved on.

"You're here because of me?"

"I promise there's no one else." She took a steadying breath. "I tried to get over you, but I only ended up missing you more. And I knew I couldn't ask you to come to San Diego. You have to be here. So I'm here to figure things out."

The confusion on Robbie's face turned to understanding, followed by a kind of hopeful look that almost did her in. Still, she pushed on. "You showed up in the middle of my divorce. I had no business getting involved with you. I knew your home was in Seattle. And the truth is, I didn't want to like you. But I couldn't help it. Every time I turned around, you did something to make me like you more." She paused, fighting the impulse to just kiss Robbie. "Then you left and I didn't know what to do."

Robbie stared at her for a moment, then scrubbed her face. "Give me a sec. I'm processing. You didn't want to do long distance, but now you're thinking of moving here?"

"It's not that I didn't want to do it. I knew I couldn't."

"Why not?" Robbie didn't wait for her answer. "Do you know how many times I wished you'd knock on my door? I finally convinced myself what happened between us didn't mean anything—you wouldn't even try long distance—and now you're moving here?"

"You thought it meant nothing?"

"No." Robbie shook her head firmly. "I'm saying I convinced myself that's what you thought. And that you didn't get attached to people and I was dumb to think—"

"Robbie, you have no idea how much you've meant to me." She spread her arms. "I'm here. I don't take risks. Not with my heart. But I'm here. Ready to try Seattle. Because of you."

Robbie held her gaze for a long moment and then let out a strangled breath. "The last six months have completely fucked with my head."

"I'm sorry. I had to figure some things out on my own. Like you said."

"I really liked you. I thought I was in love." Robbie looked down at the ground, shaking her head slowly. "If you moved here, you'd be risking so much. You'd be losing so many things you love."

"Trading." She'd guessed Robbie's feelings and wanted to savor the news now, but she understood her concern all too well. She'd had countless conversations with Mari and Elena about all of it and each time came to the same conclusion. She'd never know if things could work out unless she went for it. "Trust me, I've spent plenty of time weighing all the things I'd be trading. There's an ocean here, too. The same ocean. And Angel likes adventures."

"You're really considering this?"

"I can't get over you, Robbie. I tried."

Robbie seemed tongue-tied, and for a moment Devyn worried she'd admitted too much. Then Robbie said, "I gave myself a hard time about falling for you. We made a deal. Only sex, no getting attached."

Her chest ached at Robbie's admission. "It wasn't ever only sex."

"We could have done long distance. If you move here now, we're starting over at the beginning."

"You're right."

Robbie waited for her to go on. When she didn't, Robbie said, "I tried to figure out why you didn't want a relationship. My focus was on my uncle, I know, and I wasn't emotionally available for those first few weeks. I thought it might be that. Then I thought maybe you only wanted something with me if it was convenient. Or maybe you wanted to try new people and not be tied down after the divorce. Which made sense."

"Robbie." She felt tears building and fought to hold them back. "I knew I couldn't do long distance if there'd never be a way for us to be together. And I didn't want to make the same mistakes I made with Matt."

Robbie squinted at her. "Did you have a long-distance thing with Matt at some point?"

"No." She could see the frustration on Robbie's face and knew she had to explain. "You have no idea how much I wanted things to keep going with us. But as much as my job takes out of me, I can barely do a relationship when I'm living with the person. What happened with Matt—I wasn't there enough and I wasn't present when I was around. I wasn't the partner he needed. So he found someone else."

"Wait. Matt cheated on you?"

"For over a year. And, I found out later, there was more than one woman." Devyn thought Robbie had known all along. She could tell now that wasn't the case. "None of that really matters except I didn't want to put you in a position where you'd need someone else because I wasn't enough. I never want to go through that again, but especially not with you."

"I'm so sorry you'd think—"

Devyn shook her head, knowing where Robbie's apology was leading. "This is my issue, not yours. But it's also why I had to figure out a way to get myself to Seattle before we could go any further."

Robbie's shoulders dropped. "God, I want to kick Matt's ass right now."

"You don't need to. You already showed up and saved the day six months ago."

"I didn't save anything. I dropped into your life and took over your space. I chopped down your garden. I sliced my hand open and you had to sew me up. Then you had to do the bathroom tiling yourself. And then—"

"And then you kissed me. You fixed so many things I didn't realize were broken." Devyn stepped forward. She held out her hand, hoping Robbie would take it. After a breath, Robbie did. Their palms pressed together and a wave swept through Devyn.

"I know I don't always do things the way I'm supposed to. And maybe moving here would be a disaster. But I can't not try a relationship with you. I want you in my life too much."

Robbie looked down at their clasped hands. "You really don't do things the way you're supposed to. It's frustrating."

"I'm sorry."

"It's okay. I like you anyway." Robbie met her gaze. "Do you know how many times in the last six months I've wished I could hold your hand?"

Her own hand was tingling and a thrill seemed to zip between them. But she found herself looking at Robbie's lips. When she shifted forward, daring herself to take another chance, Robbie met her halfway.

Her knees went weak as soon as Robbie's lips touched hers. The kiss was six months in the making. Six months of working through her baggage. Six months of hoping that Robbie would wait for her. Six months of longing. When she parted her lips, Robbie deepened the kiss exactly the way she wanted, and the six months of thinking Robbie was better off without her slipped away.

She started to pull back, wanting to tell Robbie she was sorry she'd been too scared to go for what she wanted six months ago, but Robbie soundlessly asked for another kiss and she gave in willingly. She wrapped her arms around Robbie and their bodies pressed together. She could spend the rest of her life in this same spot if Robbie kept kissing her. On a sidewalk in a quiet neighborhood with the evening sky closing around them.

Never had she imagined she'd be in love with a woman from Seattle. Never had six months felt so interminable—and yet only a blink of an eye. Nothing had changed and everything had changed.

When they finally parted, Robbie's eyes stayed closed for a moment like she was committing their kiss to memory. As she opened her eyes, she looked right at Devyn. "Can I ask you out on a date?"

CHAPTER THIRTY

Robbie wanted to take Devyn on a proper date before anything else happened. Her mind spun with possibilities. Dinner and a show at the Paramount? She had a friend who worked at the theater and was good for last-minute tickets. Or they could go to a fancy lunch and spend tomorrow afternoon sightseeing. The Space Needle was always popular, and she liked the nearby Chihuly Garden with the glass displays. The Japanese Botanical Garden was another option. That one had been her favorite as a kid.

"I want to see where you live," Devyn said, slipping her hand in Robbie's as they walked down the quiet street. "Can we go there?"

"Matt's still living in my houseboat." She hated mentioning Matt now. "I rented it out to him after I moved in with my uncle. But Uncle Bruce went to Palm Springs, so I have his houseboat to myself this week."

"Palm Springs?"

"He's moving there with his boyfriend. Well, I guess I should say fiancé now. They've dated off and on for thirty years, but Paul finally popped the question last weekend. Uncle Bruce said he couldn't turn down the man who saved his life."

She had many reasons to thank Paul as well. "Paul was the one who called the ambulance. They were on the phone talking when my uncle had the stroke." She paused, thinking of that night. It felt like only yesterday with Devyn's hand in hers and yet the six months in between had been an eternity.

"Paul had asked my uncle to move down to Palm Springs years ago. I know he wanted to."

"Why didn't he?"

"Sometimes we think other things are a priority." Uncle Bruce had waited thirty years arguing against what he wanted. She knew some of that was his sense of responsibility. But some of it was simply fear—of taking a risk with his heart and having it not work out.

"So when your uncle moves to Palm Springs…"

"Then I'm officially in charge of the marina."

"You say that like it's not a good thing."

Robbie glanced down at their entwined hands. "I've spent the last six months imagining what would happen if I ran away to San Diego."

"I wish you'd told me that." Devyn stopped walking and tugged on Robbie's hand to get her to face her. "I didn't tell you a lot of the things going through my head, either. I want to change that. I want to figure out our next step together. I want us to both be somewhere that makes us happy."

"I think I could be happy anywhere with you."

"Me too. But I wish it hadn't taken me six months to be brave enough to say how into you I am." Devyn shook her head. "Being with you feels so right. And when I'm not with you, something feels like it's missing." She scrunched up her face. "Life is boring without you."

Robbie laughed.

"I want to try us being together. However it works. I think we can figure out the details."

She wanted it to be true—that they could have a future together. But she had to push away the doubts that had come up over the last several months, the ones Matt had encouraged. She had to trust Devyn. And herself. "I love details."

Devyn smiled. "Good. They're going to be a lot of them." They started walking again but hadn't gone far when Devyn stopped and said, "I want you to take me back to your place, but I really don't want to run into Matt tonight."

Robbie didn't want to run into Matt either. She didn't know what she was going to say to him. People made mistakes. Situations could push anyone to do something dumb they'd regret later. And some people simply weren't right for each other. But she hated that Matt had shifted the blame to Devyn and she hated that he'd hurt Devyn. She knew her continued friendship with Matt had probably hurt Devyn, too.

"Would you come up to my hotel room instead?"

Robbie grinned. "Are you propositioning me?"

Devyn seemed to hesitate before answering. "I know we should probably talk more, but I'm distracted."

"I was going to suggest we do things right this time and go on a date first, but a hotel room is hard to argue with."

Devyn bit the edge of her lip. "We did skip over the whole dating part last time."

"There's a lot of cool places in Seattle I'd love to show you."

"I love the idea of you showing me around, but I also love the idea of you on top of me with no clothes between us."

Robbie laughed. "Your plan sounds more fun than mine."

"I want to do both plans." Devyn stepped in front of Robbie and placed both hands on her shoulders. "I want to do all the plans." She shifted forward and met Robbie's lips with a deep kiss.

After another kiss the only thing on Robbie's mind was getting Devyn naked. As she pulled back, she murmured, "Sightseeing can definitely wait."

The walk back to the hotel felt like a dream. Devyn kept stealing glances at Robbie and finally slipped her arm around her waist. She didn't let go when they walked through the lobby and past the crowded bar, nor when they waited for the elevator. After the door had closed and she'd pressed the button for the third floor, she turned to Robbie. There was a shyness in her voice as she said, "You have no idea how many times I imagined coming to Seattle and knocking on your door unannounced."

Robbie guessed Devyn meant she'd fantasized about it. "Why didn't you?"

"Show up at your door?" Devyn pursed her lips. "I knew there was a chance you'd turn me down." The elevator opened and she immediately stepped out, heading down the hall without bothering to check if Robbie was following.

Robbie caught up as Devyn was about to unlock the room. She placed her hand on the low of Devyn's back and kissed her neck, then took the card key out of Devyn's hands. "Before we go any further, I need you to know there's no way I would have turned you down. I would have asked for an explanation—maybe—but I wouldn't have sent you away."

"You could have had company when I showed up. I didn't tell you to wait for me while I figured things out."

Robbie considered that possibility. Both Uncle Bruce and Stacy had tried to convince her to go out more. To meet someone. They thought she needed someone to distract her from thinking of Devyn.

"I didn't want anyone else's company." No one else could have come close to Devyn. "And I would have waited as long as you needed." She held the card key in the air. "Anything else we should get cleared up?"

Devyn looked from the key to Robbie's eyes. "No." She reached for the card key. "But you should know when you get that in-charge tone in your voice, I kind of stop thinking. So tomorrow I may bring up something else." She pushed open the door and reached for Robbie's hand. "Right now, though, I only want one thing."

Robbie clasped Devyn's hand but only took one step into the room before pulling Devyn toward her. She kissed Devyn as the door closed behind them—a full deep kiss. When they parted, she said, "*That* is what would have happened if you'd showed up unannounced."

Devyn sighed softly. "Why'd I wait?"

"I'm not done." Robbie took her coat off Devyn's shoulders and tossed it on the bed. She ran her hands up Devyn's arms, then pushed her against the wall. "This also would have happened." She kissed Devyn's neck, and then her collarbone, nipping at her smooth flesh, before finding her lips again.

After another deep kiss, Devyn moaned and moved against her. "What else would have happened?"

"What happened in your fantasy?" Devyn seemed to tense at the question and Robbie pulled back to look at her. "Am I moving too fast?"

"No. But…" Devyn sucked in a breath. "I don't think I'm ready to start admitting my fantasies. Maybe after that first date?"

Robbie smiled. "I can work with that." She pressed Devyn back against the wall and hiked up the bottom hem of her dress. When Devyn moved into her hands, desire overwhelmed all other thoughts.

She stroked up Devyn's smooth thighs until she reached the line of her underwear. All the pent-up longing flowed through her as she hooked the waistband with her thumb. "Can I take these off?"

"In my fantasy…you did whatever you wanted with me," Devyn murmured, going for another kiss.

The thought of Devyn wanting to be used sent her own arousal into overdrive. She tugged Devyn's underwear down and then all the way off. As she straightened, she kissed Devyn again. She forced herself to still her hands on Devyn's hips, letting the fire between them build.

It didn't seem possible that Devyn was here, that she'd stepped into her world. And Devyn had come because she wanted her— wanted her enough to leave San Diego. "I want to take my time, but six months of waiting and not knowing if I'd have you again…"

"I made you wait long enough." Devyn's hips rocked forward, pressing into hers.

They kissed, and as their kiss deepened, Robbie moved her grip from Devyn's hips to her thighs, pushing the dress up again. Devyn moved her legs apart and Robbie slid into the space, her whole body buzzing with arousal.

Devyn undid the buttons on her shirt and slipped her hands over Robbie's chest. "I made us both wait much too long." Her hand moved down Robbie until she reached the belt buckle. She pulled Robbie closer to her and groaned.

The sound of Devyn's desire was too much to fight. *No more waiting.* Robbie dropped to her knees, pushing Devyn back against the wall and spreading her. When she dipped her head, Devyn's hands gripped her shoulders. Nails dug into her skin as she tasted what she'd longed for.

She circled and licked until Devyn was dripping. She heard Devyn cuss, then beg, then cuss again. Only when she was certain Devyn was close did she stand and kiss her.

Between kisses, Devyn said, "I want…"

"I know." She knew exactly what Devyn wanted. And it was exactly what she wanted. The dress had fallen again to drape over Devyn's legs, and she pushed the fabric aside once more. She drew a line over Devyn's slit, knowing she was wet and ready for her. Devyn hitched her hips forward and every part of her begged to satisfy Devyn. And to satisfy her own desire. Still, she made herself wait.

Devyn brushed a kiss against Robbie's neck. "You want me to say please?"

"You've been saying that with your body all night."

Devyn smiled. "What more do I need to say then?"

"Tell me what you need." She slipped through Devyn's wetness and circled her opening.

Devyn gasped. "That." She moved against Robbie. "You."

So simple, and yet everything Robbie had been waiting for. In the next breath, Robbie stroked inside. Devyn pushed forward but Robbie held her against the wall. Arousal coated her hand and their moans filled the room.

Robbie thrust deep and Devyn only wrapped her arms tighter around her shoulders. She set the rhythm and Devyn followed her lead, pressing into her and begging for more.

If she could, she'd keep pleasuring Devyn all night. She'd keep her in this same place, pinned against the wall, wetness dripping down her thighs. When she moved another finger inside, Devyn tightened around the three fingers plunging into her.

"Fuck, you feel good."

Devyn only moaned in response. It was addicting how Devyn moved with her, and how she abandoned her own control. But the more Devyn gave, the more Robbie wanted to give in return. She wanted Devyn to have a release, to luxuriate in her own body, and to know how truly amazing she was.

She shifted her hand, stroking over Devyn's swollen clit, and Devyn's breathing turned ragged. "I was going to take my time," Robbie said. "But I don't want to."

Devyn nodded, panting as Robbie thrust faster.

"So agreeable," Robbie teased, stealing a kiss.

Devyn didn't respond and it was clear she was past words. Her orgasm came hard and fast, the sound filling the room. She surrendered completely to the climax and Robbie felt heat sweep through her own body. The wave took them both without warning. Robbie didn't try to fight it. She reveled in Devyn's pleasure, in Devyn's cum, and in Devyn's viselike grip on her body.

Devyn was beautiful always but stunning now. Her features were slack, the worry lines and the tension gone. They stood tangled together, both out of breath and trembling but for different reasons—Devyn with aftershocks, and Robbie with the realization that this moment was real.

In one reality, no time had passed at all. In another reality, they'd both suffered through too many lonely nights. Nights filled with doubt. Nights with impossible longing. Nights wrestling with thoughts of moving on. And now this night.

Only when Devyn sagged against the wall did Robbie slide her fingers out, letting the dress slip down to cover Devyn once more. She wrapped Devyn in her arms and then kissed her, her chest tight with emotion. "I missed that."

"Me too." Devyn nestled against Robbie's chest. "I don't really need a first date. I already know I like you."

"I already know I love you." When Devyn met her gaze, she added, "I know all the reasons I shouldn't say that yet. I don't care. I love you."

Devyn opened her mouth to say something but Robbie shook her head. "Please don't say anything in response. I still want to go on a first date. I just wanted to add a little pressure."

"You." Devyn laughed. "I do owe you a fancy dinner."

"For tiling your bathroom?"

Devyn nodded.

"You know I did that to get you to like me, right?"

"I had my suspicions." Devyn smiled. "But I didn't stop you."

"You didn't." Robbie caught Devyn's hand and tugged her the few steps from the hallway to the bed. She sat down and started to pull Devyn onto the bed, but Devyn held back.

"I need to tell you something." She put her hands on Robbie's shoulders and looked down at her with a serious expression.

"Should I be worried?"

"Maybe." The edge of her lip curved upward but she kept her serious tone. "You should know I'm only *not* saying the three words you told me because I want to add some pressure to our first date, too. And…" She reached behind her back and unzipped her dress, letting it fall to the floor. "I'm not planning on letting you sleep tonight. There are way too many things I've been waiting to do to you."

Robbie couldn't help staring—at Devyn's sexy black bra and her gorgeous body, and the confident look on her face. Devyn was everything she wanted. And so much more.

"Any questions?"

Robbie swallowed. "No questions."

"Good. Then lean back and relax."

When Devyn reached down to undo her belt, Robbie shifted back onto her elbows. She couldn't wait for what would come next.

CHAPTER THIRTY-ONE

Devyn hadn't planned to fall asleep, but sometime after three in the morning and too many orgasms to count, Robbie wrapped an arm around her and snuggled up against her back. When Robbie's breathing slowed, she couldn't fight the peaceful feeling that settled over her. The sound of an alarm not enough hours later jarred her awake as gently as a sledgehammer. Robbie groaned, rolled away from her, and mumbled an apology as she got out of bed. She silenced the alarm but didn't come back to snuggle.

After a minute, Devyn forced her eyes open. Light filtered into the room between the curtains—she hadn't thought to close them completely last night—and Robbie sat on the edge of the bed, rubbing her face. "Is it morning already?"

"It shouldn't be," Robbie said. "I have to go to the marina."

Devyn didn't want to move. Every part of her was sore. Sore in the best of ways but still sore. She forced herself to sit up. "You have to work?"

"I have to unlock things and make sure my new hire shows up." Robbie gave her a questioning look as she got out of bed. "You don't have to come with me. It's early still."

"I want to see where you live. And unless something's changed, Matt likes to sleep in. If we go early, I won't have to deal with talking to him." If Matt kept renting Robbie's houseboat, she'd eventually have to face him. Still, she intended on putting that off as long as possible.

"He does like to sleep in, but I can't guarantee we won't run into him."

Devyn reached for Robbie's hand and kissed it. She let go and said, "I've got a good feeling about today."

They both showered quickly and Devyn skipped makeup because Robbie was clearly worried about being late. As they walked out of the hotel, Robbie turned down one of the residential streets and she followed. "I have no idea what type of car you drive."

"Want to guess?" Robbie stopped walking. "I'm parked on this street."

Devyn scanned the street, eyeing the line of cars on the right side of the narrow road and then on the left. She considered pointing to a cherry-red Jeep but it didn't quite fit Robbie. Neither did the silver truck parked behind it. She stared at a white sedan for a moment, but she realized that one only stuck out because it was the most like Robbie's rental car. "I give up."

Robbie chuckled. "You didn't even try to guess." She pulled a set of keys out of her coat pocket and hit a button on a key fob. Lights blinked on the black Porsche directly across from them.

Devyn opened her mouth. "That one's yours?"

"Not what you were expecting? I can't help it if I like nice cars. And I'm not the only one." She winked and held out the keys. "Want to drive?"

"No. I want you to drive."

Robbie's car was easy to settle into and especially nice when Robbie reached across the console to rest one hand on her thigh. She didn't pay attention to the sights passing by, her thoughts swirling from what they'd done last night to the potential of living in Seattle, but then Robbie pointed to a lake lined with houses and autumn-colored trees. "That's the lake." The sun was rising but still low on the horizon, and it lit the water, turning everything gold.

"Oh, it's gorgeous. I don't know what I was expecting, but this is lovely."

Robbie nodded. "It is. Especially on sunny mornings like this."

The new hire was waiting when they pulled into the marina lot—an attractive twenty-something woman sporting ripped jeans, short blue hair, and a bomber jacket. Definitely not who she'd picture working at a marina. "That's the new hire?"

"Yup. That's Haley." Robbie's brow creased as she eyed the woman leaning against a door marked "Marina Office." The woman's dour expression broadcast how excited she was to show up for work.

"Her parents are loaded. They've got a house on the lake that they use as a vacation home and that yacht over there is theirs, too." Robbie motioned with her chin to a boat moored on a pier all by itself. Devyn didn't know much about boats, but the yacht was big and expensive-looking.

"I have a feeling this job is some kind of punishment. But Haley warned me she wasn't a morning person so maybe that's why she looks like she wants to kick my ass." Robbie opened the car door and added, "Wish me luck."

"I think you can hold your own against that one."

"All I'm hoping is she lasts longer than a week. The last guy I hired only made it two days."

Devyn didn't know what the woman's role at the marina would be, but she hoped she lasted a while for Robbie's sake. She knew managing the marina was an added stress Robbie didn't want, and she'd considered asking why Robbie had agreed to take it over for her uncle. Why not simply sell if her uncle wanted to move? She'd wondered, but she'd stopped herself from asking. Now she thought of that question, along with the dozen others she'd wanted to ask Robbie over the past six months.

So many times she'd held back from asking questions, telling herself it wasn't her place to pry in Robbie's life. But she wanted to be part of Robbie's life. And she wanted a relationship that was a partnership where things were discussed openly. After the disaster of her marriage, she didn't feel completely qualified for the position but it was what she wanted. Her therapist's words repeated in her head—*That's what we call goals.*

As Robbie chatted with Haley, Devyn walked the short path from the marina office to the water. At least two dozen boats of varying sizes lined the piers and fishing rigs were already motoring in the lake. To the left of the marina, Robbie had pointed out the dock with the houseboats. She recalled the picture Robbie had shown her and easily picked out Robbie's blue-and-white houseboat as well as her uncle's green one with the purple trim.

"Haley's all set," Robbie said, walking up to the bench Devyn had stopped at. "Want to go back to the hotel?"

"Could I see where you live?" When Robbie started to point out the houseboat, she added, "Up close, I mean. If you don't want to show me, that's okay, but I can't picture what it'd be like inside."

"Oh, sure. You should know it isn't fancy, though."

"It's not?" She feigned a sneer. "Forget it then."

Robbie laughed. "I'd love to show you."

"Thank you."

Robbie held out her hand and she took it. A feeling of contentment settled over her as they walked back to Robbie's car. She was in the right place with the right person.

"You know, you didn't have to wait six months to see my place. You could have come by any time and I would have given you a tour."

"I doubt that tour could have compared to what I got for waiting." And she'd needed to go through the last six months alone. She'd needed to finish separating all the pieces of Matt from her life. Needed to figure out what she wanted without factoring in what everyone else wanted. It hadn't been easy resisting the urge to jump on a plane to Seattle six months ago, though. Not easy at all.

They took a path from the marina's parking lot to a separate lot, and Robbie led the way down a dock lined with houseboats. "This one's Uncle Bruce's boat," Robbie said, hopping from the dock to the houseboat's deck and then adding, "I've seen your balance on a paddleboard so I won't tell you to watch your step."

"I've been told houseboats move differently."

"They do." Robbie chuckled. "And it's way harder to fall in the water."

Devyn had thought of the day she'd taken Robbie paddleboarding, and of how happy she'd felt, many times since. She'd known then she was falling in love.

"We call this the back patio," Robbie said, gesturing to a small deck area with enough space for patio furniture and a grill. "I know it doesn't look like much, but it's a perfect place to relax on a sunny day."

"You can't beat the view."

Robbie nodded. "Million-dollar view. And no yard to weed."

Devyn squinted at the deck and the water beyond it. "This does explain your luck with plants."

Robbie laughed as she went to unlock the door. "Fair warning, everything's smaller on a houseboat."

Robbie had seemed to want to lower Devyn's expectations, but it was clear how fond she was of the place the moment they stepped inside. She brushed her hand over different knickknacks, pointed out framed photos, showed Devyn the reading nook, and then joked they were once again getting the order of dating wrong since she'd brought Devyn to her childhood home before taking her on a first date.

The rooms were small, and the kitchen was barely more than a hallway, but the living area had a wall of windows looking out on the water, and Devyn could easily imagine settling in at the reading nook with a good book. When she sat down on the couch, saying she wanted a minute to enjoy the view, she felt wrapped in coziness and knew it wouldn't be hard to feel at home in the space.

"Can I make you an omelet while you enjoy the view?" Robbie asked. "It's possible I'm starving and hoping you say yes because I want one."

"An omelet sounds amazing." Her stomach had been rumbling for the last twenty minutes. "I'll help." She started to get up but Robbie held up a hand.

"Cooking is kind of a solo thing in my uncle's kitchen. There's not a lot of space. But I'm fast with omelets."

"You're telling me I don't have to help?" Devyn arched an eyebrow. "And that I have to sit right here and stare out at this gorgeous lake of yours?"

"That's exactly what I'm saying." Robbie leaned down and kissed her. As Robbie started to pull away, Devyn caught the front of her shirt and tugged her back for another kiss.

One more kiss turned to two more, and then Devyn found her hands slipping under Robbie's shirt. "You sure you need food?"

Robbie's stomach growled audibly in answer and Devyn laughed. She pulled her hands away with a soft sigh. "Go make us omelets. And coffee?"

"Definitely coffee."

Robbie padded away to the kitchen and she sank back on the cushions. The view truly was gorgeous—the silver lake, the houses bordering the water, and a band of green pines beyond.

"I could do this," she said under her breath. There would be things she'd miss leaving San Diego—having Mari and Elena close, the sunny weather, her favorite bay, and even simply the familiarity of life. But new things could become familiar.

Sounds of cooking along with the hiss of a coffee maker came from the kitchen. After a few minutes of enjoying being in Robbie's space, she got up from the sofa. Robbie was chopping vegetables and didn't look up as she hung in the doorway. She watched Robbie for a moment and realized the tension she'd felt the past long months had slipped away. Yes, she could move states for this woman.

Robbie looked over her shoulder and offered her an easy smile. "Coffee's almost ready." She motioned to a cupboard to one side of where Devyn stood and added, "Mugs are in there if you want to get two out."

The omelets were plated by the time Devyn had cream and sugar added to their coffees and they sat down at a table in an alcove of the kitchen. Devyn was again struck with how warm and cozy the place felt. *Like Robbie.*

The omelet was delicious—not surprisingly—and the coffee hit the spot. Devyn was enjoying having nothing pressing to do and being sated in all the ways when Robbie said, "I kind of hate to bring this up, but I also don't want to keep secrets from you."

"I appreciate that." She pushed her plate an inch away and straightened. "What is it?"

"Matt knows we hooked up when I was in San Diego. I wasn't going to tell him because it wasn't his business, but then…it sort of came out." Robbie paused. "He told me you don't do emotional attachment."

"Do you believe that?"

Robbie seemed to hesitate. "When we were together in San Diego, I would have said no way. But when I got back here, I started thinking…" Her voice trailed and she stared down her coffee. "Matt said some stuff that fed into my own insecurities. Now I know it was his baggage, too."

"But?" When Robbie didn't go on, Devyn reached across the table and held out her hand. She waited for Robbie to clasp it. "I'm sorry I ever made you doubt how I felt about you. There was never any question in my mind. You were exactly what I wanted. And needed. But I didn't feel like I could be what you needed."

"Are you kidding? You're perfect."

"I'm not. Not by a long shot." She shook her head. "I wanted to ask you to wait for me to do the work I needed to do, but I didn't know how long it would take. Six months was clearly too long."

Robbie shook her head. "I would have waited six years if you needed it."

"Do you think I can do emotional attachment?" It was ridiculous question, but she needed Robbie's answer. She needed to know Robbie believed they could work.

"I know you can. You're here." Robbie brought Devyn's hand to her lips and brushed the knuckles with a kiss. "The thing is…I know there will be times when you want to pull away. When it happens, can you try and tell me why? It's hard not having any idea what's going on in your head."

The hurt under Robbie's words tore at her heart. "I don't want to pull away from you again."

Robbie gave her a tentative smile. "Sometimes we need to do things alone. I just want you to tell me."

She owed Robbie that. And she owed herself the chance to open up to someone. "Okay."

"So…" Robbie scrunched up her nose. "There's one more thing we need to talk about."

She steeled herself. "Go ahead."

"Matt comes over for coffee almost every morning. I can tell him I've got company, but he's going to ask questions. What should I say?"

"Tell him the truth. If I move here, I'm hoping you'll have me over often. He's your friend. I'll deal."

"I wouldn't have to be friends with him."

Devyn pressed her lips together. "Things with Matt and I were complicated. He's not someone I recommend dating, but he's not a bad guy. And I promise I'll get used to him being around. I want to be here with you. That's what's important to me."

"What if I don't want you to move here?"

Devyn started to pull her hand back, but Robbie shook her head and said, "Hold on. Let me finish." She gently squeezed Devyn's hand. "I was so happy in San Diego. A big part of that was being with you, but I loved everything about it. When I came back here, little things that bothered me before were way worse." She looked around the kitchen for a moment. "This is home, but I don't want to be here. I don't want you to move because I'd rather be with you in San Diego."

"What about your uncle?"

"He's going to stay in Palm Springs. He hasn't formally made that decision, but I know how he feels about Paul."

"And the marina?"

Robbie exhaled heavily. "That's the part I need to figure out. Well, the marina, the dock, my houseboat, and my job."

Devyn loosened her hold on Robbie's hand. She'd had it in her head that Robbie couldn't leave. "I was getting used to the idea of Seattle, but I like the idea of you with me in San Diego even more. It'd be a lot of work for you though—selling this place and the marina and figuring out a new job…Would you let me help with some of it?"

"I can do it."

She tipped her head and Robbie gave a conciliatory smile. "I could be convinced to accept some help."

"Thank you." Devyn let go of Robbie's hand and went to her side of the table. When she held open her arms, Robbie stood. Their embrace wasn't like what they'd shared last night, but it filled her with something more. She breathed in Robbie and snuggled against her. "We'll figure out the details."

She had no reason to think things would be easy. Yet she knew it would work out. Her future was with Robbie. She'd found the person she wanted to make a new start with. The person she wanted to take chances for. The person she could trust and finally be herself with.

"You're the one," she whispered. She'd never felt so certain of anything before.

Robbie pulled back from their embrace to meet her eyes. "The one for what?"

"For me." Her heart raced as she realized what she was about to say. She didn't fall in love easily and she'd never been sure if she was truly in love before. Now there was no doubt. "I love you."

"I thought you were going to wait til after our first date."

Devyn smiled. "I changed my mind."

Robbie met her lips with a deep kiss. She knew how their first date would turn out. And she was already looking forward to all the dates that would follow.

EPILOGUE

"Is this a feng shui thing?" Robbie set her side of the bed down after Devyn let go of hers. They'd adjusted the angle of the bed six times already and Devyn still had a furrowed brow.

"I can't sleep if there's any light."

"I thought that was why we got blackout curtains."

"Curtains don't stop the light coming from under that doorway." Devyn dropped onto the mattress and turned from one hip to the other. "Can you hit the switch?"

Robbie turned off the overhead light and the room plunged into darkness. Devyn let out a contented sound. "Ah. Now that's nice."

"What is? I can't see my hand in front of my face."

Devyn laughed. "Come here. You know where the bed is."

"Do I?" Robbie took a few steps, exaggerating the stomping sound of her feet, then groaned. "Help, Angel, I'm lost in my own room." Angel's tags jingled on his collar, and he bumped into Robbie's leg a moment later. "You can't see, either? Wait, can dogs still see in the dark with blackout curtains?" Angel hopped up, placing his front legs on Robbie and asking to be scooped up. "It's okay. We're lost together." She pretended to stumble into the bed, then set Angel on the mattress and tumbled on top of Devyn. "Oh, sorry. Can't see anything."

Devyn laughed again, wrapping her arms around Robbie. Angel settled on the space next to them, and for once Devyn didn't say, "No dogs in bed."

"You sure this is the right spot? Because I'm willing to move this bed for the seventh time if it's not perfect."

Devyn kissed Robbie lightly. "It's perfect. So are you."

"Guess who's in bed with us?"

Devyn grumbled. "I'm pretending not to notice."

"Why can't Angel sleep in our bed? He's such a good dog."

"I know he is, but I can't sleep with anyone licking me."

"You sleep fine with me."

Devyn sighed contentedly. "I do. I love how well I sleep with you. But you do not try to lick my hands in the middle of the night."

"I've been tempted. With the blackout curtains, though, it's really hard to see where your hands are."

Devyn placed her hand on Robbie's cheek and guided their lips together. After a deep kiss, she said, "Welcome home to us."

"Welcome home," Robbie repeated, a tingling warmth filling her chest. "You know, since we have blackout curtains, there's no way to know where we are exactly. We could pretend to be anywhere."

"I don't need to pretend to be anywhere else," Devyn said. "I'm happy right here. With you."

"And Angel."

"And Angel." Devyn's smile showed in her voice. "Now that we've officially moved, I'm ready to talk about getting Angel a little sister or brother."

"Really?" Robbie shifted up, straddling Devyn's hips. "Angel, buddy, did you hear that? Angel? You still here?"

"He's right here." Devyn let out a happy sound and pulled Robbie down again on top of her. "I've got everyone I love right here."

"You're serious about another dog?"

"I know you've been wanting one for a while."

Robbie had only mentioned it once, when she'd first come back to San Diego. They'd all gone for a walk on the beach by the townhouse Devyn was renting at the time and Angel had wagged his tail happily when they'd run into a terrier friend of his. At the time she'd only said, "Someday I want another puppy."

Devyn had remembered. She didn't seem to forget any little thing Robbie said. She often brought Robbie little gifts—things she'd mentioned liking—and she'd surprised Robbie with a trip to Costa Rica after Robbie had casually said it was a place she'd dreamed of visiting.

The house, though, they'd decided on together. No surprises and lots of conversations. Choosing San Diego and being close to Mari and Elena, whose baby was due any minute, hadn't been hard once Robbie admitted that was where she truly wanted to be. Besides, San Diego was only a three-hour drive from Palm Springs and Uncle Bruce was happily settled there. The trick had been selling the marina. The process had taken longer than expected and there'd been months of long distance.

Devyn had worried about their time apart. Robbie had done everything she could to ease Devyn's worries and they'd gotten through it. Now they had a home together. With a long to-do list on a little house by the bay Devyn loved.

"I don't think I'm ready for a puppy quite yet," Robbie admitted.

"You still miss your Pixie?"

"Yes. But it's also all the work we have here."

"You don't think we can handle one more thing?" Devyn laughed lightly. "I think we can handle anything."

"Even dinner with your parents? We need to RSVP for that yacht club thing."

"You had to remind me." Devyn buried her face against Robbie's shoulder. "Maybe we can say one of us is sick."

"Two weeks out?"

"Mm. I feel a fever coming on."

Robbie chuckled. "If you don't want them to know about us, we can say we're roommates."

"It's not that."

"You sure? I know your parents are conservative and I'm okay being your roommate. Or a friend who needed a place to crash. Whatever makes things easier for you. It doesn't matter to me what they know or think. I know how you feel, and that's the important part."

Devyn shifted under Robbie, and a second later light flooded the room from the bedside lamp. Devyn pushed up on her elbows and locked her gaze on Robbie. "You're not my roommate. And you're not only a friend. You're the most important person in my life. I don't care what they think, but I'm not going to hide anything."

Robbie's heart seemed to press against her chest. "You sure we need blackout curtains?"

Devyn gave her a questioning look.

"Because I really love being able to see you. Especially when you're all fired up like now. You're so damn sexy."

"I'm serious, Robbie. I want my parents to know who you are to me. I want everyone to know. Not because it's going to be fun or easy having the conversation, but because you're the person I love. If they can't accept that, then maybe I don't need them in my life."

"I love you." Robbie closed the distance between them with a kiss. She pulled back and said, "I'm going to charm the pants off your parents."

"Oh, no." Devyn groaned. "I know how charming you can be. I don't want to see either of them without their pants."

"They're going to love me. Just wait." She kissed Devyn again. "Speaking of dinner plans, are we still meeting up with Mari and Elena tonight?"

"If Elena gets off on time."

"Even if she doesn't, we could still get food with Mari and bring leftovers to Elena. I've seen the food you all try to eat from that cafeteria."

"Elena would love that." Devyn snuggled closer to Robbie. "We've been focused on this bed being in the right spot, but is there anything you need set up just so?"

"There is one thing."

"Tell me."

"I may need some help arranging some seeds and some starter plants I ordered." Robbie had wanted it to be a surprise but knew it'd be better as a together project. "You know I do not have a green thumb."

"You want to work on the yard before we have a functioning kitchen?"

"We need a pollinator garden. Monarchs and bees are facing extinction. If we don't do our part—"

"You." Devyn pressed her hand against Robbie's chest. She kissed Robbie and added, "I can't believe I ever hated you."

"You forgave me. I think."

"Completely. How could I not?"

"I know we need a functioning kitchen, but butterflies and bees need flowers." She wanted to memorize Devyn's smile then, love overtaking her. "You make me happy. I want to make you happy too—with a big pollinator garden."

"You already make me happy. A thousand times over. You're the best housebutch ever."

"The best what?"

"Housebutch. You don't know the term? It's someone who's amazing with their hands and takes care of all the house stuff."

Robbie narrowed her eyes. "I don't think that's a real term."

"Look it up," Devyn said, all confidence. "I'll wait for you to tell me I'm right."

Robbie laughed, but Devyn stopped her with a kiss. A perfect kiss. A life-couldn't-get-much-better kiss. After another, she pulled back and asked, "If I'm a housebutch, what are you?"

"Yours. All yours."

Bella Books, Inc.

Women. Books. Even Better Together.

P.O. Box 10543
Tallahassee, FL 32302
Phone: (800) 729-4992
www.BellaBooks.com

More Titles from Bella Books